Murder on Display

Murder on Display

The Shepherd Sisters Mysteries

Tracy Gardner

TULE
PUBLISHING

Dedication

For the readers,
the stay-up-late, just-one-more-page,
die-hard story lovers:
I know you.
I am you.

Carson, Michigan

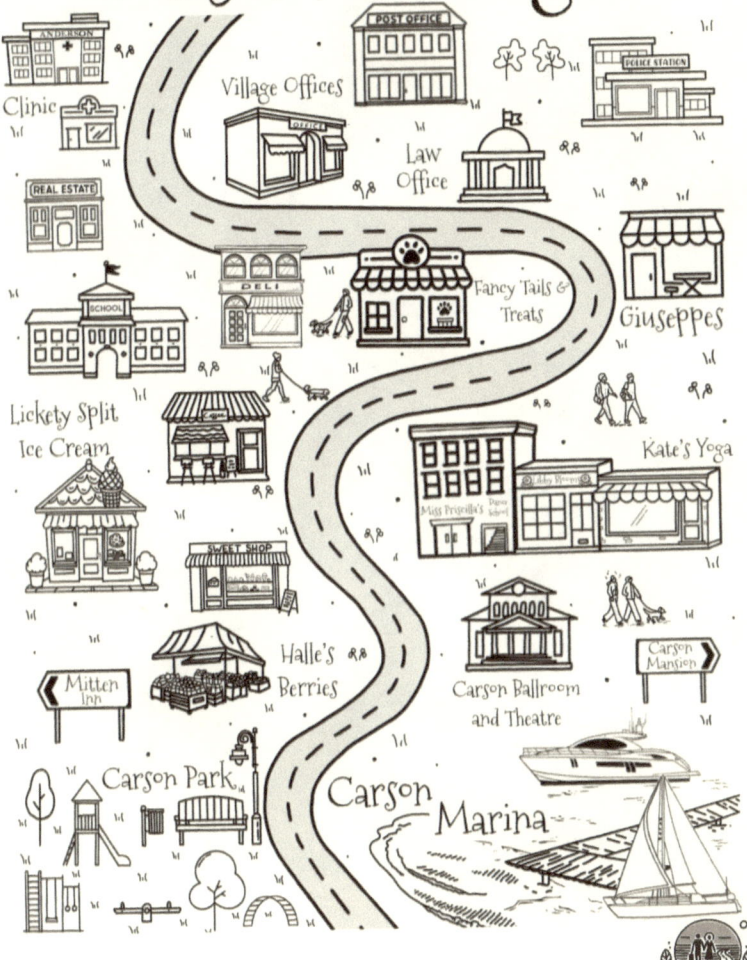

Chapter One

SAVANNA SHEPHERD ENTERED Fancy Tails & Treats backward, carrying three steaming coffees and a white bakery box of frosted cinnamon rolls. Her dog's leash was looped over a wrist, and papers were sliding out of a folder sandwiched under one arm.

Savanna's younger sister, Sydney, came around the display counter of the grooming salon, relieving Savanna of the food and coffee and taking everything over to the round red and chrome table in the corner.

"Thank you!" Savanna unclipped Fonzie's leash and followed Sydney.

"What's all that?" Sydney nodded at the papers now scattered on the tabletop just as her phone rang. "Wait, let me grab this first." She zipped through the wide daisy-decorated archway that divided the establishment to her desk, flipping her long, loose red braid over one shoulder.

Savanna took a sip of her caramel macchiato, watching Fonzie dig through the toy basket for his favorite. The shop was strangely quiet, devoid of the usual yipping, barking patrons. Sydney didn't take customers until nine a.m.

Fancy Tails & Treats doubled as a grooming salon and organic treat shop for Carson's canine population. Sydney had hit a much-needed niche in their small town's Main Street businesses; Fancy Tails had been successful from the day she'd opened. On this side of the shop, along with the gourmet treat-filled display case, Syd had created an inviting waiting area for her patrons in front of the windows, complete with overstuffed aqua couch and chair, café table, and mini-fridge stocked with complimentary drinks.

Sydney typed something into her computer, finishing the call, and then joined Savanna. "There's only a week left of school. Don't tell me you have all this paperwork?"

"No, though I do have papers at home waiting for me," Savanna said. As Carson's elementary art teacher, she still had a lot of grading to finish before summer break. "This is for the Art in the Park festival."

Sydney clapped her hands together. "Ooh! I'm so excited for that. I'm so glad you won the event for Carson. So." Syd poked through a few of the papers as Savanna put them in order. "Do you have all the details figured out?"

"I've got very little figured out. But with the planning banquet tonight, I arranged to meet with some of the committee this morning in the park to talk about logistics."

"I can help. Let me know what I can do," her sister offered. She popped a piece of icing-covered cinnamon roll in her mouth and closed her eyes. "Mmm, so good!"

"I'll need to circulate tonight and chat with the business owners who haven't volunteered goods or services yet. Maybe you can help with that?"

"That is a job I'm cut out for. I know everyone."

"I'm not surprised," Savanna said, smiling.

The bell over the door jingled and they looked up and Skylar Shepherd entered, out of breath. She tapped the smart watch on her wrist. She wore matching pink and navy workout gear and running shoes, her shiny blond hair pulled back into a short ponytail. Two years older than Savanna, four older than Sydney, Skylar was always perfectly coordinated, whether on a run or in a courtroom trying a case. She joined them at the table.

"You look cute today," Savanna told her. "I've got to go. You'll be at the banquet tonight, right?"

"Wouldn't miss it. Where are you running off to?" Skylar waved off the cinnamon roll box Sydney pushed over to her.

Savanna straightened the lightweight black blazer she'd worn today over a bright yellow shell and grabbed her coffee and notes. "I'm meeting a few folks from city council and the state committee in the park; we need to have the festival tables and thoroughfare mapped out before tonight. Can Fonzie stay, Syd?"

Sydney scratched Savanna's little Boston Terrier behind the ears. "Does it look like he wants to go with you?" He was lying on Sydney's feet, chewing on a stuffed green lizard.

"Not even a little." She and Fonzie had returned home to Carson, Michigan, last fall from a decade spent in Chicago, after losing her fiancé and her job on the same day. Starting her life over at thirty wasn't something she'd planned, but Savanna loved being here with her family as much as Fonzie did.

"Hey, hold on!"

Savanna glanced at her older sister and tapped her phone, checking the time. "Britt's on their way, early as always. I should go."

Skylar sighed. "Okay, but I wanted to hear how things went with Aidan yesterday. How was your dinner date?"

"Thank you," Sydney said to Skylar. "Savanna never tells me things. How was your date with Dr. Gallager?" She drew out his name in a singsong voice, cocking an eyebrow at Savanna.

"I don't tell you things because you do *that*," Savanna said pointedly. "We had to reschedule." She tried to keep the disappointment out of her tone.

"What? Why?" Syd's voice carried enough disappointment for both of them. "That stinks." Her expression was all pout and concern.

"He got stuck in New York. They had a trauma case come in and he had to stay."

"Until when?" Skylar asked.

"I didn't want to ask. I mean, we only had a couple of dates before this whole flying-back-and-forth stuff started. He doesn't owe me any explanations."

Sydney huffed her breath out in frustration. "He can't be the only doctor there. He couldn't tell them no?"

Savanna was slowly backing toward the door. "He feels like he has to help. He says they're still so shorthanded." Aidan had called her from the airport yesterday when he'd learned he couldn't come home yet.

His former employer in New York had tapped him a few months ago and begged him to lend them some time, as the hospital had just lost their chief of cardiothoracic surgery unexpectedly. Aidan had declined an offer to step into the position full-time, not wanting to uproot his seven-year-old daughter, but he'd agreed to help out while they looked for a replacement.

He'd explained to Savanna, over a delicious candlelight dinner at Giuseppe's in town two months ago, that the hospital, and his mentor and boss specifically, had done a lot for him. He couldn't let them down. Aidan's in-laws were more than happy to care for Mollie the two or three days each week he was in New York.

Between Aidan's absences, his family commitments, lengthened clinic hours when he was home, and Savanna's own schedule, they'd had limited time to really get to know each other. Savanna cherished the friendship they'd struck up working together to save the town matriarch, Caroline Carson. And she was in no rush to fall into a new relationship, less than a year after Rob had left her to "find himself."

But she missed Aidan. She sensed he missed her too…he'd sounded disappointed on the phone yesterday.

"Guys," she said, noting both her sisters' faces painted with sympathy. "It's okay. Things will work out, or they won't. I'm sure we'll eventually get some time to catch up."

Sydney's brows rose. "That's very chill of you, Savvy."

She laughed. "Maybe you're rubbing off on me. I've got to go," she said, halfway through the door now. "I'll see you both tonight!"

Savanna tried to push Aidan from her mind as she walked the three blocks to the park. She was still a few minutes early. Her friend Britt Nash, a colleague from Savanna's former life as an art authenticator, would likely be the first person to arrive, but she couldn't see anyone yet in the large, inviting community park that sat at the end of Main Street.

The park was lush and green now in June, with a decent stand of mature trees at the far end, a gazebo near the town statue at the other, and plenty of room to picnic, play on swings, or toss a ball in the middle. Savanna had always loved relaxing here. On quiet days, it was even possible to hear the waves of Lake Michigan through the trees. The beach was only a short walk down a sandy trail past the park.

As she approached, Savanna noticed something seemed off with the view, but she was still a block away. Her mind ran through her to-do list. She pulled a rough sketch of the park from her folder. The meeting this morning would involve herself, Britt, city councilman John Bellamy, and a liaison from the Art in the Park state committee that had awarded the event to Carson after Savanna's months of campaigning. She'd been surprised at how much competition she'd been up against, and even more surprised when Carson had finally won.

Today, the four of them were tasked with assessing the space to come up with the best layout for each of the Art in the Park facets: artwork display tents, concessions, live music stage, judges table, and more. Savanna had a rough sketch, but she wanted it firmed up by the time the planning banquet kicked off tonight. Art submissions from all over the state had been coming into Carson's parks and recreation department, which was really just an extension of Councilman Bellamy's office. Savanna and John Bellamy had been meeting every Thursday to review submissions, and she'd recently enlisted Britt to help; there were so many aspiring artists in Michigan! The first place winner of Art in the Park would be awarded a nice monetary prize and a handsome scholarship to the prestigious Michigan Art Conservatory, as well as a round of a high-visibility interviews at local and state media outlets.

Now Savanna saw what was wrong with the view. As she walked around the gazebo into the park, she stared up at the twelve-foot-tall statue of Jessamina Carson on her pedestal. Jessamina wasn't quite twelve feet tall any longer. Savanna gasped, covering her mouth in shock.

Jessamina Carson's head was missing.

Savanna took an involuntary step back, away from the defaced century-old statue, taking in the scene. What in the world?

The head of the statue lay several yards away on the ground, scattered debris littering the grass between the base of the statue and the eerily severed concrete head. Across the base of the statue, from one side to the other, spanned large red spray-painted words, *NEVER CARSON.*

Savanna whirled around at a sound behind her, hands up defensively—a reflex, considering what she'd just stumbled onto. Her friend Britt was walking toward her, eyes wide and short white-blond hair making them look paler than Savanna felt.

"What is this? What happened?"

She shook her head. "I have no idea." She turned in a circle, searching the park for any sign of the person who'd done this. No one. The park was deserted.

Britt looked the statue up and down, gaze coming to rest on the ugly words. "Well, I'd say someone has a problem with your town."

Savanna nodded in agreement. This made no sense at all. She moved closer to the statue, reaching out and gingerly touching the top of the red *C* with one finger. "It's dry. Whoever did this is long gone—look how thick the paint is. I have to call the police."

She paused, phone in hand. If she called 911, this wouldn't be considered an emergency. She guessed they'd send someone to check things out whenever they had a chance. But this was a threat. Against Carson. And on the morning of the Art in the Park planning banquet. Ugh. She groaned.

"Savanna?" Britt was looking at her, concerned.

She frowned up at her friend. "Mrs. Kingsley is on her way here now. She's sure to tell the rest of the committee about this. What if they cancel the whole event? Award it instead to the runner-up?"

"I see your point. But what can we do?"

"We need help. Now," she said. "I'm calling Detective Jordan."

"Sure, good idea. Call Detective Jordan. Who is Detective Jordan?"

"I know him through Skylar," she whispered, phone to her ear. "He handled the case last year at the Carson mansion."

Nick Jordan finally picked up. "Savanna?"

"Hi, Detective. I'm so sorry to bother you at home. On a weekend," she added, cringing.

"Don't worry about it. What's up?" His voice came through her phone, his tone dry. She never could tell if he was irritated or if this was always just him.

Britt motioned to her, pointing toward the parking area. "John's here, I'll go tell him." They headed toward the councilman just getting out of his car.

Savanna groaned inwardly. John Bellamy was here now, and Mrs. Kingsley would arrive any minute. She had to find a way to redirect attention from the statue. She followed Britt, not keeping up at all with their long-legged stride as she spoke into the phone. "I'm in the park. Someone has vandalized the statue. It's bad. And the banquet is tonight, to kick things off for the Art in the Park event, and the state committee is coming, and I really think you need to see Jessamina. This wasn't random. It's awful. Will you please come?"

She heard Nick Jordan sigh heavily. She supposed he was at home with his wife, enjoying a leisurely Saturday morning. Or maybe she'd woken him up. Savanna had a pang of guilt.

"I'll be there in ten minutes." Jordan hung up.

Savanna stared at the phone in her hand before dropping it into her purse. She jogged a little to join the councilman and Britt. Councilman Bellamy wore a suit, as he did every single time she'd ever seen him. It seemed out of place today, a seventy-degree day in the park, but Bellamy had just announced his candidacy for Carson mayor against longtime incumbent Mayor Greenwood. Midterm elections were only three months away. John Bellamy was obviously intent on making good impressions no matter where he went.

"Let's sit for a moment while we wait for Mrs. Kingsley." Savanna directed her little group to a row of park benches under a large maple tree. Each bench back bore a colorful ad for a local business or service, something Savanna had just started noticing around town. She chose a pink and yellow bench that declared *Let us pamper you*, depicting a woman relaxing with cucumber slices over her eyes, for Carson's day spa. The adjacent few benches advertised Skylar's law office, a property development company called Better Living, and a fishing charter company, Lake Michigan Expeditions.

John Bellamy stared toward the statue. "Oh, no. What happened?"

"We don't know. We found her like that. I'd really like to avoid Mrs. Kingsley seeing the vandalism up close, if possible. We need to keep this festival in Carson. I don't want her to get spooked."

Bellamy shook his head. "We can't hide this. Believe me, Carson needs the event. I want everything to proceed as planned as much as you do. But she's going to see the statue."

As if on cue, a shiny black Cadillac pulled into the parking space next to Bellamy's car. A tall, thin woman with enormous dark glasses exited and made her way slowly toward them, picking through the lawn in heels.

"You're right." Savanna cleared her throat and fidgeted with a button on her jacket. "We have to address it. It'll be fine," she said, more to herself than to the two men. She met Mrs. Kingsley halfway and shook her hand. "I'm Savanna Shepherd, Mrs. Kingsley. I'm so pleased to finally meet you in person."

The older woman took off her sunglasses and parked them atop her head. "Pleased to meet you, Savanna." She smiled. "What a lovely setting for the event!" She glanced around, obviously not yet spotting the remains of Jessamina Carson.

Savanna made introductions. "Mrs. Kingsley is the head of the state committee, out of Traverse City," she told Britt and John Bellamy. "Mrs. Kingsley, this is Carson's city councilman, John Bellamy, who runs our parks and rec department, and my colleague from the Lansing Museum of Fine Art, Britt Nash. You'll be happy to hear we've gotten hundreds of excellent submissions so far."

Mrs. Kingsley had spotted the statue at the east end of the park. It was hard to miss, adjacent to the large ribbon-and-light-adorned gazebo that Carson used for all town gatherings.

"My goodness!" She glanced at Savanna and began moving toward the statue.

Savanna matched the woman's pace, followed by Bellamy and Britt.

"Our town statue went through an unexpected, um, trauma sometime last night or early this morning," Savanna told her. "We've already reported it to the police. I'm sure they'll find the responsible party. We can begin on the other end of the park," she said, attempting to steer the woman away from the area.

Even in heels, Mrs. Kingsley had no trouble staying her course. They were now close enough to read those large scrawled bloodred words: *NEVER CARSON.* "Oh my goodness," the woman said again, stopping in her tracks. "What happened? Is this about the Art in the Park festival?"

"We aren't sure," Savanna admitted, at the same time John Bellamy said, "Of course not."

Mrs. Kingsley stared at the pair of them, her face painted with skepticism. "It certainly appears to be, with your planning banquet scheduled for this evening."

"I can see how you'd worry it's related," Savanna said. "But I really don't think so, Mrs. Kingsley. Carson is, as a community, so excited to host the event. It'll be good for the local businesses, and it's bringing in a lot of outside interest. Hotel and B&B reservations are way up—right, John?"

The councilman nodded. "Absolutely. And Carson's finest are right on top of this." John pointed now to a sheriff's department patrol car pulling up. "There isn't anything to be concerned about. I can promise you the city council will coordinate with our police force to make sure of that."

Nick Jordan and a deputy approached the statue. Mrs. Kingsley was quiet, watching them. She finally turned to Savanna. "I was the swing vote that secured the festival for Carson this year, Savanna. I'll trust this will be handled, but I do have an obligation to inform the committee."

Savanna's stomach lurched. She didn't want Carson to

lose this event. "I understand. Thank you. Please don't worry."

"Let's take a look at the rest of the area," the older woman suggested.

Savanna handed her folder to Britt. "Councilman Bellamy and my colleague Britt will walk you through our thoughts on the setup," she said, pleading silently with Britt. They could manage while she had a quick chat with Detective Jordan; he and the young woman in uniform with him were already checking out Jessamina and her disconnected head.

Detective Jordan greeted Savanna when she joined them, and introduced the woman as his forensics tech. The tech placed numbered yellow evidence markers in a series of spots and moved between the debris on the ground and statue, snapping photos.

"What do you think it means?" Savanna asked the detective.

Nick Jordan was great at his job. When Savanna was sure she'd figured out who was trying to kill Caroline Carson last fall, Jordan had actually listened to her, explored the leads she'd uncovered, and had ultimately arrested the person responsible. Savanna's sharp eye as a former art authenticator, with Sydney and Skylar pitching in and Dr. Gallager working to keep Caroline safe, all helped Jordan close the case. Since then, they'd struck up a friendly acquaintanceship, but Savanna always had trouble reading him; he was a master of the poker face.

"I don't know what it means," he said. "It could be a reference to John Bellamy announcing he's running against Greenwood for mayor. That was a front-page story in yesterday's paper; it's possible someone isn't happy about the news."

Savanna hadn't thought of that. But she couldn't imagine anyone hating Councilman Bellamy so much they'd go to these lengths.

"Or," Jordan continued, "it could be a protest of your art festival; didn't you say there's something going on tonight for that?"

"The planning banquet," Savanna said.

"Or it could just be teenagers, messing around and causing trouble."

"This seems kind of…specific. It doesn't seem like something bored kids would do. I mean, not with the 'Never Carson' thing. Right?"

Jordan shrugged. "Nothing surprises me anymore. I'm glad you called me."

Savanna was surprised. "Really? I wasn't sure. It isn't life or death, after all."

"No, but it's Jessamina Carson, Everett Carson's grandmother. She was instrumental in shaping our town, and the legacy Caroline Carson carries on. Jessamina has stood here, untouched, since 1902. This is not okay with me. We'll get to the bottom of it," Detective Jordan promised.

Chapter Two

SATURDAY EVENING, SAVANNA secured her long waves into a low ponytail, reaching for her hairspray and realizing it was still in the bathroom from this morning.

She slid to a stop in the hallway outside the bathroom door, hearing the shower running. Sydney must've just gotten in. Savanna really needed to get her own place; when she'd moved in last August, she'd never meant it to be permanent. Sydney kept saying she loved having her here, but the more time passed, the more Savanna felt like an imposition. She'd looked at a few houses but hadn't put serious effort into her search lately, with the art festival and end-of-the-schoolyear activities keeping her busy. This summer, Savanna thought. She'd find a house, and Syd could have her spare room back.

Savanna knocked. "I just need one thing! Can I come in?"

"Sure," Syd called from behind the shower curtain.

Savanna opened the door and grabbed her hairspray. "Thanks!"

"Hey, which dress are you wearing? The blue or the black?"

Savanna leaned in the doorway. "I still don't know.

What do you think?"

"Blue. Always blue! And those strappy heels we bought," Sydney said.

Savanna laughed. "Maybe the heels. I'll be standing all night—my feet will get sore."

"Have some cheese with that whine."

Savanna stuck her tongue out at the shower curtain before heading back to her room.

"I saw that," Sydney called.

"Brat," Savanna shouted. She shed her robe and pulled on the blue dress. She did love the color, and it skimmed her curves in all the right places while still being tasteful enough for the banquet she was hosting. She sat down to put the strappy heels on and admitted Sydney was right. They really were gorgeous, especially with the dress. She added tiny dangling gold star earrings.

"I'll see you there," she told Sydney through the bathroom door on her way out. She still had an hour, but the perfectionist in her wanted to make sure everything went smoothly.

Savanna entered the Carson Ballroom and stopped abruptly, taking in the room. It was beautiful. White twinkle lights were strung overhead, and the gleaming wood floor, redbrick interior walls, and a dozen white linen and crystal-adorned round tables decorated the room. Candlelit centerpieces provided a warm, inviting atmosphere. Caroline Carson's grandson Jack and a business partner had recently purchased the ballroom and the adjoining theatre with renovation in mind, and Savanna spotted the improvements he'd already made. Jack Carson's goal was to have the ballroom double as a small concert venue when it wasn't being used for town events.

The attached theatre on the other side of the ballroom's west wall was in disrepair and hadn't been used in years, but Jack envisioned a two-screen movie theatre in the space, complete with heated, reclining seats, and bottomless popcorn. He'd commissioned Savanna to paint the ambitious *Century of Cinema* mural on the entry wall, and she was set to begin work on that this summer. She couldn't wait.

She walked through to the back of the ballroom toward the kitchen, where Joe Fratelli and his staff were busily finalizing preparations for the evening's meal. Choosing Giuseppe's to cater the banquet was an easy decision. The longstanding restaurant was a town favorite, serving scrumptious Italian food and a plentiful assortment of other fare. Tonight, the owner and head chef, Joe, was preparing two of his classics, spinach-and-ricotta tortellini and chicken parmigiana. The aroma wafting from the kitchen into the banquet hall was to die for.

Two servers carried trays through the double swinging doors as Savanna entered. Joe Fratelli worked at a cutting board, wielding a large chef's knife to mince what looked like garlic and onions. A younger man, also dressed in traditional chef's whites, stood at the stove, stirring something in a deep pot. Joe smiled widely at Savanna. She estimated the man to be in his fifties; Giuseppe's restaurant had been one of the Shepherd family's favorites since Savanna was a kid.

He came over to her, giving her a quick peck on each

cheek. "What do you think?" he asked, gesturing to the stovetop. "Would you like a sample?"

Savanna agreed instantly; she was already starving. "Absolutely! It smells delicious!"

"Here," Joe said, moving to the stove and spooning generous portions onto a white plate for Savanna.

She laughed. "You're trying to ruin my appetite!" He'd given her enough for two people.

"No, no, it's just a taste. Eat, go on. Tell us how it is."

Joe Fratelli crossed his arms over his chest, waiting. Savanna had a momentary flashback of him standing at their table in his restaurant when she was little, urging her and her sisters to eat and chatting with her father about their motorcycles. His hair was gray now instead of black, and the smile lines around his eyes were a little deeper, but he was still a food pusher. If she and her sisters didn't clean their plates, he'd act personally insulted. *You don't like my cooking? It doesn't taste good? You didn't eat enough to feed a pigeon!*

She took a bite of the tortellini. "Oh," she said, closing her eyes for a second. "Oh my, Joe, this is amazing."

Fratelli motioned at her plate. "Go on, try the chicken. Remy made that. Savanna, I'm sorry, I'm so rude." He reached out and pulled the younger man by the sleeve over to them. "This is my sous chef, Remy James. He's the best. He may be trying to take my job." Fratelli winked at Savanna.

Savanna took Remy's offered hand, noting the lines of ink covering his left arm. She couldn't quite make out what the tattoos were, but there was more artwork than skin. He was taller than Joe Fratelli, thin, and probably in his twenties.

"Nice to meet you," he said.

"You too," she replied, and then, as Joe Fratelli gently gave the plate in her hand a nudge, she speared a bite of the chicken. "Mmm, this is good. So good," she said to both Joe and Remy. "You two make a great team." She took another bite to prove it. "Is there anything I can do?"

"No," Fratelli said, returning to the stove, obviously satisfied that Savanna was happy with his food. "You go do your thing—we've got this covered. I have one more server on his way. We'll be ready whenever you are."

When Savanna walked back through to the ballroom, people were already beginning to trickle in, her parents among them. They met her halfway, and she hugged them both.

"The place is lovely," her mother said, glancing around. She looked lovely herself, a simple black wrap dress adorning her petite frame and delicate earrings sparkling behind strands of her shoulder-length auburn hair. "Do you need us to help at all? You know Dad loves an assignment." Charlotte smiled up at Harlan.

Savanna shook her head. "I don't think so. I put you at a table with Caroline and Jack. I'm nervous. I hope it all goes smoothly," she said, frowning down at the note cards she'd been using to practice her speech. She wasn't used to having to speak to large crowds.

Her dad leaned in toward her. "We're proud of you, Savanna. Let us know if you need any help."

They crossed the room, her dad bending to say something to her mother that made her look up at him and smile.

Savanna still hoped she'd one day have what her parents did. Her older sister, Skylar, certainly seemed to have it with Travis. Savanna knew nobody's marriage was perfect, but it was obvious to anyone watching how much Charlotte and Harlan loved each other.

Councilman Bellamy arrived, along with the three judges who'd been appointed by the committee. Savanna joined the councilman and introduced herself to the judges, two women and a man, each with different but impressive credentials within the art world. She showed them to their seats, and a server appeared to take their drink orders, just as Savanna spotted Mayor Greenwood and his wife arriving.

She turned to tell John she was going to greet the mayor and saw he'd left her, heading toward the hors d'oeuvres table on the far wall. There was no love lost between the councilman and the mayor. Roger Greenwood ran unopposed in the last election. Savanna supposed he must be a bit unsettled having to run now against Bellamy, ten years his junior and quite well-liked within Carson.

Savanna shook the mayor's hand, thanking him for coming.

He grinned widely, taking Savanna's hand in both of his. In his midsixties, the mayor looked dapper tonight in a suit and green bowtie, his silver hair freshly cut. "No thanks necessary, young lady. Anything that's good for Carson is good in my book! Are we ready to begin? I thought I might say a few words."

Savanna was taken aback. She hadn't prepared for this; she had her opening statements on a notecard, ready to go. "I, uh, yes, Mayor Greenwood, I think that'd be wonderful! Thank you." Well, she could always wing it a little, couldn't she? Less time for her behind the podium meant less to stress about. "Let's wait another few minutes, in case of late arrivals. I'll cue you," she suggested.

"Great!"

Savanna picked up her phone to text Sydney, and then spied her sneaking in the side entrance.

Syd must've caught the look on Savanna's face. She breezed by her, holding up her iPad. "I'm so sorry I'm here now the music is all ready just let me connect," she said in one rushed breath before disappearing through the doorway next to the kitchen.

Carson Ballroom's baby grand piano was now housed in the corner on the brand-new stage, and Savanna's original plan had been for Aidan to play a little during the banquet. He'd readily agreed, and she'd been thrilled. She'd learned last year that he could play almost anything. With him stuck in New York now, Sydney was a lifesaver. She'd immediately begun creating a playlist on her streaming app and had promised Savanna there'd be music even without Aidan.

Less than a minute after she'd zipped through the door, the neutral strains of classical orchestra music came through the ballroom speakers.

Sydney reappeared and hugged Savanna sideways, around the shoulders. "All good now. Sorry I was late."

"I—" Savanna broke off, seeing Mayor Greenwood heading for the podium. "Thank you! I've got to deal with this." She hurried over to meet Greenwood in front of the podium, returning his smile. "Mayor, I'll start things off and then hand the mic over to you, okay?" She adjusted the microphone, looking out over the room. It was a good turnout, with many local business owners in attendance.

A man wearing a reporter lanyard approached her just before she began. A cameraman laden with two cameras and a backpack slung over one shoulder followed him. "Landon King," he said, holding out a hand to each of them. "Mayor, it's good to see you. And Ms. Shepherd, I assume? It's nice to meet you. I'm covering your banquet and the festival for the *Allegan County Newspaper*. Okay if we grab a few quick shots of you and the mayor before you get things rolling?"

Ah. Savanna remembered John Bellamy mentioning the newspaper was sending someone to write up the evening. The more publicity, the better, John had said, and Savanna agreed. She wanted this year's Art in the Park festival to be the best yet. "Of course," she said, nodding to Roger Greenwood. "Right here?"

She posed with Mayor Greenwood, her face feeling like it might freeze into a permanent toothy smile while the photographer snapped several photos.

"Thank you so much," King said, handing her his card. "I'll catch up with you later on with a couple of questions for the article."

With that out of the way, Savanna moved back to the podium. Happy to turn the mic over to the mayor after she thanked everyone for coming, Savanna stood a few feet away while Roger Greenwood opened with a joke. Savanna wondered, as he was waxing nostalgic about Carson through the years, how many people in town had spotted the beheaded statue of Jessamina Carson tonight. Probably most, she guessed.

He finished and stepped aside for Savanna.

"Thank you, Mayor Greenwood. A couple of housekeeping items before we dig in to the amazing dinner Chef Fratelli prepared for us tonight. I want to thank everyone who's volunteered in some way to be part of the festival. I believe the Art in the Park event will gain our town visibility and help boost Carson's tourism this season. We're already seeing a preview of that, with Rose's B&B and the Mitten Inn being booked solid through mid-July."

She heard a whoop from crowd—Mitten Inn's owner was grinning widely. Savanna recognized Mia from her mother's euchre card game group. She was seated next to elderly Rose Munsinger and her daughter, of Rose's B&B. Savanna loved that Carson's small business owners were able to be friendly with each other, despite built-in competition.

Savanna continued. "It's not too late to sign up, whether you'd like advertising, offering goods and services or anything else I might've missed. Find me tonight, or contact myself or Councilman Bellamy through the event website, and we'll be happy to work with you!" She spotted Joe Fratelli and his sous chef at the doorway to the kitchen. He gave her a small thumbs-up and a nod, smiling. "And it looks like dinner is served! Thank you to the good folks from Giuseppe's restaurant. Enjoy!"

Savanna was surprised to find she had no trouble finishing off a full serving of the tortellini. She sat back in her chair, now finally relaxed. She'd have loved to sit with her family tonight, but she'd see them at Sunday dinner tomorrow. Her table currently held the three judges, engaged in a lively conversation about something across from her, and Britt, John Bellamy, and Bellamy's assistant, Yvonne Marchand. Savanna knew the eldest judge, a gallerist she'd crossed paths with a few times at Kenilworth in Chicago. The only female judge, art critic Talia DeVries, sat between him and the younger male judge, another well-known art critic.

Talia DeVries turned to Savanna suddenly. "You'd know," she said excitedly.

"I would?" She hadn't been tuned in to their conversation.

Talia nodded, tucking a sleek strand of her platinum-blond bob behind one ear. "What medium of submitted art has won first place most often for this event?"

"Oh!" Savanna thought for a second. "I'm not sure. Michigan Arts Council started the festival in 1991, when Carson was well known for its artists' colony. We actually hosted the very first event here. But as far as the winning pieces, I have no idea."

"Hmm," Talia said. "We were just curious. Have you gotten a lot of submissions so far?"

Next to Savanna, Yvonne laughed. "Have we gotten a lot? John's office was overflowing. We had to move it all to his home office."

John Bellamy agreed. "We haven't counted. We're still going through the acceptance process," he said, gesturing toward Savanna and Britt Nash, the three of them comprising the selection committee.

"And cutoff isn't until next Friday," Savanna added. "Your judging panel will have your work cut out for you!"

Talia smiled. "I don't mind. I was thrilled to be asked to sit on the panel."

A decade ago, Savanna doubted Talia DeVries would've agreed to be part of this event; her original impressionist artwork had been showcased in one of New York's most prestigious galleries, the young DeVries touted as an artistic prodigy. But, for whatever reason, there'd never been any follow-up to her debut pieces; she'd instead pursued a career as an art critic, with a monthly column in *Galleries Galore* magazine.

Savanna excused herself, seeing the waitstaff clearing tables and a delicious array of desserts being carried out. "Everything going all right, Joe?" She poked her head into the kitchen. Fratelli was drizzling sweet sauce over a dozen small white plates holding pastries as Remy James packed up kitchen utensils into a large carrying case.

"Right on schedule." Joe nodded without glancing up. "Back out there with you, Madam Hostess! We've got it handled."

Savanna laughed. "All right then!" She hung back a bit, looking over the room. Tonight was a lovely success.

As she drifted toward the front of the ballroom, she caught a flurry of movement in her peripheral vision. In the vestibule, on the opposite side of the red-velvet-curtained wall of windows, the councilman seemed to be having words with a man Savanna didn't recognize. John Bellamy was talking with his hands, quite animated, and the other man leaned in toward Bellamy, jabbing one aggressive finger into Bellamy's chest. Both men looked upset. Savanna moved toward them, and then spotted Talia DeVries already walking through the doors into the foyer. Maybe DeVries thought she could settle things down?

Savanna hesitated, unsure of what to do. From where she stood, she couldn't hear a thing. They didn't need this perfectly executed banquet to end with some kind of drama. DeVries stood between Bellamy and the other man. He was taller than John Bellamy, maybe in his forties, and his face was flushed red as he spoke. What on earth was Talia DeVries saying to the stranger? He took a few steps back, looked down, and then turned on his heel and left, walking out into the rain.

Savanna looked around; Sydney was a few tables away. She grabbed her sister's arm, pointing. "Who is that?"

Sydney squinted. "That guy outside?"

"Yes."

"I don't recognize him. Maybe he's a husband of one of the shop owners?"

"That's Paul Stevens," a deep voice came from behind Savanna, and she turned to find the reporter just standing up from his table. "He owns Lakeside Pier Hotel in Grand Pier."

"Grand Pier? That's an hour from here. Are you sure?

You know him? He seemed very upset about something just now."

Landon King shook his head. "I don't know him well. But I've covered Art in the Park ever since I've been with the Allegan County paper, and Grand Pier hosted the last three years. Paul's normally pretty reserved. What happened?"

Savanna shrugged. "I don't know." She gestured out toward the vestibule, where Talia DeVries and the councilman now stood with their heads close together, deep in conversation. Savanna was going out there. If something related to the festival was going on, she needed to know.

DeVries gripped Bellamy's arm, frowning, looking as if she was trying hard to get her point across. Savanna pushed through the door, and the two abruptly stepped apart.

"John?" Savanna stared at him. "Is everything all right?"

"Everything's great," Bellamy said, unruffled.

Talia DeVries looked discouraged. Frustrated. Something. What on earth had she interrupted? She made a mental note to ask him about it later.

"We should get back in there," the councilman said. "I'm dying for dessert."

SAVANNA USHERED OUT the last guests—Rose of Rose's B&B and her daughter—thanking them for coming. She moved around the room among the two Carson Ballroom employees, helping put chairs away. It was a relief to have the banquet behind her; she'd planned and worried about it for weeks.

"Oh, sir, I'm sorry, we're closing up," one of the staff spoke in the now-quiet room and Savanna glanced up, hearing the door open from the vestibule.

Aidan Gallager stood in the doorway, a black suitcase trailing behind him.

Chapter Three

SAVANNA'S BREATH CAUGHT in her throat for a moment. Aidan was completely out of context, still in New York in her mind. Except he wasn't. He was here and, from the looks of it, he'd come straight from the airport. He wore a navy suit and white shirt with no tie. His dark, unruly hair was in need of a cut; he normally kept it short on the sides and a little longer on top. Combined with his five-o'clock shadow, it lent Aidan an uncharacteristic air of fatigue.

Savanna moved toward him, feeling her face break into a smile, matching his.

Aidan's deep blue eyes crinkled at the corners, and he left his suitcase as he met her in the middle of the ballroom. They each stopped, a cushion of space between them. He seemed taller than she remembered.

"Hi," she said, her voice betraying her and coming out breathier and softer than she'd intended.

"Hi," he returned, his deep voice also quiet.

If she'd allowed her body to listen to her heart, she would've sprinted across the room and leaped into his arms. Now that he was within arm's length, Savanna hesitated.

Aidan took the decision out of her hands and moved closer, hugging her.

Savanna hugged him back, flooded with warmth. Oh, he smelled good. Clean—not a generic, soapy clean, but some kind of masculine, faintly spicy scent, just a hint of it where her cheek briefly touched his lapel.

"I've missed you," Aidan said, bending so his lips were near her ear, sending shivers zinging down her spine.

"I missed you too," she whispered before they both let go. Savanna smiled up at him, her cheeks feeling like they were on fire.

"I'm so sorry—" he began.

"I thought you weren't—" she said at the same time, and then laughed. "I'm sorry," she began again. "Go ahead."

He shook his head. "I interrupted."

Things felt too formal and polite between them. She hadn't seen him in over two weeks. They'd texted a little, and talked on the phone less than that, but connecting was hit and miss between their schedules. She wished she could rewind to the comfortable, easy rapport of their last date. Every time he left, it was like starting over again when he returned.

"I didn't think you'd make it back this weekend," she said.

"I tried to get here in time for the banquet. That was the plan, anyway. But my flight got delayed. I was going to surprise you." He gave her that slightly crooked smile, shrugging.

"You did."

"Better late than never, I guess. How did it go?"

"Perfectly," Savanna said. "Everything went great. But—

yesterday you said they needed you for at least a few more days. How are you here?"

"I'm not. Not really. I'm due back again Monday."

"Oh." Savanna heard the disappointment in her own voice. She had no right to feel this way; they'd only just started dating. She tried to put a spin on it, an attempt to cover her initial reaction. "Does Mollie know you're back? She'll be thrilled."

Aidan smiled. "No. It's past her bedtime, but she's my next stop. I wanted to try to catch you here before you were gone for the night."

"I'm so glad you did."

"Are you almost finished? Do you need a ride?"

"I was about to head out, but I have my car," Savanna said.

He nodded. "Okay. I'll walk you out?"

Aidan followed her to the kitchen where she gathered her purse, laptop, and an overfilled box of flyers and registration forms from the business owners who'd signed up tonight. He took the box out of her hands as they went back through to the entrance to retrieve his suitcase.

Supplies from the evening stowed in Savanna's back seat, Aidan held the driver's-side door open for her. At nearly eleven p.m., it was full dark, and quiet in town.

Savanna was acutely aware of how close they stood to each other, but how vast the distance felt. In their paltry three dates, over the course of a couple of months, the chemistry between them had only grown. Now, Savanna focused on Aidan's neck, the small V of skin where the top button of his collar was undone. He must be exhausted. Work and then racing to the airport, trying to make it back to Carson in time to surprise her. She raised her gaze, meeting his eyes. That hadn't changed—she sometimes still had trouble looking at him. Especially this close.

"So, I got some good news today," he said, one hand resting on the open driver's-side door frame where she stood. "They finally hired a new chief of cardiothoracic surgery. She'll be up and running within two weeks."

"Oh! Aidan, that's such good news!" Savanna beamed. "Oh my gosh, wait until you tell Mollie."

"She may be less excited than we are." He laughed. "Her grandparents have been spoiling her like you wouldn't believe. But I'm so relieved. It'll be good to have my head fully in Carson again. It'll be good to see more of you, I hope," he added.

"I'd love that."

"How about Friday?"

Savanna raised an eyebrow at him. "This Friday? You'll be here?"

He made a face, drawing the corners of his mouth down. "You don't trust my crazy, unreliable promises?"

She laughed. "That's not it. I know you have no control over your schedule."

"I will soon. So, Friday?" He moved his hand across the top of her car door and covered Savanna's hand with his.

She let go of the door frame and turned her palm up in his. She kept her hand in his larger one between them now at her side. He was so warm. "Yes. Friday."

"It's date," he said, his smile reaching the corners of his eyes. Aidan's whole face smiled when he did.

Savanna could feel her heartbeat in her throat. He was close enough to kiss. Somehow, that hadn't happened yet for them. She took a deep breath; she had to get this under control. She was a grown woman. There was no reason she should be reduced to a pile of mush every time Aidan Gallager was near. "Well," Savanna said, looking down at her keys. "I should get home."

"Sure," he said. He stepped back to let Savanna get in her car and closed the door.

Once seated, she started the car and pressed the button to lower the window. Savanna smiled up at Aidan. "I really appreciate you flying home. Have fun with Mollie and your family tomorrow."

Aidan's family wasn't entirely his; he'd moved to Michigan when he got married and had stayed in Carson after losing his wife when Mollie was four, wanting his little girl to be close to her grandparents. He'd bought old Dr. Milano's clinic, added a partner, and split his hours between the clinic and Anderson Memorial in town. Aidan never talked much about his own family or the life he'd lived before, in New York. Savanna only knew he had a younger brother, Finn, and that the boys had lost their parents as kids.

He leaned down, one hand on the roof of her little car. "Be careful going home. I'll talk to you this week."

SUNDAY NIGHT DINNERS were tradition in the Shepherd family. Tonight was Sydney's turn to cook, and a delicious aroma wafted to Savanna as she and Fonzie walked around the side of her parents' house, the double French doors to the kitchen standing wide open. Basking in the sun on one of the deck chairs was Pumpkin, the Shepherd family's plump orange tabby cat. He raised his head and meowed at Savanna as she gave him a quick scratch between the ears before she followed her little Boston Terrier inside.

Sydney stood at the stove, the whole countertop strewn with recipe ingredients—orange carrot heads, the green husks from peas, scattered onion peels, asparagus stalks. Next to the large frying pan on the stove were two glass bowls, one with what looked like a chopped cilantro-and-garlic combination, the other filled with long-grain rice.

Savanna peered over her younger sister's shoulder. "What are you making? It smells so good!"

"Seafood Paella." Syd scooched Savanna away from the stove with a hip-check. "Don't even think about it—no samples until it's ready."

Savanna rolled her eyes and went around to the opposite side of the island, sitting across from her sister. "Fine. So bossy. Thank you for handling the music last night."

"I loved doing it. Your banquet was fantastic. Everyone seemed to really be enjoying themselves." She sprinkled the garlic mixture over the simmering dish, folding it in and making her bracelets jingle.

Through the doors, the sound of a motorcycle came from the driveway. "Dad's home," Savanna said. Their father restored classic bikes in his spare time. Today's weather was perfect for a ride.

Harlan came through the doors, followed closely by his son-in-law, Travis, and Savanna's nephew, Nolan. Spotting Savanna, the four-year-old zipped across the kitchen and hugged her. "Auntie Vanna!"

She bent down, scooping him up in a bundle of flying white-blond hair and giggles. She'd grown accustomed to being "Auntie Vanna." She liked that Nolan had an exclusive name for her.

"Swing me! Come on, let's go!" He was on her hip, throwing his whole body toward the yard through the open French doors and making her laugh.

Travis spoke up. "I hope it's okay it's just us today. Skylar isn't feeling well."

Both sisters frowned at him. Harlan looked over his shoulder from the sink, where he'd rolled up his sleeves and was scrubbing his hands and arms. Skylar didn't get sick.

"What's wrong with her?" Sydney asked.

"I don't think it's anything to worry about," Travis said. "She may be coming down with a little bug."

"She seemed fine last night," Savanna said.

He nodded. "She was. But today she says she just wants to take it easy. We left her on the couch with blankets and magazines. I promised to bring a plate home for her."

"She's the most stubborn of all of you," Harlan's deep, rumbling voice chimed in. He dried his hands on a kitchen towel and rolled his sleeves back down over tan, muscled forearms. "If she isn't feeling better by tomorrow, make her go to the doctor."

"Tough to *make* your daughter do anything." Travis smiled. "But I will, don't worry."

Savanna flipped Nolan onto his back, carrying him like a baby. "I'm taking this kid outside to the swings until dinner's ready," she called, tickling his tummy and eliciting a shriek.

As they were sitting down to eat at the long dining room table, Charlotte joined them. She'd been upstairs on a conference call the last hour or so; she worked as a management consultant, and often traveled on business. But the trips were usually short, a few days at most, and sometimes she convinced Harlan to join her for the more exotic locations.

Today, missing a sister, the group at the table was palpably smaller. Savanna hoped Skylar would be okay. She'd have to stop by tomorrow after work, if she was still under the weather. Travis didn't seem overly concerned, which put Savanna at ease. He doted on Skylar and Nolan. He built his work schedule around her hours as an attorney, making sure one of them was always there for their son, as Skylar headed up the Carson branch of a large law firm out of Lansing. Travis was smart, funny, and good-looking in a just-stepped-off-my-yacht manner. Nolan had inherited all those traits, especially his father's goofy side.

Sydney's Seafood Paella was amazing. When she brought a pineapple upside-down cake to the table after dinner, Savanna groaned. "I am way too full!"

"So none for you?" Sydney paused cutting pieces, looking at Savanna.

"Did I say that?" She held out her hands for a plate. "Cut one for the councilman too, please. I'll take it to go. I promised I'd drop off the registration forms from last night."

"How is John? We didn't get a chance to talk with him at the banquet," Harlan said.

"Yes, how's his campaign shaping up?" Charlotte asked.

"John's great, although I still don't know what that scene in the vestibule was about last night," Savanna said.

"We noticed that too," Harlan said. "It looked pretty heated."

"I plan to ask him about it when I see him. One of the art critics went out there, and it seemed to break things up. But as far as his campaign, he has all these new ideas for Carson. I think it's going to be a tricky choice, the election. Mayor Greenwood is great, but people might be ready for a fresh approach, you know?"

"I wouldn't want to be in his shoes," Harlan said. "Everyone loves Roger Greenwood. But you're right, he's been in office a long time."

"It should be interesting," Charlotte agreed. She took the extra plate of cake and moved into the kitchen, wrapping it up for Savanna. "Give him our best, will you?"

An hour later, Savanna stood on John Bellamy's front porch, generous serving of pineapple upside-down cake in one hand and a newly filed and organized Art in the Park binder under her arm. She was pleased so many additional businesses had signed up to be involved in the festival. She knew John would be too. She was dying to ask him what on earth all that fuss was about last night.

She rang the bell again. The light was on through the entry into the two-story foyer, which faced a double staircase, leading on each side to either the living room or his large, plush office. She knew, because she and John had met here a few times this month to go over festival details. He had a beautiful home. The hallway light upstairs was also on, and she heard something through the door—probably the TV. Maybe the volume was up too high and he hadn't heard her.

Savanna pressed the doorbell a third time and moved to the tall glass windows framing the front door. Plate in one hand, she cupped the other at the glass, peering in, hoping to spot movement. It was only 9:30—John couldn't possibly be sleeping yet.

She gasped, sucking her breath in sharply. At the bottom of the staircase, just through the doorway to the dining room, one leg was visible, sprawled on the marble floor, brown wingtip shoe half off. Completely still.

Chapter Four

SAVANNA HEARD SIRENS approaching within minutes of her 911 call. The front door was locked, so she'd raced around the back, hoping for a way in to help John, but to no avail. She'd even thought to try a few of the ground-floor windows; everything was securely closed. He must be the only person in this town who actually locked his doors.

She stood on the front walkway, watching the end of the street for the emergency vehicles. She so hoped he'd be okay; there was no way of knowing how long he'd been lying there. Savanna knew it was John, because she recognized his shoes—shoe, she mentally corrected. She could see nothing of him at all besides that one leg. Her stomach flipped over as an ambulance turned onto John's street, followed by two police cars, all pulling into the driveway.

A momentary rush of relief filled her when Detective Jordan followed the paramedics across the front lawn. Whatever had happened, Nick Jordan would make sure everything was okay. He always did.

She started talking before they reached the porch. "It's locked. The back door too—I checked. I can see him in there, on the floor. I came by to drop off some papers, and he didn't answer the bell." She could hear her voice shaking.

She and John Bellamy weren't close, but she'd come to think of him as a friend in the last month since working together on Art in the Park.

The young uniformed officer with Jordan carried a long, heavy-looking metal device. He went to work on the front door with the end that resembled a claw.

"It just takes a minute," a voice said behind her, and she turned to find Sydney's fireman ex-boyfriend, Brad. "It's called a Halligan bar. We'll have the door open in a sec."

"Oh! That's great. Thank you." Sydney had broken up with him a couple of weeks ago. From what her sister said, Brad had taken it hard.

A female emergency response worker joined them, dispelling the awkward moment. She looked down at a clipboard. "You made the call? Are you Savanna?"

She nodded. "Yes, Savanna Shepherd. I just got here. I talked to him earlier today." She heard the door open with a loud *pop*. Detective Jordan took the lead, rushing inside, one hand under his jacket on the holstered gun Savanna knew he kept there. Another officer went with him, followed quickly by Brad and two paramedics.

Savanna stood outside, watching nervously. She looked down and found that her hands were clasped together at her waist, knuckles white. He'd be okay. He had to be. Maybe he'd fallen? Or...he was too young for a heart attack, wasn't he?

On each side of the councilman's house, neighbors were emerging from their homes. It was a quiet neighborhood, with sprawling yards and one large brick colonial after the other. Savanna didn't want to hear John's neighbors speculate about what had happened. She climbed the stairs to the front porch, taking a tentative step inside, the faint sounds of a television mixed with the crackle of a police radio drifting to her.

In the foyer, facing the staircase, John's living room was on the left and his office on the right. Savanna had never set foot in the formal living room; it didn't look as if many people ever had. She was more familiar with his office, on her right. His imposing mahogany Habersham desk was pristine, over which hung his beautiful Piet Mondrian reproduction of *Red Tree*. She forced herself to focus on the room so she wouldn't have to see John in the adjacent hallway. The blues and reds in the painting were set off by the deep mahogany frame. Aside the collection of Art in the Park submissions set up on a long table near the front window, the office was as meticulously neat as John always kept it.

She heard footsteps above her, and the officer upstairs called down, "All clear up here."

Savanna glanced up and saw a navy uniformed officer crossing the hallway. He frowned down at her. "Ma'am. You can't be in here."

She knew she shouldn't be in the house. She moved back toward the front door, the hallway to the left of the staircase now coming into view. As she stood frozen in the foyer, her fears were confirmed. No one seemed to be working to revive John; there was no flurry of activity around the councilman. Most of his lower body was visible to her now. He wasn't moving at all. Savanna felt her heart lurch at the thought that John might not be okay. Brad and the other paramedic stood with Detective Jordan, who touched the screen of his phone and dropped it into his pocket.

Detective Jordan donned purple gloves and bent down, picking something up out of Savanna's line of sight, near where John's head and chest must be. He straightened, and Savanna gasped, covering her mouth with her hand. Detective Jordan held a large knife between his thumb and forefinger, carefully placing it into a clear evidence bag.

The blade was covered in blood.

Savanna's knees collapsed under her and she half sat, half wilted onto the gray marble floor of the foyer, dropping the pineapple cake that was still in one hand and shattering the plate in the process.

She dimly registered a third police officer now standing over her. She heard her name. How did he know her name?

The officer bent down, and she recognized Detective Jordan's partner, George Taylor. She'd met him last year, when she was working on the Caroline Carson case. Skylar had called him "green."

The wall behind her back felt hard and cool, and her eyes closed briefly. All she saw was that knife dangling over John's lifeless legs. Her head felt spinny, and the officer blurred as she watched him stand back up.

"A little help."

Savanna squeezed her eyes shut again; her head was pounding. When she opened them again, Brad was wrapping a coarse brown blanket around her shoulders.

His partner, the young woman, was kneeling on her other side. She had a blood pressure cuff and stethoscope on Savanna's arm. "Eighty-six over fifty," she announced, removing it.

Brad placed a water bottle in her hands. "Savanna? You're in shock. Can you drink this?"

She nodded. "I'm fine." She heard her own voice and it sounded far away. "John needs help, not me."

Brad nodded, his face close to hers, worry furrowing his brow. "Okay. Drink that, please."

She did as she was told. Beyond Brad, the group around John had grown to five or six, blocking her view. She had no idea how much time had passed since she'd found him this way. She caught fragments of discussion from the front lawn, drifting in through the open door:

"...didn't hear a thing."

"...mowed his lawn around four today."

"...can check our security camera."

Another police officer passed her on his way into the house, speaking into his radio. "Confirmed point of entry at the Michigan basement."

The blood pressure cuff inflated on her arm again, and Savanna frowned at the paramedic. Kelly, that was her name. She remembered her from Caroline's house; the woman must always keep her hair in that long blond braid.

"Better," the paramedic said. "She's up to ninety-four over fifty-eight."

Savanna's head was starting to clear. "I'm fine."

"Not really. Finish that." She pointed at the water bottle

in Savanna's hand.

Savanna tipped the water bottle back, draining it. She leaned forward, meaning to stand up, and was met with a hand on each shoulder, Kelly and Brad stopping her.

"Hold on there," Brad said.

Savanna peered down the hall, still unable to see much of anything. A man wearing a black cap that read *Evidence* was snapping photos. She'd never in a million years expected to stumble onto this awful scene. What on earth had happened? What if this had something to do with that argument at the Carson Ballroom last night?

She took a deep breath. "I'm really fine. I feel better." She tried again to stand, and this time the two flanking her helped her up and escorted her outside, both her upper arms supported. Kelly held the blanket around her shoulders closed. "This is so unnecessary." She felt ridiculous now. She was fine. It was just the sight of that knife.

"Sit here," Brad ordered, settling her on the back ledge of the ambulance. He put a small red bag down next to her and shone a light into her eyes, making her blink. He placed a little plastic clip on her finger, watching the numbers displayed on the LED screen. Pulling a stethoscope from the bag, he put the bell to her sternum, bowing his head and listening. He straightened up. "Dizzy? Light-headed at all?"

"No." She shook her head. There was no use arguing.

He checked her blood pressure once more, nodding. "Okay. Much better. Do you want us to take you in to be checked out? You didn't hurt anything when you fell, did you?"

"I didn't fall." She stared at him, insulted. "I just... I sat down quickly."

Brad's poker face was impressive. He stared back at her. "Okay."

"I've never seen that much blood before. John is my friend. Was," she said, her voice dropping. "Was?" She thought she already knew the answer.

He sighed. "He's gone. I'm sorry. There was nothing we could do. I'm sorry, Savanna."

"How? I mean, I guess I know how. But why? And I don't even understand—all of his doors were locked. I tried to get in and help him. And everyone liked him. He was a good man. Who would do this?" She sucked in a breath, finally stopping for air. Her mind was replaying that scene in the vestibule last night, but nothing made sense.

Brad glanced up at the house, and she followed his gaze. More first responders had arrived; there were four patrol cars in the driveway now, and another white-shirted paramedic was standing on the porch talking with Kelly. Brad sat down on the tailgate of the ambulance next to her. "Take some deep breaths. In through your nose, out through your mouth. Here—" He reached behind Savanna, producing another bottled water. "Drink this. We don't need your blood pressure bottoming out again."

She did as she was told.

"Detective Jordan will find out what happened," Brad said. "Forensics is in there now, and I think I saw another officer go around to the cellar door out back."

Savanna shook her head. "The cellar?"

"You know. Most of these houses have Michigan basements. This subdivision has to be from the early 1900s. It was standard then. Even with updates, most houses still have two access doors, connecting to the house and the other leading outside."

"Right, Michigan basement. Our old house had one too." She recalled a tornado from her childhood; she must've been only five or six years old. There were sirens, and the screaming howls of wind outside sounded like a freight train. Harlan had made all of them rush down the dimly lit steps into the Michigan basement: dirt floor, stone walls, damp air. Skylar had carried their hamster cage, and Savanna recalled being so worried about the goldfish they'd left upstairs. They'd had to stay there for what had felt like forever. "So that's how the person got in?"

"Sounds like it. Detective Taylor said the door that opens into Bellamy's backyard was standing wide open."

She'd tried the front and back doors. She'd never even seen the old basement entrance. That must be the way the murderer had left, as well. The possibility of coming face-to-face with a fleeing killer occurred to her, and she shuddered.

The crowd of neighbors milling around the councilman's front yard hushed abruptly and broke apart as a pair of paramedics brought John Bellamy out on a gurney, a sheet topped with a dark wool blanket covering the body. Two officers worked to herd the concerned neighbors back to their houses; Detective Taylor and another officer chatted with a couple of people in the group, jotting information on notepads.

Savanna stood, moving away from the ambulance toward her car, which was now parked in by all the emergency responders. Brad was too occupied to keep babysitting her, thank goodness. They lifted the gurney into the back of the ambulance, and she watched the vehicle roll down John's street with lights and sirens now off, making her stomach do a lurching flip. She couldn't believe this was happening.

She leaned against her car as, one by one, workers exited the home and pulled out of the driveway. By the time Detective Jordan emerged through the front door, accompanied by the evidence tech, all the neighbors had gone home.

"And your guys got the cellar door too? What about upstairs? We need to know where else the killer was in the house."

The younger man nodded. Savanna heard his reply to Jordan, even with his voice lowered. "Seems like a straight homicide, doesn't it? Not sure if the councilman was a neat freak or if he just had a great housekeeper, but nothing appears out of place. It doesn't look like they were after anything but him."

The detective nodded. "All right. I'm going to finish up here. Go ahead back to the station."

Nick Jordan joined Savanna leaning on the side of her car. Reaching into his jacket pocket, he produced a small package of M&Ms, holding it out to her.

"No thanks," Savanna said, curious. Usually, Jordan kept packs of gum in his pockets. M&Ms surprised her.

"I promised my wife I was off cigarettes for good," he grumbled. "And I'm sick of gum."

She smiled. "Good for you."

"Okay, so do you want to come in tomorrow morning and make a statement, or do you want to do it now?"

She let out a long breath. The thought of a trip to the police station now made her want to curl up right here on the front lawn for a nap. Her arms and legs felt like wet noodles, and she really couldn't wait to climb into her soft, cozy bed. "Is tomorrow okay?"

"Of course." Jordan frowned at her, searching her features. "Are you all right? You feel okay to drive?"

"Ugh. Yes. I'm totally fine, I promise. I shouldn't have been in there—"

"No," he cut her off. "You shouldn't have. For all we knew, the perp was still in the house. I think you know better."

Savanna felt herself shrink in front of him. He wasn't wrong. "I do," she said, chastised. "I'm sorry. I just didn't want John's neighbors asking me questions. And then I saw the knife. I didn't expect—It took me by surprise. I've never seen anything like that before, except in movies."

He nodded. "Understandable. We don't typically see this type of thing in Carson either," he said. "It's a shame. But we'll find the killer. The knife gives us a good place to start."

Chapter Five

THE LAST WEEK of school at Carson Elementary was controlled chaos. On Monday morning, Savanna's students were far too full of energy to sit still for long, squirrely and giggly and silly. She used the stern, no-nonsense voice she'd spent this whole first year as the new art teacher perfecting, but it lost most of its power to the warm, sunny weather out the windows and the promise of summer vacation just five days away. The Carson community pool had opened this past weekend, which only contributed to her students' lack of focus.

When Ms. Jenson arrived with Savanna's third graders for her last class before lunch, Savanna made a snap decision. She'd been stewing about John Bellamy all morning, wondering about what could've happened, worrying about the Art in the Park event; she could use a change in scenery, and she knew the kids could too.

"You know what? Stay right there." She put a hand up, meeting the teacher at the doorway before the kids could separate and find their chairs. "Our project is outside today."

The whoops of excitement made her laugh, and Elaina Jenson smiled at her. "Great idea," she said. "If I had a dollar for every time today I've said, 'stay in your seat,' I could—

well, I could buy us both lunch, at least!"

Savanna's stomach growled. She was meeting Skylar and Sydney at Fancy Tails on her lunch break, and she was already starving. She smiled at the teacher; Ms. Jenson had been immediately welcoming when Savanna had come on last fall. Her son, Carter, was in the same first-grade class as Aidan's daughter, Mollie, and he was the sweetest little boy. "Is it always like this?" Savanna thought her work at Kenilworth Museum in Chicago had been stressful, but this job required a whole different level of expertise.

"Remember how they were right before Christmas break? Multiply that by ten. You kind of have to just go with it."

Savanna's students were already herding themselves back down the hallway toward the front entrance. "Class, hold on. This way! We're taking the secret passageway." She waved them toward her, ushering them into the library, which was adjacent to her classroom.

She turned, walking backward, and put two fingers in the air, the school's universal sign for quiet. They hushed. She was impressed. She glanced at her friend, librarian Jack Carson, who was helping his computer class get started, and mouthed, *Sorry.*

He gave her a curious look.

"Secret mission," she whispered, getting the attention of his second graders. She felt immediately bad for disrupting his class, but he grinned at her. She had second grade tomorrow; she'd make sure to give them the same treatment.

Savanna led her third graders through to the far side of the library, deliberately taking them up one aisle and down the next. They were starting to whisper and giggle now.

"Almost there," she told them, and pushed through the double doors that let out into the south hallway near the bus lot—which backed up to a wide field and dense wooded area. Once outside and across the parking lot, Savanna stood in the grassy field. "Okay. We're going to make nature wind chimes! It's a super-fun project, and you can take them home at the end of the week to hang outside your house for the summer."

She explained the idea and released the seven- and eight-year-olds to scavenge for sticks, twigs, pine cones, and even small stones. Tomorrow, they'd come up with designs and begin painting and decorating their items. Savanna would help them string their adorned discoveries onto painted discs. She'd bring in the exciting find she'd stumbled across in her parents' basement this past weekend, looking for her summer clothes in the boxes she still hadn't gone through from her move. Savanna had found the huge plastic bin she and her sisters used as kids to make their own jewelry and hair clips. It was still full of beads, colored ribbon, rhinestones, and who knew what else.

The hour flew by. The students were chatty but seemed calmer when she returned them to Ms. Jenson; she hoped she'd helped them expend a little of that pent-up energy.

She was walking down the sidewalk outside the school, heading for Fancy Tails, when Aidan's car pulled into the drop-off circle. He spotted her and turned around, pulling up alongside her.

"Twice in two days!" She smiled at him through the

window of his SUV.

"I'm on my way to the airport, but I was coming to check you out first," he said.

Savanna raised her eyebrows in surprise. "Oh really?"

He grinned sheepishly. "That's not what I meant. I wanted to make sure you're okay."

"Why wouldn't I be?"

"I heard you passed out."

"Oh, for Pete's sake. I did not pass out. Who told you that?"

"I can't remember."

She looked at him skeptically. "I'm sure you can."

"Nope. Must've been someone in the ER this morning when I was leaving. Probably a well-meaning paramedic or something. What happened?"

She sighed. "You heard about the councilman, I take it? I shouldn't have gone inside the house. I just wasn't expecting—Detective Jordan picked up the murder weapon, and it kind of freaked me out. I only stopped by to bring John the forms from the banquet. And then, when I saw him on the floor, I thought at first maybe he'd fallen or something. I can't believe he's dead."

"It sounds awful." Aidan frowned. "I'm sorry you were the one to find him."

She came over and rested her elbows on the edge of the open passenger window. "I'm fine. Some well-meaning paramedic was exaggerating. When does your flight leave? I'm grabbing a quick lunch with my sisters—would you like to come?"

"Two hours," he said, looking genuinely disappointed. "With the drive to Lansing, there's no time." His phone rang over Bluetooth, and he glanced at the dash. The call screen read simply *Finn*. He tapped the red button to send the call to voicemail.

Savanna must've looked curious when he met her eyes again.

"My brother," he explained. "I'll call him back. He's been talking about coming for a visit."

"That's so exciting!" Savanna figured losing their parents as young teens must've made Aidan and his brother close, although it didn't seem as though they saw each other often. Finn was a med flight paramedic. He worked temporary assignments all over the country.

He nodded. "I miss him."

"Do you know when?"

"No. It might not even happen. He's tough to pin down."

"I'd love to meet him," Savanna said, smiling at Aidan.

"He'd like you." He returned her smile, but there were twin frown lines between his eyebrows, lending him a conflicted look. "He's a little…different. You'll have to keep that in mind. If he comes."

Savanna tipped her head. "Different how?"

He shrugged. "I don't know. Forget I said that. Finn's great—everyone loves him. I'll see if he actually has a plan this time."

She nodded. "I hope he comes." She was sort of dying to meet Aidan's brother. He knew her whole entire family, had known them for years as Carson's favorite family physician before he'd even met Savanna.

Aidan adjusted his seat belt, and Savanna caught just a glimpse of blue and purple polka-dot suspenders under his serious dark suit. "I should go. I'm using up your whole lunch break. But I'll see you Friday. Right?"

"Friday for sure. Safe flight, Aidan." It was something she said habitually; a well-wish for safe travels. Almost weekly to her mom, in Chicago to Rob, to any of her people about to catch a plane. Was Aidan her people?

"Thank you, Savanna."

A ridiculous little thrill shot up her spine. She loved the way he said her name.

She spent the rest of the five-minute walk to Fancy Tails replaying the conversation in her mind. She'd never worked up the nerve to ask him what the deal was with his odd accessories. Sometimes it was outrageous suspenders, sometimes rainbow-colored socks. It was rarely an article of clothing as visible as a tie. Unless you happened to be looking at the right moment, Aidan's look was impeccably professional and classic.

Skylar and Sydney were already seated at the red and chrome table in the corner when Savanna pushed through the door to the grooming salon. She flipped the St. Bernard sign on the glass door to the side that read: *Never trust a dog to watch your food! We don't! Closed for lunch.* Crossing to the shop side of the space, she noticed rows of delicious-looking mini-cupcakes sitting on top of the long display counter that held Sydney's homemade gourmet pet treats. Each one was decorated with a different-colored icing flower.

"Ooh, these look good! Dessert?" She picked one up.

"Only if your coat's been dull and lifeless lately. Or you're dog tired and need a pick-me-up," Sydney deadpanned.

"I should know better." Savanna joined them at the table. Skylar had supplied lunch today: turkey club wraps and Mary Ann's sodas from the deli next to her office, two blocks down from Fancy Tails & Treats in the opposite direction of Carson Elementary. "I'm sorry I'm late," she said. "I'm starving!"

"Tell us what happened last night," Skylar demanded. "You were *there* when the councilman was murdered? You didn't think maybe you should've let one of us know you were okay?"

"What? Who told you that? I wasn't there, I just found him afterward." Savanna shook her head at her older sister. "Wait a second. Are you feeling better? Travis said you were pretty sick yesterday."

"I'm fine."

Savanna scrutinized her. She did look fine. If anything, she looked better than fine. Her cheeks seemed pinker than usual. New makeup, maybe? "So it was just a bug?"

"I guess so. Now tell us what happened. My paralegal was in the coffee shop this morning, and he overheard that the whole Carson Village police department was at Bellamy's house last night. The barista told him a Shepherd sister interrupted the murder, but not soon enough to save the councilman. What on earth happened?"

"I took the pineapple cake over to John's, along with the banquet paperwork. He knew I was coming. I'd just spoken to him yesterday afternoon. But he didn't answer the front door, and then when I peeked inside, I saw him lying on the floor."

Sydney gasped, gripping Savanna's arm across the table. "Oh my gosh. How awful! Was he already dead? Did you see the killer at all? Like, fleeing?"

Savanna shook her head. "No. Sheesh, this town. I didn't really see anything. I saw part of John's leg, on the floor with his shoe falling off. I called 911 and ran around to the back to see if I could get in and help him. But everything was locked."

"And then Jordan and the paramedics showed up? They probably had to break the door down. I'm sure he called for backup once he saw John had been murdered," Skylar said, ticking off the details.

"Yes. Pretty much everyone was there. Plus all the neighbors. No one seemed to have heard or seen a thing. I feel so terrible for John—nobody deserves to die like that." She thought of something. "His poor family. I assume he has family? Does he have anyone in Carson?"

"Just Mia," Sydney answered. "His ex-wife. Oh, and I think there was a brother who lived out of state. John's been here forever though. I really thought everyone in town liked him…this is so strange."

Savanna had stopped listening at "ex-wife." "Mia who?"

"You know, Mia. Mitten Inn Mia? She's in Mom's euchre group. I've seen her at the house on a game night. Mia James."

"Oh, right," Skylar agreed. "Mia James. They've been divorced since—" She looked at the ceiling, calculating. "I'm not exactly sure. A long time. One of the partners in my firm was handling Mitten Inn's lease paperwork when I first came on, and Bellamy's name had to be taken off the contract. Something with so many years of alimony and the financials."

Savanna frowned. "I guess I didn't realize they were married. She must've reverted back to her maiden name, then?"

"Must have," Sydney said. "I wonder if they've told her about John yet."

"I don't know." Savanna sighed. "The whole thing is awful. And I'm a horrible person for even thinking about this, but I'm not sure now what to do about Art in the Park."

"What do you mean?" Sydney polished off the last bite of her sandwich and reached for another chip.

"He was my planning partner. And he was taking care of the permit and zoning stuff for the week of the festival." She scowled. "All the art submissions are still at his house, where we were going through them—there was no room in his township office for everything. Some artists actually sent full-sized copies of their work. Do you think Detective Jordan will give me access so I can collect the submissions? I'll have to get Britt's help. We were supposed to finish the acceptance notifications this week. *This* week, only the craziest week of the year at school." She groaned, resting her forehead on her palms.

"Hey." Skylar elbowed her. "It's going to be fine. You have us. We can help."

Sydney came around the table and gave her a sideways

hug. "We'll help, and Britt will be more than happy to pitch in. It'll work out."

"Thank you. Hopefully, John already took care of the permit stuff." She felt selfish even worrying about it. Poor John.

"Do you want me to email the planning director and check? We play golf sometimes—I don't mind asking him."

"Skylar, yes, that'd be great."

"Give me a job too," Sydney said, straightening up.

Savanna bit her lip, thinking. "I will. Let me think about it. I'll call Britt today. After I stop to make my statement at the police station. I told Detective Jordan I'd come in after work."

"Does he have any idea who could've done it?" Sydney sat back down.

She shook her head. "I don't think so. I don't know. He seemed confident they had enough evidence to figure it out—they have the murder weapon. And they know whoever it was came in and left through the door to the Michigan basement. Maybe they'll find fingerprints or something."

"It doesn't make any sense," Skylar said.

"It makes me wonder though," Savanna said. "What if there's a connection to the statue? What if smashing Jessamina was some kind of warning?"

Skylar sat back in her chair. "I never thought of that."

"I thought that was just kids?" Sydney frowned. "What was spray-painted again, Savvy? Carson something?"

"Never Carson." The statue had been power-washed Saturday right after Detective Jordan and his forensics tech had finished with the scene. Poor Jessamina was still headless, but the huge red words were gone.

"It's possible," Skylar said. "It's a little vague though, as a warning."

"You're right," Savanna agreed. "It probably doesn't mean anything."

"Well," Sydney said, "you'll be talking to Detective Jordan today. See what he thinks."

"I'll try. He isn't the best at letting me in on his theories. And he'll probably think it's dumb, the idea that what happened to Jessamina is connected to the councilman."

"Don't let that stop you," Skylar advised, beginning to gather up the papers and empty containers on the table. "He comes off a little gruff, but he knows you have a sharp eye."

She checked the clock over the display counter—the analog clock was a beagle with moving eyes and tail. "Oh boy, I've got to run." She helped Skylar scoop up the rest of their lunch debris and deposited it in the garbage can by the display case, and then bent to give Fonzie a quick hug and ear scratch. "Can I pick him up after I stop by the police station today?"

"Sure," Sydney said. "I'm teaching a class for Kate but not till later." She gathered her long red hair into a messy bun on top of her head and nodded toward the yoga studio across Main Street. "But my assistant will be here to close up."

"Perfect. Tell Willow I'll be here by five."

Sydney handed Savanna a bright-orange-flowered cupcake to give Fonzie. "Here, he's my best taste-tester."

The little Boston Terrier gobbled it in one bite. He'd adjusted quickly to life in Carson. She was so grateful Sydney allowed him to be the Fancy Tails greeter. He was well occupied while Savanna was gone at work.

She rounded the corner at the end of Main Street, and the school came into sight. She'd made good time; she needn't have rushed.

"Savanna!"

She turned to find Jack Carson jogging to catch up with her. "Where are you coming from?" she asked. She hadn't seen him near the shops as she walked.

"Grandmother's," he said, breathing hard and slowing down to match her stride. Jack wore his standard khakis and a light-blue button-down, pens and a pair of glasses poking out the top of the chest pocket. "I wanted to bring her some photos of the progress in the theatre. She says she remembers when it first opened, back in 1962. The very first movie shown was a black-and-white Alfred Hitchcock, can you believe that?"

"Wow! That's so cool. I'll incorporate some of the theatre's early classics into the mural. Oh!" She stopped walking and stared at him.

"What?"

"That's what you should do! Your inaugural movie at Carson Theatre should be a classic Hitchcock. To pay homage to the theatre's history. Ask Caroline if she remembers which movie played, and show that one on opening day."

"Savanna. That's a great idea! I'll ask her. I've got plenty of time to track it down."

She grinned. "It'll be perfect! I really can't wait. I miss going to the movies."

"Good. I hope everyone in town feels that way." Jack smiled at her. "So…Grandmother wanted me to make sure you're okay. She told me about John Bellamy; she heard you're the one who found him. She's worried about you."

Savanna wasn't surprised Jack had only learned about Bellamy's murder from his grandmother just now. He typically avoided the teachers' lounge gossip. "Your grandma is so sweet. Tell her I'm okay. Or I can tell her myself this week—Sydney and I owe her a visit. I just can't believe John's gone. And like that." She shuddered.

"I heard. It must've been awful."

She nodded. "I can't imagine why this happened. I've only recently gotten to know him, but everyone seemed to like him."

"Not everyone," he said, glancing at her. They were at the front entrance to the school now, and he pulled the door open for her.

"What do you mean, not everyone?"

"Well, he was a politician. I mean, sure, small town, but it's still politics. There was no love lost between him and Mayor Greenwood. John was pretty vocal about his platform and beliefs. You lose friends that way."

They stopped outside the door to Jack's library. He had a point. "Of course there was a rivalry between John and the mayor," she said. "I could sense that at the banquet Saturday. John was hoping to take his office. But, again, that's politics. Just business. And we both know Roger Greenwood. What I saw last night was…brutal. Personal. Maybe John rubbed a few people the wrong way, but there's no way what happened to him was over politics."

Chapter Six

SAVANNA WENT OVER every detail with Detective Jordan. After explaining it all to her sisters and Aidan, she couldn't wait for her part in the awful discovery to be over. But Detective Jordan was good; he asked astute questions.

"What made you look in through the window?"

"He knew I was coming. It didn't make sense that he wouldn't be home."

"When you went around to the back door, did you hear anything?"

"No, nothing."

"Think hard. Nothing? No rustling, door creaking, no sounds at all?"

"I...don't...think so." She was thinking hard.

"Why did you step into the foyer during our investigation?"

"I wanted to get away from the neighbors."

"What exactly were you looking for?"

Savanna looked at him blankly. "I wasn't looking for anything. I wanted to get away from the neighbors," she repeated.

"Officer Marsh said you were snooping around."

"I was not!" She was indignant. "I just stood in the foyer!

I think I...I was trying to find somewhere to look that wasn't directly at John. Or what I could see of John."

"How many times have you been in Bellamy's house?"

"I don't know. A few. My colleague and I were going through all the art submissions with John. We had a few more days' worth of work to do still. I'd been at his house three or four times, I guess. Not counting Sunday night."

"What parts of his house have you seen?"

"The downstairs, mainly. The front rooms, kitchen, dining room, bathroom."

"Nothing upstairs? Bedrooms?"

She raised an eyebrow at the detective. "Certainly not the bedrooms, Detective."

"So you were familiar with the main floor. To your knowledge, was anything missing, anything out of place last night?"

"I only saw the foyer and his office. You know that. And no. And by the way, Detective Jordan, your interrogation style could use some work."

Nick Jordan sat back, surprise painting his features. "What? You're not being interrogated, Savanna."

"You bark question after question, without giving a thought to the actual person sitting in this chair." Why was he treating her as if she'd done something wrong? "Did you ever stop to think you might get more elaborate answers if you didn't make the person feel immediately guilty? Even if they aren't?"

He was very still, focused on her, his expression unreadable. "No."

"Well, you should." She set her jaw and stared back at him.

He folded his hands in front of him, elbows resting on the desk. "You're right. I'm sorry."

Now she was surprised. "Thank you."

"I'll work on my technique," the detective said. "Sometimes it's the right approach, but you're right. Sometimes it's unnecessary."

Savanna laughed. She hadn't expected him to so readily agree with her. "I wouldn't try to tell you how to do your job. I'm sure sometimes it works great. But I'll tell you anything you want to know. You're already a little intimidating—you don't need to try so hard, you know?"

Nick Jordan smiled at her, and it completely transformed his features. "I get it. Let's move forward. Just a few more questions, okay?"

"Sure."

"So, nothing that you can think of was out of place or missing?"

She thought hard. There was nothing. The scene Sunday night was different, obviously, than the few times she'd been there. He typically had the television on in the background, and coffee brewing, but she'd never seen a dish on the counter or a jacket tossed over a chair. John's house was always meticulous, and last night had been no different. "Nothing seemed out of place, and I don't think anything was missing."

Detective Jordan nodded. "And the night before, at your banquet, how did the councilman seem to you? Did he enjoy the evening? Did he seem stressed about anything? Or anyone?"

"He seemed…like himself. Normal. He was excited about the festival. He did have a little, ah, argument, maybe? With a man I didn't know, out in the vestibule."

"A man you didn't know? Didn't you invite all the attendees?"

Savanna noted that his tone was now less clipped, more conversational; he was making an effort. "I did. But we also ran the invitation in the *Allegan County Newspaper* and on their website, open to all local business owners. I wasn't trying to keep sponsorship exclusive to Carson. John and I felt anything we could do to gain press and attention for Carson and the festival was a good thing, even if it meant businesses from neighboring towns could purchase vendor space or offer sponsorship."

Detective Jordan was jotting notes. "And you were never able to learn who the man was? Or what the altercation was about?"

"It wasn't really an altercation. The man was upset about something. He did kind of—" Savanna made the motion with one hand. "He jabbed his finger into John's chest. Talia DeVries was out there. Maybe she knows what the argument was about."

"Who's Talia DeVries?"

"She's an art critic. She's one of the event's three judges. She, John, and Paul Stevens were in the vestibule together. Paul Stevens," she said again, looking at Jordan's notepad. "The newspaper reporter recognized him."

The detective was scribbling furiously. "Stevens. And what reporter? Did he know who this Paul Stevens was? Is he from Carson?"

"The newspaper sent a reporter and cameraman to cover the banquet. The reporter said Mr. Stevens owns a hotel in Grand Pier. He said Grand Pier has hosted the Art in the Park event the last three years in a row."

"Interesting. Do you happen to have contact information for the judge who witnessed the argument...this Talia DeVries?"

"Of course. I can get it to you. She'll remember, I'm sure. She seemed a little upset herself about something," Savanna said.

"Really." Jordan tipped his head, curious. "Were they together? She and Stevens?"

"No. I don't think so. But after Stevens stormed out, she was talking to John. It looked...I don't know. Intense. That's when I went out there."

"Did you hear anything they were saying?"

Savanna shook her head. "No. It was brief. But afterward, John didn't seem ruffled at all."

He made a few more notes, and looked up at her. "Thank you, Savanna. This is very helpful."

She stood. "Absolutely. Um. Detective."

He stood and came around the desk to walk her out of his office. "You know you can call me Nick. Or Jordan. Right? I'm not going to arrest you if you do."

She laughed. "Okay. I know. It just sounds weird. I'll work on it," she said. "I have one question. I really need access to the collection of art submissions at the councilman's house. My colleague and I have to finish reviewing everything and send acceptance notifications by the end of this week. Is there a way I can go pack all of that up? Maybe the next time you're over there?"

Jordan nodded. "Yes, but not while it's still an open crime scene. How about tomorrow, late in the day? We should be able to grant you access by then. Just can't risk compromising any evidence."

"Of course," Savanna said. "I understand. Oh!" She suddenly remembered what she'd meant to ask the detective. They stood in the doorway to his office.

He raised an eyebrow at her. "I have a feeling you're doing it again."

She shook her head. "Doing what?"

"Details." He grinned. "You're cataloguing details in your head. I can almost see the wheels turning. What did you just think of?"

"It's probably crazy."

Jordan shrugged. "Tell me anyway. Your crazy ideas sometimes turn out to be spot-on."

"Jessamina. I was thinking about the vandalism of Jessamina. You don't think that's related, do you?"

"It's an interesting thought," he mused. "Not sure. But I doubt it. That's quite an escalation, from defacing a statue to murder."

"Right," she agreed. "I can see that."

"We can't rule anything out at this point. I'll keep it in mind. And you'll call me if anything else occurs to you." It was a statement more than a question.

"I will, Det—Jordan—Nick," she faltered and laughed. "Yeah, sorry, I can't do it. But I'll definitely let you know if I think of anything else!"

SAVANNA WAS SNUGGLED up with Fonzie on the couch, halfway through a bowl of popcorn and into her second episode of *Columbo*, when her phone on Sydney's coffee table jingled. It was Aidan. "Hi."

"Hi, Savanna." His voice was deep and quiet in her ear. "How are you feeling?"

"I'm totally fine, I swear." Her cheeks warmed. He was ridiculous, worrying about her. She imagined him in the apartment the hospital arranged for him, sitting on the couch, his long legs stretched out in front of him. Maybe the lights of the city were visible out the window behind him. Maybe he was wearing pajama pants and smelled of toothpaste.

"Just making sure," he said.

"Thank you. How was your flight?"

"Not bad. I downloaded *Hamilton* to watch, since it's apparently criminal that I never saw the musical."

"You did?" He was the sweetest. "So, aside from me shaming you into watching the film version, aren't you glad you did?"

"I am. I loved it. Feel free to shame me further if there are other important musicals I've missed and need to see."

"You're opening the floodgates like that, are you?" Savanna teased.

Aidan chuckled. Background noise came through the line. Maybe his television?

"I'll make a list to give you on Friday," she said.

"I can't wait."

She smiled into the phone as if he could see her. "Me too."

"Oh, ready?" Aidan's voice became muffled for a second.

"What?" Maybe he wasn't in his apartment. Was he talking to her?

"Sorry, Savanna. I'm walking out of the hospital now, we've got to get a cab. I'll talk to you later, okay?"

"Sure. Talk to you later," she said, but he was already gone. She frowned at her phone. Fonzie grumbled and moved closer to her on the couch.

She didn't know how he kept this schedule, constantly running. He must've been with a colleague, leaving work. She assumed later meant probably tomorrow, or sometime this week; he'd be going to bed when he got home.

Savanna forced her attention back to *Columbo*. Nearly twenty minutes later, her phone buzzed again. A text from Aidan.

Sorry, in the cab now. Was waiting for the new chief to finish up. We have a breakfast meeting tomorrow with hospital admin. She needed to go over talking points.

She. He'd just reminded Savanna that he was training the new chief of cardiothoracic surgery, who happened to be a woman. Quite likely a whip-smart, driven, gorgeous creature with everything in common with Aidan. Including a shared taxi, apparently, likely on their way home to the same apartment building. Of course they'd share a cab. The hospital probably had a contract or something for new and temporary staff. She was probably Aidan's next-door neighbor. Fan-flipping-tastic.

She typed back, *No problem. Have a good breakfast meeting.*

Thanks.

Fonzie leaped off the couch and sprinted to the front door as Savanna heard Sydney's key in the lock.

Had she misread the whole exchange? Was he only checking up on her to make sure she was okay, and that was all?

I'll let you get some sleep. Sounds like an early day, she replied.

Yes. Good night, Savanna.

Night. She shoved her phone away, across the couch cushions, as Syd set her gym bag on the bench by the front door. "Why are guys so clueless and annoying?"

"Hello to you too," Sydney said, and then glanced at Savanna's phone. "Aidan? What happened?"

"Nothing. I don't want to talk about it. He's confusing. Or maybe it's me. I'm just destined to have bad luck with guys."

"It's probably him." Syd flounced down sideways into the large, fluffy papasan chair beside the couch, stretching her neon lycra-clad legs out and pointing her toes. She glared at the television, her long red hair spilling over the wooden edge of the chair. "Why *Columbo*? Do you know how many other shows we could be watching right now? Like, ones from this century?"

Savanna held out the remote. "Fine, change it. Columbo's an underrated genius. You'd know if you ever watched an episode with me."

"It's okay. I need to shower. And speaking of guys…Brad called me twice today." She waved her phone at Savanna.

"Why? Did you call him back?"

"No. He left me a voicemail. It's been two weeks. He says he wants to talk. He doesn't understand what happened with us. I just… I never felt as strongly about him as he does me. How can I explain that without hurting him?"

"I don't know. But you have to try. If he's still hung up on you, you've got to be straight with him. Maybe it won't crush him—he's probably tougher than you think. Maybe he'll move on, and someone will fall head over heels for him instead of just putting in time." Savanna stopped and took a breath. Wow. Where had that come from?

Sydney was quiet and still, staring at her. Savanna opened her mouth to speak, not sure what else to say. Her sister scooched Fonzie out of the way and sat beside Savanna, pulling her into a tight hug. "Yes. You're right. You're a thousand percent right. I never really gave him a reason. I'll talk to him. I'll go call him back right now." She let go and stood up.

"Okay, good. Syd—"

Sydney interrupted. "Wait. You need to hear this, Savanna. Your bonehead ex-fiancé was an idiot. He wasn't just putting in time with you. He was too self-absorbed to see what he had. He did you a favor by letting you go. No one can crush you. You're the strongest person I know. Well, except Dad. Okay?" Her fists were on her narrow hips now and her gaze locked with Savanna's.

"Oh, sheesh. Don't make this about me." She sat back and pushed at Sydney's thigh with her fuzzy-socked foot. "Go. You said you're going, right?"

"Whatever. I know you hear me." She turned and pointed a finger at Savanna. "Let it sink in."

Savanna laughed. "I get it."

The doorbell rang, making them jump and setting off the bark alarm as Fonzie leaped off the couch and skittered to the front door.

Sydney placed a hand on the doorknob, glancing over her shoulder at Savanna. "Are you expecting someone?"

"No. It's late." She moved to the entryway next to Sydney.

Skylar stood on the front porch.

"Are you all right?" Syd pulled her inside.

"What's wrong, what happened?" Savanna's thoughts raced, worries about Nolan or Charlotte or Harlan. None of them simply appeared on each other's doorstep late at night.

"I just came from the sheriff's department." Skylar was breathless. "They've arrested Joe Fratelli for the murder of John Bellamy."

Chapter Seven

SAVANNA WAS ON her second cup of coffee before she left for school Tuesday morning. None of them had gotten enough sleep; Skylar had stayed until after eleven last night. How could Chef Joe have killed the councilman? Joe was one of the nicest men Savanna knew. Was it possible the knife she'd seen that night was one of his? Even if it was, someone must've stolen it from him. There was no way he was a murderer. She had known him since she was a kid, and it just made no sense.

Her phone rang as she was juggling her purse, tote bag, and the large bin of beads, rhinestones, and ribbons from her parents' house. She hurried, loading everything in, but the call had gone to voicemail by the time she got to it. It was Skylar, sounding frazzled and panicked. Savanna called her back over her car's Bluetooth system. "What's going on?"

"Savanna. I don't even know how this happened." Skylar's voice trembled as if she was about to cry.

She was instantly afraid. Her older sister never cried. "*What happened?* What can I do? Skylar, take a breath, talk to me."

"I overslept! Now Nolan is late to preschool, I'm late to my meeting in Lansing, and Travis isn't even home because he had an early consult in Grand Rapids. I never oversleep—this is terrible!"

Savanna stifled a giggle.

Skylar heard it anyway. "*Savanna!* Oh my God, stop it! Please, could you or Syd please take Nolan to preschool for me?"

"Yes. Of course, I'll be right there," she said, making sure her voice was dead serious. "Sorry. Two minutes." She glanced at the clock on her dash. She had time, and it wouldn't take long to drop Nolan at the little red schoolhouse next to Carson Elementary. Skylar never, ever asked anyone for help. She was honored to be the one she'd called.

After she arrived, Savanna kept a straight face and kneeled on the pale gray hardwood in Skylar's living room to tie Nolan's light-up sneakers. She gathered his tiny backpack and Ant-Man lunchbox, corralled her crabby, anxious sister for a quick hug, and ushered Nolan out the door.

Skylar waved to them from the front door. "Thank you," she called. "I'll call you later."

"Mama's barky today." Nolan's little voice came from the back seat.

Savanna met his gaze in the rear view mirror. "Is she?"

"All I said was that the pancakes taste funny, and she threw them away! She made me eat cereal instead." His round face was pouty, white-blond hair brushing his long lashes.

"I'm sorry, Nolan. Sometimes even mamas get barky, just like Fonzie when he can't have a treat, right?"

He nodded. "She still gave me my kiss though." He held

his chubby palm up, showing Savanna.

She'd seen Skylar do that—kiss his palm and then fold his fingers closed around it. She was a good mom having a bad day. "That's good. That means everything will be fine."

"Auntie Vanna?"

She passed the town park and turned onto the road that led to the schools. "Yes, buddy?"

"How long does Fonzie stay barky?"

She chuckled. "Not long. Your mama won't either, don't worry. You'll see when she picks you up after school today."

"Good." He nodded, as if her word was gospel.

Wow, this kid had his fingers wrapped all the way around her heart. Savanna winked at him in the mirror, and he finally gave her a smile.

She made a mental note to call Skylar later and find out what was really going on with her. Of the three siblings, their older sister was the most like their mother. Charlotte and Skylar were both organized, competitive, dependable as the tides. Skylar didn't oversleep. She didn't spend the day on the couch, either, unless she was truly sick—and she'd seemed just fine yesterday at lunch. She definitely didn't cry. The last time Savanna had seen her cry was when they were teenagers and Skylar had snagged her foot on a zebra mussel in Lake Michigan.

Savanna's busy day at school provided great distraction from worrying about her sister and trying to wrap her brain around Joe Fratelli's arrest. Her second and fourth graders loved the nature wind chime project, and she even had time to work on grades while her older kids crafted.

But on their way to Skylar's house later that evening, in Sydney's car, the worries of the day came rushing back to her. And along with the nagging feeling that she was getting way behind in her tasks for the Art in the Park festival, plus wondering if she'd even have a caterer for the event now, she'd been watching for a call from Detective Jordan all day. He was supposed to let her know by tonight when she could come pick up the collection of art submissions from Councilman Bellamy's office.

Sydney pulled her little hybrid into the driveway behind Harlan's truck and the SUV Travis drove. Skylar had asked her sisters to come over for dinner, saying she needed to talk to them.

"Mom and Dad are here?" Savanna glanced at Syd. "Did you know this was a family thing?"

"Nope."

"I think this is bad. Something's wrong with her. That's why we're all here."

Syd turned in the driver's seat and frowned at her. "Nothing's wrong with Skylar. I think this is about Joe."

She bit her lip. She hoped Syd was right. She followed her up the front steps and as Sydney pulled the front door open, they were greeted by the delicious aroma of spaghetti, Nolan's favorite and Skylar's specialty.

Skylar's house was a reflection of her personality. The contemporary exterior was complemented with pretty landscaping, neat, ornamental shrubs, and tan outdoor furniture on the stamped concrete porch. Inside, vaulted ceilings were met with neutral-toned walls and hardwood throughout, with a super-plush cream-colored rug covering most of the family room floor. Nolan's toys lived in and around a large toy chest Harlan had crafted in his woodshop, stained pale gray to match the flooring and adorned with Nolan's name in large, brightly painted wooden letters.

Skylar's square kitchen table had been widened with a leaf so they'd all fit. Charlotte and Nolan finished distributing plates and silverware, and Travis set the deep serving dish of sauce on a table mat in the center.

Once they were seated, Skylar stood, expression serious, fingertips resting on the tabletop as she looked at each one of them. Savanna swallowed around the lump in her throat; she *knew* something was up with her. That's what this was about. "I've gathered everyone here today because Travis and I have something to tell you. We've realized this house is just too big for the three of us."

"What? You're moving? Where?" Savanna was surprised; Skylar loved this house.

"You're staying in Carson though, right?" Sydney was nearly shouting. "We finally have Savanna back—you're not allowed to leave now!"

Skylar's face cracked suddenly into a smile. "Oh, for Pete's sake, you all look so freaked out."

Travis took her hand, matching her smile. "We aren't moving. But this house is too big for us."

"So," Skylar said, squeezing his hand, "we're adding to our family. I'm pregnant." She beamed.

"Oh!" Savanna clapped a hand over her mouth. The involuntary happy shriek surprised even her. Skylar laughed as she was surrounded by multiple pairs of arms hugging her at once.

Charlotte was the last to sit back down. "Not funny. That was not funny."

"Sorry, Mom." She looked sheepish. "I think it was a little funny? We did tell Nolan before everyone got here."

After a dinner filled with excited conversation about the baby, Harlan took the dish towel from Skylar's hands. "Travis and I have got this. Go talk with your mother," he said, nodding toward the table where Charlotte was chatting with Savanna and Syd. "You've just made us the happiest two-time grandparents in the world."

Skylar slid an arm around Harlan's waist, giving him a squeeze. "Thanks, Dad."

Later, after Nolan was in bed and Charlotte and Harlan headed home, the sisters gathered on the plush rug around the coffee table with three cups of fruity, steaming herbal tea Sydney had brought. Travis had some historical documentary on the television in the other room. Skylar said it was the one thing they could never agree on. He watched TV to be informed, and she watched for entertainment.

"Have you talked to Joe Fratelli? What do you think's going on?" Savanna asked.

"His arraignment is tomorrow morning," Skylar said. "I'm positive there's no way he could've murdered John Bellamy."

"Do they even have enough evidence to hold him?"

"They have the murder weapon."

Savanna shook her head. "I know that. I saw it. Is that

what's tying Joe to this?"

"It's his chef's knife. His knife was used to kill the councilman," Skylar said. "His fingerprints are still on the handle."

Sydney sucked in her breath. "That's bad."

"Okay, so it is his knife," Savanna said. "But you're sure he didn't do it. I mean, we've known him forever. I can't imagine him hurting anyone. There must be more fingerprints on the knife than his?"

Skylar shook her head. "Jordan has to loop me in on everything they've got, since I'll be defending Fratelli. There's a full set of his prints on the handle. There are a couple of partials, but they haven't identified them yet. He runs a busy kitchen, so I'm not optimistic those will even help."

"What about an alibi?" Sydney spoke up. "That's a thing, right? Can't anyone vouch for where he was when it happened?"

"The time of death was placed between eight thirty and nine Sunday night. You know Giuseppe's closes early on Sundays. They stop seating at six. I checked. The restaurant security system was turned on at 7:58 Sunday night. Joe and a few of his staff handled the closing tasks and turned on the system when they locked up."

"And then?" Savanna asked. "Maybe he stopped somewhere on his way home?"

Skylar shook her head. "No. He went straight home, showered, and was on his couch watching *America's Got Talent* by eight thirty. Alone."

The three of them were silent. Thinking.

"I'm going to argue that the knife's circumstantial, but there's some gray area there. I'm hoping to get him released on bond. I can't stand the idea of him sitting in jail until trial."

"Does *he* have any idea how this happened?" Savanna asked. Skylar hadn't said a word during dinner about his arrest. Savanna was sure she hadn't wanted to upset Harlan, since the chef was his friend. She guessed the information would probably become public tomorrow.

"I've had very little contact with him yet. We have a sit-down tomorrow, before the arraignment. I'll know more then."

"We'll figure this out," Savanna added. "I think the key is coming up with who could've wanted to hurt the councilman, and why." She'd already filled her sisters in on the argument she'd seen in the banquet hall vestibule, and the timing of Jessamina being smashed, but all of that seemed trivial in light of John losing his life.

"Tell him we're in his corner," Sydney said. "He needs to know that. The news will go like wildfire once it's out."

"I'll tell him," Skylar said. "I'll get in touch with you tomorrow after court, and at least then maybe we can come up with a plan."

On the way home, Savanna told Sydney to stop in town at Giuseppe's restaurant. "I have to pick up the catering forms," Savanna said. "I need to work on figuring out the menu for the Art in the Park opening day. If the restaurant can even still handle the event. We might need to find a different caterer. Which is a small thing to worry about, I know," she said, catching Sydney looking at her as they pulled into the parking space behind Giuseppe's.

"It is, but it's still your baby," Syd said. "Don't feel bad for worrying. If it falls through, we'll get someone from out of town. I'll help. Let's not decide anything until after we hear from Skylar tomorrow."

The two sisters were surprised to find Mia, the proprietor of Mitten Inn, at the bar, chatting with the young sous chef Savanna had met the other night during the banquet. The bartender was restocking the shelves at the other end of the space, and a woman in a serving uniform stood at the cash register, cashing out the only guests left a half hour before closing. The Italian American establishment held a warm, inviting atmosphere, conjuring old-world charm with soft lighting, starched red linen napkins on white tablecloths, high-backed wine-colored chairs, and the most delicious aromas wafting through the air.

"Girls." Mia spoke, motioning them over to the bar. "You're Charlotte's girls."

Savanna nodded. "Savanna, and this is Sydney."

"Yes, that's right," the older woman said, shaking both their hands. "Mia James. It's nice to finally meet you."

"You too. We're, uh, sorry for the loss of Councilman Bellamy." One should still offer condolences for the loss of an ex-husband, right? Had they been on good terms? What was proper etiquette for this?

"Thank you. Oh." Mia placed a hand on the tattooed forearm of the tall, thin chef behind the bar. "I'm not sure whether you've met my son? He's finally back home in

Carson, where he belongs." She smiled up at him. "Remy, Savanna and Sydney Shepherd. Girls, Remington James."

"We met," Savanna said. Remy was Mia's son? Until yesterday, she didn't even know John Bellamy had been married. Was Remy John's son? Or only Mia's? "We met at the banquet Saturday night. You and Chef Fratelli did such a fantastic job."

"Thanks." Remy pulled a rack of wineglasses across the bar and went to work drying and buffing each one with a white cotton towel and then hanging them over his head.

"Is there any word on that?" Mia looked from Savanna to Sydney and back, her voice now much quieter. "You heard he was arrested?"

Savanna nodded, not sure how much to say.

"Yes. It seems crazy," Sydney offered.

Mia was wide-eyed. "I know! I can't believe it."

"We actually stopped by to pick up the catering menu. I don't know if Joe mentioned anything to you?" Savanna looked at Remy. "About the Art in the Park event?"

He nodded. "He did. I'll grab the packet."

When Mia's son had disappeared through the double swinging doors to the kitchen, and presumably Joe Fratelli's office, she turned back to Savanna and Sydney. "You'll have to forgive him. He isn't a talker. And since the arrest last night, I think he's more than a little concerned about what'll happen with the restaurant and his job."

"That's understandable," Sydney said. "Is there a manager or someone who can help while Chef Fratelli is out? This must be overwhelming."

"Not really. Apparently there's a manager, but she's almost as new as Remy is. He's planning on working open to close until we know whether Joe will be back to work or not."

Remy reappeared, handing a large envelope to Savanna. "It's all in there. When you're ready, drop it back off, and I'll start putting orders in."

"Thank you. Should I wait, do you think? Until we…know more?" She didn't want to give the man more to fret about than was already on his plate.

A frown crossed his features, and the muscle in his jaw pulsed under his five-o'clock shadow. Remy's left eyebrow was intersected by a scar on one end, making Savanna wonder who this man had been—*where* he'd been—before he'd returned home to Carson. She didn't remember ever seeing him. She guessed him to be close to their ages. Remy shook his head. "That's okay. Chef will be back soon, I'm sure. I know he was looking forward to the job. I'll get it taken care of."

"Great. Thank you," she said again. "We should let you close up. It was nice meeting you. Both of you." Savanna looked at Mia.

"Yes!" Mia smiled at them. "Long overdue. Tell your mother I said hello."

"Have a good night," Sydney called over her shoulder as they left. The moment they were in the parking lot, Syd gripped Savanna's arm. "What. Was. That!"

Savanna stared back at her. "I know! Okay, so John's ex-wife is Mitten Inn Mia. And Mia's son is Giuseppe's new assistant chef? Or temporary head chef, I guess? Where did he come from? Do you remember him? Is he John's son too? Why don't I even remember Mia? Is it just because we were kids and didn't pay attention to boring adults?"

Syd pulled Savanna across the pavement to the car. She waited until it was started and they were on their way out of the parking lot. "I do not remember that guy Remy. I'd remember him. He's around our age, right? Late twenties, early thirties?" Syd glanced at Savanna and then back at the road.

"I think so. Syd." Savanna took a deep breath. "I'm just going to say it. If Joe Fratelli's knife was stolen to make him look guilty of killing John Bellamy, who'd have the easiest access to that knife?"

"His sous chef."

"If we don't remember Remy James, then where was he—where were *they*? How long ago did Mia open Mitten Inn? When was she married to Bellamy?"

"What did Skylar say? Remember, about her law firm and something about Mitten Inn's lease. She thought the divorce happened a long time ago, right? But Carson's a small town. We should remember Remy."

"You're right," Savanna agreed. "And we don't. But I know who will."

Chapter Eight

S AVANNA HEARD SYDNEY'S laughter before she even opened the door to Fancy Tails. She'd left school right after the last bell. She planned to grab some treats for Caroline Carson's poodles and go mine the town matriarch's memory for information about Mia and Remy James.

Fonzie ran over to her, his whole body wagging. Savanna stooped down and let him leap into her arms. He was a happy, wiggling ball of energy. She set him down, and he bolted across the shop to the toy basket.

Straightening up, she saw she was far from Fancy Tail's only customer. A middle-aged woman with a sweater-clad Yorkie in her arms stood behind the good-looking man Sydney was flirting with at the counter. She and the guy had a friendly back-and-forth banter going on about something. She could pick out Syd's flirting voice in a heartbeat—lilting, a little breathier, a little higher-pitched. She knew her sister was completely unaware—the one time Savanna had teased her about it, Syd had vehemently denied she sounded any different.

Curious, Savanna moved to the toy basket for a closer position and played tug-of-war with Fonzie while she tried to spy on the interaction at the counter. Sydney's sheer cream-

and-floral kimono over slim jeans and scoop-neck top, brightly colored strands of ribbon woven into her long, messy red side braid accentuated her already boho chic vibe. She pointed to the organic canine candies in the display case, explaining how she'd developed the recipe.

The man leaned toward Sydney, one large hand on the glass countertop. His sleeve was pushed up, revealing part of a tan, tattooed forearm. Stick-straight black hair fell over his forehead, and Savanna spied a dimple in one cheek as he flirted right back with her sister. "So you're telling me you *are* the boss? You run this place?"

"I *own* this place."

"No way. You can't be old enough for that." He shook his head, grinning.

Uh-oh. He'd hit her sister's sore spot—her whole life, growing up as Savanna and Skylar's little sister, Sydney had hated it when people treated her like the baby of the family.

Sydney's jaw squared and she stared at him. "Rude."

The man at the counter shifted, bowing his head a bit toward Sydney. "Ouch. All right, apologies, Miss...?"

Sydney moved to the register and rung him up. She handed his card back to him along with his purchase in a white box tied with a string. "Shepherd." The lilt in her voice was gone. She looked past the man and greeted the Yorkie woman. "Bernice, I'm so sorry for the wait! What are we doing today for Daisy?"

Bernice stepped toward the counter, where the man was still standing.

Syd afforded him one brief glance. "You're finished." She

held her arms out for the Yorkie, taking the dog and showering her with baby talk as she scratched her ears.

"I guess I am," the man said, one corner of his mouth rising in a half grin. He pulled aviator sunglasses off the collar of his T-shirt where they'd been tucked and put them on, nodding at Bernice and Savanna. Savanna read the white logo on the back of his jacket as he left: National Air Med Lifeteam.

Savanna tuned out the chatter between Sydney and Bernice. Her thoughts were spinning. There was no reason to think she'd just seen Aidan's brother. Literally no reason. He couldn't already be in town; Aidan wasn't even sure if he was coming to visit.

"Hello!" Sydney snapped her fingers in front of Savanna's face, jolting her back to the display counter at Fancy Tails.

"Hey, use your manners," Savanna said, pushing her hand away. She waited until Bernice exited. "Who was that guy?"

"Who knows. Did you hear what he said?"

"I'm not sure he knew he was being offensive, Syd." Savanna bit her bottom lip. Could it have been Finn? She'd never seen a picture of him.

"Okay, then he's both rude and clueless. He's not from here, anyway. I know all my customers. Hopefully he'll take the hint and shop somewhere else next time."

Savanna nodded. "I'm sure he will."

"Did you come in for something?"

"I wanted some dog treats. I'm stopping by Caroline's

before I meet Britt—I want to see what she can tell me about Mia James and her son. Have you heard from Skylar yet today?"

"No. But I'm sure we will. I'll come with you. Let me package up some chicken churro sticks for Princess and Duke." She poked her head through the doorway, calling to Willow. "Next appointment isn't until five—I'll be back by then. I'm flipping the lunch sign so you won't have to worry about the store."

Savanna clipped Fonzie's leash onto his collar. "Let's go see your friends!"

The short walk to Caroline's passed quickly, and they climbed the wide front steps to Caroline Carson's front porch. The Carson mansion was gorgeous and impressive, the rear of the house overlooking rolling dunes and the blue waves of Lake Michigan. Before Savanna even knocked, the poodles were at the front door yipping.

"Come in!" Caroline's voice came from somewhere toward the back of the house.

"She still won't lock her doors," Savanna whispered to Sydney as they entered. "Even after last year."

Fonzie and the poodles raced through the wide, two-story entry, past the gleaming, curved staircase, and down the hall toward Caroline.

Savanna and Sydney found her in the parlor, of course; if Savanna lived here, she'd spend all her time in front of these enormous windows too. The view was breathtaking: sails dotted the lake that looked more like an ocean, and to the far right, a few brightly colored umbrellas were visible in the distance on the public beach. Opposite Caroline's chair was the large mural of Lake Michigan on the far wall. She'd commissioned Savanna to paint it last fall, just before her ninetieth birthday, in the midst of someone trying to kill her.

Caroline greeted them with open arms, wrapping them in a hug. She carried her ninety years well. Her white hair was coiffed beautifully, and a tailored pale yellow blouse was complemented by a yellow and peach scarf and tasteful gold earrings. She let go and stepped back. "You two look wonderful, as always. Tell me everything. What's new?"

Sydney sat adjacent to Caroline in the other elegant wingback chair, and Savanna took the adjacent couch.

"You've heard about the poor councilman," Savanna said. "I suppose that's new. What else?" She looked at Sydney, widening her eyes. Were they allowed to spill Skylar's exciting news?

Sydney squinted, and Savanna knew she was considering. The two of them had always been able to communicate with just a look. "Savanna has a date with your Dr. Gallager this Friday," Syd told Caroline. "That's new too." She smiled sweetly at Savanna.

Savanna beamed. Her sister knew she was uncomfortable talking about her still-undefined friendship with Aidan, but Savanna didn't mind that Caroline was now laser-focused on her. She'd been thinking about the date all week. Two more days.

"I'm so happy. I think that's lovely," Caroline said. "Is he finished with all that New York craziness? Is he all ours again?"

"Not quite yet, but soon. I think another week or so. He's showing the ropes to the replacement cardiothoracic surgeon." She hoped it'd be just another week. She hadn't heard from Aidan since that interrupted phone call Monday night. Every time she thought about it, she pictured him in the back seat of a cab with a brilliant and beautiful heart surgeon, and her stomach lurched unpleasantly.

"About time he comes home. I'm starting to feel a bit neglected. I imagine you are too, dear."

Savanna's cheeks burned. "No! Oh, Caroline." She laughed. "We're really just friends. We're still getting to know each other. Truly. I don't feel neglected." That was a lie.

Caroline was scrutinizing her. "Well. Even so. We'll be glad when his attentions are back where they belong, won't we?"

She threw a look at Sydney. Her little sister had gotten what she'd wanted—to make Savanna squirm. Some things never changed. "Did Sydney mention she broke up with Brad?"

"No! Oh, my." She extended a hand out to Sydney, taking hers and giving it a good squeeze. "Relationships are never simple, are they? Are you doing all right? I'm sure it's been difficult."

Syd leaned back in her chair, letting the table lamp between the chairs block Caroline's view. She mouthed clearly to Savanna, *What the hell.* "I'm fine, Caroline. We just weren't right for each other. It was for the best—we talked yesterday, and I think he sees that now too. But it's so *fantastic* of Savanna to bring you up to date."

Caroline patted the chair beside her, and Princess hopped up, fitting her little white furry body into the space. "All right." Her voice held the stern edge they'd grown up hearing whenever their adoptive grandmother was less than pleased with them. "You two are still children, pinching each other when my back's turned. Tell me how your parents are. And how's Skylar?"

Syd gave Savanna a nod, shrugging. She looked as chastised as Savanna felt.

"Skylar's expecting! They just told us. She's due in October. I know she'd have liked to tell you herself," Savanna said, loving how Caroline's eyes lit up with this genuinely good news, "but she's so busy right now, between work and—" Could they say anything about Chef Joe?

Sydney took over. "Just between us, Skylar's tied up in the case with the councilman's murder. They've made an arrest, but she's convinced they've got the wrong person."

Caroline's gaze went from Sydney to Savanna. "Oh, my. A new baby? Skylar and her husband must be over the moon. I'll have to start a blanket—I've got the perfect soft cotton blend yarn upstairs. Thank you, girls. I do hope she isn't stressing herself. And if Skylar feels the wrong person's in custody, then I'm sure she's right." She held up a hand as Savanna started to speak. "I don't need to know, not if it hasn't been made public yet. She'd want you to keep that confidential."

"You're right. We have some questions though. We thought you might be able to help."

"You know so much about this town and all that happens here," Sydney added. "We were hoping you might tell us about John Bellamy's ex-wife, Mia James? And maybe about her son?"

"Ah. I see. I don't suppose you remember much about them, do you?"

"Neither of us can recall her son in school. He must be around our age?"

"Remington must've been eight or nine years old when they divorced. It was a bad one. I remember a lot of dirty laundry, accusations being thrown back and forth; never a good thing in a town the size of ours. I always felt Mia got the worst of it. She let him win. I don't think she could handle half the town gossiping about her. She took the boy and left—I heard she moved out west somewhere. She came back without her son."

Savanna sat on the round hand-tufted Persian rug, moving closer to Caroline, enthralled. "She came back without him? When? Where was he?"

Caroline took a sip from her tea cup on the table beside her. "Mia stayed away a good ten years. When she returned, she told everyone Remington was away at college. This must've been after you left for Chicago, Savanna."

"Why did she come back?" Sydney asked.

"Mia has a sister here. She teaches at the high school—Kimberly something. I'm sure she missed being near family. The boy did come home once, I remember."

Savanna and Sydney hung on every word; neither spoke.

"Now, that would've been when Mia opened Mitten

Inn. When was that? Five or six years ago? He worked in the kitchen for a time when the inn opened. The boy could certainly cook. Mr. Carson and I made a habit of having Sunday dinners there. Word was he'd gone to some fancy culinary school Mia paid for. Money well spent, if you ask me. One can always tell when the chef truly loves his work, and I believe Remington did. Does," Caroline corrected. "But one Sunday, Mr. Carson and I went for dinner at Mitten Inn, and it was terrible. Mia's son had gone. That was… I'm not sure. I suppose it was about four years ago, around the time little Nolan was born."

"But why? Why come home and then leave again? Didn't John have a say in any of this?"

Caroline sighed. "There was some kerfuffle at the inn. Mr. Carson and I tried to ignore it. I still don't know details. We met the young man a couple of times. He was nothing but respectful. He was a bit quiet, kept to himself, but who could blame him after all he'd been through, growing up? Anyway. Mia's son was gone before the town could even churn whatever had happened into a good piece of gossip. I really don't know much more. But it strikes me as sad, the way…" She frowned and stopped abruptly, tipping her tea cup up to finish it.

Savanna and Sydney waited.

Caroline's gaze went to the mural. "I wish John had reconciled with his son before he died. It just seems a shame. He never approved of Remington's choices. The boy got himself accepted at Yale but instead went to Europe, and believe me, the whole town heard about how angry John was with him. I think that's why he'd have nothing to do with his son when he worked at Mitten Inn. I wonder if they had any contact at all when he came back again and started working for Chef Joe."

Savanna exchanged glances with Sydney, who gave her the second affirmative nod in the last half hour. "Caroline, you do need to know; it's going to come out soon enough. Joe Fratelli was arrested for the murder of John Bellamy."

Caroline's hand went to her throat. "No."

Savanna scooted closer and placed a hand on Caroline's knee. "I know. We're working on finding a way to get him cleared. There's no way he did it."

"Of course not," she said. "Though I'm sure their history isn't helping his case. Oh, I wish I could do something!"

"What history?" Savanna asked, at the same time Sydney said, "Whose history?"

"Mia and Joe. They dated a couple of years ago. You don't—Well, I guess you wouldn't know, Savanna. You weren't here. Sydney, you don't remember? They dated for several months."

Syd was shaking her head. "I had no idea. This is *really* not going to help Joe. I wonder if Skylar knows."

Savanna made Caroline more tea before they left, and Sydney put the dog treats in the refrigerator after giving one to each poodle. They hugged Caroline goodbye with promises to come back next week.

The half-mile trip back to Fancy Tails was filled with wild speculation. Past the town park with poor headless Jessamina and back up Main Street to the shop, the walk seemed to be over in a flash.

"Mia dated Chef Joe?" Savanna asked.

"John basically disowned his son?"

"And for what? For doing what he loved?"

"So Remy's been in and out of Carson for years?"

"But what happened at Mitten Inn?"

"And how did we not know Remy was John's son?"

"They were at the banquet together! In the same room together!"

"Savanna, you'd become friends with John. You had no idea he had a son?"

"He never said a word! There's nothing in his house, no personal photos, just a few pieces of art on the walls."

"Could Remy have done something awful?"

"What?" Savanna asked. "What would be awful enough you'd have to move away?"

Sydney said nothing. She stared at Savanna in silence.

"Okay, no," Savanna said. "We're letting our imaginations get away from us. Whatever he did couldn't have been *awful* awful. His mom wouldn't have taken him back. Chef Joe wouldn't have hired him. He'd have gone to jail!"

"What if he did?"

Now Savanna was quiet.

"How long was he gone that time? Between when Nolan was born, so four years ago and just recently? Where was he?"

"Better question. Why would he want to kill his father?"

"Bad blood? Years of being treated like a bad son," Sydney said.

"No. If that's true, then why frame the one man who believed in him enough to give him a job?"

"Skylar said there were other prints on the knife. Remember? Maybe Remy didn't intend to frame Chef Joe."

"So he just recklessly stole the knife and murdered the councilman with it?" Savanna shook her head. "That doesn't make sense."

Syd put a hand on the door to Fancy Tails. "None of this does."

Savanna's phone buzzed. "I've got to run—I'm meeting Britt."

"Is Detective Jordan letting you into the councilman's house to get the art submissions?"

"No. Not yet. He says another day or two. He has to be with us. I get it. It's just going to delay the process; Britt and I will have to buckle down and get through all of them this weekend and send out the notifications by Monday morning."

"I'd offer to help, but you and Britt are better off without me. I know zip about art," Sydney said. "You're finalizing the menu at Giuseppe's tonight, right?"

"We are."

"Be careful."

Chapter Nine

THE LAST DAY of school before summer vacation began with Aidan. Savanna's wet hair was wrapped up in a towel and she'd just pulled on a summery periwinkle-blue A-line dress when her phone rang with a video call from Aidan. She glanced at her reflection in the mirror, eyes wide and cheeks still flushed from her steaming shower. She'd been missing him all week, excited about their date tonight, but the idea of Aidan seeing her without a stitch of makeup didn't thrill her.

She took a deep breath and answered. His grinning face filled the screen, and she instantly smiled back at him, trying to ignore the thumbnail video in the bottom corner of the screen of her with a pink towel on her head. "Good morning," she said. It was only 6:45.

"Good morning to you. I'm glad I didn't wake you."

Savanna took the towel off her head and shook her damp hair out, making a brief effort to finger-comb it. "You're up early too! Are you on your way in for rounds?" She was learning about a doctor's schedule since getting to know Aidan. Often, by the time a doctor arrived for clinic hours, they'd already spent an hour or two checking on their patients in the hospital.

He nodded in response to her question. "Yes, we're leaving for rounds in a few minutes. But I wanted to show you something."

Savanna caught his use of the word *we*. Apparently she'd been right, imagining Aidan sharing cab rides with the impressive new surgical chief. It sounded as if they commuted from the same apartment complex.

Aidan was off screen for a moment, reaching for something. He reappeared, holding up an airline ticket. "Look."

God, he was cute. Only a man would think to video call someone this early in the morning. His blue eyes were bright and his jawline was smooth, freshly shaved. He'd taken care of his neglected, unruly hair at some point in the last few days since she'd seen him; it was once again close cropped everywhere but on top, his black waves now tamed. Savanna squinted at the ticket between his fingers.

"Can you read it?"

"It says you leave out of LaGuardia today at 3:55."

He pointed at words in the upper corner. "It says one-way."

She was processing. "You—Aidan, so you're coming home? To stay?"

"Yes. To stay."

Savanna felt a rush of tears fill her eyes and she sucked in her breath, swallowing hard. Her cheeks burned as she blinked once, twice, carefully, trying to appear natural. She was just blinking. Everyone did it. She hoped he wouldn't notice the effect he'd just had on her; it hit her out of the blue. She smiled at him, eyes clearer now. "I can't believe it!"

Her voice sounded thick in her own ears.

"I'm not sure I do either." He grinned. "But the chief is up and running. She's doing great, she's got hospital policy down pat, the board loves her. We think she's good to go. If I do need to go back, it'll only be a day or two in the next month. That's it."

"I'm so happy, Aidan. That's amazing news. Wait until Mollie hears!"

He nodded. "Just in time for summer vacation. I can't wait to see you." He tipped his head a little. "I miss you. Are you ready for your last day? You look beautiful."

She laughed. "Okay." He was nuts, but she wasn't going to argue. "I am beyond ready. You don't understand the craziness of the last week of school. It's intense."

"I believe it. Mollie couldn't sit still when I talked to her last night. She'd better be behaving for you."

"Always. Don't worry. They're all just squirrely—" She broke off as she heard a knock on his door.

He stood, and the vantage point on Savanna's screen shifted. He was walking to the door. "I've got to run, Savanna, but I'll see you soon." The screen was filled with a view of his living room, a gray couch and chair in front of a large window, as she heard him open the door. He reappeared, turning the phone on his end from himself to the woman at the door. "Savanna, meet Alison, Alison, this is my—this is Savanna."

Savanna's heart flipped over, dropped into her stomach, and then settled back into its rightful place in her chest again, with that one sentence and the woman on her screen.

This is my what? The new chief of surgery wasn't quite what she'd pictured; she was even prettier. In the split-second glimpse on the screen, Savanna caught sleek, straight blond hair, fine-boned features, a crisp white collar with black lapels.

Savanna's hand automatically rose in a small wave. "Hi, Alison." To which she heard the woman's reply, "Nice to meet you, Savanna," as the view shifted again.

Aidan's smile filled the screen. "Tonight. Eight o'clock? I'll pick you up."

"Safe flight, Aidan." She quickly tapped the red button, and her screen went black.

Savanna stared at herself in the mirror. Her hair was drying in long, tangled brown waves. She tried to see herself as Aidan had. Without mascara and lipstick, her changeable hazel eyes wide and unadorned and her lips bare, she looked younger than her thirty years. The cap sleeves and round scalloped collar on her periwinkle dress displayed a delicate gold compass necklace, a college graduation gift from her parents, between her collarbones. Since coming home to Carson, she'd stopped wrestling with her natural waves, trying to force them to be smooth and straight and something they weren't. She'd stopped using the heavy eye makeup from her days at Kenilworth Museum in Chicago, opting for a more natural look. Savanna applied her mascara, swiped blush over her cheekbones and used her rose blossom lipstick. She gently detangled her damp hair, using a sparkly gold clip to pin it back from her face. She checked her reflection once more before leaving for school.

She looked nice. She did not look like a sophisticated, gorgeous surgeon. She looked—and felt—like Savanna Shepherd, someone she'd come to really love this past year.

While she ate breakfast alone in Sydney's kitchen, Savanna typed a quick email to Yvonne, John Bellamy's assistant. She cringed at the thought of calling her this early, plus she only had the main office number for John; email was least intrusive. She'd woken this morning with an idea about John Bellamy's murder, and there was a chance Yvonne might have key information without even knowing it.

By lunchtime, Savanna felt more like a zookeeper than an elementary art teacher. So far, she'd extracted two disgusting, sticky wads of gum from two separate heads of hair in her first-grade class, she'd broken up a fight between two third graders over whose pool party would be better this weekend, and she'd confiscated items from three students, promising to return them at the end of the day: two cell phones and one live frog.

She still had half a day to go.

The last fifth grader left for the cafeteria and Savanna rolled her chair backward to the blue plastic bucket on the floor behind her desk, peering over the edge. The small green frog inside stared back at her. He leaped into the air, one of dozens of valiant escape attempts he'd made this past hour, making Savanna jump and then laugh at herself.

"Okay, little guy. Don't worry, I lied to Ethan. I won't be giving you back at the end of the day. Let's go." She carried the bucket by the handle across the hall into the library.

Jack Carson was unpacking his sack lunch on the library counter. "Are we eating together today? Your lunch box is so fashionable." He eyed the bucket. They did often meet for lunch in the library, though Savanna hadn't brought hers today; she'd planned to grab something in town.

"No. Shortcut. Sorry. Can't talk," Savanna said, trying to maintain a smooth gait. She didn't want to jar the bucket and help her friend escape before she got him outside.

"You know, you always have strange reasons for using my library as a shortcut." He came around the counter and followed her, catching up and looking in the bucket. "Well, that's a new one. Are we taking him for a walk?"

"Yes. Back outside where he belongs. I've decided his name is Frank. That kid Ethan had him in his pocket. His *pocket*." She looked at Jack. "No idea how long he was in there, poor little thing."

"All right, that justifies your use of the shortcut." He held the door open for her, letting them out into the hallway at the bus lot exit.

Savanna and Jack went through the set of double doors out into perfect 78-degree sunny weather. They crossed the parking lot to the trees where Savanna had helped her classes search for their nature wind chime supplies this week.

She stopped in the long grass just before the tree line and turned the bucket onto its side. "Frank, be free!"

Nothing happened. She and Jack watched the bucket but the frog didn't emerge. Savanna bent down and looked inside to find him sitting comfortably on the blue plastic, staring at her. She sighed. She reached in to pick him up.

"*What* are you doing?" Jack had one hand firmly on her upper arm, and he sounded alarmed.

She looked up at him. "What? I'm setting him free." She touched the frog with her fingertips, and he hopped into her palm. She held him up for Jack to see. "Want to say good-bye?"

Jack let go of her and stepped away. "No."

The frog darted forward, balancing on Savanna's fingers, and Jack let out a loud, high-pitched shriek, his hands up shielding his face.

Savanna couldn't help laughing. She carefully set Frank in the grass and lightly touched his spotted green back so he'd take off, and he did. A stream ran through the trees several yards in; he'd be happy here.

"Don't say a word." Jack locked eyes with her.

She shook her head, straight-faced. "Not a word. I completely understand. Frank was pretty terrifying."

He glared at her. "It's a phobia, Savanna. Lots of people have phobias. Fear of frogs is common."

"Totally normal," she agreed, swinging the bucket at her side as they went back into the building.

"Very normal!" Jack held the library door for her. They crossed the library in silence. As Savanna pulled the door open on the other side, across from her classroom, he spoke up again. "They're just so slimy. I'm not afraid of spiders. Or sharks. Or even rodents. Just frogs."

Savanna smiled at him. He was her favorite person at Carson Elementary. When she'd been new last year, he'd been the first teacher to be kind to her. She remembered thinking he was a bit awkward, but now she knew that was part of his charm. "Jack. You get rid of any random spiders that take up residence in my classroom, and I'll handle any rogue frogs you run into. Deal?"

He nodded, looking more relaxed. "Deal. Hey, you got the message I put in your box from this morning, right?"

She shook her head. "No, I always forget to check it." The office had mailboxes for staff; with most communication coming in by email, the mailboxes often remained empty, and she'd never gotten in the habit of checking hers.

"Your classroom phone rang this morning when I was inventorying your art books. I should've let it go to voicemail, sorry. It was Yvonne, from John Bellamy's office. I wrote her contact info on a pink slip for you—it's in your mailbox."

"Awesome. I was waiting for her call. How much more time do we have?"

He took a bite of the same peanut butter and jelly sandwich he packed for himself every day, and checked the desk clock on the counter. "Forty-two minutes. Go call her."

Savanna was starving. She combined chores and grabbed a ham on rye and two raspberry Mary Ann's sodas to go from the deli in town, taking a couple of rushed bites of the sandwich on the short walk to the Carson Village offices.

The township officials were housed at the far end of Main Street, just past Skylar's law office. Two brown brick buildings were connected by a curving sidewalk through a small courtyard between them. The rear building held

Carson's public works and law enforcement departments, including the three cell jails. The smaller, more attractive building in front had gabled windows and an arched entry-way, and comprised Carson's parks and recreation department and Mayor Greenwood's office.

The glass door swooshed closed behind Savanna, and she stood in the lobby. A woman who looked to be in her forties looked up from a wide maple desk occupying the space in front of Roger Greenwood's office. The desk on the opposite side of the room, outside the entrance to the parks and rec department, was empty. Ugh, she hoped she hadn't missed Yvonne; maybe she was already on her lunch break.

"May I help you?" The name plate on the woman's desk read *Janice Barnes, Mayoral Assistant.*

"Yes, hi. I was hoping to catch Yvonne. I'm a friend. Is she at lunch?"

"Oh, she's here. She's clearing out Councilman Bellamy's office. If you go right through those doors, you'll find her." The intercom on Janice's desk buzzed, and Mayor Green-wood's voice came through the speaker.

"We're ready for that coffee now, Janice. Two black and one with cream."

The woman stood and moved to the beverage station against one wall in the waiting area. "Shall I make you one?" She looked over her shoulder at Savanna.

"No thank you." Savanna pushed through the double doors where she'd been just last week, popping in to see if John had secured the permits yet for the festival's parking area. Two men were in one of the small city council offices, chatting. A woman stood in the common area, putting colored pins into a corkboard-backed map as she consulted a tablet in one hand. Savanna turned to the left, toward John's office, and nearly bumped right into Yvonne, who looked like she'd been crying.

Yvonne nearly lost her balance as she halted abruptly.

Savanna steadied her with a hand on each arm; Yvonne carried stacks of papers and folders, her chin resting on top of the pile so she wouldn't lose anything.

"Here," Savanna said, taking a handful of documents from the top. "Let me help. Where were you going?"

"My desk." She went backward through the doors back out into the lobby, depositing everything onto her already messy desk.

Savanna put the rest of the files down next to them. "Yvonne. Are you all right?" she asked softly.

Yvonne nodded and then shook her head. Her gaze went to the ceiling, and Savanna could see she was fighting not to cry; her eyes were already puffy and red underneath. "Follow me."

Savanna obeyed. Yvonne led them back through into parks and rec, down the hall to the left, and into John Bellamy's nearly empty office. The desk drawers standing open, the large file cabinet now cleared out, the framed certificates and awards he'd been so proud of now packed into a box on the desk, all gave the large room a sad, eerie quality.

Yvonne shut the door and sat down in his chair behind his desk. "I don't know if I can do this." She swiped under one eye as a tear fell, and looked at Savanna. "They're moving Councilwoman Rae into his office tomorrow, like nothing happened. It's been less than a week!"

Savanna came around the desk and hugged the woman. "I'm sorry, Yvonne. This must be so hard on you. How long did you work for him?"

She sniffled. "Six and a half years. We made a good team. He relied on me. Nobody even asked me if I want to work for Linda Rae! Maybe I don't!"

Savanna snuck a glance at the clock behind Yvonne. She had twenty-two minutes before her class started. "Maybe you should take some time off."

Yvonne stared at Savanna. "Do you think so? Maybe I should."

"I think you've earned it. You need time to get through this." She patted her arm.

Yvonne stood suddenly. "I'm taking next week off. That's it." She stooped and picked up one of the boxes. "Can you grab that one? I've almost got it all cleaned out. Oh, and more submissions came in for you. They're out at my desk."

The quiet lobby was now filled with men in suits, as Mayor Greenwood was apparently wrapping up a meeting; he shook hands with one and exchanged slaps on the back with the other. "I'm going to walk these gentlemen out, Janice. We'll need you to send them the paperwork on the property deal approvals, as we discussed. Copy me on the email. Did you push my one o'clock?"

His assistant looked confused for a moment, and then recovered, nodding. "Yes, rescheduled for Monday."

Yvonne set one small and one larger box in front of Savanna from under her desk. "Here you go. I'm sure you've gotten the rest from his house by now. Oh, did you walk here? Will you be all right carrying all this?"

She eyed the two boxes. "I should be fine, don't worry. And Detective Jordan is letting us into John's tomorrow to get everything. Finally. Listen, I have a quick question for you. And I brought you a pop!" She'd almost forgotten. She pulled the bottle of raspberry soda from her purse and set it on the desk.

"Oh, for goodness' sake, I completely forgot you needed to talk to me. That's right. I'm sorry, I'm just not doing well today, or this week in general. Sit down, let's talk." She twisted the cap off the bottle and pointed to the chair facing her desk.

Savanna checked her phone. Eighteen minutes until the bell rang at school. She perched on the edge of her chair. "I'm afraid I can't stay. My lunch break is almost over. But I wanted to ask you something about John." She shot a look over her shoulder at Greenwood's assistant, then scooted closer to Yvonne.

Yvonne leaned closer as well, elbows on her desk. "You can ask me anything. Don't worry about Janice. She's a good friend—we talk about everything."

"Well, this might sound strange. But I'm wondering if John ever had meetings with anyone else about the art event?"

"You mean, besides you and Britt?"

Savanna nodded. "Yes. Perhaps, I don't know, someone

you wouldn't have recognized, someone out of the ordinary. Or possibly someone on the judging panel. Or what about his ex-wife?"

Yvonne squinted, looking up at the ceiling. "Oh! Hold on." She pressed a button on her computer. "We keep a log to reconcile against his appointment calendar. You know, for walk-ins, or if someone misses an appointment." She clicked though, eyes scanning the screen.

"I'm thinking just in the last month or so," Savanna said. "If that helps." She didn't know exactly what she was looking for. But she'd gone to bed last night thinking about the argument in the vestibule at the banquet. And then she'd dreamed that Mia and Remy James were plotting to destroy what was left of Jessamina. Dreams didn't always make sense, but she couldn't shake the creepy feeling that one had left her with.

"Okay, yes." Yvonne nodded. "John met with Mia James on June first, last Monday. Oh, and also May twentieth, about two weeks earlier."

"Was that normal? For them to meet?" It struck Savanna as odd.

Yvonne shrugged. "A little, I guess. He was grouchy the whole day after the second meeting." She went back to scanning the screen. "Remind me of the judges' names so I can check?"

Savanna ticked them off on her fingers. "Talia DeVries, Robert Wallace, and Grant Hoffman."

"Yes, Talia DeVries. John had me call and schedule an appointment with her. He met with her the Friday before he...before he passed."

Savanna was jotting notes on the back of a grocery receipt she'd found in her purse. "Thank you, that helps. How did that meeting go?"

"Fine, I guess. She was very nice. I only saw her when she arrived; I had to leave early that day. Does that help at all? Should I check for anyone else?"

"Did he have appointments lately with anyone from out of town?" Savanna asked, thinking about that hotel owner from Grand Pier.

"Oh, well, that happens all the time. Especially since he announced his run for mayor. Like Jeremy Payne, a radio DJ from the county station, for an interview. Edward Takoma, president of Raisin River Farms, for possible sponsorship. Elizabeth Quincy—" She stopped as Savanna put a hand up.

Savanna shook her head. "Can you search a specific name?" She leaned in closer. "I mean, maybe you aren't supposed to, but I promise I won't tell a soul."

Yvonne tapped her fingertips on the desk, quiet for a moment, then said, "I don't see how that could hurt. What's the name?"

"Paul Stevens."

Yvonne typed, and looked up at Savanna. "Nothing. Any other names?"

Savanna felt deflated. "No. Any way to know what those meetings with Ms. DeVries or Mia were about?"

Yvonne sat back. "No. Not unless he took personal notes, and I'd never violate his privacy, not even now. These are all being picked up today by the estate attorney." She gestured at the boxes. "Savanna, I hope whatever you're trying to figure out helps the police get to the bottom of this. I know they've got Chef Joe, but if you're still tracking down information, it makes me believe the rumors in town are true; everyone is saying he didn't do it."

Her words buoyed Savanna's spirits. If the town was convinced Fratelli was innocent, that could only help her and sisters' efforts to gather information. They'd need to find out more about Remy and Mia James, and also why John had met with Talia DeVries. She came around the desk and gave Yvonne a quick hug. "He didn't. We'll find out who did, don't worry." She hoped she'd be able to back up her words.

Mayor Greenwood's group was breaking up as Savanna crossed the parking lot to head back to school. The two men were pulling out of the drive in a white sedan with a logo on the doors that jarred Savanna's sense of déjà vu. She was sure she'd seen it somewhere before: Black capital letters *B.L.* inside a black triangle.

Mayor Greenwood raised a hand in the air as they pulled out onto Main Street. He smiled at Savanna as he passed her, walking back toward the building. "Beautiful day, Ms. Shepherd, isn't it?"

"It is." She couldn't disagree. It was a perfect day, warm, sunny, blue sky overhead, just a short afternoon in front of her until the start of summer vacation, and seven hours until her date with Aidan.

Chapter Ten

SAVANNA HURRIED INTO the living room for the third time in the last five minutes, turning in a circle for Sydney's appraisal. Aidan would be here in just a few minutes. "How's this?" Dark denim cropped jeans left room at her ankles, where she'd wrapped the long ribbon ties of her wedge heels in a crisscross pattern and secured them with a bow. Her lightweight, not-quite-sheer turquoise top was perfect for the warm summer evening.

"Gorgeous!" Sydney was at the window and she peered through the curtain. "He's here!"

"Hey! Stop that," Savanna whispered, shooing her away from the large picture window. "You're so embarrassing." She picked up her purse. "Don't you have something to do? Somewhere else you could be?"

"I could answer the door for you," Sydney replied cheerfully, trying to shove past Savanna into the foyer.

"You're seriously the worst. Go away!"

Syd made a pouty face. "Fine." She sat on the couch and stretched one arm along the back. Fonzie hopped into her lap. "We're ready to receive your gentleman caller, Savvy."

She groaned. The doorbell rang, and she pulled the front door open.

"Hi." Aidan's smile was instant, crinkling the corners of his eyes.

"Hi." She fought the intense urge to hug him. Standing in the foyer, with her heels, she was almost eye to eye with him.

Fonzie skittered over and did his happy dance for Aidan, his body wiggling so fast he was nearly impossible to pet, but Aidan tried. "I know, I know. I missed you too," he said, laughing.

Sydney had joined them in the small entryway. "Have fun, you two." Savanna was nearly in Aidan's car when she heard her sister call, "Not a minute past curfew, young lady!"

"Sorry." She glanced at Aidan. "She thinks she's funny."

"Not sure I'll have you home by curfew," he said. He met her eyes briefly. He put a hand on the edge of her seat near her shoulder and turned to check behind him as he began backing out of the driveway.

Savanna caught a hint of aftershave when he moved. She spotted her pain-in-the-neck sister standing in the open doorway, waving. Brat.

"So, our dinner plans are a little unconventional," Aidan said once they were on the road.

"Hmm. I'm intrigued."

He took the turn at the end of Main Street that would take them along the lake, and eventually out of Carson if they stayed on Lakeview Drive. It seemed they might. The sun had started to drop in the sky, creeping toward the horizon, but it wasn't getting dark now until nearly 9:30. Savanna watched the coastline beyond Aidan on his side of the vehicle, the sky painted with faint streaks of pink now.

They drove for almost twenty minutes. Small talk gave way to short periods of comfortable silence. Savanna leaned her head on the headrest and snuck occasional glances at him as they chatted. She'd missed him more than she'd let herself admit.

Several miles outside Carson, Aidan checked a map he'd pulled up on his phone and turned down a narrow street that led to a rectangle of pavement in front of a split rail fence, bearing a sign that read *Private Access.*

She looked at him curiously. He winked at her and quickly got out of the car, opening her door for her while she was still gathering her things—sweater, purse, phone.

When she stepped out of the car, Aidan had an actual picnic basket hanging on one arm. It was wicker, with double flap closures on top, complete with red-and-white-checkered lining peeking out over the edges. He reached past her into the back seat and grabbed the blanket he'd brought. He'd dressed slightly more appropriately than she, with black and gray Vans sneakers, jeans, and a short-sleeve gray chambray shirt.

Savanna checked behind her when he told her to follow him, hoping no one would be there to see them; she was sure *Private Access* didn't mean Aidan and Savanna. She felt an idiotic smile on her lips that she had no control over the entire time she followed him down the sandy path laid with round paving stones.

Over the top of a small dune, Lake Michigan came into view, vast and blue, waves rolling in. There wasn't a single person on the beach. She bent and untied her sandals, stringing them together over one purse handle. It'd been far too long since she'd felt sand between her toes.

She sat where Aidan told her to on the blanket while he emptied the picnic basket: small, individually wrapped sandwiches he'd made himself ("These have mustard, and these don't," he told her); a plastic container of grapes, strawberries, and watermelon; sea salt crackers; dark chocolate; and a bottle of white wine. He picked up a bundled set of dish towels and carefully unwrapped them, revealing two wineglasses. He handed them to her and opened the wine bottle with a corkscrew.

"You're unbelievable," she said.

He looked up from pouring. "Why?"

She was in awe. He'd worked all day, caught a plane home, greeted his daughter, showered and shaved, and created this lovely picnic dinner. Was he even real? "This," she said simply.

He tipped his head to the side and finished pouring. "I don't know what you mean. Maybe I just wanted a cheap date idea."

She handed him his glass. "I love it."

He settled onto the blanket, one long leg stretched out alongside hers. A thin band of rainbow-striped sock was visible between the hem of his jeans and his Vans. "I've missed you." His voice was quieter now. He held her gaze.

Savanna's cheeks were hot. She felt her heartbeat in her neck, in the notch between her collarbones. "I missed you too." She finally broke eye contact, looking down at her glass; he made it nearly impossible to be this close to him, meeting his eyes, without losing her cool. She took a deep breath. "We should have a toast."

"You're right." He raised his glass. "To...new beginnings."

"New beginnings." She clinked with him.

The sun was kissing the horizon by the time they'd finished their picnic, the sky a brilliant palette of reds and pinks. Savanna sat next to him, facing the sunset, leaning lightly on the arm he'd propped behind her. His warmth transferred to her where they touched, shoulders, hips, the length of her leg against his. She bent one knee and dug her foot into the cooling sand.

"You know that feeling?" Aidan spoke, his voice near her ear. "Where it seems like you've known someone forever, even though you just met?"

A zing shot through her, from the middle of her chest to her throat. "Yes," she said, watching the building waves, not moving.

"And things are better, you feel more...whole...when you're with them."

She looked at him. "And even when you're not, just the idea of them makes you smile."

His face was inches from hers, the low light making his eyes dark and even more intense than usual. "Exactly."

Her heart might race right out of her chest. He was so close she could see the faint freckles across the bridge of his nose and the way his black lashes curved up at the corners. His lips were inches from hers. His breath smelled like strawberries.

A loud whistle broke the spell between them. Savanna jumped, looking around. A large yellow dog was bounding down the beach toward them, tail flying and mouth wide open, biting at the waves, his owner jogging after him. The dog got closer, running straight at them, and it became obvious he had no interest in listening to his master. She whistled again, short and ear-piercing.

"Norman!" The girl had picked up speed and was now at a full-out run. "Nor-man!" Her shout was authoritative and no-nonsense, and had no effect on the dog.

Norman sprinted the last few yards to them and leaped onto their blanket, wreaking havoc in every direction with his inquisitive nose and fluffy, wagging tail, and Savanna burst out laughing. She jumped up along with Aidan, giving the dog what he wanted—pets and scratches behind the ears and what was left of the sandwiches on the paper plates.

"I'm *so* sorry!" The young girl finally caught up to her dog, breathing hard. She looked stricken. "Bad dog!" She reached out and caught him by the collar.

"He's not a bad dog," Savanna said, smiling at the girl. She patted Norman's head. "He couldn't help it. That was the best joy run I've ever seen."

"Ugh! He doesn't usually do that." She was taking in the crumpled picnic blanket, overturned plates, and the two wineglasses now in the sand. "Really, I'm awfully sorry. We didn't mean to ruin your picnic." She clipped the leash onto Norman.

"Nothing could ruin our picnic." Aidan bent and began

packing up. "Don't worry about it."

Savanna helped him, waving back to the girl as she led Norman away. "Bye, Norman!" She carefully wrapped the wineglasses in their dish towels and handed them to Aidan. "Cute dog."

"Cute dog with terrible timing," he said, looking down at her.

"Really bad timing," she agreed, pulling her sweater on and grabbing her shoes. The beach had gotten chilly when the sun had disappeared.

"All right." He slung the blanket over one arm, followed by the basket. "On to the second stage of the evening, then." He held his hand out to her.

She took it, loving her hand enclosed in his larger, warmer one. "There are stages? Nobody told me there would be stages. I'd have planned a wardrobe change."

He looked at her. "No need. You're perfect."

He had a way of leaving her speechless.

"So," Aidan said, in the car on the same road back to Carson. "You have to tell me what's been going on in town. My mother-in-law says Chef Joe was arrested? Does she have that right?"

"She does. It's crazy. Skylar got him released at his arraignment, but he's on house arrest until it goes to trial—or until we can find out who really killed the councilman."

Aidan looked at her sharply. "We? You mean the police, right?"

"Detective Jordan seems to believe he's got the right man. I don't know how he can think that!" Savanna huffed out the words in frustration. "The detective has dinner at Giuseppe's just like the rest of Carson; he knows Chef Joe. He's got to know he's not capable!"

"Yeah, I don't believe it. But they found his chef's knife at the scene, right? At least, that's what Jean heard."

"That's true too. But anyone could've taken that knife. Chef Joe and his staff were at the banquet the night before, and most of the town's been in and out of his restaurant. His prints were on the knife," Savanna admitted. "But Skylar says there were other prints too, though not full sets. The police can't know for sure that it wasn't someone else. Did you know Chef Joe's sous chef is John Bellamy's son? And Mia from Mitten Inn is his ex-wife?"

Aidan was nodding. "Yes. I mean, yes, I knew about Mia. I remember Remy from when he worked at Mitten Inn, after his mother opened it. I guess I didn't realize he was back. I don't think I've seen him yet at Giuseppe's."

"How did you know about Mia and Remy at Mitten Inn?"

He glanced sideways at her. "You were born and raised here, but you missed a decade or so. I'm in my seventh year here. I remember when Mitten Inn opened. Even when you try to avoid gossip in Carson, it finds you anyway. There were a lot of rumors flying around back then. Remy was arrested for something that happened at the inn. Mia defended him and tried to get his father involved, and it backfired on her. Bellamy made things worse, bringing up things that'd happened in their son's past. Remy was eventually cleared of whatever the charges were, but not before the town had already tried and convicted him. I was brand-new, still figuring out how things worked here. I wasn't surprised he left."

"Wow. That's so horrible." She tried to reconcile the John Bellamy she knew with a man who'd turn on his own son, and couldn't; the thought of it made her heart feel heavy.

"Are you thinking Remy got ahold of Chef Joe's knife?"

"I don't know. Honestly, I don't know what to think. We've been talking about possibilities, and it seems like the persona John presented to the public wasn't exactly who he was. I think we have to look at who might've had a grudge against him. As far as I know, Chef Joe had nothing against John. But Remy sure could've. And Jack Carson thinks there was bad blood between John and the mayor, since John announced he was running, although it's ridiculous to think Mayor Greenwood would resort to murder. Plus, I saw John having an argument the night of the banquet. There was something going on between him and one of the Art in the Park judges, and then this hotel owner from Grand Pier was yelling at him too; the reporter told me Grand Pier has hosted the last three festivals. I'm thinking maybe the hotel owner was angry—"

"Savanna," Aidan cut her off. "You're getting yourself all tangled up in the middle of this? I think it's under control. You said Skylar got Chef Joe released, at least until the trial. If he's innocent, I'm sure Detective Jordan will figure that out."

"I'm not so sure," Savanna said. "Without another lead,

Chef Joe is the only suspect he's got. We can't just do nothing."

He frowned at her. "Have you thought about what happens if you're right?"

"What do you mean?"

"If the real killer is still out there, and you're poking around trying to find him, you're in danger. Just like last year. I remember finding out you'd been chased and run off the road on the expressway. I want you safe." The muscle in his jaw pulsed, twin frown lines etched between his eyebrows, and their car was speeding now.

Savanna put a hand on his arm; his muscles were tensed. "Hey. It's okay. Aidan, slow down."

He took his foot off the gas. "Sorry."

"I remember too; I won't let anything like that happen again, don't worry. I'm not getting tangled in anything. I'm just asking some questions, talking to people I trust. Caroline, Jack, you. I promise I'm not doing anything dangerous."

He gave her a sideways glance.

"Maybe next week, you'd like to come with me for a drive up to Grand Pier. It's a gorgeous trip, takes about an hour."

He cracked a smile and rolled his eyes, shaking his head. "You're so transparent. Yes, I'll definitely be checking out Grand Pier with you. Seems like there's a hotel owner there we might end up chatting with."

She shrugged. "Could be. It crossed my mind that someone who was really upset at losing a big event for their town might try to sabotage it for the winning town. Maybe by vandalizing town landmarks. Or killing one of the organizers."

"Savanna." He stared at her so long that she pointed back at the road in front of him.

"Aidan! Eyes on the road, please."

"So, you think possibly this guy from Grand Pier smashed our statue and murdered the councilman because he's trying to ruin the festival *you're* planning, and your great idea is to go have a talk with him?"

"Well, when you say it like that, it sounds crazy and reckless."

He laughed. "Listen," he said, pulling the car into a parking space, now back in town. "Let me help you. I know you aren't asking, but I want to. I'm back, and I'm not going anywhere. Promise me you'll be careful. Please. Don't follow any of these hunches without backup—me or one of your sisters or Nick Jordan."

"I promise. For real." She looked up at the sign they'd just parked under. "Lickety Split? I love stage two!"

They stood in line under the ice cream shop's red awning with a handful of other people who'd had the same idea, despite the fact that it was already past ten. Lickety Split was Carson's original ice cream establishment, having occupied this space in town for the last seventy-some years. Lickety Split even provided free Pup Sundaes for patrons with dogs, a scoop of lactose-free ice cream topped with a dog biscuit. Savanna had forgotten all about that until right now, seeing it on the posted menu. She'd have to come back with Fonzie this summer.

Aidan suddenly bumped into her as a pink blur slammed into his side; Mollie had her arms around his waist, hugging him tight and grinning up at him through white-blond bangs ineffectively held back by her signature bluebird barrettes. "Daddy!"

"Hey, bunny!" He scooped her up, hugging her back. "What are you doing here? Where's Uncle—"

"Right here." A voice came from Savanna's left and she turned, finding herself face-to-face with the man Sydney had gotten so irritated with the other day. He wore a wide grin that could've passed for Aidan's own. His eyes were as vividly green as Aidan's were blue. He was slighter, though just as tall. Of course.

"Finn." Aidan looked at his brother and then at Savanna, setting Mollie down. "Finn, this is Savanna. Savanna, my brother, Finn."

Finn held out a hand. "It's my pleasure. I've heard a whole lot about you, Savanna."

She shook his hand. *And I've heard almost nothing about you.* "Finn. It's so nice to meet you." She smiled, gaze going to Aidan.

"Didn't I mention Finn was in town? I must've forgotten."

Chapter Eleven

THE EVENING DIDN'T end the way Savanna had imagined. She wasn't sure exactly what she'd imagined, but as soon as the four of them finished their ice creams, Finn left them at Lickety Split for some pressing engagement.

Aidan pulled into Sydney's driveway, and the moment the car was in park, Mollie unbuckled herself from her booster and hung over the front seat, looking first at Savanna and then at Aidan. Savanna had grown very fond of this little girl in the past several months; she loved seeing her smiling face twice each week in her art class. In keeping with Mollie's love of rabbits, she'd gifted Savanna a Mrs. FluffyPants Teacher-Bunny earlier today, for the last day of school. She'd spent two weeks sculpting it and painting it, and then someone at home—Savanna wasn't sure if it was Aidan or her grandmother Jean—had helped her add a bright blue dress and a dollhouse-sized paintbrush and palette in one hand.

Mollie tapped Savanna's shoulder with one finger, and then did the same to her dad. "Uncle F-F-Finn says you're on a date. Does that mean you kiss Ms. Shepherd goodbye, Daddy?"

Savanna's cheeks burned. And on the heels of that, she

registered surprise at the little girl's stutter; she'd only ever heard it in school, but never when Mollie was with Aidan. It must be the combination of this new circumstance, being in a car with her father and his potential date, whom she only knew as her art teacher.

She met Aidan's gaze, her eyes wide as she tried not to laugh. He looked stricken, like he had no idea how to answer his daughter. "Mollie," she said softly. "Sometimes people might kiss if they're on a date, if they really care about each other and they both want to. But sometimes people also like to hug goodbye, or shake hands too." There. Pressure removed. She didn't want her first kiss with Aidan to be with his seven-year-old daughter scrutinizing them. *If* they got a first kiss. If.

"Oh." Mollie looked disappointed, giving Savanna a boost of optimism; maybe the girl didn't mind at all that they were dating.

"On that note," Aidan said, "I'll walk you up." He gave Savanna a half smile.

She could feel Mollie watching them on Sydney's porch. She stood a good three feet from him and clasped her hands behind her back, looking up at him. "So. Maybe we should shake hands then?"

He laughed. "She spooked you, huh?"

She threw her hands up in the air, laughing with him. "I don't know how you do it. Being a parent must be the toughest job in the world."

He leaned in just a bit toward her. "You do know how I do it. You take care of how many kids on any given day?

They love you. You're a natural at it. And that?" He tipped his head toward the car where his daughter waited. "That couldn't have been more perfect. You gave her a good answer."

"Thank you." She loved the sound of his voice. Especially when he showered her with compliments.

"I think," he said, taking a step toward her, "a hug would be acceptable. It's not going to scar her. What do you think?"

"I agree." This had to be the oddest end-of-date conversation she'd ever had.

He moved into her space and wrapped his arms around her, his face turned into her hair. She hugged him back. Her cheek rested near his neck, and she could hear his heartbeat under her ear. She didn't want him to ever let go.

When he loosened his hold, she looked up at him, glad he couldn't hear her heartbeat too. He'd know the full extent of how she felt around him.

"I wanted the kiss," he murmured, his gaze dropping briefly to her mouth. He ran one hand down her arm as they moved apart. "I always have the best time with you, Savanna."

Her entire body flushed hot. She swallowed hard. "Me too. I mean, with you. Thank you for the picnic."

"It was my pleasure. I'll call you."

She nodded. "Okay."

He turned and looked over his shoulder at her when he was halfway down the walk toward his car. "I'm sorry my brother's clueless." Even in the dark, she caught his aggravated expression.

"It's fine, no worries. He was very nice. And funny." Aidan's brother was certainly all right in Mollie's eyes. The little girl had chattered to him about summer plans the whole time they'd finished their ice cream. He'd been nothing but nice to Savanna, asking her questions about Carson and her job. Other than leaving them abruptly with Mollie, Savanna didn't see what Aidan's issues were with him.

"Finn is always nice and funny. But he's also impulsive. I didn't know he was here until a few hours ago when I got home. Anyway…" He walked backward toward the car. "I'll talk to you tomorrow."

SAVANNA AND BRITT Nash stood on John Bellamy's front porch Saturday morning, waiting for Detective Jordan. As soon as they could collect all the art submissions from the councilman's office, they'd cart everything back to Sydney's house, where Savanna had stowed her art supplies in a corner of the sunroom and borrowed three of Charlotte's portable tables she used when it was her turn to host her euchre group.

A perk of being back home was getting to spend more time with Britt. They'd hit it off instantly in Chicago from their first meeting five years ago, when Kenilworth had contracted with Lansing's Museum of Fine Art to bring Britt in for additional help on a particularly extensive acquisition.

Since then, they'd crossed paths infrequently, once or twice a year. But they now had a standing lunch date every month, and Savanna counted Britt as one of her best friends.

"I fully approve the vibe you've got going on today," Savanna said, smiling up at them. Britt was tall and lanky; today's white linen slacks and button-down floral print shirt were topped off with a white, wide-brimmed hat, effortless and chic. "I feel like we should be in a cabana somewhere, holding tropical cocktails with little drink umbrellas and maraschino cherries."

"That's just what I was going for." They tapped the brim of their hat with a finger, gaze going to the driveway as Detective Jordan's police cruiser rolled into the driveway.

Nick Jordan joined them on the porch and reached up, removing the crime scene tape from the front door. "I appreciate your patience. I thought we'd get you access sooner, but I had to send the evidence tech back out on something, and it's taken a while to get the house cleared." He took a key from a small manila envelope and turned it in the lock, pushing the door open and moving out of Savanna's way.

She caught movement out of the corner of her eye as she stepped inside; an SUV sped past John's house, blowing through the stop sign and turning onto the adjacent street much too fast. She glanced at Detective Jordan.

His gaze was also on the car and he shook his head, groaning. "People. This is a residential street, twenty miles an hour. That's a good way to kill someone, all so they can get somewhere a minute sooner."

"Yeah, I hate that." She'd half expected the detective to jump in his patrol car to give the driver a ticket, but she supposed he couldn't ticket everyone.

"Anyway." Jordan followed them into the house. "I hope we didn't hold you up too long."

"It's okay, Detective. We plan to send out acceptance or denial emails to the applicants by Monday. It'll be fine." She and Britt moved through into the office to the right of the foyer, Savanna deliberately avoiding looking toward the hallway beyond the staircase where she'd seen John's lifeless body.

"Give me a shout when you two are ready to go," Jordan called over his shoulder, heading toward the back of the house.

Savanna began shuffling through art submissions. When the first several started arriving a month ago, through the designated PO box and also a dedicated email address, the three of them—Savanna, Britt, and John—had decided to print a copy of every electronic submission, for a more hands-on approach to choosing the eventual one hundred pieces of art that'd be entered into the Art in the Park contest. All one hundred would be displayed during the festival, but only three lucky artists would win first through third place, with the overall winner earning full tuition to Michigan Art Conservatory and substantial exposure through interviews with multiple media outlets. The scholarship alone was worth over $50,000. The Art Conservatory and a handful of the school's benefactors offered the handsome scholarship every year, a huge incentive to applicants.

"What a mess," she murmured.

Britt nodded. "Well, we thought we'd be sorting all of it out days ago. This was a 'maybe,' wasn't it?" They held up a charcoal portrayal of an elderly man on a tractor.

"Yes. I remember talking about that one. Here." She dug around in her purse and produced a black magic marker, and wrote *MAYBE* on an empty box, handing it to Britt. "We can't possibly go through all of them here. But as we're packing up, if anything strikes us as great, we can at least categorize it." She bent and pulled two more empty boxes from under the table, writing *YES* on one and a large question mark on the other.

"Then everything else goes in this one," Britt said, dropping two pieces into the question-marked box. They worked for a while in silence, the stacks of paper thinning as the boxes filled.

"What's this?" Savanna held up a printout of an online submission. It was an abstract painting in deep blues and purples; the printed version of the artist's submission still showed interesting textures on a horizontal composition. A bright orange sticky note in the upper righthand corner bore John's block writing: *DISQUALIFY.*

Britt moved to her side, taking the paper copy from her. The top of the page held the entrant's name and contact information, and the title of the piece. "John wrote this. The artist is Nina McCullen; she's a senior at Romulus High School."

"Why would he disqualify her?"

"No idea," Britt said. "What gets applicants disqualified

from the event? Plagiarism, obviously…what else?"

Britt held the submission at arm's length as they both studied it. "It's good, especially for an emailed copy. Look at what she did with the negative space." Savanna pointed to areas between brushstrokes on the left third of the painting. "It has a bit of a discordant quality, doesn't it?"

"It does." Britt nodded. "She's very good. And it's not reminiscent of anything I've ever seen before. Does it ring a bell for you?"

Savanna shook her head. "No. And how would John recognize a plagiarized copy anyway? He was the business portion of our team."

"So what else? Oh! Age, right? Applicants have to be twenty-five or younger."

Savanna was already typing into Safari on her iPhone. "Okay, look, this is a Nina McCullen. It's got to be the same one—Romulus, Michigan. Hold on, there's a Facebook link." She turned her phone toward Britt, displaying a profile picture of a young woman who looked to be seventeen or eighteen.

Britt squinted at the screen. "That says she's a senior at Romulus High. And look," they said, swiping a finger over Savanna's phone screen. "All of her posts are pictures of her artwork. So, same girl. She looks young. There's no way she's over the age limit."

"But what if she's related to someone? That's the only other thing I can think of that'd get someone disqualified. Did John discover she's a relative of someone on the state committee? Maybe Mrs. Kingsley?" Savanna tapped the search icon at the top of Nina McCullen's Facebook page.

"What are you doing?" Britt looked over her shoulder.

"Checking to see if she's Facebook friends with anyone on the committee, anyone involved at all. Okay, no Mrs. Kingsley. Let me try a few others. Hector Ramirez," she spoke as she typed. "Nope. Oooh! What about the judges?" She tapped her screen, muttering "Nope, nope," and then sucked in her breath. "Oh, wow."

"No. Way." Britt saw the name and photo at the same time Savanna did, listed in Nina McCullen's friend list.

"Talia DeVries. The judge."

"How?" Britt frowned. "How are they friends? Talia DeVries lives up north and is in her thirties or forties, isn't she?"

"Hold on." Savanna went back to Nina's profile information. "Sydney knows how to navigate all the newer apps out there, but I know Facebook. I know how to do this. Look!"

"Oh my heck. They're related?" Britt pointed at Savanna's screen. "This says Talia DeVries is Nina's aunt!"

"Do you think she knew?"

"Who," Savanna asked. "Talia DeVries or Nina McCullen?"

"Both?"

"Britt." She gripped her friend's forearm. "That argument. The night of the banquet. Did you see any of that?"

"What argument? Your little town is too picture-perfect for arguments at banquets. That was the loveliest evening. I don't remember anything like that going on."

"It was brief. John was outside in the vestibule, having a conversation with Talia DeVries and Paul Stevens—a hotel owner from the town that hosted Art in the Park the last couple of years," she offered. "It wasn't really a conversation though. Mr. Stevens was angry, and he jabbed John in the chest." She poked Britt, scrunching up her face, demonstrating. "He stormed out right after that, but Judge DeVries stayed to talk to John. She looked upset about something, like she was pleading with him. Ugh! I wish I'd gotten out there sooner!"

"Sounds like you saw plenty! What did John say when you went out? Was he upset?"

She shook her head. "Not by then. He seemed completely unfazed."

"Did you ever get a chance to talk to either of them? Talia DeVries or that hotel owner?"

"Not yet." Her mind was already racing, planning. "I'm driving up to the hotel in Grand Pier this week for Stevens. I can track down the judge—she shouldn't be hard to find. We need to know what the deal is with this." She took the art submission out of Britt's hand.

"Right. I mean, this girl is talented. It's a shame to disqualify her if we're wrong."

Savanna nodded, looking down at the submission and tapping the orange sticky note. "But this is a high-profile art event. If they are related, what are the odds she didn't know her art critic aunt was a judge? Better question, what are the odds Talia DeVries hoped she'd get in and planned to skew the results in favor of her niece?"

"John must've talked to her," Britt mused.

"It's the best explanation," she agreed. "So she was out there with John that night, trying to convince him to let it slide? To let her niece participate."

Britt was quiet.

"I'm getting derailed here. None of that would be reason enough for her to want to hurt John. And not the way he died." She shuddered. "That knife—that was such a violent way to go."

"You never know what someone's capable of." A deep voice came from the doorway, and Savanna jumped. She hadn't even seen Detective Jordan standing there. "Especially when something important's at stake."

"What? An art scholarship? That's ridiculous."

"Well…" Britt spoke. "To be fair, it's more than an art scholarship."

"What exactly does the winner get?" Nick Jordan walked over to their cluttered corner of John Bellamy's office.

"First place comes with a full ride to Michigan Art Conservatory, interviews and media exposure, and a monetary prize as well," Savanna said.

"My office put a call in to Ms. DeVries earlier this week, based on what you told me the other day about the argument in the vestibule. She hasn't gotten back to us yet. I'll check her out."

She tipped her head at him. "I don't mind talking to her. Wouldn't that seem a little more natural?"

Detective Jordan raised an eyebrow at her. "Why would I be concerned about keeping things natural in a murder investigation?"

Savanna laughed. "Good point. But I think this is kind of silly. You must have better leads? Have you looked into anyone else who might've had a problem with John? Like—" She cut herself off. She'd been about to say Remy James, but she felt bad throwing him under the bus after hearing from Aidan how terribly his father had treated him.

"Like...?"

"I don't know. That hotel owner in Grand Pier, the one I told you was so angry with John the night of the banquet. Or anyone else who could've had access to the restaurant's kitchen? Anyone could've gotten their hands on a knife from Giuseppe's if they really wanted to."

"It's an active investigation, Savanna."

She heard the hint of condescension in his words—*leave the crime solving to the professionals.* "Got it." She returned to their task of packing up boxes, she and Britt now working in silence.

Twenty minutes later, Savanna stood in the doorway to John's home office, the last box balanced between her arm and hip. She couldn't believe he was really gone. She turned to join the detective and Britt outside, but she couldn't leave. Picturing him behind that imposing mahogany desk, she had the oddest sensation. She wasn't sure at first what it was. Something was just...off. She moved to the center of the arched doorway, squarely facing his office, the Piet Mondrian reproduction of *Red Tree* centered on the wall behind his desk. Except, it wasn't. Savanna blinked and turned her head slightly to the side, feeling her brow furrowing. The painting was crooked. Had it been crooked the other night?

She'd bet her life it hadn't. Now that she saw it, there was no way to unsee it. And she knew there was no way she'd have missed it the night of the murder. The painting was at a distinct angle, glaringly disturbing to Savanna's keen art authenticator's eye. "Jordan! Detective Jordan!" she shouted, not wanting to take her eyes off the painting.

Nick Jordan appeared beside her. "You need help with that one?" He took it from her arms before looking at her and following her gaze. "What's up?"

"The Piet Mondrian is crooked. Who was in here after you took John away Sunday night? Did your guys go through his office?"

"No. Nothing more than a cursory walk-through. This room looks like something out of a museum; nothing's been touched."

"Nothing except that painting. Don't you see it?"

Detective Jordan stood beside Savanna and stared at the painting. He tipped his head and then straightened. "I don't know. Maybe?" He set the box on the floor and walked over behind John's desk, pulling on a purple latex glove before Savanna could even see where he'd produced it from. He applied pressure to the bottom corner, and the heavy painting moved.

Savanna gasped. She went quickly to the detective's side. He pulled the edge of the painting a couple of inches away from the wall and shone a small flashlight behind it, and she poked her head into his space, peering behind it to see a wall safe.

He cleared his throat.

Savanna stepped back, letting him get a better view. "It's like something right out of a Nancy Drew novel!"

He cocked an eyebrow at her. "Or it's just something the wealthy think will help conceal their assets. The lock is broken. Look. *Don't* touch anything." This time he stepped aside and held the flashlight so she could see.

The door to the safe stood open about an inch. It was about two feet square and who knew how deep, and sat in a recessed compartment in the wall.

"I'll get my evidence tech back out here. Good catch, Savanna."

Wow. That was high praise coming from Nick Jordan. "What do you think it means?"

"Not sure. I can see why we missed it," he admitted. "I'm surprised you—Well," he said, "I suppose I'm not surprised you saw it. You were probably too shaken up on Sunday to notice anything."

Savanna bit one side of her bottom lip, frowning. "I would've noticed. It's a classic painting, even if it is a repro- duction. I did see his office Sunday, and nothing seemed off."

"Hmm." He was quiet. "We'll have to see whose prints we can pull from the frame."

"Oh!" Savanna tapped his arm excitedly. "And then see if they match the ones your guy got off the cellar door! Which probably aren't a match for Joe Fratelli, right?"

He scowled at her.

She read his mind. It'd been worth a try, but she knew

he couldn't divulge any details. "I can't help that I was here the night he died. I'm just going off what I heard when your team was finishing up, Detective." She stuck her hand in the pocket of her jeans, feigning a more relaxed posture and trying to appear less enthusiastic.

Jordan picked the box up again and moved toward the front door. "You and your colleague can go. I appreciate your find, really. I have more work to do here."

Everything loaded into her car, Savanna watched the detective head back to the house, phone to his ear. How she wished she could be fly on the wall when his evidence tech got here!

She and Britt spent the bulk of the day and evening sorting through art submissions in Sydney's sunroom. The light shifted as the sun moved across the sky, and Savanna finally pushed her chair back from the long table she and Britt shared, arching and stretching her back. "I can't do anymore today. How about you?"

Britt's summer fedora rested on the far end of the table, and their white-blond hair had had a hand scrubbed through it a few too many times; it was spiked up at odd angles, giving her friend a comical horned appearance. "Thank God."

Sydney poked her head around the corner into the sunroom and turned on the ceiling lamps. "Guys. It's getting dark. Aren't you starving? Come and eat, I ordered pizza."

In the kitchen nook, Savanna opened her sparkly pink notebook and made checkmarks next to items on the running to-do list she'd started two months ago for the festival. Tomorrow's assignment was to send out notifications to all the accepted entrants. She and Britt split the list alphabetically, giving them fifty each, minus the uncertain decision on Nina McCullen. That would have to wait until Savanna could speak with Talia DeVries. She could cross the emailing task off her list by noon and still have plenty of time to start preparing Sunday dinner for her family. It was her turn. She was making Yooper Pasties and Mixed Berry Shortcake.

She swallowed a bite of the delicious veggie pizza Sydney had picked up in town just as her phone dinged. "She answered me!" She turned her phone toward Britt. "Talia DeVries. I emailed her after we left John's, asking if I could meet with her. We're going to have to remove either her or her niece from the event."

"What did she say?"

She scanned the message. "She's in Grand Rapids next week for work. I'll ask if I can meet her somewhere for lunch to go over details of the event. I'll tell her we're doing the same with each of the judges."

Britt pointed a finger at her. "Smart. Meeting in public, in case she's the killer."

"What?" Sydney looked from Britt to Savanna. "The female judge from the banquet? You think she murdered John? How? She's tiny!"

"*You're* tiny, but you're freakishly strong." Savanna raised her eyebrows at her sister.

"Okay, good point. But still."

"And she's not actually tiny," Britt said. "She's about Savanna's height, and twenty years younger than John."

"I'll go with you," Sydney said. "If you suspect her, you can't meet her alone."

Savanna felt that little thrill, the one she got whenever she realized she was working on something big. At Kenilworth, it had happened occasionally when an acquisition had turned out to be even more valuable than the curator had originally thought. Last year, figuring out who was trying to kill Caroline Carson, she'd felt the thrill every time a new piece of the puzzle had fallen into place. Some pieces didn't contribute as much as others to the ultimate result, but each was instrumental to seeing the big picture at the end.

Chapter Twelve

CONTINUING THE SHEPHERD family tradition of preparing Sunday dinner at their parents' home, Savanna sprinkled flour onto the granite countertop and began rolling out dough for her Yooper Pasties. She wasn't sure, but the beef pasty seemed to be purely a Michigan thing. She'd never found one in Chicago; Skylar had once sent her a dozen of them packed on dry ice for Christmas, and she'd eaten well for weeks. Rob had hated them, but that'd just meant more for her. Pasties were a delicious concoction of diced skirt steak, onion, potato, carrot, rutabaga, and a light peppery seasoning, wrapped in a circle of pastry with one edge crimped into a crust. Savanna always considered the rutabaga the key ingredient—it lent the pasties their unique flavor. They had to bake for a solid hour, but she had plenty of time.

Savanna had finished emailing the accepted applicants for Art in the Park, and that in itself was probably the most exciting process so far in running the event. Several of her fifty must've been constantly refreshing their inboxes, as she'd almost immediately gotten replies back from a bunch of the artists. Savanna had never received so many expressions of gratitude in her life. She and Britt had left Nina

McCullen on the fence for now until after her lunch with Talia DeVries.

Savanna spooned the beef-and-vegetable filling into each pastry shell, pinching the edges closed and then pressing them lightly with the back of a fork. When she was finished, she had twelve of them on two baking sheets loaded into the oven. Fonzie sat patiently by her feet the entire time she worked, cleaning up little scraps of anything she dropped. Once the oven door snapped shut, he ambled over and curled up in the sun near Charlotte, seated at the round kitchen table by the window.

"I've got to grab the berries," she called over her shoulder to her mother, heading out the kitchen door. Carson had the best fresh produce market on this side of the state. Halle's Berries had been in business since Savanna was in grade school; back then, it'd been a handmade wooden booth across the street from the village park. Now it was a real pop-up market, a large red and white food-truck-style trailer with an awning and shelves of farm-fresh fruit and vegetables. The family who ran it owned a huge farm east of town. Halle herself, the girl the market had been named for when she was a baby, was now in her twenties and often helped her parents behind the counter. They greeted Savanna by name every time she went.

Savanna rounded the corner of her parents' house, heading toward the front yard and driveway, and was startled by squealing tires. She whipped her head in both directions, up and down the street. A gray SUV was speeding away, leaving behind black skid marks on the pavement. It looked a lot like the vehicle that had raced down John's street yesterday. Was it the same one? She squinted after it, but couldn't read the license plate number. She hoped she was just feeling paranoid. It was probably kids.

She carried cartons of blackberries, raspberries, and strawberries into the kitchen, and Charlotte jumped up to help, taking the top two cartons off the stack between her arms and her chin.

Her mom set them on the counter and popped a blackberry in her mouth. "Mmm." Charlotte closed her eyes for a moment. "My favorite. You got them from Halle's?"

"Where else?" She pulled packages of shortcake shells from the paper bag over her arm. She'd already stowed the ice cream in the freezer earlier. "Shortcut. I'm cheating a little. The pasty dough is homemade; I lost the will to bake the shortbread from scratch too."

Charlotte grinned. "'Shortcut' is my middle name when it comes to cooking."

"Shall I assemble them, or let everyone make their own?"

"Oh, let them make their own. Nolan will love that. I'll help you clean the berries."

Savanna stood side by side with her mother at the sink, rinsing berries and halving the strawberries.

"Tell me about your date."

She glanced at her mother. "Sydney told you."

"Of course. Tell me about Aidan. And who's the mystery man you all had ice cream with at Lickety Split?"

She laughed. "Oh my gosh. Now who was that from?" She bit her lip, trying to remember who exactly had been at the ice cream parlor whom Charlotte would've spoken to.

"Apparently Rose Munsinger sent her daughter out for a banana split last night. When your ninety-two-year-old mother wants ice cream, you get her ice cream. Rose's daughter told Mia that my daughter was enjoying sundaes with not one but two handsome men."

Savanna rolled her eyes. "Rose's daughter knows who Dr. Gallager is, I'm sure. So Mia called you to ask about your daughter's scandalous behavior?"

"No, Mia's not that bold." Charlotte laughed. "I actually called her—I had to call all the ladies in my euchre group to reschedule our game night to Thursday. Mia asked me about what Rose's daughter told her before we hung up. She said she ran into you girls at Giuseppe's the other day."

"Oops. I was supposed to give you her regards. She was there talking to her son—did you know the new sous chef there is Mia's son? With John Bellamy."

Charlotte nodded. "Sure. You didn't?"

"How would I? It sounds like his relationship with John was complicated." She was treading lightly. She really didn't know how close Charlotte and Mia were, or what Charlotte thought of Remy James.

"That's a nice word for it. You don't even have time for that story." She glanced up at the wall clock over the sink. "Everyone will be here soon."

"Mom, I do have time. I need to know."

Charlotte frowned at her. "Skylar told me you're helping her with her case, trying to learn who framed Joe Fratelli. I'm not sure I like any of this, Savanna."

"I'm fine. No one needs to worry, really. I'm just working on figuring out connections. And everything I'm hearing lately about John contradicts what I thought I knew about him. Did he really turn against Remy when he got in trouble for whatever happened at Mitten Inn?"

"Yes, he did." She sighed. "The whole affair was awful. I'll tell you. I will, I promise. But your sisters and Travis will be here in twenty minutes, I've still got to pack for my flight tonight, and I think you're trying to avoid my original question."

Savanna hugged her mom around the shoulders with one arm, trying not to touch her with her dripping-wet hand. "I'm not."

"Let's chat this week. I'm back from Denver on Tuesday, and you're out of school now. You choose when and where, and I promise I'll fill you in. Now please. Tell me something, anything, about *you*." Charlotte turned off the faucet. "Tell me about your date on Friday." She dried her hands on a dish towel and handed it to Savanna.

Oh, good grief. Why were mothers so good at guilt trips? "You don't have to pry anything from me! Our date was great. Aidan is…" Savanna bit her lip. How to describe him? How to explain how he made her feel, without worrying she was going to jinx the whole thing? It was all so new and tenuous.

Charlotte set the large glass bowl of plump berries in the center of the island and moved to the coffee maker, pouring two cups. She added a small spoonful of sugar to each.

Patience and guilt, a powerful combination, Savanna

thought. She couldn't help smiling, knowing exactly what her mother was doing. She didn't mind. She'd missed this in Chicago; the familiarity of family, even when it meant she couldn't hide from her feelings.

Charlotte moved to the table in the sun with her coffee and began packing up her laptop. She was silent. Waiting.

"Aidan's like no one I've ever met." Savanna sat at the table and helped gather up the few pens and papers scattered around the laptop.

Her mother packed the laptop cord into the case and took a sip of her coffee.

"He's generous and caring and smart, and it's terrifying. He's—What's his story? Has he dated much since his wife died? I can't be the first person to see how great he is." Savanna had been wondering, but she didn't want to ask Aidan.

"I've never heard of him dating at all, until you."

"Not at all? His wife passed away three years ago. That's surprising. Maybe he was just low-key with it, with dating? Because of Mollie."

Charlotte shook her head. "I guess that's possible, but I don't think so. Oh, he's had opportunity, believe me. Barb from my yoga class works at his clinic, and she says several of his office staff have tried. All I know is he seems to be very focused on his work and his daughter. Until you." She tapped Savanna's hand.

She was quiet. She hadn't wanted to hear that Aidan dated tons of women…but she wasn't sure how to feel, knowing she was the first woman he'd gone out with since his wife had died. Maybe he was testing the waters. He'd been with Olivia since med school. Maybe he finally wanted to get back out there, and Savanna seemed as good a prospect as any; better in some ways, low risk since she didn't work at his clinic or the hospital, and she wasn't tangled up in the interwoven relationships in town, after being gone for ten years.

"I think he wasn't ready before." Charlotte was watching Savanna. "Maybe you've made him realize he is now."

"Ready for what?" Savanna met her mother's gaze. "To start dating people again? What if I don't want to be part of his recovery?"

Charlotte's eyebrows went up. "Don't you?"

"Yes! I mean, no. I know I can't even imagine what he's been through. I don't want to be a stepping stone as he works through everything. I don't know if I want to be the very first person he's dated after losing Olivia. What are the odds that'd even work out?"

"Oh, honey." Charlotte squeezed her hand. "What do odds have to do with love?"

Savanna swallowed hard around a lump that appeared in her throat at that word. Love? What was that? Was it what she'd thought she'd shared with Rob in Chicago? Because whatever that was had left her feeling more alone when she'd been with him than she'd ever felt on her own.

Charlotte let go of her daughter's hand and zipped her laptop into its case, studying Savanna's disturbed expression. "All right. Listen to me. You're putting way too much thought into this. You enjoy being with Aidan. He clearly enjoys being with you. As you said, he's caring and smart. I don't believe for a minute that he's callous or has ulterior motives. And you, my dear, can't let your past experiences dictate your future happiness."

She blinked at her mom. "Sydney's been sharing her self-help books again, hasn't she?"

Charlotte burst out laughing. She shook her head. "How did I raise such a snarky daughter? Punk." She slung her computer bag over one shoulder and moved toward the doorway and the staircase beyond to the bedrooms.

"Sorry."

"You're not. How do you feel when you're with him, Savanna?"

She thought about it, unconsciously wrapping her arms across her chest. She felt too many things for words. "I feel seen."

Charlotte nodded. "Perfect. I'm going to pack. Can you let your dad know we're eating soon?"

Harlan was the only one at the table to finish off two entire Yooper Pasties, complete with gravy. Savanna was surprised that even Nolan ate most of his—for a four-year-old, he was good about trying almost anything at least once.

Savanna carried the large bowl of strawberries, raspberries, and blackberries to the long dining room table, followed by French vanilla ice cream, strawberry syrup, shortcakes, and Nolan's favorite, whipped cream topping in a can.

He stood up in his chair and clapped, reaching for the can. "I can do it!"

"Okay, buddy," Skylar said. "That's your job. We'll pass

our berry shortcakes to you for the final touch. But no sampling until you're finished!"

Nolan proved to be skilled at doling out ample swirls of whipped cream. Savanna suspected he'd had plenty of practice.

"Skylar," she said as they dug in. "Have you heard anything at all from Detective Jordan?"

"Not since the arraignment last week. Why?"

Savanna filled her sisters in on the discovery behind the painting, and then about John's apparent discovery of a relationship between Judge DeVries and one of the applicants. She and Britt had agreed that if Talia DeVries graciously stepped down as a judge, they'd grant Nina McCullen entrance to Art in the Park; her talent wasn't the issue. That scene in the ballroom vestibule nagged at Savanna. In light of that sticky note in John's handwriting, it now seemed DeVries had likely been pleading with Bellamy to keep the information to himself.

"And the weird thing about that crooked painting is, I'm positive it wasn't like that the night John was—" She interrupted herself abruptly, glancing at Nolan, whose face was completely covered in whipped cream and reddish-purple berry goo. "The night he fell asleep. But I can't figure out why whoever…helped him fall asleep…would've come back to the house afterward. That seems so risky."

"Did Jordan have any ideas?" Skylar asked, leaning over and swiping at Nolan's face with a baby wipe.

Travis stood and scooped him out of his chair. "You got more berries on your face than in your tummy, big guy.

We're going outside to play with Fonzie," he told Skylar, carrying the little boy at arm's length toward the kitchen sink.

"I think Detective Jordan assumes I probably missed it that night. I know I didn't; the Mondrian wasn't crooked when I was in the house last Sunday. I was trying so hard not to look at John, and the blood." She lowered her voice, even though Travis was making Nolan shriek with laughter at the sink now. "I got a good look at his home office that night. Someone came back for something in that safe—and knew the safe was hidden there."

"Or, someone was searching for something and looked in an obvious spot," Sydney said, playing devil's advocate.

"Right," Skylar said. "I can see that. Or else they made John give up the information the night they killed him, but then had to get out of there when Savanna rang the doorbell. It could be that the killer came back later last week when the coast was clear, to get whatever was in the safe."

"If they find fingerprints on the safe and they aren't Chef Joe's, that'll help clear him, won't it?" Savanna set her spoon down and leaned forward, looking at Skylar.

"Not necessarily," Skylar answered. "The prints from the cellar door aren't Chef Joe's, but it doesn't change the fact that his fingerprints are the only identifiable ones on the murder weapon."

"Oh."

"The sheriff's department did get video footage from two of the councilman's neighbors, and I'm told they're going through those. And I requisitioned any video we can get from the intersection cam outside the Carson Ballroom the night of the banquet, I should have that tomorrow morning. Chef Joe thinks that's when his knife was stolen. He doesn't remember having it after that."

"There's an intersection camera?" Sydney asked.

"Just at the four corners in town. I'm not sure if anything was captured—maybe someone who didn't belong there, or anything suspicious; the angle won't be great, but it's better than nothing."

"Oh!" Savanna slapped the table. "What about the photographer at the banquet? The *Allegan County* reporter had a photographer with him. Maybe he accidentally caught something in one of his shots."

"Even better! He'd have shots inside the ballroom," Skylar said. "Can you get in touch and ask him?"

"Sure, I've got the reporter's card somewhere. I'll look for it tonight. And listen, I'm driving up to Grand Pier tomorrow to talk to that hotel owner John was arguing with." She put a hand up as both her sisters started to protest. "Aidan's coming with me."

"I'm off," Charlotte spoke up from the doorway. "Flight to catch. Be careful. All of you." She looked pointedly from Savanna to Sydney to Skylar. "Lunch Wednesday when I'm back, girls. Let me know what time works."

Harlan put the last dish in the dishwasher and dried his hands on a towel, taking Charlotte's suitcase from her. "I'll walk you out."

"Tuesday we're going to Grand Rapids to find out what's up with that art critic judge, right?" Sydney asked. "I've got

Willow lined up to run the shop for the day."

"Awesome," Savanna said.

"We're having lunch with Mom?" Skylar tapped her phone and then her calendar app. "Wednesday?"

"She promised to fill us in on the big scandal years ago at Mitten Inn with Remy James and Mia. She says it's a long story." Savanna summed up what she'd learned so far from Caroline and Aidan.

Skylar frowned. "That was right after I had Nolan. I was off on maternity leave. I know Mia hired my firm to defend Remy, but he was released and cleared after just a few days. Those records will be sealed—I don't have access, since I wasn't part of the defense team."

"I'll pick up sandwiches for us Wednesday from the deli," Sydney said. "By then, we should have some answers. I'm just glad to know Chef Joe is back home, even if he's stuck there for now."

"We've got a problem." Harlan stood in the dining room doorway, his face somber. "Follow me."

Savanna exchanged curious glances with her sisters as they followed their dad out the front door to the driveway.

Savanna's car, parked in the driveway behind Harlan's truck and in front of the SUV Travis drove and Sydney's hybrid, had four flat tires. One hand over her mouth, she walked in a circle around her little car, now resting much lower to the ground than it had when she'd arrived. The other vehicles in the driveway were untouched. She made it around to the front driver's side and gasped. A stainless steel knife jutted out, still stuck in the rubber tire treads.

Chapter Thirteen

"**D**ON'T TOUCH IT."

She stared at her dad. "What does this mean? Who did this?"

"We'll find out. Don't worry." Harlan's calm, low tone was betrayed by his expression; fury furrowed his brown. "Do you have your phone?"

She handed it to him, her hand shaking.

He scrolled through her contacts and tapped one, putting the phone to his ear. "Detective Jordan. Harlan Shepherd here. Someone's taken a knife to my daughter's tires."

Savanna saw Sydney hurrying toward the side of the house, where Skylar and Nolan were coming around the corner. They turned abruptly and retreated toward the backyard, redirecting Nolan's attention with a quick Frisbee tossed to Fonzie.

"Jordan will be here in a minute. Let's sit." His hand was still on her upper arm and he led her to the front porch, where they sat on the wide steps.

"Dad." That SUV. The one that'd raced down her parents' quiet street earlier today when she'd come out to get the berries—it looked like the car that had sped past the councilman's house. What if it was? "What if someone's watching me, following me?" She told him what had happened at John's.

"You think it was the same car?"

"I don't know. It's probably crazy to think that."

Detective Jordan's black-and-white police cruiser pulled into the driveway.

Savanna met him at her car, Harlan right behind her. The detective looked strange like this, in jeans and a Detroit Pistons T-shirt. She felt bad for dragging him away from his relaxing weekend; she was making a habit of it without meaning to.

"Did you see anything? Hear anything at all?"

She told him about the car. "What if it was the same one we saw on John's street yesterday morning? I think it could've been. They were both gray."

The skeptical look he wore was beginning to grate on her. He didn't answer, instead pulling out a notepad and jotting notes as he walked around her car.

"Okay, I know there are lots of gray SUVs," she went on. "But they were both speeding on quiet residential streets where I happened to be, two days in a row. What if someone thinks I'm getting too close to whatever happened to John?"

Detective Jordan shot her a sharp look. "If someone's targeting you for poking into things better left to the police, the safest thing to do is to leave those things to us."

Harlan spoke up behind Savanna. "Explain to us exactly how collecting artwork from the councilman's house and then having a family dinner is poking into things she shouldn't be, Detective."

Savanna didn't have to look back at her dad to know he was angry. "Detective," she said, making her voice polite but no-nonsense. "What now? I'll have to take the car in for new tires." She cringed; four new tires wouldn't be cheap, even with insurance.

He finished typing something into his phone and looked at her. "My evidence tech is on his way here. We'll have to collect what we can before you can do anything with the car. But it looks like you've got plenty of help in terms of getting where you need to be?" His gaze rose to Harlan.

"What are you going to do to make sure she's safe?"

"I'm not thinking she's in danger. If someone wanted to hurt her, they wouldn't have stopped at the tires," the detective said.

"That's some weak reasoning."

"Okay," Savanna said. The two of them were making her nervous. She didn't need Nick Jordan and her father fighting on the front lawn. She looked up at her dad. "I'll be fine. Don't worry. Syd will drive me home, and I can come back for my car tomorrow. You can pull around me to get out, can't you, Dad?" She pointed at Harlan's truck.

The muscle in his jaw pulsed. "I'll follow you two back to Sydney's house and stay there tonight. I'll bring you your car with new tires tomorrow." His gaze went to the detective, and Savanna had no doubt the evidence collection would be wrapped up in plenty of time for Harlan to do exactly what he said. She loved her dad like crazy, but he'd always been able to wield that intimidating edge effortlessly.

SAVANNA LAY IN bed, wide awake, for much too long that night. Was someone watching her? Following her? If John's killer had come back to the house to retrieve something from that safe, they would've been nervous seeing her enter the house, accompanied by Detective Jordan. If someone thought she knew too much, they were wrong; Savanna still had no idea who killed John Bellamy. She hoped to gain some answers this week.

When the hundredth glance at her clock told her it was 1:12 a.m., she huffed out a sigh, flipped the clock facedown on her nightstand, and turned over in bed. At least she didn't have to get up for school in the morning.

Savanna's eyes snapped open at the crack of dawn. Fonzie was snuggled up against her feet, and he grumbled as she climbed out of bed. So much for sleeping in. It was probably going to take her the first month of summer vacation just to override her internal alarm.

She pulled on jeans and the *Hamilton* tee she'd bought when the musical came to Chicago. She tiptoed out to the kitchen to feed Fonzie and found Harlan already up and drinking coffee at the kitchen counter.

"You know that's decaf, right?" She poured herself a glass of orange juice and stood across from him.

"I know," he grumbled. "How'd you sleep?"

"So-so," she said honestly. "I'm going to grab coffee at the corner. Should I bring you one?"

Harlan stood. "I'll walk with you."

"Dad. I'll be on Main Street—it's a block away, and people are already out and about. I'll be okay."

He stared down at her intently. She got the feeling he still saw her as ten-year-old Savanna. "You've got that pepper spray I gave you in Chicago?"

She smiled. "I do. I'll bring it, okay? I won't be long, just coffee and a quick walk. Do you want anything with yours? Maybe a bagel?"

He shook his head. "I'll make breakfast." He opened the refrigerator. "Take your dog with you."

Town center was only a one-block walk from Syd's. There was no caffeine to speak of in the house; Sydney had been trying hard to convert her to decaf, but it would never happen. The coffee shop was bustling, even in the pinkish light of dawn.

She hooked Fonzie's leash to the bicycle rack in front of the coffee house window, bending to scratch his chin. "I'll be right back. Be good!"

Inside, waiting for her mocha latte with an espresso shot and her dad's black coffee, she spotted Yvonne through the window bending to pet Fonzie, her tiny chihuahua wiggling and wagging as the dogs greeted each other. The barista handed her the cup holder with two steaming cups and she went outside, joining Yvonne and giving her a quick hug.

"Are you getting coffee? I can stay with your little cutie if you want."

Yvonne nodded. "Oh, that'd be great. Thank you! Mayor Greenwood has me doing his running this morning, and he starts much earlier than John did. I've still got to drop Goliath off at home and then head in."

"What?" Savanna frowned. "What about the mayor's assistant?"

"Janice quit. She just *quit*!" Yvonne was wide-eyed, shaking her head. "She didn't even give notice, and right in the middle of the Better Living negotiations. I even had to work Saturday for Mayor Greenwood. Would you believe he made me take his car to the shop so they could add windshield wiper fluid? Like that's in my job description? They need to find a replacement, or else give me a big raise. The new councilwoman starts today, I can't do both jobs. I wanted to take a few days off." She looked close to tears.

"Oh my gosh. That's ridiculous. And windshield wiper fluid? Why can't he do that himself? I know how to add my own, for Pete's sake. That's not your job. I'm so sorry." Savanna gave Yvonne's arm a sympathetic squeeze. "Go, get your coffee."

Savanna took a seat at one of the small iron tables, letting the dogs prance in circles around her feet as she took turns petting them. She was surprised to hear about Janice. The mayor's assistant had been a little brisk, but she'd appeared efficient, and Savanna had thought it was nice Yvonne considered her a friend, especially having to work in such close proximity.

When Yvonne came back out, she had a carrier with three cups and a brown paper bag. She seemed calmer. "I'm sorry, I know I'm grouchy. I don't mean to be." She took Goliath's leash from Savanna.

Savanna put a hand on the woman's arm. "Maybe you

need to ask the mayor what the plan is for replacing Janice. This all sounds like it happened suddenly. I'm sure he'd listen. I doubt he'd want to lose another employee."

She nodded. "You're right. I'll ask him. I'm waiting for Janice to call me back. She was behind closed doors with him Friday afternoon, and then she just cleared out her desk and left without a word." Her phone rang from her purse. "I've got to run. Hey, enjoy your first day of summer break!"

Savanna sipped the chocolatey goodness in her cup and let Fonzie lead her to the park. She'd leave her dad alone in the kitchen for a bit; he loved cooking breakfast. She followed the curving sidewalk through century-old trees toward the expansive green lawn. The area was deserted but for a man and a fluffy collie at the other side, walking near the trail to the dunes of Lake Michigan.

Savanna sat at one of the park picnic tables and stared up at Jessamina Carson. The twelve-foot statue on the raised pedestal was in the process of being repaired. Scaffolding was set up around her, and her head was now reattached, albeit roughly and in need of a lot of patchwork and refinishing. She hoped Jessamina would be intact by the time the festival rolled around a week and a half from now.

The hands of the tall town clock above the gazebo displayed the time: eight a.m. Savanna pulled a plain black-and-white business card from her back pocket and stared at it. Was eight on a Monday morning too early to call? *Landon King, journalist, Allegan County Newspaper* was followed by the reporter's phone, fax, and email information. She dialed the number.

"Landon King," he answered on the second ring.

"Mr. King! Hello. This is Savanna Shepherd, from Carson. With the Art in the Park event? We met last weekend at the banquet."

"Ms. Shepherd, it's nice to hear from you. I've almost got the article ready to send you, if you'd like, to approve before it goes to print. It'll run in next Sunday's paper. I thought the timing would work well for the festival."

"That's perfect," she said. "I'm so grateful for the exposure. I know it'll help bring in more people. I, um, I have a question for you." She hesitated. How to make this sound normal and not like she was trying to be some rogue private detective?

"Sure, shoot. What can I do for you?"

"I'm sure you heard about our councilman, John Bellamy, and the, uh, his unfortunate, er, passing. Last Sunday night."

"I did. I'm so sorry for Carson's loss. It sounds terrible."

She took a deep breath. "It was. Is. He was a friend, and we're—I'm—still trying to wrap my head around what could've happened. I wondered if I could possibly have you put me in touch with your cameraman from the night of the banquet?"

The other end of the line was quiet.

"Mr. King?"

"Landon. Please. Sure, I can connect you with him. I'm not certain I see why, though? I read that the police have someone in custody for the murder of Councilman Bellamy. And the banquet was the night before it happened, right?"

"Yes. It's just…" She wished she'd thought this through better before dialing. But why should she care if Landon King thought she was meddling or being ridiculous in trying to find out what had happened? "I'm just hoping maybe, by some small chance, the photographer may have accidentally captured something important during the banquet, probably without even knowing it. We don't believe the man in custody is Councilman Bellamy's killer."

"Oh." More silence. "Well. I have to say, I'm intrigued now. I'm happy to help. Why don't we meet? I'll reach out to my photographer for you, but I'd love to hear your thoughts on what really happened."

Savanna swallowed hard, feeling her pulse speed up. This wasn't at all what she'd been aiming for. It was one thing to discreetly try to clear Chef Joe. She didn't think Skylar would approve of her talking to a reporter about their theories on who really killed John Bellamy.

"I'll come to you," King was saying. "I'm out that way a few times a week. What works for you?"

"I'll have to get back to you on that. My schedule is a little up in the air right now," she said, improvising. "But it sounds like a great idea. And in the meantime, maybe you could have your photographer call me?"

"Absolutely. At this number?"

When they hung up, Savanna left Jessamina and headed back toward home, mind racing. King had promised to have his photographer get in touch with her this week. She picked up her pace, nearing Sydney's and already thinking about her plans this afternoon. Aidan was picking her up to drive to

Grand Pier. First day of summer vacation, and Savanna had already loaded her schedule. She didn't mind. She came in through the kitchen door to the delicious aroma of Harlan's signature cinnamon French toast and bacon.

An hour later, Savanna was kneeling behind the gourmet treat counter at Fancy Tails, restocking Syd's Peanut Butter Pupcakes. She'd offered to help out in exchange for Sydney letting her borrow her car to pick up paint and supplies for the Carson Theatre mural. The shop had been open only a few minutes when the bell over the door jingled.

"Appointment only," Sydney spoke from her desk on the other side of the shop near the grooming intake area. Her voice was short and terse, nothing like her usual proprietor tone.

"Oh, we don't need the fancy tail today. Just the treats."

Savanna swore she recognized the voice. She peered over the edge of the glass countertop. Finn Gallager. With Aidan's shaggy mixed breed, the dog's fluffy tail wagging in anticipation of snacks or attention from Sydney. Jersey visited often enough that he knew the drill. Finn rested one hand on the edge of her sister's desk, wearing that hint of a smile from the other day when he'd been here. He exuded effortless confidence. Or was it arrogance?

Sydney looked pointedly at Finn's hand on her desk, then reached out and scratched the pooch behind the ears, completely ignoring the man on the other end of the leash. "Such a good boy, aren't you? Where's your real dad, Jersey? Do you want a treat?" She headed over to the display case.

Savanna stood up quickly, not wanting to look as if she

was hiding and eavesdropping.

Finn's face transformed into a full smile when he saw her. "Hey, I know you."

Sydney stared at Savanna, who was sure there'd be a hole burned right through her if laser eyes were a real thing and not just a superhero power. "Right! Uh. Syd, this is Aidan's brother, Finn. Finn, this is my sister Sydney." Savanna gave her sister her best poker face before returning her attention to Finn. "What were you looking for today?"

Finn peered into the display case. "Something...impressive. What are those? With the swirls on top?"

"Bacon Biscuits," Sydney answered. "How many?"

"I don't know yet." Finn made eye contact with Sydney, and she looked at Savanna.

Sheesh. She knew they'd gotten off on the wrong foot, but she'd never seen Sydney so rude to a customer. Savanna reached into the case underneath the Pupcakes and set a small tray of cookies decorated like tennis balls on the counter. "Maybe these? Who are you hoping to impress? Not Jersey, I hope. He likes all this stuff."

"My brother's in-laws. They need a little incentive. I get the feeling they don't like me much."

"Can't imagine why," Sydney spoke behind Savanna, her tone dry.

"Okay." Savanna turned and glared at her sister. "I've got this. You have a nine-fifteen appointment, don't you?"

Sydney spun and left them, grabbing her pink smock from her desk chair before disappearing into the grooming area.

Savanna sighed, stifling the impulse to apologize for her sister's behavior. It wasn't her place. But the least she could do was show Finn that Carson could be a welcoming town. "What makes you think his in-laws don't like you?"

He shrugged. "Not sure. Just a feeling I get around them. Same as with your sister," he said, nodding toward the back of the shop.

"I'm sure that's not true. Don't worry." She didn't really know if she meant Jean and Tom Beckett or Sydney.

"Well, maybe these will help." Finn tapped the tray of tennis ball treats. "I'll take a dozen. Wait, do you know the Becketts' dog? I think it's a pug or beagle, something like that. Does she like these?"

"Yes." Savanna smiled, glad she had a little inside knowledge. "She's a beagle mix, and she loves these. I'll wrap them up." As she packaged the treats and rang him up, she was aware of Finn watching her. "Six twenty-nine, please."

He handed her cash. "So, you and my brother, huh?" He nodded. "Good." She wasn't sure how to take that. She must've looked surprised, because he laughed. "I just mean I'm glad. It's about time he let someone in. You like him?"

"Of course I like him," Savanna said, tipping her head curiously at Finn.

"But, you *like* like him, right?"

Now she laughed. "I suppose I do."

Finn nodded. "Awesome. All right, Savanna. I'll see you around. And please thank Sydney for me too."

Savanna glanced at the wall clock as he left. She really had to go! She zipped over to the grooming area and poked her head in, shouting to Sydney over the running dog bath. "Rude!"

"Yes, he is!" Syd didn't even look up from the tub.

God, her sister could be so stubborn. The guy made one bad impression and was now a persona non grata. Savanna shook her head, hurrying through the back to the house so she could shower and start her day. She'd have to talk to Aidan on the way to Grand Pier; maybe they could all have dinner together one night before Finn left. She didn't like the idea of her sister and Aidan's brother hating each other.

Chapter Fourteen

SAVANNA SET TWO strawberry lemonades in Aidan's cupholder and buckled her seat belt. He'd appeared in Sydney's driveway at exactly five fifteen, as promised. She'd changed out of blue jeans into a summery lavender wrap dress and wedge sandals. "Highway 22 will take us all the way into Grand Pier; it's the next town past North Haven."

"So, does Detective Jordan know yet who slashed your tires?" Aidan's turn signal clicked on and off, and he looked straight ahead at the road as Savanna stared at him.

"Who told you about that?"

He glanced sideways at her. "Who didn't tell me? It was the topic of the day in my waiting room. You can't keep these things secret from me, Savanna."

"I'm not!" She hadn't intended to. There were no secrets in Carson. "So what's the consensus among your patients? Mob hitmen from Chicago trying to knock me off?"

Aidan laughed. "That's pretty close."

"*What?* Oh, for goodness' sake."

"Let me think. The most popular theory was your jilted ex-fiancé sending someone to do his dirty work, because you've been seen at Lickety Split recently with another man."

"Wow! That's pretty good!" She laughed. "So illicit and

dangerous. But it's been almost a year! And does no one remember *I* was the jilted one?"

Aidan didn't reply.

She glanced at him and saw the muscle in his jaw working. "I mean," she said, "he did me a favor. I would've done it if he hadn't." Looking back, she hoped she would've. Rob really had done her a favor.

"Let me think. I know there were a few other exciting theories." He moved past the topic without any comment. "My receptionist thinks one of the teachers at Carson Elementary did it; apparently, the teacher is threatened by your relationship with Jack Carson, so she's trying to send you a message to bow out."

She shook her head. "What in the world? That's a pretty violent message. Which teacher? What relationship? He's my friend."

"I can't remember. I don't know many tire-slashing teachers, so not sure I believe that theory." He gave her a half grin. "Oh, and one of my patients this afternoon thought the same person who beheaded Jessamina also destroyed your tires, because they were jealous of you dating the eligible town doctor."

"Oh, my." She giggled, her cheeks flushing with warmth. Dating? So she and Aidan were dating. If the town was talking about it, there had to be a nugget of truth to it. Hearing him say it out loud warmed her and made her heart beat a little faster. "I'm glad to see you aren't immune to the gossip. Sounds like someone has a secret crush on you—you should be careful."

He raised an eyebrow at her. "*You* should be careful," he advised, feigning seriousness. "My admirer will stop at nothing to get rid of you."

"I'm not scared. My ex has mob connections, remember?"

He laughed, and she joined him.

"But wait, so what about the councilman's murder? All these potential perps killed an innocent town official just to send me a message?"

He shrugged. "The overall consensus among my clinic patients is that Councilman Bellamy's murder was unrelated."

She nodded. "Really. I've been thinking about that too."

"Anyway. Don't let it get to you. People will redirect their gossip as soon as the next big thing happens."

"Of course," Savanna agreed. "I unfortunately know how it works."

They rode in silence for a while, dense forest and the occasional glimpse of blue water visible out Aidan's driver's-side window.

"Savanna. Even though we're joking about it, someone is obviously troubled at the interest you're taking in the councilman's murder. Or at something. Please be careful."

"I *am* careful. I'm getting plenty of worry and advice from my dad, believe me. I don't want you to worry too." She fiddled with the radio stations as the signal got fuzzy. They were about twenty minutes away from Grand Pier now. Something was nagging at her. "Aidan?"

He looked at her.

"An answer for an answer. Okay?"

His eyebrows were raised in curiosity. "Sure."

"Have you dated much since...since losing your wife?"

"I haven't."

"You haven't dated much?"

"I haven't dated."

"At all?"

He glanced at her and then returned his gaze to the road. "I haven't wanted to."

"Oh."

"Mollie was so young," he said. "After her mom was gone, I felt like I owed it to her to try to give her all my attention."

"As it should be," Savanna said, nodding. "That makes perfect sense."

"I never wanted this for her." His tone dropped slightly.

Savanna wanted to turn the radio volume down to hear him better, but she kept her hands in her lap; she didn't want to spook him, make him feel as if he was under a microscope. She waited.

"Finn and I had no one after our parents died. We lost them both at once. He was twelve, and I was fourteen. I wanted Mollie to have what we didn't, two parents, an uncomplicated life. I worry every day about what she's missing. I try, but I can't be both parents to her."

Savanna's chest burned as she took in the uncharacteristic angst written in Aidan's features. "But you're a wonderful dad." She matched his quiet tone. "I don't think Mollie feels like she's missing out."

"She remembers bits and pieces, little snippets of time spent with her mom. She's very attached to her grandparents. It was the right decision to stay in Carson, I'm sure of that. Jean isn't exactly Olivia, but she's a good grandma to Mollie."

"I can see that."

"So. Your answer for an answer. No, I haven't dated. At all. I had no interest until I met you." He met her gaze and held it for a beat longer than he probably should've, sitting behind the wheel.

She knew her cheeks were red and she didn't care. She didn't think she'd ever received a nicer compliment.

"My turn. What really happened between you and your fiancé? Would you have left him if he hadn't beaten you to it? Were you in love with him?"

Her eyes widened. "Um. That's three questions, not one." Her mind was racing. How to explain what had happened between her and Rob?

"My bad. I get one question. What would you do if he showed up today and asked you to come back?"

She laughed. "That's too easy. I'd shoo him away to Chicago without a second thought." She knew her answer was unsatisfactory after he'd opened up to her. "We weren't right together, looking back. I think I knew it from the beginning. But I was young... And then, by the end, I think I'd convinced myself that eventually we might grow into the kind of couple I wanted us to be. I thought I loved him, but what I felt was...what's the right word? Insufficient. Ambiguous. It never felt the way I thought it should—like, you know when something really great happens, and you can't wait to tell that one person, *your* person? Because it's just a given that you have that connection, and they matter more to you than anyone else? We never had that. I don't think I was ever in love with him."

"That connection," Aidan said. "I do know what you mean. If you didn't have it with him, how do you know you should have?"

Because you're the person I want to tell—you are that person. Savanna bit her lip, stopping the words before they could roll off her tongue. Oh, she absolutely could not say that to him. Not now, not at this early stage. "Because I see it. In my parents, in Skylar and Travis. I know it exists."

"This is it," Aidan said.

Her heart did a happy little nauseating flip until she saw him point ahead out the windshield. They'd arrived at Lakeside Pier Hotel.

Elegant and *stately* didn't begin to describe the establishment. Savanna and Aidan stood on the expansive front porch, taking in the view. The hotel sat high on bluffs overlooking Lake Michigan. A plaque mounted adjacent to the front door declared the hotel an historic landmark, in the Stevens family since 1922, with 198 guest rooms and the five-star Lakeside Pier Bistro on-site.

"Wow," Savanna said, glancing up at Aidan.

He held the door for her, and they entered a completely empty lobby. The reception desk was vacant of staff, and not a soul was around.

She checked her phone for the time. "It's six thirty. This

should be peak dinner crowd, right?" She read a directional sign for the bistro and pointed down the hallway to the left. "Let's go check it out." They turned the corner and were greeted by a formally attired maître d' at a black podium.

"Two in your party tonight?"

Aidan nodded, shooting Savanna a quick look. "Yes, please."

They followed the man through a nearly empty restaurant to a table near the windows facing the lake. He set two menus in front of them and disappeared.

A hostess took his place, also dressed in black and white, complete with an elegant black satin vest and tie. She took their drink orders and informed them their server would be with them shortly.

"Fancy," Savanna said once she'd gone.

"Empty," Aidan replied. "Is it because it's a Monday?"

"Maybe?"

After the server had taken their order, Savanna put a hand up to stop him from leaving. "Excuse me. We wondered if Mr. Stevens is on-site somewhere? We hoped to meet him."

"I think so. I'll find out for you. Is everything all right?" The young man's brow furrowed.

"Oh yes, of course. We just wanted to ask him a few things about the hotel."

That seemed to satisfy the server. He walked around the bar toward the kitchen and stood chatting with a young woman for a minute or two.

Savanna leaned toward Aidan across their little candlelit

table. This would all be very romantic if they hadn't arrived hoping to interrogate a murder suspect. "Giuseppe's is busy even on Mondays. This is weird," she whispered.

"You're right."

Savanna saw Paul Stevens appear at the podium for the briefest moment. He met her gaze, and then turned and walked quickly away; he was out of sight before she could even tell Aidan to look.

The server came back to their table. "Mr. Stevens is unfortunately away on business right now. I'm happy to have him call you tomorrow if you'd like to leave your contact information before you go."

"Yes, thanks, I'll do that," Savanna said. She reached for her purse, waiting for the server to leave.

Once he was gone, she pushed her chair back and grabbed Aidan's hand. "Come on." She tried to appear unhurried as they crossed the dining room. Once they rounded the corner beyond the maître d', she broke into a sprint.

Aidan easily kept up with her, her pace no match for his long-legged stride. "What are we doing?" His words were hushed and intrigued.

"He's here, I saw him." She pushed through the tall double doors onto the porch just in time to spot Stevens climbing into the passenger side of a sedan in the parking lot. A younger man was already seated behind the wheel.

"Paul Stevens," Aidan's deep voice boomed near her ear.

Stevens halted, one hand on the door frame. He looked defeated.

Savanna and Aidan stopped ten feet away from him in the parking lot. "We just want to talk to you," she said, breathless.

"Fine." He got out and shut his car door. He stuck one hand in a pocket, then removed it, adjusted his belt, and cleared his throat. "We can talk in my office."

Aidan held out a hand. "Thank you. Lead the way."

As Stevens pulled the door open to the lobby, the three of them were startled by squealing tires. Savanna jumped and whipped around. The car Paul Stevens had just tried to flee in was speeding out of the parking lot, leaving black skid marks and smoke from burning rubber in its wake.

She stared at the hotel owner. He sighed, holding the door open for them.

In his office, with Savanna and Aidan sitting opposite him in two red leather chairs, Stevens rested his elbows on his paper strewn desk and laced his fingers together in front of him. "Savanna Shepherd. And I don't think I know you?"

"Dr. Gallager. From Carson."

Savanna leaned forward in her chair. "What's going on? I know you saw me. Why were you trying to leave? Who just took your car?"

Stevens shook his head. "That was my son. We've...been having some trouble with him." He ran a hand through thinning hair. "I apologize, Ms. Shepherd. I suppose I was trying to avoid an inevitable conversation. I know about your councilman."

She frowned. "What do you mean?"

"I know he was killed. I'm sure you and probably a lot of

people saw us arguing the night before he died. I figured it was just a matter of time before someone came to talk to me."

Savanna was taken aback.

"If you expected it, why didn't you come forward?" Aidan asked the question on Savanna's mind.

"With what?" He stared at them, his tone incredulous at the question. "With information that I'm one of the last people to see John Bellamy alive and we didn't part amicably? Would *you* come forward with that information?"

"Fair point." Aidan looked at Savanna.

"What were you fighting about? It appeared pretty heated. I saw you poke your finger into John's chest."

"We weren't fighting. That's a strong word. I'd been in touch with the councilman weeks earlier, when Art in the Park was awarded to Carson through your efforts. Carson was never even in the running until this year, you know."

"I'm aware of that. But the event can be awarded to any Michigan city or township that meets the criteria. You've had the distinction of hosting the last three years in Grand Pier—why not give another town the opportunity?"

"Why not? Because we also met all the criteria. We entered early. Our city council lobbied hard for the event, and I even sent an appeal. I compiled data on how we can better accommodate the tourist crowd than most other coastal Michigan towns, with Lakeside Pier Hotel being part of that. Grand Pier should've won the festival. We're not going to make it through this tourism season without it."

Savanna shook her head. "How's that possible? You can't

mean that one event sustained this place through three entire tourist seasons."

Stevens sat back in his chair. "Ms. Shepherd, I'll be honest with you. This hotel was on the brink of bankruptcy three years ago before Grand Pier was awarded Art in the Park. The event saved us. You've seen what it's already done for your restaurants and lodging by now, I'm sure. Look around." He spread his arms out wide, though they were enclosed in his small office. "A paltry eighteen percent of our rooms are booked. And that's for the whole season. You were in our restaurant. Does that look like a normal dinner rush?"

Savanna took a breath and crossed her legs. "Okay. I get it. Not that I agree that Grand Pier deserves the festival more than Carson. But I see why you're upset. Is that what you were arguing with John about?"

"Between your Rose's B&B and Mitten Inn, Carson can't accommodate the event's tourism crowd by a longshot. It just doesn't make sense to allow such a small town to host."

"It's true that Rose's B&B and Mitten Inn are booked solid. But there are several establishments within fifteen minutes that are running Art in the Park deals. The festival will boost tourism for all the neighboring areas. Maybe even Grand Pier."

He shook his head. "No. We're too far. No one wants to drive this far. I've got a meeting with the bank on Thursday to discuss bankruptcy versus foreclosure." He was nearly glaring at her.

She stood up, and Aidan followed her lead. None of this

was her fault. "Mr. Stevens. I'm not responsible for the failure of your business. I'm very sorry this is happening, but it doesn't justify anything you might've said or done to John Bellamy."

Stevens didn't bother to get up. "I did nothing to your councilman. I asked him to concede when Carson won the event, and I told him again at the banquet that he was making a mistake by insisting Carson could handle the magnitude of the tourism traffic. I still say it's a bad decision."

"Where were you last Sunday night, Mr. Stevens?"

"Really? I don't see a police badge or warrant." He stared at Savanna and then at Aidan, silent behind her.

She shrugged. "No, you're right. You don't. I'm sure my friend Detective Jordan will be up here soon enough to talk to you. Since, as you said, you're one of the last people to see John Bellamy alive, and you didn't part on good terms."

Now Paul Stevens stood, his chair rolling out from under him and smacking against the wall. "It's time for you to leave. Not that I owe you any explanation, but last Sunday was my wife's surprise fiftieth birthday party. My family and I were here with her and dozens of witnesses all night." He moved to his office door and opened it, standing back.

In the hallway outside, Savanna turned to at least thank him for his time. She was met with the door being slammed abruptly, hard enough to make the frosted glass window rattle. "Okay then." She looked up at Aidan.

"It's still a win," he said quietly, bending so she could hear his words. "Come on, I'm starving. Let's find somewhere to eat on the way home."

In the car, she turned in her seat to face him. "How was that a win? I'd basically figured the argument with John was sour grapes over his hotel losing the tourist traffic. I didn't expect him to be so unpleasant," she mused.

"Well, if nothing else, we can cross him off your list of possible suspects. Right? He has an alibi; he was throwing his wife a birthday party all night."

"True. But was his son at the party?"

Aidan stared at her, and then returned his gaze to the road. "Savvy."

She laughed. "What did you call me?"

He shook his head. "No. Savvy of you. To look at the son. But...maybe I should call you Savvy? It fits." He winked at her.

"The only person who calls me that is Syd. It sounds odd coming out of your mouth." She closed her eyes in the darkening car, just briefly. Why had she mentioned his mouth? Now all she could think about was their almost-kiss on the beach last Friday. She shook her head to clear it. "But listen. I saw that guy in the car, when we were yelling at Stevens to stop. I didn't know it was his son. He looked to be late teens or early twenties. Maybe this is a stretch, but what lengths might someone go to if they knew their father was about to declare bankruptcy and lose the family business—potentially their own future source of income?"

Aidan was frowning, obviously deep in thought. "You think that kid could be responsible for the councilman's murder? Maybe for wreaking all the havoc going on in

Carson?"

She shrugged. "I don't know. Probably not. But I could see a disgruntled teenage kid taking matters into their own hands and vandalizing a town monument to make a point. I mean, maybe his father even knows what he did! Paul was getting into the car with him to get away from us. I bet Sydney can help me find him on social media. We can try to learn more about him."

"Very good idea."

After dinner at a small diner about a half hour outside of Carson, they rode in comfortable silence the rest of the way home. The inside of the car was enveloped in darkness but for the dash lights. The radio had gotten turned off at some point since Grand Pier, when static had taken over, and the quiet hum of the road lulled Savanna into a sleepy, content-ed state. Aidan pulled off the highway onto the long, winding stretch of road that led back to town, lit every so often by streetlights.

Savanna had assumed the same position she'd been in before dinner, her body angled in her seat toward Aidan, her head now leaning on the headrest. Her eyelids felt so heavy; she should've had coffee with dinner. Panels of light from the streetlamps rolled across the cabin of the car, followed by darkness, followed by rolling light, followed by darkness...

She opened her eyes when the SUV stopped moving. They were in Sydney's driveway. She blinked, getting her bearings and trying to clear her slowed, sleepy processing.

Aidan sat just a foot or two away from her, looking at her. His lips were curved slightly into a half smile. "Hi."

"Oh, wow. I'm so sorry. I cannot believe I fell asleep!" She rubbed one eye as she apologized. She was mortified. Last night's tossing and turning had obviously caught up with her.

"Don't be sorry. It's not your fault I'm boring."

"No! You are *not*—" She watched his eyes crinkle as he gave her a full smile.

"I'm just messing with you." He tipped his head the slightest bit toward her. "I'm sure you're worn out after last night. I'm glad you were comfortable enough to get a catnap."

"I'm always comfortable with you." He was so close Savanna caught a faint hint of his aftershave, spicy and clean.

Sydney's car pulled past them in the driveway, parking just ahead of them by the garage. Savanna could see her leaning down, gathering her things.

"Come on, I'll walk you up," Aidan said. He took her hand in his on the way up the walk. Syd at least had the sense to go in through the garage, leaving the front entrance to them.

On the porch, Savanna looked down at their linked hands; his was much larger, and so warm. She looked back up to find Aidan watching her. He pressed his other hand gently to her upper arm, sending electric tingles through her skin where he touched her, and leaned down.

High-beam headlights illuminated them as a second car pulled into the driveway: Harlan bringing Savanna's car back.

Aidan had already dropped his hand from her arm. His

gaze went from Harlan climbing out of the car back to Savanna.

She laughed. "Fantastic," she whispered, rolling her eyes at him and then dropping her head and letting her forehead rest for a moment on his chest. She felt his laughter start with a low rumble as he joined her.

"I'm gonna go. We really have to work on our timing." He placed a hand on the back of her neck and bent, kissing the top of her head through her hair. "Good night, Savanna."

Aidan headed down the walk to his vehicle, and she stood on the porch, her heart racing, skin glowing from the light touch of his hands.

"Sir." Aidan nodded at her father as they passed each other on the walkway.

"Dr. Gallager."

Harlan handed her keys to her, turning next to her to watch Aidan leave. She raised a hand in a small wave as his SUV rolled down the street.

"Well." Harlan looked down at Savanna. "Did I interrupt something?"

She blinked at him.

"All right. Better luck next time then."

She could see him working not to crack a smile. She smacked his arm. "Thank you for the tires, Dad. Come on in, and I'll write you a check."

He shook his head. "Forget about it. It was all covered."

"I doubt that."

He shrugged. "I can stay again tonight if you think I

should. Anything out of the ordinary happen today?"

"Nope. We'll be fine. I'll double-check all the locks, I promise."

"Make sure you do. Tell your sister I said good night."

She gave him a quick hug. "I will. Love you."

"Love you too."

Savanna locked the front door behind her, sitting on the entryway bench to give Fonzie all the pats he demanded. She could hear the shower running; Sydney must've just come from yoga.

Her phone dinged, and she fished it from her purse. She was sure it was Aidan.

It wasn't. The text message was from Skylar, in all caps: *YOU WILL NOT BELIEVE WHAT'S ON THE TRAFFIC CAM FOOTAGE!*

Chapter Fifteen

S AVANNA AND SYDNEY were waiting for Skylar the next morning when she arrived at her law office. A stack of salted crackers was under one arm with her briefcase, and she sipped Coke from a can as she took her seat behind her desk. Skylar's normally rosy skin had a clammy, faint green cast.

Sydney spoke first. "You look awful."

"You don't look awful, Sky," Savanna said. "Still queasy? That's miserable."

Skylar popped a cracker in her mouth and followed it with another sip of the pop. Skylar rested her palms on her desktop planner and closed her eyes. "Just give me a minute."

Her sister's assistant crossed to her and set a steaming cup of tea and a scone in front of her. "Mornings are bad," she whispered to Sydney and Savanna. "The ginger tea helps, and she says the carbs do too. She'll be okay soon."

"Ginger tea is natural and so much healthier than Coke—" Sydney started to speak, and Savanna stared at her wide-eyed, making her hush.

"Whatever helps," she said. "A few sips of pop never hurt anyone. Remember Mom giving us cola syrup over ice when we had the stomach flu?"

Sydney nodded. "You're right, I forgot. That or Vernors always worked. Did you try Vernors yet?"

Vernors was actually a good suggestion; it was a Michigan ginger ale cure-all. Savanna was sure Skylar was on top of any and all morning sickness tricks.

Their sister had followed up that message last night with a quick call, telling them it'd be easier to show them in person this morning what she'd discovered. Savanna couldn't wait to find out what the camera had caught.

Skylar opened her eyes, squeezed them shut, and then opened them again. "I'm fine. Mornings are the worst. It's not just the nausea—my head spins too. I'll be okay."

"How long will this last? I feel so bad for you." Savanna made a sad face at her.

"It should be over by now. So, any day, I hope." She took a drink of the ginger tea and ate another cracker.

Sydney turned her phone toward Skylar. "I just ordered you these. They're pregnancy lollipops in ginger and spearmint. And these," she said, turning the phone back to herself and tapping the screen. "These are acupressure wristbands, for motion sickness and that spinny feeling. You'll have them tomorrow."

Skylar gave them a weak smile. "Thank you. Okay, this isn't what you came here for. Let me show you." She turned her desktop monitor toward them and tapped a few keys.

A silent black-and-white video played on the screen. It took a moment to understand the perspective of the camera; Savanna tipped her head a little, seeing the fish-eye view of the corner the Carson Ballroom occupied. Scattered patrons were exiting; thirty seconds went by, and she could see the crowd was thinning.

"The intersection cam is on a motion-activated sensor. Real time is at the bottom." She pointed at the clock on the screen. "So this is as your banquet is ending, and the last few people are leaving. Watch. It starts at 10:27 p.m."

She and Sydney both sat forward, staring at the screen. When the real-time clock registered 10:27, a trio of people exited the ballroom. They looked to be chatting on the sidewalk at first, and then the man—Mayor Greenwood, Savanna caught his face when he turned—turned and walked toward uptown, while the two women—the mayor's wife, wearing the cute pillbox hat Savanna had admired at the banquet, and her sister—headed in the opposite direction.

"Mrs. Greenwood gets into her car down the street, here, with her sister," Skylar said, pointing at the edge of the screen. "That's captured from the camera's other directional lens. This lens loses sight of Mayor Greenwood about halfway up this block. But watch."

Savanna caught movement at the edge of the screen Roger Greenwood had just walked off. He was moving back down the sidewalk and stopped just short of the tall ballroom entryway windows.

"What's he doing? Why didn't he leave with his wife?" Sydney asked.

"Just watch."

At 10:31 p.m., John Bellamy exited the ballroom. He turned to the left and began walking in the same direction the mayor's wife had gone; he abruptly stopped and spun around. At the opposite end of the screen, Greenwood was quite obviously talking to him, and John moved back up the sidewalk toward the mayor.

The two men met, and even in the silent black-and-white footage, it was clear they were having an animated conversation. The two figures went from standing a couple of feet apart to John taking a quick step in toward the mayor, and the mayor matching him, so they were nearly nose to nose. The screen froze.

Savanna stared wide-eyed at Skylar. "What. Was. That."

Skylar's index finger rested above a function key; she'd paused the video. She dunked her scone briefly into her tea, taking a bite and then a sip. "That is Mayor Greenwood and Councilman Bellamy having a good old-fashioned yelling match. Look at them. Their body language is aggressive and rigid."

"God, I wish we had sound!" Sydney groaned. "There isn't any, right? No chance of getting the audio of this?"

Skylar shook her head. "Nope." She tapped the keyboard and nodded at the screen. "But watch."

Roger Greenwood's hand shot out and before Savanna was sure she'd really seen it happen, the councilman's body jerked forward. She and Sydney both leaned in toward the screen. The mayor's shoulders shook as he shook John by the collar.

John hit the mayor with the heels of both hands against his shoulders, shoving him backward and causing the mayor to lose his grip.

The mayor struggled for a moment to regain his footing,

and as he did, the councilman moved toward him, leaning in and pointing at him. John then stepped back, smoothed his suit jacket and ran one hand over the top of his head, and turned to walk away. Roger Greenwood had the last word, it appeared; the mayor took a few steps after him, gesturing wildly and saying something no one would ever hear. The councilman kept walking. The mayor stood still, watching him, until two last stragglers exited the ballroom, and then Greenwood spun and walked off screen.

"What the heck happened?" Savanna breathed. "I mean, seriously, what in the world. That cannot all have been over the campaign and John's candidacy."

Skylar shook her head. "I'd be surprised if that's all it was."

"I've never seen the mayor like that. He looked like he could kill Councilman Bellamy," Sydney mused.

"I wonder what Roger Greenwood would have to say about this," Savanna said.

"I've got a message into Detective Jordan. He needs to see this. Mayor Greenwood can't know the video exists, and we need to keep it that way until Jordan can deal with it, hopefully today. Chef Joe is still on house arrest, which is better than being in jail, but I'd love to find concrete evidence to get him exonerated as soon as possible."

"Speaking of which," Sydney said, looking at Savanna, "you wanted me to try to find that hotel owner's kid on social media, right?"

"What?" Skylar frowned at them.

Savanna summed up the meeting with Paul Stevens for

her sister; she'd already filled Sydney in this morning at home.

"No offense, Savanna," Sydney spoke. "But what teenager is capable of murder?"

"Okay. Guys, I'm actually not thinking this boy is capable of murder. But it's totally possible the vandalism going on could be separate from the councilman's murder. Right? I mean, we've said since the beginning that it's a huge escalation, going from destroying a statue to killing someone. Can you just look him up, Syd? On the Instagram app or that Snap-talk thing you use? Somewhere? I'm sure we can find him. His name is Alan James Stevens."

"How do you know his full name?" Skylar asked.

"It's on the hotel website. The place has been in their family for decades; they have the whole history listed."

Sydney pulled out her phone. "See, you're more tech-savvy than you think you are. I can teach you how to do this," she said, leaning over Savanna and facing her iPhone screen toward her.

"No way," Savanna said, shaking her head. "It's too complicated. Besides, that's what I have you for."

Sydney worked over her phone for no more than a minute. "Got him. This is him, right? Same name, and this guy's location is set to Grand Pier, Michigan."

Savanna peered at the screen. "I'm sure that's him. We only saw him for a moment, but it looks like him."

Sydney scrolled through Alan's posts. "Oh hey, is this the hotel?"

"Yes, that's him at the reception desk," Savanna said.

"Oh! Holy cow, look!"

Savanna and Skylar peered at the screen. Savanna snatched the phone out of Sydney's hands, staring down at it. "You have *got* to be kidding me. No one's this dumb."

"Let me see!" Skylar reached across the desk and took the phone. "No way. Alan James Stevens really is this dumb."

Sydney took her phone back and screenshotted the picture Alan had posted ten days ago. "I just sent it to both of you. Detective Jordan needs to see this."

The photo was stamped the date of the planning banquet. It was a close-up shot of the still-dripping red words *NEVER CARSON*, with a portion of Jessamina's head on the grass in the background and the edge of a red spray paint canister in the foreground.

Sydney was shaking her head. "At least we know who vandalized Jessamina. Do you think he also got your tires?"

Savanna tipped her head and frowned, considering. "Gosh. I don't know. It's possible, I guess, right? But that was a full week later. And it seemed so personal, compared to Jessamina."

Skylar's assistant spoke from the doorway. "Your ten o'clock is here."

"Oh, boy. I've got to run." Savanna stood. "Jack's probably wondering what happened to me. I'll pick you up in an hour?"

Sydney nodded, walking out with her. "Sounds good. Send that picture to Detective Jordan so he can start checking on the kid."

JACK WAS WAITING at the future Carson Theatre for Savanna with two whipped-cream-and-caramel-topped iced coffees. She followed him up the winding stairway to the balcony, loving his running commentary. "These steps will be covered in red carpeting, with wrought-iron railing all the way up. The main level concession will have a smaller, sister concession up here, for when people need a quick refill on their popcorn or drink. I'm having the painters strip all the crumbling old wallpaper, and sand, patch, and paint. We'll add footlights in each aisle here, here, and up there. I found vintage 1960s replacement bulbs for the chandelier; they're being shipped from a tiny company in Santa Clarita." Sitting in the front row of the balcony, Jack gestured with a sweeping hand from one side of the theatre to the other. "I've also ordered two hundred forty-four heated, reclining leather seats, with a third of those being cuddle seats."

Savanna laughed. "Did you make that up?"

"I wish. The chain theatres have kind of coined the term, but they're a big hit. Your mural will take up that entire wall." He pointed.

"Wow." She breathed the word. "I can do this. I'm going to have a blast doing this." She grinned at him. "When's your projected opening? How long do I have?"

"I'm not sure. Permits are a nightmare, and there's a lot of labor involved before everything is operational. We have a while."

"Okay. We'll have the words *Century of Cinema* on a

painted scroll at the top," she said, pointing. "I've got some of my ideas sketched out, but I'll run everything by you before I begin. I'm planning on starting right after Art in the Park wraps up."

"Sounds great." Jack smiled at her. His sandy-brown hair was perpetually mussed, and even now, on this warm June day, he wore his standard khakis, albeit with a short-sleeved polo shirt instead of the button-down he wore for school. His expression was painted with anticipatory excitement.

"You're super psyched about this, aren't you?"

"I am."

"I am too. It's exactly what Carson needs. You'll be a hero."

He shrugged. "I just want a place to kick back and see a good movie without an hour drive."

"You and the rest of this town!"

Outside, Jack gave her a quick hug goodbye. She headed over to her car outside Fancy Tails, where Sydney was waiting to go meet Talia DeVries for lunch.

Sydney narrated directions from Savanna's phone as they got into the city; Grand Rapids was the largest city on this side of the state. In recent years, it'd become a cultural hub, offering museums, concert venues, a botanical garden, and excellent restaurants. They drove past the place Talia DeVries had chosen for their lunch today, looking for parking.

"The Old Goat." Sydney read the sign, aptly set behind a large carved wooden goat standing over the entrance. "This place isn't what I expected."

The interior was industrial-chic, with oil-drum lighting suspended over a mixture of standard and raised tables, and patio seating visible through doors off one side. As the hostess led them through to their table, they checked out some of the fare; by the time they joined the art critic, Savanna knew she wanted the pierogis, and Sydney had clutched Savanna's arm, pointing to a delicious-looking salmon platter being carried out.

"Ms. DeVries," Savanna said, smiling, and offered her hand to the woman, who was already seated. "This is my sister Sydney. I couldn't resist bringing her—we've both been wanting to try this place." It was a lie, but a white lie, and if the food was as good as the atmosphere, it might not be a lie at all.

"Nice to meet you, Sydney."

Five minutes of studying the menu didn't change either of their minds; the server took their order and then brought Talia DeVries a glass of white wine, Sydney a lemonade, and Savanna an iced tea.

Now that they were seated across from the woman, she was suddenly nervous about broaching the topic of why they were here. She reached into the large purse she'd brought. Best to rip off the bandage, right? She set the manila folder containing Nina McCullen's artwork submission on the tabletop, resting one hand on top of it.

"I was glad you contacted me." The art critic spoke first.

"Talia…Ms. DeVries."

"Talia," the woman said. "That's fine."

"Okay. I'm not really sure how to say this, but we have

an art submission—one that was likely going to be accepted—from a young artist we think may be related to you."

Talia set her wineglass down. She propped elbows on the table and clasped her hands in front of her, looking at the folder.

Savanna pushed it across the table to her.

The woman examined the printed submission, John's orange sticky note still attached. She slid a finger under one corner, frowning at John's handwritten, block print words: *DISQUALIFY.*

"The artist is Nina McCullen." Savanna pointed to the corner, which bore the contact information, watching the woman's face.

The corners of her mouth turned down, and her shoulders visibly slumped. "I resign." She looked up at Savanna. "I'm dropping out. This artist is obviously talented. You can't disqualify her," she pled.

Savanna sat back, frowning. This was so…tawdry. When she'd won the Art in the Park event for Carson, she'd never once imagined she'd have to confront a cheater. And especially not a grown woman and well-known artist!

Talia closed the folder and pushed it back across the table to Savanna. "Nina is my niece. I *swear* I didn't know she'd applied."

"What do you mean, you didn't know?" Sydney took a bite of breadstick. Her gaze was bouncing back and forth between the women as she took in the exchange.

Talia scowled at Sydney for a second, and then rearranged her expression into something more benign. She looked back at Savanna. "I had no idea until last weekend that Nina had submitted this." She tapped the folder.

"Last weekend," Savanna said. "When John— Councilman Bellamy—told you?"

She nodded. "Yes. Honestly. She and I aren't close. You know I live in Mackinac City, up north. Nina is my brother's daughter. They're at the southern end of the state, at least six hours from me. We see each other on holidays, if that."

"You're telling me your niece, this very talented artist, didn't know you were signed on as a judge in the statewide contest she decided to enter? Your niece knows who you are, doesn't she?"

Talia scoffed. "You mean, who I was? That era is long over, Ms. Shepherd. I was a one-hit wonder. I made a couple of feeble tries at a follow-up collection, but nothing was any good. I burned it all."

Savanna gasped. "You burned it? How—how could you do that?" She knew the energy she poured into one of her own pieces of art. Even with the ones she was less than happy with, she still felt a kind of connection; there was no way she'd ever destroy her own work.

"How could I not do it? I'm much better as a critic. I've always known that. Anyway, by the time Nina was getting into art, I was already freelancing and working for the magazine. She doesn't think of me as an artist. I don't think she knew I was judging. And I had no idea she was an applicant. Please," she said, "don't disqualify her. I'm out. No one else knew about this besides me and Councilman

Bellamy."

"What did he say to you that night? You know, I saw the two of you arguing."

Talia took a sip of her wine. "When he told me about Nina's submission, I was shocked. I told him the same thing I'm telling you—to let me step down so she could be accepted."

"You were pleading with him."

"Yes, I was. He wouldn't listen. He was convinced we were in it together, plotting so she'd win. He wanted me out, and he refused to consider her submission. I'm surprised he didn't tell you."

"He died before he had the chance." Sydney daintily patted her mouth with a white linen napkin, then smoothed it on her lap.

The server appeared with their food, distributing their meals on white square plates: the salmon platter, the pierogis, and a Michigan cherry salad for Talia. All conversation halted until he was gone.

Talia's expression registered full understanding now. "You cannot think I had anything to do with his death." She leaned in toward them, her words sharp and hushed. "That's why we're here, isn't it?"

"We don't know what happened to John Bellamy," Savanna said. "We're trying to find out. How did the two of you leave things the night of the banquet?"

"You should know," she answered. "You interrupted the end of it. He was totally unreasonable. I don't think he even cared that I felt he was being unfair. The next day, I tried to bring myself to call Nina and tell her what had happened, but I just couldn't. I figured she'd get a rejection like the rest, and maybe she'd never know it was because of me." She looked down.

"But then the councilman turns up dead, and now maybe you're thinking your niece will get in," Sydney said. She speared a bite of fish with her fork, looking at Talia.

The woman was quiet. She pushed the food around on her plate.

"That's why," Savanna spoke, "you never came forward with the information yourself, isn't it? You hoped Britt and I didn't know about Nina being your niece."

"I planned on telling you," she said, the waver in her voice betraying her uncertainty about that. "I called my brother yesterday. I made up a reason, and he ended up telling me about Nina applying for Art in the Park. She was upset she hadn't been notified yet either way, this far past the deadline. So I guess I knew I had to talk to you. If you hadn't reached out, I would have."

Savanna believed her. She looked tortured, weighed down by all that had happened in the last week. But she still had to ask her last question. "Talia, where were you last Sunday night? The night the councilman was killed."

Talia picked up her purse from the empty chair beside her, and for a moment Savanna thought she was going to storm out. She rummaged around and pulled out a long, white, heavy-weight cardstock, folded in half vertically. "I was working. I took this at the end of the night; I always do. I was in Detroit last Sunday, from four p.m. until very late."

"Detroit Institute of Art Charity Ball, Renowned Art Critic Talia M. DeVries," Savanna read.

Next to Savanna, Sydney had pulled out her phone and was typing on the screen. "She's not lying. She was there." She showed Savanna a photo of the panel of judges, a tiny thumbnail picture but still clearly Talia DeVries.

Now Talia stood. She set three twenty-dollar bills on the table and slung her purse over a shoulder. "Let me cover lunch. I'm sorry, I just don't have an appetite. Ms. Shepherd," she said, meeting Savanna's gaze. "Please consider allowing my niece the chance to participate, if you feel she's good enough. None of this is her fault. I'd offer some names of other art critics who might be willing to step in for me, but I'm sure that wouldn't be appropriate; you should select someone on your own."

"I promise I'll talk it over with my colleague, Britt Nash." Savanna was earnest. "Thank you for being candid with us."

Talia DeVries nodded. "I'm sorry it wasn't sooner. And I'm sorry you lost the councilman; it's a tragedy, no matter how I felt about him."

Later that afternoon, Savanna turned onto Main Street and headed toward Fancy Tails to drop Sydney off.

"Ugh." Sydney stuck her tongue out. "I'm so full. That place was awesome. Why did you let me order the carrot cake?" She rested one hand on her belly.

Savanna laughed. "Let you? Like I could stop you. It was good though." She parked in front of the grooming salon. "I'm going to take Fonzie for a quick walk, and then I've got to call that reporter from the Allegan County paper back; he left me a voicemail."

"Just leave me here," Sydney moaned. "I'll be in when some of this food settles."

"Sure thing. I'll tell Willow you're in a food coma and can't come back to work."

Sydney pushed the car door open with a foot and climbed out. "It's okay. I'll suffer through." She followed Savanna into the shop.

A huge bouquet of daisies sat in the center of Sydney's desk, tied with a bright peach-colored ribbon.

"Oh! So pretty!" Sydney pulled a card from the small white envelope sticking up from the bouquet.

"Someone must be really happy with their beautifully groomed pooch," Willow called in her lilting voice from the back of the shop. "Those arrived about an hour ago."

Sydney perched on the edge of her desk, frowning at the card.

"What's wrong?" Savanna joined her.

She handed it over, and Savanna read aloud:

Sydney—

I'm sorry we got off on the wrong foot.

Would love a redo.

Finn Gallager

Chapter Sixteen

T HE BELL OVER the door of Fancy Tails jingled, and Skylar poked her head in, making both sisters look up from the card.

"Good, you're both here. I got a meeting at the station with Nick Jordan tomorrow morning to sit down and go over our recent discoveries. You should be there. The two of you are now officially on my defense team for Chef Joe; Jordan will have to listen to what you've found. Pretty flowers."

Sydney held up the card from Finn. "Aidan Gallager's brother sent them."

Skylar stepped into the salon, glancing down at her watch. "I'm meeting a client in four minutes. What's going on now?" She read the message and cocked an eyebrow at Sydney. "What's this about?"

"It wasn't a big deal. He made a rude comment, and I called him on it; I didn't know he was Aidan's brother at the time."

Savanna spoke. "Honestly, I don't think he meant to offend you. He just mentioned that Syd didn't look old enough to have her own business," she told Skylar, bringing her up to speed. "You could've taken it as a compliment."

Sydney was quiet. She looked back down at the card.

"You've always had a chip on your shoulder about being the youngest, but he should know better than to comment on any woman's age." Skylar gave Sydney an affectionate squeeze around the shoulders. "It's a sweet gesture though."

Sydney sighed and placed the pretty card back in the bracket among the daisies. "You're right. It's very sweet. All right, you have your meeting, and I've got to get back to work." She made shooing motions at her sisters.

"Actually, we're caught up," Willow spoke from the doorway, holding a newly washed and groomed fluffy Pekinese in her arms.

Savanna scratched behind the little dog's ears. "You're so cute!" Sydney's young assistant was also adorable. She wore her hair in a short rainbow-colored pixie cut with long bangs, several earrings adorning each ear, and she always had the brightest neon manicure. Her sunny attitude complemented Fancy Tails & Treats' sunny atmosphere.

"I'm out," Skylar said. The greenish, clammy tinge of her skin from this morning was now replaced with a rosy glow and her eyes were bright. "I'll see you tomorrow for lunch." She was out the door before Sydney could reply.

"How did he know daisies are my favorite?" Sydney looked at Savanna.

"It's a small town, with one flower shop. I'm sure Libby knows your flower preference by now. Finn probably just asked." Her phone rang; she didn't recognize the number, but it was a local area code. "Hello?"

"Savanna, this is Landon King. From the newspaper? I'm

glad I caught you!"

"I was just about to call you back," she said, grabbing Fonzie's leash from the hook on the wall and clipping it to his collar.

"No worries. Are you free right now?"

Savanna put a hand on the door and motioned at her sister, indicating she'd be back shortly. "I am. Sort of. Why?"

"I'm in town, and I have the files you asked for—I put my photographer's photos on a flash drive for you. I can meet you at the coffee shop if that works for you."

"Actually," she said, side-stepping Fonzie as he excitedly sniffed every tree, flower and blade of grass as they walked, "I have my dog with me. Could you meet me in the park?"

"Of course. I'll head over there now. Can I bring you something to drink?"

"Oh, no thank you. I just came from lunch. See you in a few." She felt as full as Sydney had lamented, and she'd shared Syd's carrot cake along with a cup of coffee; she certainly didn't need another cup.

She sat on a bench under the maple trees, near the center of the park this time, where she unhooked Fonzie and granted him playtime. He sprinted over to the couple of other dogs present; raising Fonzie from a pup in Chicago had given him a clear sense of his boundaries. He never got too far away from her, and he was very obedient whenever she called him back.

The reporter crossed the green lawn toward her, carrying a canvas messenger bag and a cup of coffee. She guessed him to be in his mid- to late-thirties; he was of medium build, his wavy hair with hints of gray at the temples. Today he wore a tan sportscoat and brown loafers.

Fonzie came bounding over to them as King reached the park bench. The man bent down and put a hand out to the Boston Terrier. "This must be your little guy."

"That's Fonzie," Savanna said as her dog retreated and took off again. "Lots of energy," she said, laughing.

He joined her on the bench, pulling a silver and black flash drive from the bag and handing it to her. "This is everything my photographer got at the banquet. There are a lot," he cautioned. "He always takes more than he needs. Maybe you'll see something useful in one of them."

"Thank you so much. I'm not sure there's anything to see, but we're just trying to cover all angles."

"Right, right." He crossed his legs and took a drink from his coffee cup. "So, you said you don't believe they've got the right man. You must have a theory," he said, tipping his head toward her and lowering his voice. "Who do you think the killer is?"

She was a bit taken aback. She looked at him, and he immediately sat up straight, moving back into his own space.

"Sorry. I've been doing this so long, sometimes I forget not everything's a story. I'm just curious; I'm not thinking of writing anything about the case, don't worry. Off the record." He gave her an apologetic smile.

"I honestly don't know." Savanna hesitated, frowning at him. He was a reporter. He probably knew more than she thought he did. "My sister's representing the man the police think did it. My family has known him a long time. Skylar feels the facts don't add up, and I believe her. So I'm doing what I can to help."

"Makes sense. I've covered a lot of our county's more...unsavory events. Maybe I can be a resource for you. Typically, investigations take into account who might've had something to gain with the victim's death. You said Councilman Bellamy was a friend, so you knew him pretty well? Can you think of anyone who'd want to hurt him?"

"I thought I knew him. But as I've been talking to people, I'm not so sure."

"How's that?"

She thought for a moment. "How long have you worked for the paper?"

King looked up at the sky, exhaling through pursed lips. "Let me think. Eleven—no, twelve years."

"And you've covered the Art in the Park event for most of that time?"

He nodded. "That I have."

"Do you recall anything odd about Paul Stevens, or his family? He runs the Lakeside Pier hotel up in Grand Pier."

Now King frowned. "Not really. Though, I did think it was a strange choice of his to attend your banquet. Of course, I don't know for sure what that little scuffle was about, between him and your councilman that night, but I think we can make a pretty good guess."

"We'd be guessing right; I've already spoken to him. He confirmed he was trying to convince John to decline the event so it would go to Grand Pier."

"Did he now! Has Carson's investigatory team talked to

him?"

"He has kind of an airtight alibi. But his son might be another story."

"I'm intrigued."

Savanna shrugged. "It doesn't matter. I don't actually believe that kid could've hurt John. We also caught some potential fraud within the festival, but I think we've ruled that person out as well."

"You don't appear to be having too much trouble on your own with this investigation," he said. "Your sister's lucky to have you on her team. Or, should I say, Joe Fratelli is."

She looked at him sharply. "His name was withheld from public record during the arraignment, and I didn't tell you. How do you know that?"

Landon King sighed. "It's a pitfall of my profession. Even when I'm not on a story, I still hear things. I have sources, and they pass information to me. Sometimes it's information I can't officially use, like the fact that Fratelli's fingerprints were found on the murder weapon. But..." He met Savanna's gaze. "Do they even have a motive for him?"

She bit her lower lip. She'd been trying to keep things vague, but all the messy details seemed to be scattered out in the open, between what she knew and what this reporter knew. "I don't know what the police have as motive. But Chef Joe dated the councilman's ex-wife, Mia James. It was a while ago, last year I think. Caroline Carson told me."

King was nodding. "Hmm. A jilted lover always makes a good murder suspect."

"Except he didn't do it. My sister says Chef Joe told her nothing was serious, that they dated for less than a year. He thought it was ridiculous as a possible motive."

"Well, to play devil's advocate, if your Chef Joe was love-sick and did something about it, would he admit they'd had a serious relationship?"

"No," Savanna said. "You're right. But it doesn't make sense. It's not like Mia left Chef Joe to go back to the councilman."

King laughed. "Well, I'd think not."

"Do you know her?"

"Not really. I know of her. I've covered a few stories at Mitten Inn. No offense to your late councilman, but after the way he treated Mia James during the whole scandal with their son, pigs would fly before she'd have gotten back together with her ex-husband."

"Oh! You covered the story involving Remy James? I suppose you must have!" Savanna felt a surge of excitement. Finally, someone who might tell her what exactly had happened. She knew her mother had promised to fill them all in tomorrow, but she had a feeling Landon King might have a slightly different version, as an impartial reporter.

"There was no story. Nothing was ever printed, anyway, after the initial report of the incident. Even after John Bellamy's smear campaign against his own son, with the whole town certain he'd done it, our judicial system let him go due to insufficient evidence."

Savanna turned toward him on the park bench. "Insufficient evidence of *what*?"

He pressed his lips together. "I can't say."

"Seriously? I've been trying to be discreet, and you just blew all my vague information out of the water. I'm obviously not going to tell anyone you have inside information about Chef Joe's arrest. Anything you tell me about what happened with Remy will stay between us. You can trust me."

He stretched one arm out on the back rest of the bench, the opposite direction of Savanna, and uncrossed his legs, then recrossed them in the other direction. "I really shouldn't say." He looked at her. "I'll tell you, but anything you decide to do with the information, it can't have come from me. Okay?"

"Yes. I promise."

"They never proved for sure that it was murder," he mused, almost to himself. "It was a wealthy couple from Arizona, visiting family in Michigan. Room 112. I can't believe I still remember that."

"Oh my God. What happened? There was a double murder at Mitten Inn?" Savanna tucked one leg underneath her on the park bench, hanging on every word.

King looked at her. "Not double. The husband. I wish I could recall the name, but I guess it doesn't matter. The husband was found dead in their hotel room the morning they were supposed to check out. He drowned in the bathtub."

Savanna shook her head. "What? How does that even happen? They thought someone, what, held him under until he died?"

"There were fresh bruises on his chest and arms. The authorities put the time of death between midnight and three in the morning, a few hours before his wife discovered him. There was a half-full bottle of gin on the bathroom floor."

"Where was his wife while he was drowning in the bathtub?"

"That was part of the problem. She was gone for a good portion of that window of death. She had a valet ticket for a club in Grand Rapids; she didn't get back to Mitten Inn that night until after two a.m. She said she entered the room and fell into bed with her clothes on; she never turned on the light."

"Okay. Well…her husband is drunk, falls asleep in the bathtub, and drowns. It's sad, but it doesn't sound like murder."

"Right, right. But then the wife finds all of their prescriptions missing, along with the cash they had in the room safe. All things they'd logged when they checked in."

"Did they do a tox screen?" Savanna caught Landon King's look. "My sister's a lawyer, and I watch way too much *Columbo*."

He laughed. "They did. Other than the alcohol, it was clear, and the blood alcohol level was pretty nominal. There was a room service delivery at twelve thirty a.m., a half hour after the kitchen had closed. The concierge was gone for the night, and probably most of the kitchen staff by then. Mia's son, Remington, delivered the food."

"And that's what led the authorities to believe Mia's son was the killer?"

"He was the only one who had contact with the guest during the time of death window."

"Besides the man's wife, in the last hour of the time frame," Savanna added.

"There is that," King acknowledged. "But apparently the woman's phone call that morning, and her condition when medical responders arrived, left no doubt that she was truly shocked to find her husband dead in the bathtub."

"So Mia James got Remy's father involved—Councilman Bellamy. Maybe she thought John would have some pull with the prosecutor or the sheriff's department?"

"I'm sure that was Mia's thought process. But it back-fired. Bellamy did the opposite: he provided the investigation team with Remy's juvenile records detailing a history of petty theft. I'm not sure if the councilman was also the one who tipped them off on the assault at knife point when Remy was living in Paris for culinary school, but once they got hold of that incident, things unraveled from there."

"All right, slow down. Assault? At knife point? Remy has a record?"

"Officially? I'm not sure. But you can't escape your past."

Savanna shook her head. "Wow. So, Remy James was arrested, but it never went to trial. What happened?"

"Mia hired Jillian Black."

Savanna looked at him blankly.

"Jillian Black of Black, Jones, and Sydowski. The parent firm for your sister's branch, Michigan largest legal firm. Jillian Black is a barracuda. She got the charges dropped and the case tossed out."

Landon King was tough to read. Savanna studied his expression, unable to discern what he wasn't saying, the thoughts between the lines. "What do you think? Do you think Remy did it?"

King sighed. "I'm still not sure. I know Mia James never for a moment believed her son was guilty. But isn't that a mother's job? To protect her son? I also know Bellamy seemed convinced Remy was bad news. Listen—" He stared at Savanna intently, frowning. "I can see how deeply involved in all of this you are. Don't underestimate the gravity of the things you're working to uncover. Be careful around Remy James."

Even after Landon King had gone, Savanna remained on the park bench, her mind reeling. She watched Fonzie playing without really seeing him as she tried to imagine the events that unfolded at Mitten Inn four years ago. There were too many possibilities. She dug around in her purse, coming up with the sparkly pink notebook she kept her Art in the Park notes in. She flipped it open to the last page and began jotting notes, hoping to clear her thoughts.

Savanna spent the evening on her laptop, clicking through 176 photos on the flash drive King had given her. She tried to focus specifically on the shots that captured any of the people she was interested in for Chef Joe's case, and any near the kitchen, where Chef Joe's knife was stolen, or the front entrance, where some of the drama had occurred. She dragged a handful of photos to a separate folder on her screen, wanting to take a closer look at them. In one, in the doorway of the kitchen, Chef Joe was having an animated conversation with his sous chef Remy; in true Joe Fratelli fashion, his hands were caught midmotion in the air as he made his point. In the background of another, Mayor Greenwood and John Bellamy stood not ten feet apart, each holding a drink and facing opposite directions despite no one else being in the frame.

There were far too many photos of people going in and out of the kitchen—she didn't know why she'd thought that would be the missing piece in the puzzle. Had she expected to find a photo of the killer leaving the kitchen carrying the large chef's knife? At various points in the evening, the waitstaff, Chef Joe, Remy James, Talia DeVries, Yvonne, Mayor Greenwood and his wife, Paul Stevens, John Bellamy, and Mia James had all entered or exited the kitchen, mostly in the backgrounds of the photographer's photos. They seemed to be in order of the evening's events, judging by the food and empty dishes on trays caught here and there. Savanna flipped between the series of photos, zooming in on the one of Mayor Greenwood too many times, and another with a profile view of Mia James walking away from the kitchen.

Wednesday morning, walking to the Carson Village police station, Savanna typed a short to-do list into her phone:

Pick up festival decorations.

Lunch with Mom.

Stop at Giuseppe's and finalize catering order.

Visit Chef Joe.

She planned to ask Skylar if it'd be okay to go talk with him. He'd be able to tell them why so many people had been in and out of the kitchen the night of the banquet. She had a twinge as she remembered that even she had popped into the kitchen at the beginning of the night, and then she'd sent Sydney in briefly toward the end to ask for more tarts to be brought out. Maybe it wasn't so odd.

Taking the sidewalk up to the front door of the police station, she stopped as someone shouted to her.

"Savanna!"

She turned to find her real estate agent climbing out of his car; Carson Community Homes was right across the street from the police station. "Hey, Mike! How are you?"

"I'm great! I was going to call you. I know you've hit pause for a bit, but I have the perfect house for you. No exaggeration, the perfect house. It just went on the market. Lake view, huge yard, nice Cape Cod style. A bit of a fixer-upper, but it has your name all over it."

She laughed. "Okay. I believe you. I'll make some time and get in touch! Try not to show anyone else, okay?"

He took his briefcase from the back seat. "No promises! Call me. It's not going to last long."

Savanna bounced into the police station, unable to keep the grin off her face. Oh, she hoped he really had something. So far, the ones Mike had shown her were either perfect and way out of her price range, or not at all what she hoped to end up in. She stopped short a few feet from the desk sergeant, taking a moment to add to her to-do list: *Call Mike!*

Skylar waved to her from down the hallway, and Savanna joined her outside Detective Jordan's office.

"Syd isn't with you?" She wore the set of gray acupressure wristbands Syd had ordered her, a Vernors in one hand today.

"Nope. She was still out last night when I went to bed, and gone already this morning. She's probably teaching a crack-of-dawn yoga class. I'm sure she'll be here."

"It's fine. Come on." She gave two quick knocks on Detective Jordan's door and opened it, holding it for Savanna.

When they were seated across from him, Savanna asked, "Detective, did you get the screenshot of that social media post showing the destroyed statue? I sent it yesterday."

He nodded, tapping a few keys on his computer. "Got it. Alan James Stevens. Thanks for that. My partner is up there this morning having a talk with young Mr. Stevens and his father."

"We met with Paul Stevens on Monday. He was hosting his wife's birthday party the night the councilman was killed."

Detective Jordan raised a single eyebrow at her. "That's helpful. You know there's a process for this, right?"

"I do know, yes. But Dr. Gallager and I took a drive. It's so pretty up in Grand Pier, and then I thought since we were already there, why not stop at the bistro for dinner? We just happened to run into Mr. Stevens."

"Mm-hmm. That was convenient. And he happened to mention his whereabouts the night in question." The detective's tone was dry.

"He did, actually." Savanna smiled. "But while we were there, we, uh, learned that they've been having a little trouble with their son. Which is how I ended up finding that picture on social media. Well, Sydney found it."

Skylar pulled a yellow legal pad and a sheaf of papers from her briefcase. "So, while the connection between the Jessamina incident and Paul Stevens's kid is interesting, I don't believe it's relevant to Joe Fratelli's case. But we do have some information that is."

The detective pulled his own notepad over in front of him, looking at Skylar. "Good morning to you, Counselor."

Skylar glanced up from her papers. "Morning, Jordan. How's things?"

"Oh, you know. Murder, vandalism. The usual. Hit me. What do you have?"

She slid a micro-SD card in a tiny plastic case across the desk. "Traffic cam footage from the intersection cameras the night before Bellamy was killed. It shows a pretty heated argument between the councilman and Roger Greenwood. While you get that up and running, I'd like to hear about the findings from Savanna's discovery in John's home office."

Detective Jordan met Skylar's gaze. "I was waiting for evidence to finish up on that. I planned to email you."

"Would you mind checking to see if the results are back? You can speak freely in front of my sister—she's working for the firm as my research assistant on Joe Fratelli's case."

A hint of a smile played around Nick Jordan's lips as he looked from Skylar to Savanna. "Of course." He turned his attention to his computer, typing and browsing through websites that required him to enter and reenter clearance passwords, all in a protected view.

Skylar sat back in her chair while they waited.

"We've got a hit from IAFIS on the prints pulled from the broken door of the safe. They match the fingerprints on the picture frame you noticed was crooked, the—what did you call it?" Detective Jordan glanced up at Savanna.

"*Red Tree*. The Piet Mondrian painting," she said, thrilled they'd uncovered evidence as a result of her find. She sat forward. "What's IAFIS? Does it tell you who the fingerprints belong to?"

"It's a federal database, the Integrated Automated Fingerprint Identification System. It matches evidence collected at crime scenes to any possible existing data in the system."

"So the person who broke into the safe, are they in the system?"

The detective nodded. "Yes. We still don't have a definitive answer though." He looked at Skylar. "The findings raise more questions than they answer. The prints on the safe and the frame of the Mondrian painting are a match for Remington James."

Savanna nearly jumped out of her seat. "Remy?" She stared wide-eyed at Skylar.

"Hold on." Jordan looked from his screen to the two of them. "There were two sets of prints on and around that safe, not including Bellamy's. One set is still unidentified. And listen. Remington James's prints are nowhere to be found on the point of entry, the cellar door. They're unknown, which means whoever broke into Bellamy's house the night he was killed isn't in the database."

Chapter Seventeen

"SAVANNA." DETECTIVE JORDAN leaned forward, elbows on his desk. "How certain are you that the painting was moved after the night of the murder? Isn't it possible you missed it that night? You fainted, didn't you? I'm sure it was difficult to process everything you saw."

Savanna recalled her impression from that night— nothing was out of place, which was the norm for him. She was positive she'd have noticed if the painting had already been crooked. And she'd noticed the state of his office well *before* she'd nearly fainted. "I'm sure," she said firmly. "I'm certain the painting hadn't been tampered with the night John was killed. Because when we went back, it jumped out at me. Like, I couldn't *not* see it."

"Maybe you saw it that Sunday night too, but you were too stressed to register it. Is that possible?"

"No. I really don't think so. I looked at the painting the night John was killed; I remember admiring how the frame coordinated so well with his desk."

Skylar spoke. "Jordan, don't the prints speak for themselves? What does it matter when the painting was tampered with? Perhaps the killer came back. You know that happens. A frazzled murderer, not getting to complete what he came there to do. People return to the scene of their crime all the time."

Detective Jordan sat back and his chair creaked. "Sometimes. But if that's what happened, why not retrieve whatever was in the safe after killing the councilman?"

Skylar shrugged. "Who knows. A neighbor stopped by? Savanna rang the bell? Someone startled him, and he took off prematurely."

"It doesn't explain the other set of prints on the frame and safe, or the unidentified set of prints on the cellar door. If Remington James is the killer, he had help."

"Mia," Savanna said.

Detective Jordan and Skylar both stared at her.

Savanna put a hand up. "I know it sounds crazy. But what if John's ex-wife was with Remy? What if they went there that night, hoping to get something from John's safe. Everyone knows their split wasn't amicable, and John and Remy were estranged. Heck, John and Mia were estranged too. I'm sure after the Mitten Inn incident, there was no love lost between them. Mia and Remy went to John's house, and things took a bad turn. Maybe they fled before getting what they came for. Then they came back later on to get something out of the safe."

"All right," Detective Jordan said. "So Remy does the stabbing. He'd have had the easiest access to Joe Fratelli's knife. He's wearing gloves, and he's careful with his grip, making sure enough of Fratelli's prints will still appear on the handle. Why frame Joe Fratelli? And what about the other set of prints that isn't in the database?"

"And," Skylar added, frowning now at Savanna, "who have you been getting information from about the Mitten Inn incident? Those records are sealed. Remy James was exonerated."

Savanna ignored her sister for a moment. "Maybe Remy didn't want to frame Chef Joe, but he knew he'd be scrutinized, with the history between him and his father. He had to somehow get suspicion cast elsewhere; Chef Joe would've been the easiest target. He could get his knife, and he probably knew Chef Joe's routine, no alibi that night. Could the unidentified fingerprints belong to John himself? Or Mia. I assume she probably isn't in the system?"

Detective Jordan laced his fingers into a steeple under his chin. He had no quick response this time.

"Do you think it's possible?" Skylar sat forward.

"We've already done elimination prints on Bellamy. We know the prints aren't his. But we'll bring James in for questioning. Remy," he clarified. "We've got no cause to look at Mia at this point."

"Other than the fact she'd have motive, after how John treated Remy before," Savanna offered.

"So she waited four years to exact her revenge?" Jordan cocked an eyebrow at her.

"No. I mean, not exactly," Savanna said. Now she wasn't sure about her theory. "But I think she'd do whatever she had to, to protect Remy. She did before." Skylar cleared her throat, and Savanna deliberately avoided looking at her; she knew she'd have to answer her sister's question at some point.

Detective Jordan hit a key on his computer and played the black-and-white footage from the SD card Skylar had given him. He watched in silence, and then clicked a few keys and replayed it twice more before letting the screen go black. "Well, this is something."

"That's what we thought," Skylar said coolly.

Savanna marveled at her sister's restraint. If the detective thought the video was significant, it had to be. But then, what about her Remy and Mia James murder-team theory?

"Have you said anything to Greenwood about this? Does he know you have this?"

"Of course not."

"Do we run our village officials through IAFIS?" His question wasn't meant for them; Savanna could nearly see the wheels turning in Detective Jordan's head as he mused. "I'm not sure," he said, answering his own question and frowning at Skylar.

"I don't know either. That's a good thought."

"But who would kill over a political seat?" Savanna asked. "I mean, are we really thinking Mayor Greenwood would've followed up that argument by killing John Bellamy just so he could run unopposed? To be mayor of a town most people have never even heard of?"

"Mayoral offices are often stepping stones to bigger goals," Skylar said.

Savanna nodded. "True. Well, you can rule out the mayor as one of those fingerprint sets, if it turns out our officials are registered in the system, right?"

Jordan nodded. "I'll find out today. If he hasn't been

registered, we'll take a closer look at him and what he was doing the night the councilman was killed."

"Their platforms were starkly different from each other, from the little I know," Skylar said.

"So maybe the argument was over something more specific than the campaign?" Savanna looked at Skylar. "You know there's some kind of drama going on over at the mayor's office, right? Roger Greenwood's assistant just quit without notice."

"I hadn't heard that."

"I'll ask Yvonne if she knows anything more about it when I see her today," Savanna said. "I have to pick up the decorations and banners for the festival."

Jordan stood, signaling their meeting was over. He walked them out to the front door.

"Detective," Savanna said before following Skylar out. "Were you able to learn anything about what happened to my tires?"

"So far nothing. I'll let you know when Detective Taylor reports back after talking to the Stevens family today. Seems in line with something that kid might do if he had no qualms about smashing Jessamina."

She nodded. "Thank you."

Skylar stopped Savanna with a hand on her arm before they headed in opposite directions outside the police station. "Did someone from my office give you all that information about the Mitten Inn incident? It's important that I know, if that's the case."

"No," she said quickly. "It was that reporter from the

banquet."

"That's right. Syd said you met with him? He certainly has a lot of inside information about Mia and Remy James."

"He was assigned to cover the story, but then he said there was no story, after the authorities cleared Remy of the murder. Did you know about that whole thing? Landon King said it was handled by a bigwig at your firm."

"Jillian Black was the attorney. I was off on leave after having Nolan. I don't know many details. But I'm sure Jillian wouldn't have gotten Remy cleared if she was suspicious he was guilty."

"Hmm."

Skylar laughed. "I know that look. We're getting close, I can feel it. I'll see you at Fancy Tails for lunch?"

"Yep! Mom said one o'clock, and Syd's grabbing sandwiches from the deli. I'm heading over to talk to Yvonne; I'll fill you in when I see you."

Savanna poked her head into the lobby of the building next door, which housed Carson's parks and rec department and the mayor's office. It was completely deserted. The door to Mayor Greenwood's office stood open, which she supposed meant he hadn't yet hired a replacement for his assistant.

She walked through the oddly silent lobby, peering through the glass door to where John Bellamy's office had been, among the other city officials. There were a few people working, though Yvonne's desk was empty.

"Can I help you?"

Savanna jumped and spun around. Roger Greenwood

was standing in the doorway to his office, holding a cup of coffee. "Oh! Hello, Mayor. I'm sorry to disturb you. I was looking for Yvonne? She was going to help me collect the decorations for the art festival, and the Michigan Council for the Arts sent a couple of large banners to display as well." Savanna was suddenly acutely aware of the fact that she was alone with Roger Greenwood, on the heels of speculating with Detective Jordan over whether the mayor could be the killer. That quick, violent outburst in the silent video flashed into her mind. Without meaning to, she took a step back, toward the door to the city council offices. Could anyone see or hear her out here? "Um…maybe Yvonne's on break. Do you know when she'll be back?"

"I wish I knew. I think she must be out sick. Do you know where she'd have put your items?"

Savanna groaned inwardly. She had no clue. "I'm not sure. Maybe one of Councilman Bellamy's coworkers would know?" She put a hand on the doorknob, feeling her heart pound as the mayor crossed the lobby to her.

Less than two feet from her, he reached past her, and she held her breath, ready to dart away from him. "Let's find out." He held the door open for her.

Savanna followed him down the hallway, trying to calm down; this area was more populated. There were witnesses here. Mayor Greenwood poked his head into the new councilwoman's office, but Linda Rae didn't know what they were talking about. A young man in the office next door overheard them and came to Savanna's rescue.

"Everything's back here," he said. A name badge hung

off his shirt: Jason Patterson, Assistant Recreation Director. "Follow me." He led Savanna down a hallway, and the mayor left them to it, thank goodness. The young man held a storeroom door open and flipped a light switch. "All the tables and chairs will be trucked to the park and set up next Wednesday, before Thursday morning kickoff; the councilman gave us your layout. These came on Monday," he said, bending and opening a large box to reveal enormous colorful banners that would be stretched across Main Street. "And these were in the councilman's personal belongings when we finished clearing out his office. He must've been keeping them to give you." He handed her a thin stack of official-looking letters.

"Thank you, this is great! Do you know the timing for the banners?" Savanna would've liked them up a week ago; she didn't even know they'd come. Between John's unfortunate death and Yvonne doing double duty as the new councilwoman's assistant as well as the mayor's, plus being out sick today, Savanna supposed it was inevitable there was a little lag time with some of the details.

"I finally got a firm yes on the banners. Honestly, Ms. Shepherd, they were supposed to go up this past weekend. I'm sorry about that. We were waiting on the tree trimmers—they've got the boom lifts to string the banners up. They're doing it today. We're planning one at the beginning of Main Street, one at the four corners in town, and the third at the park, is that right?"

"Yes. That's perfect." Savanna clapped her hands together, rocking back on her heels. She couldn't wait; it was all coming together. "So we can come through and get the displays decorated next Wednesday night, then?"

Jason nodded. "You got it. We can allocate a few people to help if you'd like."

She shook her head. She'd already recruited her whole family, Aidan, Jack, and Sydney's Willow to help. "I think we've got it covered."

The assistant director accompanied her on the way out.

"By the way," Savanna asked. "Could you let Yvonne know I hope she feels better, if she's back tomorrow? I'd hoped to catch her."

He stopped walking. They weren't yet out through the door to the lobby. "Yvonne is never sick. She was a no-call, no-show this morning, which can get you fired around here. It's not like her at all." Worry painted his features.

A chill crept up Savanna's spine. She pulled out her phone and checked it. Yvonne had never replied to her text this morning, a quick message saying she'd be stopping by. The lack of response hadn't seemed strange until right now. "I should check on her. Listen," she said, appealing to him. "I don't have Yvonne's address, but we're old friends from high school. I know you don't know me, but most folks around here know my family. Would you be comfortable giving me her address? I'm worried about her too."

Jason nodded. "I'm okay with that. I know your sister— we take our dog to Fancy Tails. I'd feel better too if you checked on her. I know her workload has been a lot lately. One sec." He disappeared through a doorway and returned less than a minute later, handing her an address scrawled on

TRACY GARDNER

a yellow sticky note. "Tell her to get better soon."

"Thank you so much." Savanna left him, typing the address into the map app on her phone. It looked like she'd need to drive, as Yvonne lived a couple of miles outside of town.

She shuffled through the mail on her walk home. She'd been managing the dedicated email inbox she and Britt had set up, but John must've tossed these in with his things to pass on to her. Among a few pieces of junk mail, there was a letter from Mrs. Kingsley at the Michigan Arts Council, something from the *Allegan County Newspaper*, and an envelope bearing a bold *B.L.* inside a triangle in the return address area, addressed to her in care of the festival.

She'd seen that logo before; it had been on the car in the parking lot the last time she was with Yvonne at the village offices. Better Living Properties was printed on the back of the envelope, along with a Lansing, Michigan, address. Savanna slid a finger under the flap to free the seal and was surprised to find it already unglued. Frowning, she pulled out the letter and scanned it. The real estate company was offering sponsorship of the Art in the Park festival, to the tune of $10,000.

Holy cow, the crowds she could reach with that kind of advertising money! Not to mention amped-up displays, a major boost to her decorating budget, more concessions and contests, and who knew what else.

But it was too late. The festival was a week away. She flipped the envelope over, checking the postdate. May! This had come in over a month ago. Why had John held on to it so long? Had he read it? No. There was no way; if he had, he'd have jumped at the offer, she was sure.

She read the letter again. Better Living Properties called Art in the Park a "boon to Carson's tourism," stating they felt it was never too early to build their presence and garner town support for their "upcoming development." What development? Now she wanted to turn around and ask Mayor Greenwood if that's what his meeting had been about that day, with the gentlemen who'd left in the Better Living vehicle. She'd do some research later today; they also had an ad on one of the park benches too, if she remembered correctly.

Savanna's phone rang, jarring her from her thoughts. She unlocked the door to Sydney's, dropped her mail on the kitchen counter, and answered her phone as she grabbed her car keys. "Hello?"

Aidan's deep voice came through the phone to her ear. "You sound like you're running."

She laughed. "I'm not, just rushing. How are you?"

"I'm great. I have a proposition for you. Would it be all right if I stopped by after work to run it by you?"

"Yes!" *Oh Lord, Savanna, calm down.* "I mean, sure, that'd be fine."

Now Aidan laughed. "I'll see you around six. Is everything okay? Where are you rushing to, if you don't mind me asking?"

"I'm just going to check on a sick friend, and then meeting my mom and sisters for lunch. Hey," she said. "Did you know that your brother sent my sister flowers?"

"Finn?"

"Um, yes? Finn's the only brother you have, right?"

Aidan's confusion carried through the phone. "Yes...but...he sent flowers? Oh, no. What did he do? Finn doesn't send flowers."

"He and Sydney got off on the wrong foot when he stopped by Fancy Tails the other day. I was there for most of it; I don't think he meant to offend her."

Aidan groaned on the other end of the line. "He never means to offend. He just does. Were the flowers at least nice?"

"They're beautiful. He must've asked the florist what she'd like. Sydney wasn't sure what to think. But it was a very nice gesture."

"Okay. I apologize in advance for whatever my brother said and will say at any given moment in the future; please extend my apologies to Sydney too when you see her."

"Aidan." Savanna smiled. "I think it's all fine. They just sort of clashed right off the bat. It'll blow over."

"I'm sure it will. Right around the time he heads out next week." He paused. "I'm sorry, I know I sound harsh. I love my brother. Finn is...real. He says whatever he thinks, and he rarely worries about who he offends. Which can make things difficult. We should have dinner sometime before he leaves. I'll make sure he brings his filter."

She chuckled. "If he does, maybe he could share it with Sydney."

Savanna enjoyed her drive on sun-dappled, tree-shrouded country roads to Yvonne's house. She was looking forward to lunch with her mother and sisters, and now she was extra excited that she'd see Aidan this evening.

Following her GPS, she turned from one long, winding road onto Yvonne's road, Blue Heron Way. Maybe her friend could shed some light on the Better Living people, or even what all the animosity had really been about in that scuffle between John and Roger Greenwood. The woman sat right across from the mayor's office, after all, and was friends with his assistant. Maybe Janice had called her by now about what caused her to just quit her job without notice. Savanna could make Yvonne soup and come back to pick her brain about the goings-on at the mayor's office.

She spotted flashing red lights up ahead, coming at her at an alarming speed on this narrow dirt road. She slowed down, moving her car to the shoulder, and an ambulance screamed by her, kicking up dust as it went. Savanna glanced at the GPS screen; Yvonne's house was less than a mile away.

The front door to Yvonne's ranch-style home was pulled open before Savanna could ring the bell. A woman who looked like an older version of Yvonne scowled at her. "What? Now's a bad time."

Savanna felt her eyes widen. "I'm, uh, I'm a friend of Yvonne's. From the city council office," she said, improvising. Goodness, she hoped that ambulance hadn't just come from here. "I heard she was sick. I was just checking in to see if she needed anything."

"Sick? Do you call being thrown down the basement stairs and nearly dying 'sick'? Who said she was sick?" The woman's voice cracked into a higher pitch, bordering on hysteria.

A middle-aged man appeared behind the woman. "Hon? What's going on?" He placed a hand on the woman's shoulder, looking at Savanna.

"I'm sorry," Savanna said quickly. "I—I had no idea. The ambulance just passed me. She fell down the stairs? Will she be all right?"

The woman separated herself from the gray-haired man, moving down the hall off the entrance. "I've got to feed the cat, and we have to get to the hospital. Ed." Her voice was sharp as she glanced back over her shoulder once before disappearing into what must be the kitchen.

Her husband remained in the doorway. "The paramedics called it in to the police, and they're coming to check it out. They think she was pushed—it looks like there was a struggle in the front room. It's lucky we came over, I was going to fix Diane's sister's refrigerator. She might've already been lying down there for hours." His voice was quiet and laden with concern.

"That's awful." Savanna's words came out in a whisper. "I'm so sorry. I hope she'll be okay!"

Diane reappeared, purse in one hand. "Ed! Let's go." She pulled the front door closed as they stepped out onto the porch with Savanna.

Savanna walked with the couple to the driveway. "Can I do anything? Anything at all?"

The woman sniffled, swiping under one eye. "They said she must've known whoever did it. The door was standing wide open when we got here, and her coffee table is smashed to bits, and a chair…" Her voice trailed off as her husband opened the car door for her.

Savanna covered her mouth with one hand. She hated to think of what had happened to Yvonne. And when? Last night? Early this morning? "My God. I hope she'll be okay."

Diane started to cry. "I don't know if she will. I just don't know."

Her husband handed her purse to her once she was seated in the passenger seat. "Honey, she's in good hands now. She'll be all right." The man's worried gaze went to Savanna. "She was still unconscious when they took her. I'm sorry, what was your name? We can let her know you're thinking about her, if she—*when* she—wakes up," the man said, his own eyes widening as his faux pas elicited sobs from Yvonne's sister.

"Savanna. Savanna Shepherd. Ma'am," she said, tentatively reaching out and patting the woman's arm. "Yvonne's a wonderful person. I'm so sorry this happened. I know a great doctor at Anderson Memorial; I can ask him to check on her. I'm sure they'll take good care of her."

"Yes." The woman met Savanna's eyes and clutched her hand, her expression tortured. "Please, have your doctor friend check on her. Who would do such a horrible thing to someone like my sister?"

Chapter Eighteen

SAVANNA BURST THROUGH the door to Fancy Tails. Charlotte, Skylar, and Sydney all looked up from the table in the nook by the window. "Yvonne is in the hospital. Someone tried to kill her."

"Yvonne?" Charlotte asked.

"Councilman Bellamy's assistant—now Mayor Greenwood's assistant, since his own quit last Friday. Janice. Janice something...what was her last name? We need to find out what happened to her. What if she's lying at the bottom of her basement stairs too? What if Mayor Greenwood killed John, and now he's taking out everyone who knew anything? What if it was *the mayor* who slashed my tires, as a message to stop digging for information?" She dropped into the empty chair, mind racing.

She was aware of Sydney, Skylar, and their mother all staring at her. Syd's sandwich was paused in midair; she'd been about to take a bite. Charlotte set hers down and opened a bottle of raspberry Mary Ann's soda, handing it to Savanna.

Skylar took another bite of her sandwich and pulled out her phone. "Aren't you the one who called me paranoid earlier today?" She tapped her screen. "Let's call Janice and ask her if she's still alive and well or dead at the bottom of her basement stairs."

"Skylar!" Savanna stared at her. "Hold on, you're really calling her?"

"Sure." She put the phone to her ear. "She's in my spin class. I'll see her tonight. But you're clearly freaking out, so let's just make sure she's fine right now. Janice? Hey girl, how are you?"

"Is she okay?" Savanna meant to whisper but it came out much louder than she'd planned.

"No, no, nothing's wrong," Skylar said into the phone. "I'm sorry to bother you. I know we never call each other. No one has time for that nonsense. But my sister is a little concerned. Something about Yvonne being in the hospital? Did you quit your job? You don't work for the mayor anymore?"

The suspense was killing Savanna as she sat watching Skylar, straining to hear any of what Janice was saying. She grabbed the phone from her sister and tapped the speaker icon, and Janice's voice came through, clear and relaxed.

"—shady was going on with him, and I wasn't comfortable staying. He'd become more and more demanding, and last Friday he actually asked me to lie for him. Who does he think he is?"

Savanna opened her mouth to speak and then thought better of it. She had a pang of guilt over the fact that Janice had no idea she was on speaker with most of Skylar's family.

"That's crazy," Skylar lamented, leaning toward the phone. "What did he want you to lie about?"

"It was some stupid thing to do with those property development guys. I don't even really understand it. I was supposed to say the zoning went through, but we were still waiting on the approval letter. He meets with them almost every week...I don't know why he was so fussed about it last Friday. Between that and him cutting my breaks, and then adding Saturdays, I just had enough. No job is worth your peace of mind, you know?"

"Absolutely," Skylar agreed. "So, nothing to do with Councilman Bellamy then?"

"No, why? Wait, did you say Yvonne's in the hospital?"

"Yes. Hold on, Savanna's walking in. She has the details. Let me put you on speaker."

Savanna mouthed the words *thank you* to her sister. "Hi, Janice, this is Savanna. I just came from Yvonne's house— her sister accidentally found her. She's at Anderson Memorial now. They think she was attacked and pushed down her own stairs."

"Oh, no! Poor Yvonne! Who on earth would do that? She's sweet to everyone!"

"I know. I'm worried about her. I was—we were—a little worried about you too."

"Me? I'm fine. I've got to run, I'm with my kids, but Skylar? I'll see you tonight!"

Savanna let Skylar take her phone back. "I'm glad she's okay. I really am. But something's going on. Whatever happened to Yvonne is related to John's death, I'm sure of it."

Charlotte pushed Savanna's paper plate over to her. Her

club sandwich was wrapped in brown deli paper with a foil-covered pickle beside it. "Have some lunch," her mother advised. "I'm sure you'll feel better with some food in you."

Savanna unwrapped her sandwich and took a bite. Her mother was probably right; she hadn't eaten breakfast at all.

"I hope your friend will be okay," Sydney said. "Are you going to go see her?"

Savanna shook her head, taking another bite and a swig of raspberry pop. "No, not yet. She was still unconscious last I heard. But I promised to ask Aidan to check on her."

"So are you thinking now that Mayor Greenwood is our prime suspect?" Sydney asked.

Charlotte shook her head. "Girls. I don't like this. Let the police do their job. None of you need to be involved in this."

"But we do," Skylar said. "I do, and I can't prove Chef Joe's innocence alone; it's taking the three of us to make any headway. We're being careful, I promise."

"Honestly, I really was leaning toward Remy as the prime suspect," Savanna said. "Now I just don't know."

"Remy isn't a killer," Charlotte said firmly, as if putting that notion to bed without further discussion.

"What happened at Mitten Inn four years ago? Do you know Mia's side of the story?"

"There really isn't a story. A guest was killed at Mia's inn, and her son was an unfortunate scapegoat. There was no truth to it."

"The reporter who covered what happened said Remy was the last person to see that man alive," Savanna said.

"And that things were stolen from the room safe, like medications and money."

"And John made sure the police knew about Remy's troubles with the law before he came back to Carson. He had a few shoplifting incidents when he was a teenager, after the divorce. And then more trouble in Paris, where Mia sent him for culinary school."

"Did he attack someone with a knife?" Savanna remembered Landon King's words. "That reporter said something about him being involved in an assault at knifepoint."

Charlotte rolled her eyes. "No. He and his girlfriend were out to dinner when they were mugged. Remy pulled out a knife he carried with him and used it to discourage the attacker before anything could be stolen. Paris police confiscated the knife as evidence. Somehow that story made it back to the councilman and got distorted in the process."

Sydney spoke. "Did he stab the attacker?"

"No," Charlotte said. "Mia said the mugger was arrested. Remy not only saved himself and his girlfriend, he also carted the mugger to the police station, where the mugger tried to flip the truth and accuse Remy of attacking him. But there were witnesses outside the restaurant who backed up Remy's story."

"So, Mia's son stops a mugger, drags him in to be arrested, and by the time the story makes it across the ocean to us, Remy's become a knife-wielding criminal." Skylar shook her head. "No wonder he has a love-hate relationship with this town."

"To be fair," Charlotte said, "I don't think too many

people around here believe the darker side of Remy's history anymore. I know John Bellamy was your friend, Savanna, but he was a very flawed father. With what happened at Mitten Inn, Remy got as far away as possible after Jillian Black cleared his name. We were all surprised when he came back."

"Why did he?" Savanna asked.

"I'm not sure. I know Mia's happier when her son's in Carson. And he's been a great asset to Giuseppe's, especially lately."

"Mom," Savanna said. "Did Skylar tell you Detective Jordan found Remy's fingerprints on the safe that was broken into in John's home office? What do you think that could be about?"

"People can be ugly." Charlotte shook her head. "Mia had been after John for years to straighten out their assets; I think there was an estate issue from when Mia's parents passed away. There was some property, a few investments, that kind of thing. I'm just guessing, but I wonder if Remy and Mia felt they needed to get something from John's house that he shouldn't have had. I know you were gone during the time trouble was brewing between the councilman and Mia, Savanna. Mia has always maintained she was treated unfairly in the divorce. I'm guessing whatever was in the safe might've belonged to her or Remy."

"Wow," Savanna said, once again forcing herself to imagine John Bellamy as the man he actually had been, rather than the person she'd thought he was. He'd been adept at showing her the face he'd wanted her to see. To say he was a flawed father to Remy was an understatement; Savanna didn't think she'd have liked the real John Bellamy at all.

"Nothing else was ever discovered about the murder at Mitten Inn?" Sydney looked at Skylar.

"Not officially," her sister said. "But I looked into the little information I could find in our files. Jillian Black was certain the wife did it. She was smart enough to clear out the room safe too, to make it look like an outside job. But there was no evidence to arrest her. The man was probably pretty easy to drown, with half a bottle of gin in him by the time the wife returned and held him underwater in the bathtub."

"There's an added piece to that theory," Charlotte said. "The couple had come here together. But the wife was seen at that dance club with another man. The valet at the club swears she left with him, but the wife maintained that she returned to Mitten Inn alone."

"What about security cameras at the inn?" Sydney asked.

Charlotte shook her head. "Only at the front desk. You know the inn has all private lake-view entrances. I don't think anyone but that poor man's wife, and maybe her accomplice, will ever know what really happened that night."

SAVANNA SPENT THE rest of the afternoon in front of a large drawing pad on her art easel, diagramming the festival setup in detail, down to which decorations would go where and placement of all the tables, chairs, temporary stage, concessions, and the like. Fonzie jarred her from her work as she was putting the finishing touches on the itinerary for next week's setup. She followed her dog from Sydney's sunroom to the front door.

Aidan stood on the porch, Mollie by his side and shaggy pooch Jersey at the end of a leash. The little girl grinned up at her, swinging her arms from side to side.

"Hi, Ms. Shepherd." Her voice was soft and lilting.

"We've come to escort you to an impromptu picnic in the park. Unless you already have dinner plans?" Aidan wore gray dress pants and a blue pinstriped Brooks Brothers button-down. His top button was undone, and Savanna spied a hint of five-o'clock shadow, but he didn't look like he'd spent the day catering to needy patients. He handed Jersey's leash to Mollie, and Savanna caught a flash of green and gold turtle-shaped cuff links. She vowed to ask him, the first chance she got, about his little fashion quirks.

"I'm totally free," she said. "Come in for second. Let me grab my purse. And maybe drinks?" She eyed the bag full of paper cartons that hung from Aidan's right hand. The front of the bag bore the swirly red *LILLY'S* logo for the Chinese restaurant in town.

"Ah, drinks," Aidan said, looking at Mollie. "That's what we forgot."

Savanna left Aidan and his daughter in the foyer with the dogs, who were excitedly sniffing and pouncing on each other.

She jotted a quick note in the kitchen for Sydney, then reappeared at the front door, carrying a small lunch cooler and Fonzie's leash.

Mollie pranced and skipped ahead alongside Fonzie and Jersey on the walk to the park, strawberry-blond hair flying around her head like a halo.

"This was a great idea," Savanna said.

Aidan took her hand. "We thought so."

"You said you had something to ask me?"

He nodded. "I do. I have a barbecue to go to, and I'm hoping you're free. I'd like you to come with me."

"A barbecue? When is it?"

"Saturday. I think you know the hostess—you teach with her. Elaina Jenson?"

"Oh! Yes, we've crossed paths quite a bit. She's nice."

"Yes," he said, glancing at her. "Elaina's son and Mollie are friends, so she invited us. I feel sort of strange. I don't usually go to these things, but Mollie really wants to go. She loves Carter's pool."

Savanna's mind raced. She knew Elaina's son Carter was in Mollie's grade, so it made sense they were friends. But what if Elaina had invited Aidan—just Aidan—to come with Mollie, because she wanted him there? Was she interested in him? Was Aidan clueless enough not to realize?

"Savanna?"

"Sure! I'd love to go." She hoped she was wrong about Elaina. Either way, she wasn't going to miss it.

"Great! Elaina lives four houses down from me. Why don't you come over Saturday and walk with me and Mollie?"

"That sounds perfect."

They arrived at the park, and after they'd eaten, Mollie

took off across the lawn to the play area. Savanna filled Aidan in on the events of the last couple of days, bringing him up to date on her new "role" as part of Skylar's legal team, along with Sydney, as they worked to prove Chef Joe didn't kill the councilman.

She remembered to ask Aidan for a small favor before they parted at Sydney's front porch, Jersey and Fonzie tangled around their legs and Mollie practicing cartwheels on Sydney's front lawn. Aidan agreed to check in on Yvonne at the hospital and make sure everything possible was being done for her.

"I won't be able to tell you anything, but I promise I'll see that she's being taken care of," he said. "Do you know yet what the police think happened?"

Savanna shook her head. "I haven't heard anything. I plan to stop by and see Detective Jordan tomorrow. But I have an idea." She leaned in a little as she let him in on her plan, not wanting to cause Aidan to have to answer questions later from Mollie.

He nodded, giving her a look that was half worry, half surprise. "I think that's a great idea. But be careful," he stressed as they parted.

THURSDAY AFTERNOON, AS promised, Savanna arrived at Charlotte's house to sit in for a missing member of Charlotte's euchre group. Leslie was in North Carolina meeting her first grandchild.

It took a few rounds before she remembered the details of how to play, but her mother's friends were so helpful and patient, Savanna was enjoying herself more than she'd expected. The game was a Michigan staple she'd learned years ago. By the time the evening began to wind down, she'd gotten to spend small portions of time chatting with Mia here and there. She saw what her mother liked about the woman. Mia James was charismatic and smart, with an easy laugh that seemed to set those around her at ease. Her sleek, nearly black hair fell in long waves past her shoulders, and tonight her all-black outfit was adorned with a shimmery, sheer gold scarf thrown over one shoulder.

Savanna almost felt bad about what she was planning. But it was the only way to get answers, one way or another. She reminded herself of this as the ladies began filtering out, amid laughter and promises of coffee dates. Savanna began bringing dishes and glasses from the large living room to the kitchen.

Her mother was still by the front door, saying goodbye. Savanna carefully carried the last of the items into the kitchen. She put two wineglasses in the sink and took painstaking care to set the third one on the counter; she held it in a tenuous grasp through a thin dishtowel, between her thumb and forefinger.

Harlan came in through the kitchen door, startling her. She jumped a mile, whipping her head around to look at him. He laughed at her, coming over and giving her shoulder a light squeeze. "Sorry, didn't mean to scare you. I figured things were breaking up by now. Am I allowed to be here yet?"

She hugged him around the waist. "It's your house, Dad. I think you're allowed to be here. There's a ton of food left. Are you hungry?"

"I'm stuffed. Travis and I had burgers at Jake's. But I can eat. These look good," he said, eyeing the collection of hors d'oeuvres and desserts littering the island countertop.

She handed Harlan a plate, and he gathered a few of each concoction, carrying his plate around the island and pulling up a stool.

"Did euchre come back to you pretty easily? I know I get rusty if I haven't played in a while," Harlan said, taking a bite of spinach pie.

Savanna turned on the water and kept her back to him, making motions as if she was washing dishes. She couldn't toss her plan out now. "It took a few rounds. I had a good partner. How's Travis doing?" She moved over enough to block the movement of her left hand, covered again in a towel, picking up the wineglass she'd set on the counter. She cleared her throat loudly to disguise the sound as she shook open a small lunch-sized brown paper bag over the sink and deposited the glass quickly into the bag.

"Travis is tired," Harlan said. "Sounds like work's been busier than usual lately, but he says that's a good thing."

Savanna shut the water off and bent down, keeping the paper bag close to her body. She reached over and opened a bottom cupboard, then banged some pots and pans around, scooting closer to the open door. She chanced a glance over one shoulder at her dad, but he was involved now in a cannoli, trying not to knock all the mini chocolate chips off as he took a bite.

She stashed the paper bag in the cupboard and shut the door, straightening up. God, she hoped she hadn't just erased whatever fingerprints were on the glass, with all her furtive juggling of the evidence. She faced the counter and her dad. "Well, I'm glad he's enjoying the busier schedule!"

Savanna moved to grab the extra-large, slouchy yellow leather purse she'd brought specifically for tonight's task, and made a concerted effort to drift slowly back to the exact spot she'd just been standing: in front of the cupboard with the package in the soup pot.

Harlan polished off a second cannoli and rested muscled forearms on the granite countertop. "You're really digging having some downtime this summer, aren't you? Your Chicago pace sounded a little crazy every time you'd call home and give us updates." He stirred a spoonful of sugar into his coffee. "I'm glad you're back home." His voice became quieter and gruffer at the tail end, and she saw her dad swallow hard, though he was done eating.

She came around the island and hugged him. She was lucky. She had two of the greatest parents a person could ask for. "I'm glad to be home."

Savanna heard Charlotte heading their way, and her gaze darted to her big yellow purse on the kitchen counter. Her mother would come in, move it out of the way, start washing dishes, and she'd never have a chance to retrieve her package.

She quickly went to her purse, sweeping it onto one fore-arm, and bent down and scooped the paper bag into the purse in one smooth motion with her back turned to her dad. She was standing, purse slung casually over one shoulder, when Charlotte entered the kitchen.

"That was so much fun!" She moved to her mom and hugged her goodbye. "I cleared all the dishes, but I didn't get a chance to load the dishwasher yet."

Charlotte shook her head. "Don't worry about it. Your dad loves helping me with the dishes." She winked at Harlan.

"Thanks for including me tonight. I'll talk to you tomorrow." She backed toward the kitchen door, trying not to sound as if she was rushing out. Fortunately, Harlan had come to the rescue and joined her mom at the sink.

"Bye, honey! Thanks for coming!" Charlotte turned back to the sink, slapping Harlan's arm with the wet dishtowel.

Outside, safely in her car, Savanna called Detective Jordan over Bluetooth. It was past nine at night, and she felt bad infringing on his family time, but she wasn't sure how long fingerprints stayed on glass, and she wasn't comfortable keeping this until morning.

He picked up on the second ring. "This had better be important."

She let a big breath out she hadn't even been aware she was holding. "It is. I'm sorry to bother you."

"It's all right, I'm just giving you a hard time. You got the message earlier from my office, right?"

"No." Savanna backed out of the driveway. "Should I have?"

Detective Jordan groaned. "Why can't people just do

their job? Yes. That Stevens kid, the genius who posted the incriminating photo on social media? He definitely vandalized Jessamina. We're charging him. He'll get a slap on the wrist and community service. That's one mystery solved, thanks to you and Sydney. But he didn't slash your tires, Savanna. The knife was wiped clean."

Savanna sucked in her breath. Her mind spun. "What? What does that mean? Who do you think did it?" Her mind was racing. A yellow traffic light directly in front of her turned red and she slammed on her brakes, too hard, eliciting a squeal of protest from the rubber on pavement and throwing her purse onto the floor of the passenger side. "Ugh!"

"It's all right," Detective Jordan replied. "We don't know who did it, but confirming it wasn't tied to Jessamina doesn't automatically mean the killer slashed your tires. What would be the point of that? It's possible it was random."

"Random?" she scoffed.

"I'm not satisfied with that explanation, either, but we have no other leads. I'm still working on it, don't worry. In the meantime, be careful, stay mindful of your surroundings, and keep your family updated on where you are. I promise to let you know the minute I have any updates. Now, what did you call me about?"

Chapter Nineteen

NICK JORDAN HELD the door to the precinct open for Savanna. "Let's talk in my office."

Savanna set her purse on the detective's desk and took out the brown paper bag. The wineglass had miraculously not shattered into pieces when her purse had hit the floor of her car.

Detective Jordan pulled on a purple latex glove and extracted the glass from the bag. "So you're positive this is Mia James's glass? And it's from a dinner party at your house?"

"My mom's house, yes."

The muscle in his jaw worked and his brows furrowed as his gaze went from the wineglass to Savanna. "Your mom's house. Is she aware you took it?"

"No. Does that matter? I read online that police can check ordinary objects used by someone, during a crime investigation, if they're left in a public place."

"Right. But your mother's house isn't a public place. And it's not a residence owned by you. I can't technically do anything with this without your parents signing off on the knowledge that you took it from their house and we're testing it to rule out a suspect."

"Oh." She felt deflated. She wasn't giving up, not if this

glass could either prove that Mia never touched John Bellamy's safe, or that she did. "Okay. I'll get their permission. How should I do that?"

Detective Jordan sat back, making his chair creak. "Why don't you give your parents a heads-up tonight that we'll need to come by tomorrow morning so I can explain this to them. Is your mother going to have a problem with it? I assume she and Mia James are friends."

"I think she'll be all right with it. I'll explain it's a way of hopefully showing Mia wasn't involved in John's death; maybe it'll help clear Remy somehow too. Who knows."

The detective opened a drawer at the bottom right side of his desk. He placed the wineglass in a large plastic evidence bag, wrote on it with black Sharpie, and then used a key on his key ring to lock the glass in the drawer. "That can't be checked into evidence until after we talk to your parents. Will one of them be home tomorrow morning around nine?"

"My mom should be. I'll make sure she is—I'll call them tonight."

He stood, and she followed him out of his office. He locked the door and ushered her out to the parking lot, talking half to himself and half to Savanna on the way. "If those prints match one of the sets from the safe and the painting, but not from the cellar door, it'll show that she, likely with her son, attempted to get something from Bellamy's safe after the night of his murder. You're still sure about that?" He looked at her.

"I'm very sure. The painting was perfectly straight the

night he was killed."

The detective nodded. "And if the prints match nothing, it means Remy acted on his own."

"My mother says there was some longstanding dispute between Mia and John, after their divorce, over property or her parents' estate or something. Isn't it possible she or Remy were just trying to retrieve something that already belonged to them? What was in the safe?"

"Nothing at all," Nick Jordan said. "It was completely bare."

"Hmm." Savanna didn't know what to think of that. They were now standing outside her car. "Detective, do you know anything yet about John's assistant, Yvonne? Your people were at her house yesterday, checking things out after her sister found her at the bottom her basement stairs. You think she was pushed?"

"We're sure she was. We found fibers under her fingernails, and there are bruises that can't be explained otherwise. She either let whoever did it in, meaning she knew them, or else she just leaves her front door unlocked all the time."

"Like practically everyone in Carson," Savanna added, recalling how much trouble that had caused last fall in trying to save Caroline Carson's life.

"Except you," he said sternly.

"Except me," she agreed. "Don't worry. I broke that habit the minute I moved away."

"Good. We can't talk to Yvonne yet, as she's still unconscious, but we did get ahold of the other assistant at the village offices. She's coming in tomorrow morning to give a statement. Apparently she resigned her job with the mayor just last week, and in light of Yvonne's situation, we want to be sure no one else is in danger."

"Janice," Savanna said. "She told us she quit because the mayor asked her to lie. Well, that among other reasons."

Detective Jordan stared at her, saying nothing.

"I'd planned to let you know about that. I'm not sure it's important?" She felt herself shrinking under the detective's sharp gaze. "I mean, maybe it is important. Janice said it was over a real estate deal through Better Living. The mayor wanted her to say zoning or something had already been approved, but it hasn't yet."

"Interesting. Anything else?"

"No. Really, no. Nothing I can think of." She opened her car door and got in.

The detective pulled out his keys. "I'll meet you at your parents' house at nine a.m."

"Got it," Savanna said, pulling her door closed. She had the distinct feeling that she and the detective were both going to be doing research tonight on the same thing: Better Living Properties.

By the time she'd hung up the phone with her mom, trying hard to explain why it was a good idea to let the police compare Mia's fingerprints to those found at John's house, she was exhausted. She hoped Nick Jordan did a better job than she had. She was pretty sure all she'd accomplished was making her mother mad. No, not mad. Disappointed.

"I'm not angry with you, Savanna," Charlotte had said over the phone. "I'm disappointed. You should've trusted me enough to tell me what you wanted to do and why. We'll discuss this in the morning."

Savanna carried her laptop into Sydney's bedroom, she and Fonzie settling onto her sister's fluffy, canopied double bed to wait for her. Fancy Tails was closed, and yoga classes didn't run this late. Had Sydney perhaps met someone? She dismissed the thought. Syd was such an open book; if she'd started seeing someone new, she'd be shouting about it. She was probably just out with friends.

After a few false starts, Savanna found useful information on the *Allegan County Newspaper* mobile site. A search for Better Living at first brought up decorating tips from the Home and Garden section. When she changed her search to Better Living Properties, several articles came up over the last year. She scrolled through, absorbing as much as she could about the company and its plans for Carson's lakefront.

By the time she heard Sydney's key in the front door, Savanna had learned a lot. Better Living Properties was a relatively new commercial property company that was growing fast. They'd been eyeing a large piece of land at the north end of Carson's waterfront since last year. A few months ago, back in February, they'd submitted plans for a proposed boardwalk development on Lake Michigan that would house an eighteen-story luxury hotel, rows of shops, and a handful of restaurants, all targeted at the tourist crowd.

"Watcha doing?" Sydney appeared in the bedroom doorway.

"Research." She groaned, rolling her eyes. "Where were you?"

"Oh. Um, out. I feel so gross—I'm jumping in the shower. Stay there, I want to hear what you're researching." She spun and headed toward the bathroom and Savanna saw that the ends of her hair were damp, twisting themselves into red ringlets while drying. Her khaki shorts were splotchy shades of darker and lighter color tan, as if they'd also been wet.

Interesting. Had she been swimming somewhere? Savanna refocused her attention on the screen. From what she could gather in these articles, the proposed development was thought to be a sound, lucrative plan from all angles. It'd boost tourism, bringing revenue into Carson. The high-end eateries and shops would raise property values. She tried to imagine the plot of land in question and couldn't. She might need to go take a look tomorrow. Where was it in relation to Mitten Inn, which was also on the lake?

Sydney entered the bedroom wearing a fuzzy pink robe, her hair wrapped up in a towel on top of her head. She peered at the laptop as she removed the towel and shook out her now completely wet hair. "Ew."

"What?" Savanna looked at her curiously.

"Those Better Living weasels. They're never going to get approval for that. It'll totally block the view of the lake. Did you read about how many tons of sand they'll have to take off the dunes just for the boardwalk? Actual *tons*. Which'll lead to beach erosion up and down the coast, not to mention the traffic volume through town. Their proposal would mean no more Main Street! They'd have to add three more lanes, and the road goes right through the middle of Carson Park.

Why are you reading about it?"

Savanna stared at Sydney, stunned. "That's crazy! Why would it even be on the table, and why would Mayor Greenwood be meeting with the developers? I haven't read anything yet about what you're saying. But wow." She bit her bottom lip. "It makes sense. You're right. How else would all that tourist traffic get through to the development? I mean, they could go through the forest north of town, I guess," she mused.

"No they can't. Manistee Forest is protected. The only route is right through town."

"No." She scrolled through to the next article. "It can't happen. Wait! So is that why Mayor Greenwood wanted Janice to lie? Is he trying to push their proposal through?"

"He'd better not be! He wouldn't do that to Carson." Sydney sat next to Savanna and finger-combed through her curls, detangling them.

"Were you at the lake?"

"What?"

"Just now. Your hair and shorts were damp when you came in. I wondered if you went for a late swim."

"Oh!" She leaned over, bumping her shoulder against Savanna's. "You can't help it, can you? Always picking up details, even if you aren't trying."

Savanna shrugged. "I don't know, I don't think I do that. So were you?"

"Yes, I went for a swim. You should try it sometime at night. It's so peaceful, especially with the full moon tonight. It's still almost eighty degrees out there right now."

"You went alone?" Savanna chastised. It'd been drilled into them as girls to never, under any circumstances, swim alone. Ever.

"I didn't go alone. I went with a friend."

Savanna closed her laptop and leaned back against Sydney's mountain of throw pillows. "A friend?"

"Oh my God! Yes, a friend. We went for a spur-of-the-moment swim. It was fun!"

"So, is this a new friend? Did you go for a moonlight swim with a guy?"

Sydney sighed, leaning on one elbow and peering at Savanna wide-eyed. "Yes I did, Mom. If I end up seeing him again, I promise I'll clear it with you first, okay?"

Savanna laughed. "Sorry. I'm happy for you, Syd. I'm glad you're moving on. Will I get to meet him?"

"It's not even a thing. I had dinner with a cute guy, we went for a walk on the beach and decided to jump in the lake. It was a lot of fun. That's all," she emphasized.

"Okay! Then I'm happy you had a good evening. I'm going to bed. I have to meet Detective Jordan at Mom and Dad's early tomorrow morning." She changed the subject and filled Sydney in on her covert operation at Charlotte's game night.

"Dang, look at you! Ooh, Mom is going to be so mad when she finds out. Are you going to let Nick tell her what you did?"

"She already knows. I told her. And she isn't mad, she's just disappointed."

Sydney laughed. "That's perfect. I love it. Good luck

tomorrow—better you than me."

Friday morning at Harlan and Charlotte's went better than Savanna had hoped, until they were about to leave. Detective Jordan explained that even if it backfired and it turned out Mia's fingerprints matched those on the cellar door, Mia would be able to explain herself, and the police would've learned about that eventually once Remy was questioned—as he was scheduled to be today, based on his own prints on the safe.

Charlotte stopped the detective at that point. "It wouldn't have been Mia going in through the Michigan basement access door though. I'm sure of that."

"How do you know that?"

"They used a key."

"There was a key?" Detective Jordan and Savanna echoed each other in Charlotte's sunny kitchen nook.

"Remy had a housekey from when he was a teenager."

Savanna looked at Detective Jordan.

"I don't know that John even remembered Remy had that key. I only know about it because Mia mentioned once that she should just have Remy let her in the house so she could get her things he was keeping from her. But she seemed afraid to cross John. He'd have known instantly that they'd broken into the safe. Once he was gone, maybe Mia felt differently," Charlotte said carefully, her gaze going to Detective Jordan and then back to Savanna. "I'm not sure I should have said anything." She pressed her lips together.

Outside, as Nick Jordan and Savanna parted, he paused climbing into his patrol car. "This just opens a whole new can of worms," he said, shaking his head.

She imagined he was right. "But hopefully, Mia's wine-glass prints won't match a thing in John's house, right? Then, poof, no can of worms at all."

He groaned. "Let's hope."

Savanna spent the rest of her day working through an errand list a mile long. With kickoff for Art in the Park just days away, by late afternoon, she'd been to Grand Rapids to finalize plans with the concessions company, to the bank handling the funds for the festival, and to Parties Are Us for all the odds and ends she needed for decorating that weren't being supplied as part of the event. She even remembered to stop by Carson Lock and Key to check out the display cases for all the submitted artwork and make the final payment to the proprietor.

She edited the to-do list in her phone; she still needed to speak with Remy at Giuseppe's one last time about the catered items and make the last payment, and she and Skylar had talked about popping in on Chef Joe, just to let him know they were making progress. And she really needed to stop by Carson's library; she had an idea she wanted to check out. *And* she really needed to make an appointment with Mike to see that house. She'd probably have to delay the last few items until tomorrow or later.

Savanna dragged her feet into Fancy Tails, dropping heavily into one of the overstuffed aqua chairs.

"Be right with you!" Sydney called out from the back of the salon as the bell over the door jangled.

"No need, it's just me!" She was tired and starving. On

impulse, before she could lose her nerve, she scrolled through her contacts and called Aidan.

He picked up on the second ring. "Your timing couldn't be better. My last patient just left. How are you?"

"I'm great! Hey, are you hungry?"

SAVANNA CROSSED THE street and walked down a block to Giuseppe's after letting Sydney know she'd see her later at home. She got a table, and the waitress brought her iced tea just as Aidan joined her.

"I'm glad you called," he said, taking the seat across from her. He ordered a coffee, waiting until the waitress left and then leaning across the table and lowering his voice. "How did your covert operation go?"

Savanna laughed. "Pretty well, all things considered. My intensive online research was a little off. Detective Jordan still had to get permission from my mother to run the tests, since I took the wineglass from her home without her knowing. I don't know anything yet."

Aidan stood briefly and shed his suit jacket, folding it and draping it over the chair next to him. Blue suspenders with purple polka dots matched the blue and purple tie Savanna had already noticed. He sat back down, turning his cuffs up twice. "Better. I'm so glad it's Friday and the clinic is closed tomorrow. This first full week back has been intense."

"Aidan. I just have to know. You have so many

fun...accessories to your wardrobe. Are men's wardrobe items called accessories?" Savanna mused. "I've been wanting to ask you about them. I love the suspenders and tie, by the way. Do you do it for your younger patients? I imagine seeing rainbow-colored socks on their doctor would put them at ease."

Aidan shocked her. For the first time ever, Savanna saw a hint of red flush his cheekbones and he looked down for a moment, not meeting her eyes. When he did, his expression was unreadable. "It's for Mollie," he said. "I started it when—" He broke off as their server appeared with his coffee, asking if they were ready to order. "Sure," Aidan said, glancing at the menu briefly and then up at Savanna. "Have you decided?"

"Yes, I'll have the chicken limoncello, please, with a side of brussels sprouts. They're amazing here," she told Aidan. "Get the brussels sprouts."

"They really are. Chef Remy is a magician," the server agreed.

"Well, then, I'll have the brussels sprouts," Aidan said. "And the beef tenderloin medallions. Let's start with your bruschetta. Good?" He checked with Savanna.

"Mmm. Yes, absolutely. Oh, and could you ask Chef Remy if he has a few minutes to spare at some point? We need to finalize the catering menu arrangements for Art in the Park opening day next week, but we can schedule a better time if he's too tied up."

She nodded, dropping her order pad into the pocket of her apron, and turned to head toward the kitchen. "I'll let him know you're here, Ms. Shepherd."

"You're on their radar," Aidan said. "Is the restaurant handling all the food for the festival?"

"Not all of it. We'll also have a food truck, plus two booths with carnival-type items, like elephant ears and corndogs. Giuseppe's is handling the banquet dinner opening night for the judges and participants, and also the closing ceremony dinner for the judges and the winners. Chef Joe was so thrilled to—Hey. Stop distracting me." She frowned at him. She reached impulsively across the table, lightly tapping the back of his hand. "I really want to hear about the suspenders. And socks. And turtle cuff links."

His mouth turned up in a half smile. "I try to keep it subtle. Nobody really notices."

"I do."

"It began when we lost Olivia," he said. "Mollie was so connected to her mom. She was only four. It started small. She'd bring me little gifts as we were going out the door each morning to preschool. A unicorn sticker to wear on my collar for the day, or a fuzzy pen so I wouldn't forget about her during the day at work—she said it like that." He swallowed hard, looking away for a moment. "'So you remember me.' God. Who really understands what goes on in the mind of a child? I noticed little things, like she'd purposely put a mitten in my suit pocket or a barrette in my briefcase. Maybe it was her way of making sure we wouldn't lose each other, after she lost her mom." He stopped, and took a deep breath.

Savanna was silent. She reached across the table and took

his hand.

"I took her shopping. We made it a weekend. By then, she was nearly five. We went to Chicago, to the American Girl Doll store, and then a dozen other shops. She loved the doll she chose, the outfits and little accessories, but that wasn't the purpose of the trip...and it wasn't the best thing we bought. By the time we came home, we had an entire collection of items for me: ties, socks, suspenders, watches, a money clip." He reached into a pocket and set a money clip on the table, clasped around a few twenties. The bright, gaudy paint on the clip was beginning to wear off, but Savanna could see it was a bunch of cartoon cats in various colors.

She smiled at him, surprised to feel her eyes welling up. She had no idea what it was like to be a parent, but Aidan obviously cherished his role as Mollie's dad.

"Anyway." Aidan cleared his throat. "Every day since then, she selects an item for me to wear. We've picked up a few more in the last couple of years. My two bottom dresser drawers are filled with these things. Believe me," he said, grinning, "some of her fashion choices for me would hurt your eyes. I try to just go with it."

Savanna's whole body ached to hug him. She sat across the table from him and tried to settle for less for now. She covered their linked hands with her other one, feeling her chest rising and falling too fast. He'd gotten through that entire story relatively calmly. *You will not burst into warm-fuzzy tears like a lunatic, Savanna.* She frowned and tried to regain control over her emotions.

She was saved by the bruschetta. The server deposited the plates as they separated their hands, making room on the table. It gave Savanna time to find her voice. "You're a wonderful father," she said. "I'd say her fashion sense is actually pretty good. She matched your tie and suspenders today."

He glanced down. "Yes, she did."

"I'm glad you told me," Savanna said softly.

Aidan reached out and interlaced his fingers with hers. "I'm glad you asked." He met her eyes. "I've missed you, Savanna. You have no idea how good it feels to be home."

She tipped her head to the side, smiling widely. She swore there were little tendrils of electricity zinging through their fingers, and in the air between them. "I know how good it feels to have you home."

They polished off the bruschetta and then their meals. Savanna sat back in her chair, one hand on her middle, as Remy came out to their table. "You are a magician," she told him, looking up—way up—at the tall, thin man in chef's coat and hat.

Remy set a clipboard on the table. "Is this a good time?"

"Sure." Savanna looked over the catering plan on the clipboard he turned around to face her. "This looks good. I have your deposit check." She reached into her purse and handed Remy an envelope. "Oh, and what about the dessert table?"

Remy flipped the page for her, revealing another, several items listed with quantities, dates, and times.

"Perfect. Remy, this is Aidan Gallager. Can you sit for a

moment?"

Remy pulled a chair over from the table behind them, facing it backward and sitting, draping his ink-covered forearms over the backrest. "Nice to meet you," he addressed Aidan.

"Dinner was delicious."

The young chef nodded. "Thanks."

Savanna wasn't sure how to start, but she really wanted to hear what Remy had to say. "Listen, I don't know if you're aware, but my sister is defending Chef Joe. She works for the law firm up the street."

"Yeah, Joe told me. I talk to him every couple of days to go over the books."

"Oh! Well, good. So, um, I don't know what you think about the arrest—"

Remy interrupted her. "Arresting Joe was a bogus move. They should know better."

"We agree with you. We don't believe Chef Joe killed the councilman either. Which brings me to my question." She paused and took a deep breath, mustering courage.

"That detective already talked to me," Remy said. "I went in and gave a statement this morning. I know they have my fingerprints on the Mondrian reproduction and the safe."

Savanna blinked at him, trying to catch up. "You know that painting? Or—Right, you probably remember when your dad acquired it?"

Remy shook his head. "Are you kidding? My father doesn't know art. One of the interior decorators he dated after the divorce got it for him. He likes people to think he has taste. He *liked*." Remy's animosity was apparent in his tone and his expression.

"Oh." One more example of John Bellamy showing two different faces to Carson versus his family. How willingly Savanna had accepted him as a friend; it bothered her immensely that she hadn't seen through his act. She'd picked up on the fact that John had been constantly intent on making good impressions, but she'd connected that to his political aspirations. Now she saw it was a much deeper character flaw. She forced her attention back to Remy. "Were you able to explain to the detective how your fingerprints got on the frame?" She raised a hand in a gesture of peace before he got the wrong idea. "Remy, I know you don't owe me anything. You don't have to answer any of my questions."

He shrugged. "It doesn't bother me. He had my mother's things. Sentimental items and jewelry she'd kept in a lock box, a diamond ring worth a fortune that belonged to her mother, the deed to my grandparents' summer home. He refused to be fair and give them to her after my grandparents died. My mother even had a lawyer pursue it, but Ms. Black was never able to prove to the court that the jerk had anything of hers."

"Oh, wow. So, after you and your mother learned what happened to your father, you went to retrieve the items? You weren't worried about, um..." She was walking a fine line. How could Remy not have been concerned the police would implicate him in John's murder? Or at least arrest him for breaking and entering?

"No." Remy stood abruptly. He stared down at them, scowling, though he kept his voice low; it was still early, but the Friday night crowd was starting to trickle in. "It was just me. Not my mom. I went to get her things Tuesday after he died. And no, I wasn't worried about what might happen to me when the police found out. I didn't break in to his house, and the only things I took didn't belong to him in the first place. I just took back what belonged to my mom."

"You didn't break in?" Savanna was pushing him, but he said his mother hadn't been involved.

"I unlocked the front door and let myself in," Remy said firmly. "With the key I've had since I was a teenager. After the divorce, when he was still acting like a halfway decent dad." He put the chair back at the table behind him. "Is that everything?"

Savanna sighed. "I had to ask. I'm sorry." She looked at Aidan, widening her eyes. She hadn't expected that conversation to escalate the way it did.

"I believe we're ready?" Aidan asked her. He placed his card in the leather check binder and handed it to their server who was just crossing behind Remy.

"I've got to get back to work," Remy said. He picked up his clipboard. "We're good to go for next week."

"I appreciate your help," Savanna said, but the young man was already heading toward the kitchen. She let out a breath, shaking her head and standing along with Aidan. "I'm sorry to you too. I shouldn't have prodded him that way. But he was lying."

Aidan raised an eyebrow at her. "I sort of got that too.

He was very defensive."

"Mia had something to do with him breaking into the safe. He's protecting her. I think she was with him. Did you notice how quickly he jumped to the conclusion that that's what I meant when I asked him? It set him off. I wish there was a way to hurry the testing they're doing on that wineglass."

She tried to contribute her portion of the bill when the server brought the receipt back to them, but Aidan waved it off.

Savanna led the way out of Giuseppe's, Aidan a few steps behind her, as their path narrowed through patrons standing around the bar now, waiting for tables. Savanna stopped abruptly, and Aidan bumped into her, nearly knocking her over. He grabbed her shoulders, steadying her.

"Savanna, what—" He stopped, understanding.

She could hardly believe her eyes. At a table directly in front of them, Finn Gallager and Sydney were seated, cozily, on the same side of a booth. Finn's arm rested along the back of the booth behind Sydney and she leaned into him, absorbed in some story that was quite obviously riveting as she hung on his every word.

Finn saw Savanna and Aidan first. Sydney followed his gaze as he stopped talking, turning in her seat to find Savanna staring at her.

Chapter Twenty

"SAVVY!" SYDNEY SHRIEKED, extending a hand toward her sister. "Dr. Aidan! Sit. Come on, guys, join us!"

Savanna had a split-second thought that Sydney might try to deny what was happening here. Something had definitely changed. The opportunity to see what this was really about was tempting. But one quick glance at Aidan told Savanna everything she needed to know. "Oh, no, that's all right. We don't want to interrupt."

"Right. We were on our way out," Aidan said. He didn't sound happy.

"We are. I'm so full. Everything here is delicious." She looked from Sydney to Finn and then back to her sister, unable to suppress her grin.

Sydney's cheeks were flushed and her eyes bright. She was dressed for dinner in a rich copper-colored halter dress with sparkly gold necklace and earrings; she looked gorgeous. "Isn't it funny? We started talking yesterday at Fancy Tails, and Finn asked what was going on with Jessamina—did you notice they've got her head back on now? We ended up walking through the park to the lake. And then this morning when I found out he's never eaten at Giuseppe's, I had to bring him."

Savanna nodded, incredulous. "That's great! You'll love it," she said to Finn. "The food is amazing." She couldn't wait to check in with Sydney later tonight.

Aidan spoke up, his gaze on Finn. "Last night?"

"I lost track of time. I figured it was all right. Your in-laws wouldn't care I was a no-show."

"Mollie cared." Aidan's voice was cutting. Savanna had never heard that edge before.

Finn's face fell. "Oh." He looked truly remorseful, worry lines appearing around his green eyes as he cringed. "I'm sorry. I'll make it up to her."

Aidan's expression was stony.

"We should let you have your evening," Savanna said. She stared at Sydney, her eyes wide. Ugh, she wished she'd never seen them here at all.

Sydney pressed her lips together, remaining quiet now, but too late.

"It was good seeing you again, Finn," Savanna said, meaning it. "You guys have a nice dinner. Talk to you later, Syd."

She followed Aidan outside; his long-legged stride made it hard to keep up. He finally stopped just past the long red awning at the side of the restaurant. There was a light but steady stream of pedestrian traffic on the sidewalk, with it being a temperate Friday evening.

"I'm sorry," she said, taking a few steps off the walkway so they could talk. "Are you all right?"

Aidan had twin creases between his eyebrows, stress written in his features. "This is what he does. He makes casual promises and breaks them. Your sister's going to get hurt. He probably started out by royally teeing her off with some off-the-cuff remark. Finn loves a challenge. He's reeled Sydney right in, you saw them. But he's flighty and unreliable and never stays in one place long enough to see the damage he causes."

Savanna put a hand on Aidan's arm, feeling how tense he was. "Sydney's a grownup. She's impossible to fool, so don't kid yourself. I'm sure she saw right through him. I should've known she'd go for him—your brother is exactly her type. He's even a paramedic," Savanna said, laughing. "She can't help it. Firemen and paramedics are her kryptonite."

"So you're not worried?"

"I'm not. Well," she said, reconsidering, "maybe I'm a little worried about Finn. I love my sister like crazy. But she's never really gotten serious with anyone."

Aidan looked visibly more relaxed. He moved to the side to let a couple pass him. "Perfect. Then they're perfect for each other. You're right, they're both adults and not our problem. Oh, no." He pulled out his phone as it jingled with a tone she hadn't heard before. "That's the hospital."

"Oh! Go. This was nice, Aidan, thank you."

"My pleasure," he said, closing one hand loosely around her forearm as he stepped closer to her, pulling her into a hug.

She hugged him back, self-conscious of the passersby probably gathering gossip about them for later. Or maybe not, she thought. She and Aidan hadn't tried to hide their…whatever it was they had together.

"Tomorrow, my house, right?" he called as they headed in separate directions.

"Yes! I'll see you then." She was looking forward to Elaina Jenson's party, despite the smidge of nerves she had about what Elaina's motives were for inviting Aidan.

SAVANNA WAS AT the Carson Public Library bright and early Saturday morning to check that task off her list. She recalled the delightful anticipation of leaving the stately red brick building and rushing home to dive into the tall stack of borrowed books every Saturday.

"Little Savanna Shepherd." Violet Lyle beamed at her from the help desk. Violet's brother, Bill, and his wife, Maggie, were neighbors to town matriarch Caroline Carson. Violet had been a librarian here ever since Savanna could remember; as kids, they'd lived in fear of returning their books even a day late. Now, standing in front of Violet Lyle, she instantly recalled the shrinking feeling of that eagle-eyed stare when she had a late fee or, even worse, had dog-eared a book. It was probably no coincidence that now, as an adult, every single book she owned had folded pages. Sometimes, if she read something really gripping or profound, she'd even fold the page *and* highlight it with marker to go back and read again later.

But she'd never tell Violet Lyle. "Hi, Mrs. Lyle!"

The older woman peered at her over her readers. "You look just as you did the last time I saw you, Savanna!"

Savanna wasn't sure how to take that; the last time she'd seen Mrs. Lyle, she was probably in high school. "Thank you. So do you!" Now that was true—the woman hadn't changed a bit in twelve years, right down to her bold hibiscus-print blouse and red-framed glasses.

"What can I help you with today?"

"I'm hoping the library has access to newspaper articles? I can get to some of them at home or on my phone, but so many newspapers now require subscriptions in order to read more than one or two articles online."

"Of course. We can access anything from almost any paper. Are you looking locally or out of state?"

"Sort of locally? I'm researching a little about that proposed boardwalk and hotel development in Carson, but I'd like a wider perspective, so probably any large-circulation Michigan news source. I'm mostly finding articles in the Allegan County paper. A few came up listed in the *Detroit News* and the *Mid-Michigan Gazette*, but I don't subscribe to those. May I check them out or read them here?"

"You can't take anything out of the library, but we can print for you if you find something you need. I'll set you up with our system so you can research your articles."

"That would be great, thank you!"

Within minutes, Savanna was scrolling through articles in newspapers from all over the state. Searching key phrases "Better Living Properties," "Better Living Carson Michigan," and "New Lake Michigan Hotel," she found several pieces over the last eight to twelve months in the *Detroit News*, the *Mid-Michigan Gazette*, and the *Lansing Press & Argus*, in addition to the *Allegan County Newspaper*. She perused as many as she could, jotting notes as she went and starring the ones she wanted to have Mrs. Lyle print for her.

Many of the articles simply presented the facts, with no real new information from what Savanna already knew. But there were a few editorial pieces, and a handful of others, that made it clear the development was a poorly planned environmental and architectural nightmare. Aside from the eighteen-story hotel obstructing much of the view that lakefront homeowners prized, there was the likelihood of destroying the ecosystem of the dunes in Carson, as well as a good twenty miles north and south, up and down the coastline. One article cited wildlife studies that estimated nearly a quarter of the area's bird and amphibian population and sea life would be affected, with beach erosion and loss of habitat. No more Carson fishing trade.

And then there was the question of access. Just as Sydney had said, Better Living Properties had submitted a proposal for a restructured Carson Main Street, which involved raising the speed limit to fifty miles per hour through town, with an adjacent parallel service drive zoned for the current twenty miles per hour as a method of still allowing for local residential traffic. The service drive would run behind the pretty storefront area that currently made up Main Street. Savanna could hardly imagine what would happen to Carson's small businesses in light of the expansion. Small shops like Fancy Tails would never survive. The Carson City Park would be obliterated, replaced by a triple roundabout for tourist traffic.

Savanna sat back and rubbed her eyes. Why on earth wasn't the Allegan County paper reporting any of these things? She leaned forward again and opened the search bar, clicking through the last several *Allegan County* articles. Every single one painted the proposed development in a rosy light, praising the benefits, which all boiled down to one thing: an enormous boost to tourism not just for Carson, but Allegan County in general. Which, Savanna supposed, was a good thing. But not at the cost of everything she loved about Carson. Heck, everything every Carson resident loved about this town.

She was struck by an idea. What if the newspaper was owned by Better Living Properties? Or by the company that owned them? How would she even find out if that was true?

She squinted at the screen, scanning for information related to sources cited, people quoted, and byline. The byline for this *Allegan County* article on the screen read: Landon King, Senior Journalist.

She clicked back to the previous article, checking. Landon King. The two before that were written by a Byron Kolczyk, and then a few previous to that by Landon King again.

It made sense. King himself had told her he was usually the assigned reporter for Carson area happenings. So him being the reporting journalist on the Better Living plan might not be strange at all. She bit her lip and typed "Landon King, Senior Journalist" into the search bar.

Dozens and dozens of articles populated her screen, and she groaned. There must be over a hundred. She scrolled down, catching articles on literally everything, from two orange kittens stuck in a willow tree in Grand Pier, to a spotlight on the three-time winner of Allegan County's annual spelling bee, and going back at least ten years. She glanced at the clock in the bottom righthand corner of the screen and nearly jumped out of her chair. She'd completely lost track of time! It was almost one p.m. She was supposed to be at Aidan's house in an hour.

Savanna hurried to the front desk, planning to ask Mrs. Lyle if she could print the articles on her list, but the woman was nowhere to be found. The help desk was unmanned. Ugh. The librarian was likely off helping someone, but the timing was terrible. Savanna would have to come back another time to get what she needed.

By the time she made it home, she was racing the clock. This morning, she'd thrown on jeans and the red T-shirt she'd gotten at an off-Broadway musical, *Be More Chill*, now a permanent favorite, and rushed to the library with a granola bar and coffee. She'd had every intention of allowing plenty of prep time before needing to leave for Aidan's and the pool party. Now, she dropped her purse at the front door and sprinted down the hall toward the bathroom, Fonzie galloping alongside her, thinking it was a fun game.

She took the fastest shower of her life, and then ate up a huge chunk of her remaining time trying on swimsuits and hating every single one. Perhaps the pool portion of the party would be mostly meant for the children? One could hope. She stuck her tongue out at her reflection, deciding there was no good choice, and settled on a black one-piece with gold accents. Luckily, it was halter style, which would work well underneath the black and white sundress she planned to wear.

Savanna flipped her head upside down, yanked a brush through wet brown waves, and popped on delicate gold earrings that complemented her gold compass necklace. She crossed the hall and sat at Sydney's vanity, applying light makeup and dropping a red tint lip gloss into the pocket of her dress. Dresses with pockets were the best. She took a deep breath and peered at her reflection. Good enough. She used a few pumps of Sydney's fancy cupcake-smelling lotion on her bare arms, then carried her strappy black sandals to the front door. It was ten minutes to two.

Savanna scooped up her dog and gave him a hug, setting out food and refilling his water bowl. "Be good, Fonzie!"

She easily found Aidan's house from the directions he'd given her; he and Mollie were playing in the front yard with Jersey. She joined them, bending to give Jersey pats and ear scratches. When she straightened up, Aidan was staring at her.

"Savanna. You look beautiful." His body jerked as Jersey yanked at the Frisbee in his hand, obviously impatient with the pause in their game.

"Throw it, Daddy!" Mollie yelled from the other side of the lawn.

Aidan laughed and tossed the plastic disc, and Jersey took a running leap, catching it midair.

"Wow! Good boy! Oh, is it my turn now?" Savanna giggled as Jersey bumped her in the thigh with the Frisbee in his mouth. "You have to let go if you want me to throw it, goofball."

Her throw went sideways, but the dog still snatched it up, panting around the toy.

"All right," Aidan said. "He'll do this for hours. Mol, would you please take him inside and we'll go?"

Aidan slung a glittery purple beach bag over one shoulder as they stood in the driveway, waiting for Mollie. She tried not to stare at his legs; she'd only ever seen him in jeans or long pants. Bare below the knee in white denim shorts, Aidan's muscled legs were a shade paler than his arms.

He caught her looking. "I know. Looks like I work in a hospital or something," he joked.

"They don't see a lot of sun."

Savanna shook her head. "Sorry. That's not what I was thinking." She was embarrassed. She'd been paying more attention to his general firm build than his skin, but wasn't about to say that. His navy blue polo shirt stretched across his chest nicely, and she noted a yellow and black bumblebee pinned just below his collar. "Nice touch," she said, pointing to the bee.

"Wait, you'll see." He watched as the front door snapped shut and Mollie approached them. Now Savanna noticed she wore a white and navy sundress, matching her dad's color scheme. Her blond hair was clipped back on each side with yellow and black bumblebee barrettes.

Warm little tingles zinged through Savanna's chest. She felt like a privileged insider in Aidan and Mollie's special accessory tradition. "I love your little bees, Mollie. And the one you chose for your dad."

"Thank you." Mollie skipped ahead of them on the sidewalk. "Come on!"

The little girl stopped and waited for them to catch up at what must be Elaina Jenson's front walk. The driveway was filled with cars, and several were parked in front of the house in the street. A teenage girl answered the door, motioning them through the house. "Everyone's out back—my mom's at the grill." She could only be Elaina's daughter; the resemblance was striking.

"Aidan!" Elaina Jenson came toward them on the patio. "And Savanna!" She leaned in and gave Savanna a quick hug. "It's good to see you!"

She felt instant relief. Elaina seemed genuinely pleased she was there. "Thank you for having me."

"I'm so glad you came. You'll find a few familiar faces here…you'll have to give me your number before you leave. I lost my staff directory right after we got it last fall," she said, smiling. She turned her attention to Aidan momentarily, frowning. "Should we call you Dr. Gallager here? You've probably seen half these people in your clinic."

"It doesn't matter. Aidan is fine. Do you need any help with anything?"

"I don't think so," she said. "Food will be ready soon. Help yourself to drinks at the tiki hut, and feel free to cool off if you'd like." Elaina turned and gestured at a small thatch-roofed drink station set up in the driveway, decorated with straw and huge flowers to match the overall theme of the party. A large oval pool took up much of the backyard, surrounded by gatherings of parents in deck chairs and a lot of little faces Savanna recognized, plus a couple of teachers from school. Soft rock music played from somewhere near the pool.

Jack Carson came out of the house, carrying a platter of burgers ready to be cooked. "Hey there!" He and Aidan shook hands, and he gave Savanna a one-armed hug around her shoulders before turning to set the plate at the grill. "How great to see you two!"

Savanna hadn't realized Jack and Elaina were friends, but it didn't surprise her. They were two of the nicest faculty at Carson Elementary.

"Oh, Jack, the Millers are here." Elaina placed a hand on his arm as she looked through the open door wall into her house. "They brought more chairs. Would you mind helping carry them in?"

"No problem. Here, watch the grill." He handed Elaina the spatula and planted a kiss on her lips before stepping back into the house.

Savanna's eyes widened.

Elaina leaned in toward her. "I know!"

"You're… You and Jack are a thing?"

Elaina nodded. She was beaming. "Isn't it crazy?"

Savanna shook her head. "No! It's fantastic. Good for you. Both of you!"

"It just happened. I've been trying to send him signals for months. But you know Jack. He can be a little…"

"In his own head?" Savanna supplied.

"Yes, that's it. He's really great." Elaina's eyes held a

dreamy, faraway look. The scent of burning hot dogs wafted to them, and she whipped around, swinging the spatula. "No! Gotta go."

Savanna took Aidan's hand, squeezing it and looking up at him. "So cool. Did you know?"

"Sure. I told you," he said, lowering his voice and bending so only she could hear him. "I'm up on all the town gossip. It's a hazard of working in the clinic. They started dating last week."

"I'm so happy for them." Savanna loved the idea of Jack with a partner; he could be such a loner. She was glad Elaina's signals had finally been successful.

That evening, as the crowd began to thin, Savanna and Aidan sat at poolside watching Mollie, Carter, and a handful of other kids still splashing and playing. The sky over the trees in Elaina's backyard was streaked with pinks and oranges, and the air was balmy. Aidan's arm was draped along the back of the swing where they sat, and Savanna leaned comfortably against it.

Aidan's phone buzzed against her thigh, startling her.

He shifted and pulled the phone from his pocket. A number with an area code Savanna didn't recognize flashed on the screen. Aidan hit the button on the side and dropped it on the canvas seat next to him.

"You don't need to get that?" She was curious.

"They can leave a message."

The phone buzzed again, as the caller apparently did leave a message. And then it began ringing again. Aidan groaned.

Savanna waited, watching him. It was his phone, his business, but it must be urgent.

He picked it up, showing the same number on the screen. "I have to take this. I'll be back." He stood, putting the phone to his ear as he walked away from her.

He moved to the far corner of the backyard, leaning on the gate with one elbow while he dealt with whomever was calling. Savanna assumed it must be work. But that area code worried her. Was that a New York area code? Probably silly to assume. Savanna bit her lip, watching Aidan and trying not to look like she was. She did make sure to keep one eye on Mollie in the water in front of her as well, though there were still several parents also policing the pool.

Aidan's call had ended now, but he remained alone in the driveway by the gate, stock-still, his head tilted back and one hand at the back of his neck. Savanna's stomach suddenly hurt. Something was wrong. She was on her feet and moving across the lawn before she even decided to do so.

She stopped a couple of feet away from him. "Aidan?"

Those lines between his brows were back, and his posture was rigid.

"What's wrong?" She kept her voice quiet.

"That was the hospital."

Savanna's heart lurched, and she forgot for a moment that the call hadn't come from a local number. She only thought of Yvonne. She stared up at Aidan, holding her breath, afraid to ask.

"I have to go back. My boss was just brought in by ambulance. He's had a massive heart attack." He focused on

Savanna, and now she understood that the look in his eyes wasn't anger, it was grief. Or fear. "It's called a widow maker. They're working to stabilize him, but he needs me. Henry's wife will only let me do the surgery. I've got to get a flight out tonight."

New York. His boss in New York. As it registered, she remembered a piece of what he'd told her from his past. "Your original boss, the one who hired you after your residency?" She recalled Aidan saying the man was the reason he'd agreed to help out at the New York hospital this past year. Aidan spoke about him almost like a father figure.

He nodded, dropping his hand.

Savanna stepped into him and wrapped her arms around him, hugging him tightly. "I'm so sorry. Tell me what I can do."

He hugged her back, not speaking.

She was sure his mind was reeling. Could he even get a flight tonight? She loosened her hold and tipped her head back, facing him. "He'll be all right. You'll get there in time. Let's go. I'll get Mollie." She started to pull away from him, but he held on.

"I don't want to leave." He brushed a strand of hair back from her temple, his hand slowing in midair as he hesitated, his gaze moving from her eyes to her mouth. And then he leaned down and kissed her.

Savanna kissed him back, melting into him, heart thrumming wildly. Aidan's warm, inviting lips, his clean, spicy scent, the heat from his wide palm on the bare skin of her back overwhelmed her, the party around them vanishing, leaving only them. She was falling and soaring at once.

They were knocked off balance suddenly, and Savanna felt clammy, wet little arms clutching her as Mollie hugged the two of them, giggling wildly. The girl shrieked and let go, veering off toward the grass as Carter chased her.

Savanna burst out laughing, and Aidan shook his head. He was fighting a smile and losing. She shrugged helplessly.

She reached up and briefly touched his cheek, feeling light scruff under her fingertips. "You have to go. It's okay."

"I'll be back as soon as I can. I miss you already," Aidan said. His lips were near her ear and sent little shivers down her spine, a promise of things to come.

Chapter Twenty-One

S AVANNA'S FEET WEREN'T entirely back on earth yet when Skylar arrived Sunday morning to take her and Sydney for a visit with Chef Joe Fratelli.

Last night at Elaina's, she'd helped Aidan wrangle Mollie, getting her home, dried off and into pajamas while he threw together a small suitcase and arranged a car to the airport. Within twenty minutes of the call from New York, Aidan was dashing out the front door as Finn was walking in. When Savanna left, Finn had Mollie set up on the couch with popcorn, juice box, and *The Princess Bride* playing on television. Jersey was settled against the girl's side mooching snacks, and Finn promised to have Mollie up and ready for church tomorrow when her grandparents came to get her.

Savanna had one foot out the door when Mollie called her back.

"Ms. Shepherd? You can hug me goodbye if you want."

Savanna instantly complied, leaning down and giving Mollie a hug. "Enjoy your movie. It's one of my favorites."

"You should stay and watch!"

Savanna laughed, glancing at Finn. He was kicked back in Aidan's leather recliner, Mollie's pink stuffed unicorn next to him, popcorn bowl in his lap, looking comfy and relaxed and not at all like the hip, edgy guy she'd seen last night at Giuseppe's. She had a feeling he'd been with Sydney again tonight when Aidan had texted him to come home ASAP. "That's okay, you guys have fun. Fonzie's waiting for me, remember?"

As she pulled the front door closed behind her, she heard Mollie and her uncle Finn both crack up at something on-screen. He didn't seem as bad as Aidan made him sound.

Savanna arrived home at Sydney's on autopilot. During the short drive, she replayed those few brief moments with Aidan over and over in her head—the way he'd looked at her, his lips on hers, one warm hand in the middle of her back, gentle yet firm. It was bittersweet, sandwiched between his intense worry over his friend and Mollie's interruption. But, even bittersweet, it sent tingles zinging through her just thinking about it.

Sydney was on the couch when she came into the house, but Savanna wasn't quite ready to share what had happened. Not yet. For now, it was just hers.

Now, Savanna sat in Skylar's passenger seat with Sydney nearly hanging over the front seat, chattering to them both.

"What I really want to know is why Savanna won't talk about what happened last night."

Skylar turned and shot Savanna a look. "What happened last night?"

"*Something* happened," Sydney said. "Finn got a text from Dr. Aidan and had to run home, and Savanna came in, like, two minutes later and went right to bed!"

"Why do you feel the need to know everything about

everyone all the time?" Savanna turned in her seat to face Sydney.

"This is just because you're upset I didn't tell you I was dating Finn." She flounced back against the back seat, making a ridiculous pouty face.

"You're dating? You're dating Aidan's brother, who's in town for a short visit?" Skylar glanced at Syd in her rearview mirror.

"Not everything is about you, you know," Savanna told Sydney.

"You only said you saw them at dinner," Skylar said to Savanna. "This is a thing? They're dating? How's that going to work if he's leaving?"

Sydney was back, hanging over the front seat again. "I'm right here. You could ask me. Finn isn't sure now that he really will leave. He likes it here."

Skylar and Savanna both whipped their heads around, staring at Sydney.

"Drive!" Syd nudged Skylar's shoulder, pointing ahead out the windshield.

"He's staying?" Savanna was stunned. "He decided that after a couple of dates?"

Sydney shrugged, eyebrows raised as if she'd had nothing to do with it. "He's thinking things over. He's a med flight paramedic, so he can work from anywhere. He takes travel assignments all over the country."

"Oh my God." Skylar's eyes were on the road and she was shaking her head. "This isn't going to end well."

"Hey," Sydney protested. "You could both be a little

supportive. Finn is the coolest guy I've ever met. Ever. He's funny and smart and super sweet. You don't know him. And you've never even met him, Skylar. You could get to know him before you decide the whole thing will go up in flames."

Savanna fell silent. Skylar gave Savanna a sideways glance, lips pressed together.

"Syd," Savanna said, softening her voice. "I don't think we're trying to slam Finn. You know we love you, but you tend to keep things light, even when the other person might feel more strongly. Like with Brad."

Skylar spoke up. "And with Alex before Brad. And Milo before that."

"You have walls," Savanna said.

"Major, impenetrable walls. But you don't think you do."

Sydney's hyped-up demeanor crashed. She leaned to one side and rested her temple on Savanna's headrest. "I know," she groaned. "I do realize that. I'm working on it. Kate's helping me, I've been taking her meditative yoga sessions. I know it's an issue. I realized it with Brad. Dang, I feel like this is an intervention to save Sydney from herself."

Savanna took a strand of Sydney's hair and wrapped it around one finger, meeting her sister's eyes. "Maybe it'd be good to take things slow with Finn, before anyone makes any big decisions?"

"Yeah. I know you're right. But he's so..." Sydney sighed. "I've never met anyone like him before. I swear, you'd both like him."

"The most important thing is that you like him," Skylar

said. "If you start feeling like he's more invested than you are, Syd, you've got to tell him. Before he turns his life upside down for you."

Sydney shook her head. "I hardly know him. I mean, seriously. All of this is crazy. I know you're right." She leaned back, returning to the back seat.

They rode in silence for a few minutes. Skylar's GPS showed they were six minutes away from Chef Joe's house. The mood in the car was dark and heavy; Savanna felt bad for reining Sydney in, but she didn't regret it. The last thing she wanted was for her sister to end up hurt or stuck in a self-defeating cycle.

She had to do something to change this stuffy, depressing mood. The air in the car felt stifling. "Aidan kissed me."

"Aha!" Sydney screamed, instantly back in Savanna's face and clapping her hands on the leather of the front seat. "I knew it!"

Skylar laughed, keeping both hands on the wheel. "You're lucky I'm a good driver. Sheesh." She rolled her eyes at Sydney.

"I actually thought maybe you broke up," Sydney admitted. "But a kiss is so much better! It's about time."

Heat crept into Savanna's cheeks as she thought about last night. "I know."

"Oh-my-God-tell-us-everything-was-it-amazing?"

"Yes. It was beyond amazing." She couldn't stop smiling. "I can't… There's just nothing else I can say."

Sydney let out one more little shriek. "I love it. Good for you."

"I'm not surprised," Skylar said. "I'm shocked it took this long."

"Um, we've both been a little busy. And he's only recently back in Michigan. He had to fly back to New York last night." She explained what had happened as they pulled into Chef Joe's long, winding driveway.

A pretty young woman opened the door for them, introducing herself as Fratelli's niece, Angela. "He said you were coming. Thank you so much for helping him," she said, leading them through the open-floor-plan house to a large room with a vaulted ceiling, done in gleaming oak with massive beams framing the two-story-high windows on the back wall. The view was woodsy and breathtaking, looking out over an elevated deck and a small lake, surrounded with lush green forest. The aroma of some delicious concoction grew stronger as they entered the room.

"Gorgeous," Savanna breathed, going to the windows.

Chef Joe stood at a large island cooktop, frying round slices of ham and stirring something in a sauce pan. "Ah, you're just in time!" He spread his arms wide, welcoming them. He handed the wooden spoon in one hand to his niece. "Don't stop stirring."

She did as she was told, and Joe came around the island, giving each of them a hug. He seemed smaller, somehow. Savanna remembered Chef Joe being taller.

"Thank you. Thank you so much, all of you, Skylar's been keeping me updated. I'm so fortunate to have you on my team." His eyes were glossy. "Come, sit. We're having eggs Benedict, my special recipe."

The long oak table was set for breakfast. Joe made the finishing touches at the stove, and then, one by one, delivered plates to each of them, still steaming. The meal was almost too pretty to eat, with a light sprinkle of paprika on the yellow hollandaise sauce over English muffins, Canadian bacon, and poached eggs, a sprig of parsley adorning the decorative drizzled sauce on the square white plate.

"We should've visited Chef Joe days ago," Sydney whispered to Savanna.

"This looks incredible," Skylar said. "You really didn't need to feed us."

Angela chuckled. "He can't help it."

Joe sat at the head of the table, beaming at the four of them. "This makes me happy."

"So, to update you on—"

Chef Joe put a hand up, stopping Skylar. "First, we eat. Then we'll talk, okay?"

"This is the way," Angela said, closing her hand affectionately around her uncle's forearm and smiling. "You can't sway him on this."

Joe looked at her. "This *is* the way, young lady. Stress is bad for digestion. No one wants a good meal ruined. Eat!"

Breakfast tasted even better than it looked. Savanna hadn't even thought she was hungry, but she cleaned her plate.

Angela carried their empty dishes to the sink and returned with the coffeepot, refilling cups. She sat back down and spoke to the Shepherd sisters. "My family's taking turns coming to stay with Uncle Joe. Being on house arrest takes its toll after a while, and we don't want him to be alone. We're hoping you might have some news. Is that why you came to see him today?"

Savanna had momentarily forgotten why there were really here. She'd spotted the flashing light on his ankle monitor when they'd walked in, but the breakfast and conversation had been so enjoyable she'd been lulled into an overly satiated relaxed state, hands wrapped around the warm cup of coffee. She looked worriedly at Skylar; as far as she knew, they didn't have any earthshaking updates that would mean Chef Joe's freedom.

Skylar set her briefcase on the table, taking a folder, yellow legal pad, and pen out and returning the case to the floor by her chair. "We're getting close, I promise. There are a few things. First, Detective Jordan has questioned both Mia James and her son, your sous chef Remy. Fingerprints were identified on a picture frame and the hidden safe behind it, belonging to Remy and Mia. Your wineglass results came back," she said to Savanna.

"So they were Mia's prints! She was with Remy when they got into the safe. He was lying to protect her."

"But," Skylar said, glancing up from the papers in front of her, "the evidence collected from the Michigan basement access door doesn't match either of them. There was an initial party who entered the house illegally, through that door, to murder John. And it confirms the theory that whatever was in the safe wasn't the motive. The painting was moved and the safe was opened after the night the councilman was killed. Jordan believes your authenticator's eye," she said, looking again at Savanna. "He feels if that painting was crooked the night you were in the house with his response team, you'd have seen it."

"You can't blame Remy for taking back what belonged to him and his mother," Chef Joe spoke up. "John Bellamy never should've had that ring or deed in the first place."

"Remy told you about that?" Skylar asked.

"No, Mia told me. We dated a while back."

"How did that end?" Skylar asked.

"We realized we were a poor match," Fratelli said. "It only lasted a few months. We're still friends. She's moved on—I hear she's dating someone."

Sydney spoke up. "So we can cross Remy off the suspect list. And Mia, I assume. If either of them were the murderer, there wouldn't be any reason to break in. Unless they were trying to throw off the police by making it look like a break-in, and got scared away by Savanna ringing the doorbell before they could grab what was in the safe."

"That doesn't make any sense," Savanna said. "It doesn't explain the unknown fingerprints on the cellar door."

"Which means we have to go at this from a different angle," Skylar said. "The murder weapon. Chef Joe, we know with reasonable certainty that your knife was stolen the night of Savanna's planning banquet at the Carson Ballroom. You're positive you started the evening with it?"

"I am. I used it to chop the scallions. I discovered it missing when we got back to the restaurant and began cleaning up."

"Savanna has photos of attendees who were seen entering

or leaving the kitchen that night. Do you think you'd remember why a given person was in your kitchen?"

Joe nodded. "I don't enjoy non-staff in my kitchen. Let's see the photos."

Skylar set a tablet in front of him on the table and scrolled slowly through each one Savanna had dragged into the separate file.

"All right. Councilman Bellamy wanted butter, not the margarine Savanna and I had agreed upon as a healthier choice, but real butter for his dinner roll. He was a bit rude when I told him it wasn't an option. And this next one is Bellamy's assistant, isn't it? Can't think of her name, but Bellamy sent her to ask when dessert would be served." He swiped to the third photo, showing the inn owner Paul Stevens. "This fellow was a piece of work. He started giving me and Remy the third degree about average turnout for Giuseppe's dinner crowds and the number of waitstaff I employ. Remy got rid of him. Who is he?"

Savanna answered. "He owns the hotel and restaurant in Grand Pier that handled the Art in the Park event the last three years. His interrogation of you two was just sour grapes, nothing personal against you."

Fratelli nodded. "Ah. And here's Mia—she poked her head in to say the food was delicious. All right, and this next lady said she was one of the judges, right? She needed to know if the tortellini dish was gluten free. It is," he added, speaking about Judge Talia Devries. "And there's the mayor and Mrs. Greenwood, God love 'em," he said, laughing.

They all looked at him curiously.

"Oh, it was nothing. Roger came to tell us the sauce was running out; he was a little panicked. I think he was worried he wouldn't get seconds. And Mrs. Greenwood burst through the door after him...well, come to think of it, that was a little odd. The mayor's wife has never said two words to me, but she felt it necessary to reassure me I shouldn't worry about the new restaurants going in on the lake." He frowned. "I thought it was strange, but Roger waved it off. He told her she was mixed up, getting me confused with someone else or something. I don't know. We were in the middle of glazing the pastries and if you don't move fast, the sauce congeals."

"What do you think she was talking about?" Savanna asked.

"I honestly haven't thought about it since that night. She had to be mixed up; we aren't getting a new restaurant in town as far as I know."

"That's everyone." Skylar reached for the tablet, but Chef Joe touched the screen again, swiping back through to the beginning and then slowly perusing each photo again.

"There were two others," he murmured. "Those two guys from the paper, the reporter and his photographer, wanting to know if they might do a piece sometime on Giuseppe's. I said absolutely, that'd be great for business. The photographer took some shots in the kitchen when we were plating dessert."

Savanna nodded. "That makes sense. His cameraman gave us these photos. The article's running in this morning's paper, since the festival kicks off Thursday morning." She'd nearly forgotten about the article.

"I canceled my subscription last year," Chef Joe said. "I'd love to see what they printed. Would you pick up a copy for me when you're in town?" He looked at Angela.

"Of course!"

"Try Happy Family. They always have plenty," Sydney said. "We need to grab a copy too."

The drive home went much faster than it had on the way to Joe Fratelli's. Savanna filled Skylar and Sydney in on her research yesterday at the library, and the huge discrepancy in stories between their county newspaper and most other media outlets covering the Better Living proposal on Carson's waterfront.

With it being Skylar's turn to cook Sunday dinner, she dropped off her sisters at Sydney's house with a plan for the three of them to go over all the new pieces of information that evening.

Savanna had just pulled up at Charlotte and Harlan's late Sunday afternoon when a text from Aidan came through on her phone. She opened her car door, letting Fonzie scamper around the side of the house ahead of her while she followed, reading his message.

Just out of surgery. All went well. Henry's in post-op. I think he has a good chance. Wanted to let you know that your friend Yvonne woke up today, a good sign. You didn't hear it from me, but I spoke with her sister who said she'd be reaching out to Yvonne's friends to visit as soon as she's out of ICU this evening.

Thank you, Aidan! So happy to hear on both counts. Henry has a wonderful surgeon—I know he will be just fine. xo

She typed the last bit, the "xo," and hit send before she

could second-guess herself. She dropped the phone back into her purse, her step lighter with happiness at hearing Yvonne had finally woken up. Savanna had been so afraid things might go the other way. She'd visit tomorrow.

Her parents' orange tabby, Pumpkin, meowed at her from the porch chair and she patted him on the head. She opened the French door to the kitchen and entered the second house that day filled with delectable aromas.

Travis worked over a large pan full of what looked like beef Stroganoff. He added a small portion of beef broth to the pan, stirring vigorously, then a spoonful of something from the other pan on the stove, and turned up the heat.

Skylar was at the counter, with Nolan standing on a chair beside her. They were carefully placing thin strips of pie crust dough in a crisscross pattern over the tops of several mini rhubarb pies.

"No way." Savanna grabbed a spoon and swiped it through the sauce in the mostly empty mixing bowl. She popped the bit of sugary pink concoction in her mouth, closing her eyes. "Oh, I love you guys! Rhubarb is my favorite."

"First of the summer," Skylar said. "I've been craving it."

"The little pies are so pretty. You're doing a great job, Nolan. They look delicious."

Skylar helped him put on an oven mitt and they slid the two large baking sheets full of little pies into the oven.

"Dinner will be ready soon," Travis announced. "Nolan, would you please go tell Grandpa we're eating in about ten minutes? I think he's in the pole barn working on a bike."

Nolan and Fonzie were out the kitchen door in a flash, nearly knocking Sydney and Charlotte down coming in, laden with bags from a spur-of-the-moment Sunday shopping trip. Savanna had opted out, choosing instead to spend her afternoon at the library trying to make sense of the Better Living proposal issues and articles. She couldn't wait to show her sisters what she'd found.

She tried not to rush dinner, but once everyone seemed to have finished, Savanna stood and began clearing plates, carrying them to the kitchen sink. She helped Skylar carry in the pies and vanilla ice cream, the aroma of rhubarb wafting behind them. "You're probably too full for pie now," she joked with Nolan, ruffling her nephew's hair.

He threw his head back, arms out to the side. "Never! *You're* too full for pie!" He stared up at Savanna, eliciting laughter around the table.

Skylar scooped the ice cream and Savanna distributed the plates around the table. By the time the family was done, Nolan's face was a sticky pink mess. Skylar started to stand, but Travis put a hand on her shoulder, stopping her.

"I've got him. Grandpa wants to show us the motorcycle he's almost done restoring."

Harlan pushed his chair back, rising slowly. "I'm stuffed. Who let me have that second serving of ice cream?"

Travis pulled Nolan's chair out. "Okay, little man. Let's go clean up. Don't. Touch. Anything."

Nolan minded, walking stiffly to the kitchen sink with arms straight out in front of him like a robot.

"Are we done? Everyone?" Savanna circled the table

again, collecting plates and utensils.

Sydney laughed. "Okay, she's got something up her sleeve. What did you find, Savvy?"

"Help me, and I'll show you."

Once the table was cleared, and the tablecloth wrapped up and tossed into the laundry room, Savanna set her laptop on the table, opening it and hitting the power button. "I think I've figured it out." She couldn't keep the excitement from her voice. She looked around the table at Sydney, Skylar, and her mom, then down at her computer. The screen was black.

"Oh shoot, sorry!" She'd let the battery die again. She sprinted into the nook, snatching the cord from her case and then searching in the dining room for an outlet close enough to reach. She finally got it plugged in and powered on, and turned it around to face her family.

"All right, watch this." She had YouTube open and tapped play on Mayor Greenwood's campaign video for the upcoming election. The video opened with the mayor itemizing the great things he'd already done for Carson, set against a collection of photos in town and an uplifting instrumental tune.

"What are we watching? We all know he's running, and now he's unopposed."

Savanna shushed Sydney. "Listen."

At around the minute mark, Greenwood's ad shifted to another montage, with his voiceover listing plans for his next term, including an exciting new boardwalk with shops, restaurants, and a luxury hotel with four hundred guest rooms. "Our new Better Living development is perfect for Carson as Michigan's premiere tourist destination," Mayor Greenwood promised. He ended with his slogan: "Good things are happening in Carson."

Savanna spoke before anyone else had a chance. "We already know Mayor Greenwood supports the proposal, from what I saw when I was at the village offices. And with what his assistant, Janice, told us, we know it's important to him that it goes through. But did you know John also had a campaign video?"

"How?" Skylar asked. "He'd only just announced his candidacy."

"He was prepared, apparently. Both ads are small scale," Savanna said. "Greenwood's plays on mid-Michigan channels in prime time, something like three times a week. John must not have secured an ad spot yet when he died, but it's still on YouTube. Watch."

She typed on the laptop keyboard and then stepped out of the way as Councilman John Bellamy's ad played. The quality was impressive, similar caliber as the incumbent mayor's ad. But the content was almost entirely about the Better Living development. Bellamy highlighted the drawbacks, including a blocked view of the lake, expected beachfront and animal ecosystem results, and the disastrous effect on Carson's Main Street. Bellamy's ad finished with a simple statement: "If you love Carson, don't let Roger Greenwood destroy it. Vote Bellamy."

The screen went black. The four women at the table were silent; Charlotte sat with one hand over her mouth, staring at the screen and shaking her head.

"I told you," Sydney said. "You didn't know?" she asked her mom. "Most of this town is probably in the dark."

Savanna snapped her laptop shut. "John's video has sixty-three views. Mayor Greenwood's has over six thousand. If someone—"

"Roger Greenwood," Skylar interjected. "Let's call it what it looks like."

Savanna nodded. "If Greenwood wanted the proposal, and his campaign, to succeed, he'd have had to make certain this town stayed in the dark. What better way than taking out his competition?"

Chapter Twenty-Two

SKYLAR WAS THE voice of reason. "This is enlightening, but I don't think Detective Jordan is going to see it as motive for murder."

"You're right," Savanna said. "But when you combine that with the yelling match Mayor Greenwood and John had in front of the ballroom the night before he was killed, I think he'd want to know about it, don't you? They still don't know whose fingerprints are on the door to the Michigan basement."

"I meant to tell you," Skylar said, "I looked into whether we require our government officials to be fingerprinted. Every system has varying rules. There's no actual mandate, so each county, city, and township has a protocol in place for procedures elected officials must complete to hold office. Carson requires a federal background check, based on name and Social Security number, but no fingerprints."

"So it's possible those prints belong to Mayor Greenwood?" Sydney asked. "I mean, assuming he's never been arrested and processed, Jordan wouldn't be able to match them to him so far, right?"

"Right. Jordan was going to talk to Greenwood last week, after we showed him that video. With a lack of actual evidence, I doubt he brought him in for formal questioning, but I'd think he'd at least know if the mayor has an alibi for the night John Bellamy was killed."

"Let's ask him. Tomorrow?" Savanna asked. It was already Sunday evening, and she didn't want to bother the detective again on his own time unless she had to.

"First thing," Skylar agreed. "I don't have any meetings until after lunch."

"We can tell him about the major slant the Allegan County paper has for the Better Living deal too," Savanna said. She opened the folder on the table in front of her, flipping through a stack of papers. With help from Mrs. Lyle this afternoon, she'd printed, collated, and stapled together every article she could find mentioning the Better Living proposal. "I printed them all. You'd be shocked at the huge discrepancy in how our county paper is covering it compared to most other newspapers." She pushed the folder over to her mother on her left.

"Let me guess," Sydney said. "Our newspaper says it's the best thing ever, and everyone else says it's a nightmare and should never pass. Anything for tourist dollars."

"Look at the bylines on all the Allegan County paper articles." Savanna leaned over, pointing it out to Charlotte. "Landon King. Why is he writing almost every single article?"

Charlotte scanned the first few. "Is he?" She flipped through. "Hmm. Most of them… No, here's one, *Allegan County Newspaper*, April of this year, by a Byron Kolczyk. Wait, this one too, last October, journalist Byron Kolczyk."

"King's done the majority," Savanna said. "It's just odd."

"It's a county newspaper for a moderately populated rural area west of mid-Michigan," Skylar said. "A far cry from the *Detroit News* or the *Lansing Press*. I doubt there's an abundance of reporters. But we should find out if Landon King has any stake in the company. That could be something."

Savanna looked up at Skylar. "Yes. And Roger Greenwood, while we're at it."

"That'd be a conflict of interest," Charlotte said. "Mayor Greenwood can't have any ownership in the company and still push it as part of his campaign agenda."

"Well," Savanna said, "I also wouldn't think Landon King could be the primary reporter for a story he stands to benefit from either."

Charlotte was slowly shuffling through the articles, perusing as she went. "According to this, the proposed development has made it through several hoops so far. This one says the Better Living boardwalk proposal has passed their environmental survey, at least for the first stages."

"How?" Sydney stood and paced as she spoke. "That's impossible! There's no way they can do what they're promising without disturbing the Lake Michigan aquatic habitat, not just in Carson but for miles around."

Charlotte pushed the sheaf of papers across the table. "They seem to have a plan for everything; sand retention equipment for use on the dunes during construction, that kind of thing."

"Ugh!" Sydney stopped and perched on the edge of the

buffet against the wall, color high in her cheeks.

"Okay," Savanna said. "We're getting off track. We can't fix all of this. But tomorrow morning, I'll meet Skylar at the police station and give Detective Jordan the articles, plus show him the video. It's a good start. Maybe he can look harder at Roger Greenwood and also check into Landon King."

"How was Joe holding up when you saw him this morning?" Charlotte asked.

"Not great," Skylar replied. "He was so hopeful, and we really didn't have anything new to tell him. But we'll get some answers from Jordan; I want to know if he's actually ruling out the Remy/Mia James team as suspects."

Charlotte stared at her.

"Mom. I know Mia is your friend. But she and Remy broke into John's house, opened his personal safe, and took everything inside. Two days after he was murdered. Jordan has to follow up on that. And there's still the question of whether it's possible either of them was there the night he died."

"They weren't." Charlotte's jaw was set; she had that look each of the sisters knew well.

"You can't know that for sure," Savanna said, keeping her tone softer and gentler than her older sister had. "I don't think they had anything to do with John's death, Mom. But Remy was hiding something. He lied about Mia being there. What if there's more he's lying about?"

Charlotte pushed her chair away from the table and stood. "Well, then someone had better figure it out. Because

Mia isn't a killer, and I don't believe her son is either. He probably lied to protect her reputation. I'm finished with this conversation." She went out the kitchen door, leaving them watching after her.

Skylar and Savanna exchanged wide-eyed glances in silence.

Sydney stood at the head of the table, leaning forward, palms down. "Let her cool off. She'll be fine."

SAVANNA WAS WAITING for Skylar outside the police station Monday morning. She sat on the little half wall that separated the sidewalk from the two Carson village offices, an iced caramel mocha with whipped cream in her hand and a black iced decaf for Skylar.

Skylar joined her, coming from her law office next door. She nodded at the parks and recreation parking lot, and Savanna turned to look: two white sedans bearing the Better Living logo, the black *B.L.* inside a triangle, were in the lot with the other handful of cars.

"Must be a big meeting today." Savanna frowned. "I wish we could spy on them."

"If only. Let's go pick Jordan's brain." Skylar held the door open for Savanna.

Detective Jordan was ready for them. The YouTube videos were already cued up on his computer screen as they sat in the two chairs across the desk from him. Skylar had emailed him last night.

"I've taken a look at these. While it's interesting, I wouldn't call it motive. But I can tell you that Mayor Greenwood has an alibi for the night the councilman was killed. He and Mrs. Greenwood were together all afternoon and evening. They ate dinner together, Roger worked in his study for a while after, and then they watched *The Voice* at eight p.m."

Savanna leaned forward. "His wife can act as his alibi? Dinner and television at home with his wife is really all he needs to be clear of this?"

"I caught him at home on Friday and spoke with him. He let me in and answered my questions amicably. And he wasn't required to do so—I didn't have a warrant."

"Was Mrs. Greenwood there when you talked to him?"

Detective Jordan shook his head. "No, she was out. But she confirmed what her husband had told me when I spoke with her later."

"You don't think that's a little weak?" Skylar had her yellow legal pad out and was jotting something as she asked the question. "You questioned Greenwood, and then he told his wife to lie and say he was home with her at—What time was time of death again?" She flipped back through several pages.

"Between eight thirty and nine p.m.," Savanna supplied.

"Weak or not," Detective Jordan said, "it's a witness corroborating his whereabouts at the time of the murder."

"What did he say about the fight we saw on camera?"

"Oh," Detective Jordan said, hesitating. "That wasn't exactly what it looked like."

"What do you mean?" Skylar asked.

"Roger Greenwood and John Bellamy apparently both have VIP standing at Carson Country Club. I checked, and it's true, they do. But Greenwood has seniority by four years there. He said the councilman took his prime tee time for the season, even though the mayor's seniority means he has higher standing. The argument was Roger Greenwood calling John Bellamy out for stealing his tee time."

Savanna looked at Skylar.

Skylar looked at Jordan. "You can't be serious."

He sat back in his chair and sighed. "I am. Greenwood explained it without any hesitation."

"Wait a minute," Savanna said. "What does that even mean? It sounds ridiculous."

"It is ridiculous!" Skylar set the legal pad on the desk. "Carson Country Club has this elite status for members in good standing of longer than ten years. It's not cheap, but it comes with unlimited play for each day's green fees. Solo golfers and groups vie for the most-coveted tee times, but VIPs get first choice at bids on times. Bellamy must've gotten his bid in first and somehow had it accepted before the board realized Greenwood had seniority?"

Jordan nodded. "Exactly."

"That fight—that pushing, shoving, yelling match—we saw on video, was about tee times?" Savanna couldn't hide the disbelief in her tone.

"According to Mayor Greenwood. Carson Country Club would only verify their membership status. We obviously have no way to prove or disprove Roger Greenwood's explanation of the argument, but as ridiculous as it sounds, it's also plausible."

"Wow," Savanna said, shaking her head. "So Roger Greenwood's wife is his alibi, and he picked a fight with the councilman after the banquet over tee times. In spite of those two opposing campaign videos involving the Better Living proposal. None of that sounds plausible, I'm sorry."

Detective Jordan met her gaze. "Mayor Greenwood maintains that he and Bellamy left politics at the office. If anything else develops, I promise to let you know."

"Moving on," Skylar said, shooting Savanna a look. "We want to talk to you about a couple of other things. My sister noticed the Allegan County paper has a significant bias in favor of that Better Living development Greenwood and Bellamy opposed each other on. And almost every article has been written by one reporter, a man named Landon King."

"Right." Jordan nodded. "He covers Carson, Grand Pier, and other areas of the county."

"But," Savanna started, not really sure where she was going with the protest. "What do you mean? He's always assigned to cases around Carson?"

"Pretty much," he said. "Once in a while, another reporter will handle a story, but King's been covering Carson and the surrounding area since before I made detective."

"Even so, is there any way you can question him about where he was the night John was killed?"

"We can have a conversation; I can ask him. But I can't bring him in for questioning without cause," the detective replied. "Do you have anything other than his articles?"

"Not really."

"You mentioned the other day that a reporter provided you with photos of your banquet, the night you think Joe Fratelli's knife was stolen from him, right? That was King?"

"Yes, he had his photographer put the photos on a flash drive for me." She dug around in her purse and handed it to him. She felt silly; she could hear how this sounded, first doubting everything the detective had told her about Roger Greenwood, and now pointing the finger at Landon King, who'd been nothing but helpful to her. "Detective, you know Skylar and I feel strongly that you have the wrong man in custody. We don't believe Joe Fratelli could possibly have killed the councilman. How do you explain the fingerprints on the cellar access door?"

Nick Jordan sighed, leaning on his elbows on his desk, his expression earnest. "I don't have an explanation yet. Bellamy's water softener is in the Michigan basement; the salt company used that door to refill it every month. We also learned he'd hired Carson Plumbing to replace some copper pipes down there recently. We don't know that everyone in and out latched the door when they left. We don't know for certain that the killer came in through the access door. It was our working theory, but it's possible Fratelli didn't come in that way. Bellamy could've let him in—they knew each other.

"I can't fingerprint the salt deliveryman and every plumber who's worked down there. Unfortunately, the primary evidence points to Skylar's client. Without proof that someone else committed the murder, or proof that Fratelli didn't, I can't change the course of this." He snapped off his computer and pushed his chair back, standing up to signal that they were done.

Skylar gathered her briefcase and purse and stood, dropping her empty coffee cup into the trash can next to Detective Jordan's desk. She turned to Savanna. "Ready?"

Savanna marveled at her cool and collected demeanor. She knew Skylar's mind was spinning, constantly working to free Chef Joe, but her exterior betrayed nothing.

"One last thing." Skylar stopped, a hand on the door to the office. "What's going to happen to Mia and Remy James? Are you certain they were completely uninvolved in Bellamy's murder?"

"Mia confessed to being at the house with Remy two days later, when they decided to get her belongings from Bellamy's safe. Your wineglass fingerprints allowed me to bring her in," he said, looking at Savanna. "But as it turned out, I never had to mention we had them. She gave us a much fuller version of what happened than her son did."

"Will they be charged with breaking and entering?"

"Doubtful. They used a housekey Remy's had since he was a teenager. We'll be watching their accounts for any unusual activity, but they seem to have been truthful about what they took. We finally heard back from the councilman's brother, his only surviving family aside Mia and Remy. The brother told us that all Bellamy kept in that safe were his ex-wife's things. It'll be up to the brother as to whether he wants to press charges, and I don't think he will."

Savanna and Skylar trudged outside after the depressing meeting with Detective Jordan. Skylar gave Savanna a quick hug before heading back to her office, both of them noting the white Better Living cars were gone now from the village offices.

"It's not over," Skylar said. "You look so defeated."

"I know we're close. I can feel it. I'm going to the hospital to try to see Yvonne. She's awake now, and I got myself on the approved visitors list—they have an officer stationed outside her hospital room. They still don't have any answers about who pushed her down the stairs. Maybe she'll remember something."

"Keep me updated. I'll dig into Better Living's shareholders. Wish me luck that one of them is Landon King or Roger Greenwood!"

Chapter Twenty-Three

M ONDAY AFTERNOON, SAVANNA showed her ID to the Carson police officer at the door to Yvonne's hospital room. He gave her the go-ahead to enter with one quick, somber nod. Savanna had never seen him at the precinct; he looked very, very young. His neat military haircut and the creases in his uniform accentuated his fresh-out-of-the-academy vibe, but even so, he was a bit intimidating. Good choice of armed guard, she thought, pushing the door open. The officer sat back down on his stool as she entered.

Yvonne smiled widely at her from the bed. "Savanna!"

Savanna set flowers on the windowsill, a pretty peony planter with a Get Well balloon tied to it, and went to give her friend a careful hug. "Are you okay? Does anything hurt?" She let go, pulling up a chair to the bedside.

Yvonne had been here at Anderson Memorial for nearly a week, since last Wednesday. She looked better than Savanna had expected, having just woken up in the ICU yesterday. Her hair was freshly washed, her short curls light and fluffy around her face. Her complexion was pale, and there were gray circles under eyes. The plain white hospital bedding was covered with a fuzzy yellow blanket pulled up to Yvonne's waist, and she wore a pastel floral robe over the drab blue and white hospital gown. "My head hurts a little, but mostly I feel fine. I've got a pretty good-sized lump." She put a hand gingerly at the back of her head. "I want to get out of here."

"I'm so glad you're okay. This must've been terrifying. You look great, by the way."

"My sister brought all this." Yvonne glanced down at the yellow blanket and robe. "The minute they transferred me down here from the ICU, Diane wrangled a nurse's aide to wash my hair and get me settled. I just can't move my head very fast. And I feel nauseated whenever I stand up. They say I have to stay a couple more days because of the concussion and swelling."

"It's amazing you didn't break anything. I mean, other than your head!" Savanna made a sad face. Her friend was lucky to be alive; the concussion sounded awful. "Do you need something for the pain? I can call the nurse."

"I'm all right for now. It's not too bad."

"Do you remember…" Savanna hesitated. "Maybe you'd rather not talk about it."

"I don't mind, but I don't remember anything." Yvonne exhaled in a huff, frowning. "I don't even remember opening the front door for anyone. The last thing I remember is having breakfast Wednesday morning, before work. A detective came by here last night, but I don't have anything to help them. I know they seem certain I didn't just fall down the stairs. They're hoping something comes back to me."

"Can you think of anyone who'd want to hurt you? Any reason at all someone might've done this?"

She shook her head, and then grabbed her temples by both hands, wincing. "Ooof. Not smart. No one. I get along with everyone."

Savanna proceeded carefully. She so wanted to jog her memory or at least help her recall more than the start of her day last Wednesday. But she didn't want to scare her friend. "You know, my older sister and Janice are in the same spin class together. When I found out what happened to you, we called Janice right away to make sure she was okay. You have to admit it's strange that you two worked forty feet apart and now you're off work within a week of each other."

"Is Janice all right?" Yvonne's brows furrowed, her tone concerned.

"She's totally fine; she's worried about you. She was angry at Mayor Greenwood. She said she quit because he wanted her to lie to those Better Living people about zoning or something. Well, she said that was the last straw; she was aggravated in general with him."

Yvonne frowned. "Zoning. For the boardwalk proposal, right?"

"Yes. It sounded like it hadn't gone through yet, and she said the mayor wanted her to tell Better Living it had. They seem to be at his office a lot. Skylar and I just saw them this morning."

Yvonne was frowning, one hand still at her right temple.

Savanna stood up. "How about an ice pack? Or I can leave and let you rest." She gently touched Yvonne's ankle through the yellow blanket.

"Would you mind asking my nurse for an ice pack? They

help a lot."

"Of course. Be right back." Savanna pushed the door open, halting when the officer stood up. "Oh. I'm just getting the nurse. I'm coming back."

He gave her a curt nod and sat back down.

Savanna stopped the first person she spotted with a name badge, securing a promise that Yvonne's nurse would be notified she needed an ice pack.

Back at Yvonne's bedside, Savanna redirected the conversation. "It was nice to finally meet your sister. I don't think I ever did when we were in school together. She's older, right?" It'd been stressful meeting Diane, but Yvonne needed a distraction to get her mind off the pain.

"She's six years older. She was already moved out when we were in high school. She's bossy and controlling, I'm not sure how nice it was for you to meet her." She smiled at Savanna. "She's exactly what I need in here though. She keeps everyone on their toes." She lowered her voice. "I think the cops outside my door are even a little afraid of her."

Savanna laughed. "I can believe that. Well, she cares about you a lot. So does her husband. He was very sweet. They were in panic mode when I met them, worried about you."

The nurse entered, a tiny paper medication cup in one hand and an ice pack in the other. "Here we go," she said, helping Yvonne lean forward slightly so she could place the ice pack behind her head on the pillow. "And you're due for a pain pill and your steroid."

Yvonne took the cup from the nurse, then her disposable cup of ice water, washing the medication down. "Steroids," she said to Savanna. She held an arm out, bent at the elbow and flexing as if showing her muscles. "I'm going to get buff."

"They aren't that kind of steroid," the nurse said, smiling. "They help make sure the swelling in your head stays down. I'll be back to check on you, but press your button if you need anything."

When the nurse was gone, Yvonne looked at Savanna. "Everyone here is so nice. But I can't wait to be at home. My poor cat must wonder where I am. Diane and Ed took him to their house until I'm released. I hope they're giving him his medicine."

"I'm sure they are," Savanna said.

"He takes it twice a day. I forget some mornings, if I'm rushing, and I've had to go back..." She paused, frowning. "To give it to him. I hope they don't forget." Yvonne's brow remained furrowed, and she seemed distant, despite being two feet from Savanna.

"Do you need anything while you're stuck here? Magazines, junk food? I feel kind of useless." Yvonne was too fragile right now; Savanna gave up on pressing her for information. The least she could do was offer some added comfort. "A smoothie? Gourmet cookies from the bakery?"

"No, I'm fine. I'm mostly sleeping. It hurts my head to read, and I'm not very hungry."

They sat in silence for a bit, a muted cooking show playing on the wall-mounted television. Yvonne started to doze off after a while; the medications were probably working. Savanna quietly stood, careful not to scrape the chair legs on the floor. She draped her purse over one shoulder and tiptoed to the door. Yvonne snorted once, loudly, and opened her eyes.

"I'm sorry. I'm not much fun right now." She looked tired and sad.

Savanna moved back to the bedside, taking Yvonne's hand. "You're in the hospital! You aren't supposed to be fun, silly. I want you to rest. Listen, I'll have Skylar tell Janice you said hello and you're okay, and I'll come visit again tomorrow."

"Janice." Yvonne squeezed Savanna's hand. "Wednesday after breakfast, I was running late for work. I forgot to give the pill. Janice said Roger didn't tolerate lateness, and I knew I'd be late, but I had to bring the papers he kept texting me about. I forgot the day before. John was such a neatnik, it was easy to find the Better Living file, but then I had to go back and give Mr. Meow his pill, and I knew I'd be late." She stared wide-eyed up at Savanna.

"Yvonne." Savanna sat on the side of the bed, careful not to jar her friend. The thoughts were so muddled together; she tried to pick out the pieces that might be important. "What file?"

"The Better Living file. Oh my goodness. I remember. I scanned copies, I knew it was going to make me late, but I didn't want to disrupt John's records and I had the file in my car under my purse, but then I realized I forgot Mr. Meow's pill."

"John had a file the mayor wanted?" She kept her tone soft and level.

"John had all the data on how the boardwalk would hurt Carson. He'd been gathering it for months. I do remember that." She squeezed her eyes shut momentarily. "Stupid brain. I think maybe Roger was ready to accept the facts. He sent me a few messages, Monday and then again Tuesday, asking if I still had anything of John's about the proposal. He said I could just put it in his box in the parks and rec office. It's what John would've wanted, I'm sure. I planned to print the scans I took and put them back though. John would've hated the idea of something missing from his records." Yvonne gripped Savanna's hand suddenly. "I need the phone. I need to call my sister. I have to know they're giving him his medicine."

"Okay," Savanna said, nodding. "The room phone? Or your cell phone? I can get it." She stood up, eyes on her friend but her mind racing with a plan. The file had never made it to Mayor Greenwood. No matter what was in there, she needed to see it. She had to get it from Yvonne's car, probably still parked in her garage at her house. Or the scans...on her laptop, Savanna assumed. She needed to call Detective Jordan. She had to get out of here.

"My cell phone. I think it's on the table?" She pointed to the bedside table, out of her reach.

It wasn't. But Savanna knew she'd seen it when she'd come in. By the peonies. She picked up the cell phone, smiling at the squishy cat charm and purple tassel attached to the corner, and handed it to Yvonne.

"Who was I calling again?"

"Your sister, to check on your cat?"

Yvonne groaned. "That's right. Sorry."

Savanna leaned down and gently hugged her. "Stop saying sorry. Call Diane, okay? And then take a nap. I'll come back tomorrow, Yvonne, I promise." She'd come back and bring a smoothie to celebrate Yvonne's help in exposing the mayor.

She thanked the officer on her way out, slowing when she spotted Yvonne's nurse sitting at the nurses' station in front of a computer. "Excuse me?"

The woman glanced up. "Yes?"

"My friend Yvonne is, um… I know I'm not family, so maybe you can't tell me, but is she okay? Her thoughts are kind of jumbled. Like, she's all over the place. She asked me for her phone so she could call her sister and then forgot she was calling her sister."

The nurse nodded. "It's normal. It typically improves over time. Try not to worry."

"Okay. Thank you. I'll be back," she said, feeling a little pang of guilt for leaving her in such a fragile state.

Savanna called Detective Jordan first, relieved when she was routed into his voicemail. She left as short and concise a message as possible, giving basic details of her conversation with Yvonne and what she planned to do. By the time he got the message, she hoped to already have her hands on John's files that Yvonne was going to deliver to the mayor. Yvonne was under police guard, and if someone knew she had paperwork she shouldn't, they'd already have taken it from her house. Savanna hoped the file would still be sitting on the front seat of Yvonne's car; she had nothing to lose by trying.

She made a second call over Bluetooth in her car as she pulled out of the hospital parking lot.

Sydney picked up on the second ring. "What's up?"

"Is Willow working today?"

"Yeeess, why? That makes you sound stalker-y."

"I'm hoping you can come with me to Yvonne's house."

"Oh. She's home already? Sure, probably. When?"

"Now? I can explain when I get there. Pick you up in five minutes?"

"Hold on, let me check my books. I can't leave Willow here alone if we have back-to-back grooming appointments."

Savanna heard Sydney's clicking footsteps across the tile floor and already knew she'd be able to go. Syd wore boots or sneakers on heavy grooming days, and usually cute heels or sandals the other days. Savanna had always assumed Syd checked her books the night before, so she'd know how to dress, but maybe it was something she did subconsciously, knowing what the day held and dressing for it without realizing she was planning for it.

"It should be fine. There's a two-hour block between the puppy Willow's working on and the next appointment. Pick me up!"

Savanna pulled up in front of Fancy Tails, and Sydney slid into the passenger seat.

"Are you nervous about going to see Yvonne alone? Did they figure out who pushed her down the stairs?" Sydney fiddled with the radio stations as she spoke.

"She's still in the hospital with a police officer outside her door. But she told me about a file I need to grab from her house. I kind of didn't want to go alone."

Sydney turned in her seat, and Savanna could feel her stare. "So Yvonne doesn't know you're going to take the file from her house."

She shrugged. "It's not technically in her house, it's in her car. She wouldn't mind!" She looked at her sister. "I'm positive. The morning she was shoved down her basement stairs, she was going to be taking some information of John's on the Better Living deal and giving it to Roger Greenwood. She says she assumed the mayor asked her about it because he was starting to agree with the councilman that it was a bad plan."

"I really doubt that's why the mayor wanted those documents."

"You and me both. I think Janice left her job with the mayor just in time and didn't know enough. I think Yvonne, unfortunately, knew more than she realizes about the Better Living proposal, plus she still has what's left of the councilman's files. If John had proof—"

Sydney interrupted her. "Of the mayor using the proposal for his own agenda, like if he was a shareholder…"

"John's killer would need to get ahold of that information before anyone else did," Savanna finished. She made a left turn onto the long, winding road that led out to Yvonne's woodsy location a few miles outside of town.

"You rolled right through that stop sign," Sydney accused.

"Really, that's your biggest concern? No one does a full stop at that corner," Savanna justified. She'd meant to come to a full stop, but her brakes felt a little soft; she'd have to get them checked tomorrow. She eyed her GPS screen, seeing she had three miles to go before she reached Yvonne's dirt road, Blue Heron Way, and picked up speed.

Sydney giggled, looking down at her phone. She held the phone up in front of her face, snapping a selfie and then tapping the screen. "Oh! He's so funny," she said, turning the phone briefly to face Savanna.

She caught a brief glimpse of the photo Finn sent back, of his own goofy, cross-eyed selfie. "I like him, Syd. He was very sweet with Mollie the other night, when Aidan had to fly out."

Syd leaned back against the seat, rolling her head to look at Savanna and smiling. "I'm glad. I really like him. A lot."

She shot a sideways look at her. "A lot?"

"Yeah." Sydney's voice was soft and breathy. "Savvy. He's so different. Fun. Exciting. I can't imagine ever being bored around him."

Savanna smiled at her, easing off the gas and putting her turn signal on as she approached Blue Heron Way. "I'm happy you guys have hit it off so well." She tapped her brake, coming up on the red light. Nothing happened.

Sydney put a hand on the dashboard. "Hey. Slow down."

Savanna pressed her foot hard on the brake pedal, and still nothing happened. The pedal went all the way to the floor, and her car barreled forward toward the intersection.

She gripped the steering wheel, hazarding a quick glance at Sydney. "I'm trying—I can't stop!"

"What?" Sydney whipped her head from side to side, trying to see out into the intersection as Savanna did the same thing.

A semitruck was headed straight for them from the cross road, his traffic light green. "No!" Savanna heard herself shriek and cut the wheel hard to the right onto the dirt road, narrowly missing a car as it swerved around her. The sound of the driver's horn blared in her ears as it passed her, too fast.

The sharp turn at thirty-plus miles an hour sent the back of her car into a fishtail, and she wrestled with the wheel, stomping on the brake to no avail. "What do I do what do I do?"

"I don't know!" Sydney screamed. She had one hand braced on the dashboard and the other tightly gripping the cotton blend of Savanna's cargo pants at her thigh.

Savanna saw the semi in her rearview mirror but had no time for relief when it crossed the median line and sped past her. She steered toward the shoulder, hoping the grassy ditch would slow them down, and the nose of her car tipped down faster than she'd anticipated, knocking her hands off the wheel. Green rushed by the windows as she grappled for control, and then everything came to an abrupt, crunching halt.

Chapter Twenty-Four

S AVANNA MOVED IN slow motion, unbuckling her seat belt, then reaching over and unbuckling Sydney's. In the aftermath of the crash, the air was still and silent, and she felt as if she was moving underwater.

Sydney stared at her, wide-eyed. "We're okay."

Savanna nodded. "I think so. We're okay." The entire front end of her car was smashed, compressed, the steering wheel airbag pressing on her chest and stomach. The enormous maple tree they'd hit towered over the car, and a branch had shattered the windshield. Her car was smoking. From under the collapsed hood, a trail of smoke rose into the air like a signal fire.

"Get out. We have to get out." Savanna reached across Sydney and pulled on the door handle, but nothing moved. She went to reach for her own door handle with her left hand and yelped the moment she tried to move her arm. It looked fine. But oh holy cow, it hurt.

She looked to her right to find Sydney climbing over into the back seat. She got the back door open and half crawled, half fell out of the car. When she made it around to the driver's side, she was limping, her face twisted in pain.

Syd tugged on Savanna's door, but it wouldn't give.

"Can you push? Or kick it?"

Savanna cradled her left arm with her uninjured one, tipping her body sideways onto the front seat where Sydney had just been, and kicked the door with both feet. Hard. It opened.

Sydney pulled her out of the car, the two of them moving a good distance away in the grassy ditch that butted up to the tree line.

"You're limping. Let me see."

Sydney stretched her legs out in front of her, skin bare from her shorts to her sandals. Her left ankle was already puffing up. "Ugh. That's ugly. It better only be sprained— I'm running the yoga booth all week for your festival." She frowned, touching the ankle gingerly.

Everything she'd just said sounded ridiculous to Savanna's ears. She giggled softly, then stopped, staring at her sister. Then she burst out laughing. "It better just be sprained, I've got yoga," she repeated, struggling to get the words out between guffaws, copying Syd. "Look." she pointed to her car, which was now billowing smoke.

Sydney joined her, laughing, lying back onto the hill where they sat. "What the heck," she gasped. "What the heck happened?"

Savanna wiped her eyes, getting her outburst under control. She had zero answers. "Do we need to move back more? What if it blows up?"

"I think we're okay. We're pretty far. I think that only happens in movies," Syd said, sitting up. "Let me see your arm," she said, turning to face her.

Savanna still had her painful left arm cradled with her right one, right hand cupping her left elbow. "My wrist hurts." She tried wiggling the fingers on her left hand and cringed. "And it's worse when I move the hand."

"Keep it still. It's probably broken."

"But I have yoga!" Savanna wailed, making them both laugh again.

Sydney hugged her suddenly. "I'm glad we're okay. Oh, no. Your car. Don't look."

Savanna looked. Orange flames were now snaking out from under the left front area of the hood.

"Hello! Are you all right?" A man was approaching them from the road, heading carefully down the slope. "Can you move? I've called 911."

Sydney was apparently right about cars only exploding in movies. While they were both being assessed and helped into the back of the ambulance, the front of Savanna's car had turned into a full-on bonfire. Emergency response workers were able to extinguish it quickly, leaving it a blackened, smoking mess.

Neither of them tried to protest being taken to the hospital. In the back of the ambulance, Savanna startled as her leg vibrated. She unbuttoned the thigh pocket of her cropped cargo pants and pulled out her phone.

"I still have my phone!" Aidan was calling.

"Mine's in your car," Sydney said sadly.

She answered, putting it to her ear. "You have really weird timing." She told him what had just happened, making sure to start with the fact that she and Sydney were both fine.

"Why are you in an ambulance if you're fine? I should be there. They'll take you to Anderson, it's closest. Man, I should be there!" His distress was clear through the phone.

"We're really okay. Sydney's ankle is banged up, and so's my arm, but that's all. I don't get it. The brakes just wouldn't work. At all." Savanna had image of that slow roll through the stop sign on the way to Yvonne's. What if someone had tampered with her brakes? What if the person who'd slashed her tires was getting serious? She and Sydney could've been killed just now.

"That's strange. Have you noticed they've been going?"

She started to answer; it was the only thing that made sense. But they must be nearing town, the ambulance now filled with the loud scream of the siren.

She pulled the phone away from her ear, unable to hear anything but the wailing above and around her. She hit the red hang-up button; it was useless. She'd text him once she and Sydney got checked out and released. Maybe an officer would come talk to them; if not, she had to tell Detective Jordan about her suspicions.

The paramedic in the back of the ambulance with them ran another vital sign check, jotting down results on two pages on his clipboard. He used a pen light to assess both their pupils, and then moved to the foot of their gurneys and gently touched Sydney's swollen foot and ankle, explaining that her peripheral pulses were fine.

Five minutes later, they were settled side by side on emergency room beds, surrounded by a privacy curtain.

Their paramedic handed off their report to the nurse, a clean-cut man in blue scrubs bearing a name badge that read Andy, RN, CEN. The nurse repeated his own assessment and informed them he'd be back with pain medicine as soon as the doctor saw them.

"Do we have to call Mom and Dad?" Savanna turned her head to the left, looking at Sydney. "Or maybe just Skylar?"

"Aidan already called your sister," a deep voice said. A hand pulled the curtain aside, and Finn entered their little holding room.

Sydney's face lit up. Finn closed the ten feet between them, bending to hug her, and she wrapped her arms around him. She squeezed her eyes shut and turned her face into his neck, her shoulders shaking with sudden sobs as the events of the day caught up to her.

Finn held her, not letting go. "You scared me," he murmured into her hair.

Savanna looked away, feeling like she was intruding. Her throat was suddenly congested, her eyes hot, and she wished fiercely that Aidan was here. She took a deep breath, exhaling slowly. He'd immediately called Finn to come, knowing he couldn't be here.

Sydney let go, swiping at her eyes.

Finn straightened, standing between them and looking from Syd to Savanna. "You're really all right? Can I do anything?"

Savanna shook her head. "We're just glad you're here."

Finn stepped outside the curtain and dragged a chair into their room, pulling it up between their beds. His cuffed, dark denim jeans contrasted with his gray V-necked shirt. He reached out and took Sydney's hand in his, resting his on her bed, while he addressed Savanna. "I stopped in the ambulance bay on the way in and talked to your paramedics. That was some crazy-good NASCAR driving you did, from how the crash looked. I can't believe all you hit was that tree."

"How did you—?"

"Oh." Finn nodded, understanding. "Didn't I mention I'm your very concerned brother who needs all the details? Sounds like your brakes went out. Did you know they were going?"

Savanna shook her head. "They weren't going. I just had the brakes done last fall, so they should've been fine. I think someone tampered with my car. Remember"—she looked at Sydney—"when I rolled through that stop sign today? I didn't mean to. My brakes felt soft but I didn't think anything of it. When we came up on that light at Blue Heron Way, I had no brakes at all. Nothing."

"The brake lines," Finn answered. "If someone cut—not even cut, but just made a small hole—in your brake line, the car would make it through a few stops before the brakes went."

"I drove it from here, after seeing Yvonne upstairs, to Fancy Tails to grab Sydney, and then out toward Yvonne's house. I probably stopped a total of three or four times."

"It makes sense. So who wants you dead? Or at least out of commission?" Finn asked.

Savanna frowned. "Maybe the answer to that is in *when* someone tampered with my brakes. It had to have been done today, right? You said the car would've made it through a few stops. What if it happened right here, while I was visiting Yvonne? Someone didn't want me to get those files from her place." She instantly thought of the cop stationed outside Yvonne's door. Could he have heard their conversation? She shivered involuntarily. She didn't want to even consider a police officer being mixed up in something this awful.

The emergency room doctor came around the curtain just then. Finn stepped out, giving them privacy. The doctor checked them each over thoroughly, determining their injuries were exactly where they described and nowhere else. "Someone will come take you to X-ray shortly. Your arm," he said to Savanna. "And your leg. No group discounts, sorry," he deadpanned. "Do we need something for the pain?"

"Yes," Savanna said. "Please."

Sydney declined.

When Finn came back in, Skylar was with him.

"Oh my God." She moved between their beds, hugging Savanna and then Sydney. "I saw the pictures. You two...you're lucky to be here."

Finn moved the chair closer to her, motioning for her to sit. "Please."

Nurse Andy entered, handing Savanna two pills in a little cup, followed by hospital-issue apple juice and graham crackers. The nurse turned and set juice and crackers on Sydney's table, hesitating. "Ms. Shepherd, you might have a broken ankle. X-ray will be uncomfortable, and so will anything we have to do after that. Are you sure you don't want something for pain?"

"She does," Finn said, frowning at Sydney. "There's no need for you to be in pain."

"I do not," she said firmly. "I actually don't feel too bad. I promise. I'll let you know if I change my mind," she told the nurse, and he nodded and left.

Finn leaned against the wall, his arms folded across his chest. "By the time you realize you need something, it's not going to help."

"Possibly. I'll take that chance." She held a hand out to him and he took it. "I'm okay right now. Finn, have you met Skylar yet?"

"We met in the hallway," their sister said. "He explained about your brake lines. I called Jordan, and he's having his forensics team go over your car as soon as it's brought in. He's on his way here to talk to both of you directly."

Waiting for X-ray seemed to take forever. Savanna filled Skylar in on what she and Sydney had been trying to do, after first listening to an in-depth lecture from her older sister about total disregard for safety and lack of common sense. She tried to defend herself. "I notified Detective Jordan where we were going, I didn't go alone, and even if I had, there was no reason to think it'd be dangerous. I figured if anyone knew about the file Yvonne was going to give Mayor Greenwood, they'd have already taken it."

By the time they'd learned that Sydney's bad sprain could be treated with a walking boot and rest, and Savanna had returned from having a bright pink cast applied for her fractured left forearm, Detective Jordan had joined the small group in the room.

Skylar stood. "All right. Listen, ladies, and no arguments. I'm heading to Mom and Dad's to tell them you're both fine, and then let them know what happened. This is going to freak them out too much over the phone. Savanna, Jordan has information for you. I can be back here in an hour, unless you're both discharged before then."

"I'm staying," Finn spoke up. "I've got Mollie spending the night with her grandparents. I'll bring them home; they'll be done here soon."

"Sky, listen to him," Sydney said. "Go talk to Mom and Dad and then please, go home. You need rest, and Nolan needs you. It's getting late."

Skylar looked at Savanna.

"You know she's right. Go." She held out her good arm, giving her older sister a quick hug.

She sighed. "Text me when you're home. Promise."

When she'd gone, Detective Jordan took her vacated chair, pulling his notepad from inside his jacket and flipping through it. "We need to go through the details of your accident. That can be now or tomorrow at the station. You've both had a long day."

Savanna and Sydney exchanged a look.

"Tomorrow, please," Savanna said. "We'll come in the morning."

"Come whenever you're up to it, or I can come to you," Detective Jordan said. "Let me know. Now, from what you told me of your conversation with Yvonne Marchand today, the morning she was found pushed down her basement stairs, she'd left the information Roger Greenwood wanted on the front seat of her car. I spoke with her while you were in X-ray. Her memory is patchy, but she backed all of that up. She said she was about to leave for work, but she ran back inside to feed the cat or something. The front seat of her car is empty. My partner got there to check it out not even an hour after your crash."

"No! Someone got to them." She groaned in frustration. "It was a folder of information John had been compiling. Yvonne thought the mayor was changing his mind about endorsing the Better Living proposal, but I'm sure he wasn't. We're thinking he was financially benefitting—"

"All right." Detective Jordan put a hand up, stopping her. "Skylar told me about your theory, so I looked into it. Neither Roger Greenwood nor Landon King are shareholders in Better Living. But listen. I've got the files you wanted that were stolen from Yvonne Marchand's car." He held up the cell phone Savanna had handed Yvonne earlier that day, the purple tassel and cat charm hanging off the corner.

"Yvonne's phone? How? She said she scanned them. She meant in her phone? Oh, jeez." She smacked her right palm to her forehead. She'd had her hands on the files hours ago and hadn't known it.

"Take a look," Nick Jordan said, tapping the screen a few times and handing her the phone. "Scroll through. The councilman wasn't compiling facts proving Better Living was going to hurt Carson. He had screenshots of transactions. You were right. Greenwood and Landon King were being handsomely paid off by Better Living Properties." He sat back and waited.

Savanna swiped through, stopping to zoom in on several spots. She sucked in her breath. "What—Each of these shows money being sent in the NowFunds app. They originate here; I don't recognize this name. Then that amount...is sent to Greenwood, and one day later, from Greenwood to King. Since when?" She continued through, answering her own question. "Since last November. We were right," she said, looking at Sydney then Detective Jordan.

"What does that mean?" Sydney asked. "Better Living was giving money to Roger Greenwood so he'd push the proposal?"

"And Greenwood was paying Landon King to bombard the Allegan County population with nothing but a glowing view of the boardwalk development," Savanna finished. "They used one of those fast-cash apps so it wouldn't link to their own bank accounts, but John Bellamy knew. He had proof." She waved the phone in her hand and then gave it back to the detective.

Detective Jordan stood. "That's what it looks like."

Savanna's mind was racing. "John's no longer a threat, but Greenwood must've suspected he had proof. That's why he tried to use Yvonne to get John's files—the only real proof of what he and Landon King were up to. He must've asked her more than once. Yvonne said she'd forgotten to bring the papers the day before. Oh! That argument outside the Carson Ballroom! John was so aggressive with the mayor. It was never about golf!"

Detective Jordan nodded. "The theory is that John Bellamy confronted Roger Greenwood, either in an attempt to get in on the money being funneled from Better Living, or—"

Savanna jumped in. "No. He would've tried to force Greenwood to come clean. John was staunchly opposed to the proposal, plus if he got Greenwood to confess, the election would've been his. He must've threatened to expose the mayor and Landon King. He had the proof."

"Right. That seems most likely."

"So Roger Greenwood knew he had to do something. Get rid of John, or lose his office and his extra income." Savanna frowned. "But what about my brakes? I'd just learned from Yvonne about the files she was going to give the mayor. We're thinking someone raced to Yvonne's and beat us to the files, right? Taking steps to make sure I never got there?"

"This is tough for me." Detective Jordan scrubbed a hand through his hair. "One of my officers has gotten involved in this, pulled in by Roger Greenwood or the reporter. We've moved Ms. Marchand to a different room, with Detective Taylor stationed outside for now. When I got your voicemail, and then learned what happened to your car, we swept your friend's hospital room and found two hidden listening devices. One of my officers had to have been paid off to plant them. I *will* find out who it was," Detective Jordan vowed, his tone restrained but furious.

He went on. "Greenwood and King are being picked up as we speak. I'm not dealing with them tonight; they can sit in holding cells until morning. I have to go through all of this with the prosecutor, make sure we have our ducks are in a row; it needs to be airtight. By the time we formally charge them, we'll have confirmation of Greenwood's fingerprints on Bellamy's cellar door, and possibly even on your brake lines if we're lucky."

Something nagged at Savanna. Everything added up—it all made sense. But it was that sensation of a small detail out of place, similar to last year when she'd noticed the discrepancy in Caroline Carson's Laurant painting. She tried to shake off the feeling and at least put it away for the moment. "Can I do anything? Are we safe, then, as soon as your men make the arrests?"

He nodded. "I'll check in with you the moment I have word they're both in custody. All right? But until then, my friend Officer Zapelli will be with you. She's going to follow you home and stay outside until I give her the all clear."

"Thank you," Sydney said. "We appreciate that."

"Talk to you soon." Detective Jordan moved to leave, stopping at the curtain and looking back. "I'm glad you're both all right. Thank you."

With Nick Jordan gone, Savanna stood, antsy to go home. Her left arm was sheathed in a pink cast, Sydney had her bulky gray walking cast and crutches, and all they needed was the doctor to sign them out.

Finn cleared his throat, and Savanna thought he was going to tell her to be patient, but he stepped out of the room, coming back in under a minute with their doctor.

"Ready to get out of here, are we? You're both all set. I'll sign for your discharge, and the nurse will bring in the papers. Follow up with your own doctors, eight weeks for the cast, and"—he looked at Sydney—"I need you to make sure you limit how much you're on that foot during the next two weeks. The boot is meant to protect your ankle, not to get you right back to a normal activity level."

"Yes, sir," Sydney said, nodding. She waited until he left, then said, "That's what the crutches are for. I can't leave Willow on her own; I'll just be careful."

Finn shook his head, and Savanna protested. "Nope," Savanna said. "You can sit your butt on a chair at Fancy Tails and supervise. You've got plenty of help with Willow, Dad, and my one good arm."

"And both of mine," Finn added.

"You have a flight out on Saturday," Syd said.

He shrugged. "Canceled it. I'm not leaving yet."

Sydney's cheeks flushed. "Oh. Good."

Chapter Twenty-Five

S AVANNA WOKE UP in the middle of the night, that nagging feeling of something being out place still with her. She shuffled out to the kitchen, Fonzie following her. She stood in the dark, staring at the refrigerator for a moment. She rubbed her eyes, looking into the living room. Both her parents were set up on the sofa bed, and her dad was snoring. Loudly. They'd been here when Finn had brought her and Sydney home last night. Charlotte had been upset, peppering them with questions. Harlan had been very, very quiet. When she'd hugged him good night and tried to let go, he'd held on. Even after she and her sister had been settled in comfortably, with Officer Zapelli outside, they'd refused to leave.

Savanna pulled a bowl from the cupboard, careful not to make any noise when she set it on the counter. Sydney only kept ultrahealthy cereals in the house, but Savanna needed something other than flax-seed fortified triple-grain oat flakes. One-handed, she filled her bowl from the box of Captain Crunch she kept behind the cake pans, added milk, and sat on a stool at the counter.

While she ate, she carefully used the free fingers of her casted left arm and scrolled on Sydney's iPad through Mia

James's social media posts, taking care not to turn her hand sideways or palm up. The pain medication from the hospital must still be working, as she wasn't too uncomfortable, considering. She stopped scrolling; she'd found exactly what she'd hoped she would. It didn't necessarily prove anything, but it helped support the idea she'd woken up with.

She opened the map app and typed in Mitten Inn, Carson, Michigan. When a map of the inn and surrounding area populated the screen, she switched to Google Earth view and zoomed in. Ugh. While she could make out a fuzzy view of the property, it wasn't what she needed. She didn't have the tools to find what she was looking for.

The police did. But she'd have to wait until morning. There wasn't a thing she could do to confirm her theory at 2:52 a.m…or was there?

She moved to the sink and ran a splash of water into her empty bowl, got Fonzie a bone from his cookie jar to keep him busy for a minute, and tiptoed to the front door. She carefully, quietly, unlocked the dead bolt. She turned and peered wide-eyed behind her into the dark, holding her breath in case her parents heard her, but there was no change in her dad's snoring, no movement from the sofa bed.

Savanna padded down the sidewalk in bare feet to where Officer Zapelli still sat in the police cruiser in front of the house. Savanna halted, hands up, her arm in the pink cast starting to throb, as the officer caught sight of her and whipped around in the front seat, one hand at her side holster.

She hit the window button, looking up at Savanna.

"What are you doing, Ms. Shepherd?" Her tone was low and authoritarian.

Savanna instantly remembered the officer from Caroline Carson's house last fall; she'd been there the day of the break-in. "Sorry! I'm sorry. I can't sleep. I need help with something."

The officer turned her radio down. "What happened?"

Savanna moved closer to the window, leaning down a little. "Nothing at all. But… Okay, you know all about this case, right? Detective Jordan filled you in?"

"Of course."

"I'm really hoping you can look something up for me. Please. If you don't mind."

"This isn't how this works, Ms. Shepherd. I'm here to keep you safe. If your family finds you gone, they'll call it in, and Jordan will have a conniption."

She nodded. "They won't, I swear. I'm not gone—I'm thirty feet away in the front yard. It'll only take a minute, please?"

Zapelli looked irritated. Her gaze went to Savanna's pink cast. Savanna could feel her assessing her, the cast, the messy hair piled on top of her head, her ancient T-shirt bearing the *Phantom of the Opera* logo. Zapelli reached across the front seat. "Get in. Two minutes."

"Thank you!"

Savanna was back inside, snuggled into her bed, less than five minutes later. She slept more soundly than she had in days.

Harlan had a smorgasbord of breakfast foods waiting

when Savanna emerged in the morning. Sydney was already at the table eating, and Charlotte had gone to work. Her dad set a plate in front of her with a strawberry-and-whipped-cream-topped waffle, already cut neatly into small squares.

She laughed, spearing one with a fork. "I could've cut it, Dad. But thank you."

"Skylar says you two have to go in and give a statement to Detective Jordan. She'll meet us there whenever you want to go later."

"Now." She took two quick bites, turning to Sydney. "I figured out what was nagging at me last night. When will you be ready?"

"Anytime. I'm not the one who slept in 'til almost eleven."

She gasped, looking up at the clock. "No. That's impossible. Ugh." She stabbed three more pieces of waffle, trying to eat faster. There was no way her dad was driving them to the police station without breakfast.

Within the hour, she and Sydney were at the front desk of the precinct, waiting for Detective Jordan. Harlan promised to wait in the parking lot for them.

Skylar pushed through the double front doors, giving them each a hug. "You two are a sight. Does it hurt? Did you take something?" She looked pointedly at Sydney.

"It's not even broken. It's ridiculous how much it hurts," Sydney said. "Any time I bump it. Yes, we took our Tylenol this morning, boss." She rolled her eyes at Skylar. "And we'll take our ibuprofen as soon as it's due."

Nick Jordan came around a corner, motioning them

over. Sydney went first, maneuvering carefully with the crutches. He led them down a long hallway, turning back now and then as he spoke. "We've got Greenwood and King both in custody, as you know. They've been read their rights, and both have called their lawyers. Greenwood has made every threat you can think of. According to him, I'll never work again. Oh." He stopped walking, letting them catch up. "Sorry. I'm on my fourth cup of coffee. Joe Fratelli is clear. They removed his ankle bracelet about an hour ago."

He started walking again, more slowly, and stopped at a window in the middle of the wall that was clearly a two-way mirror. Through it sat Landon King, alone in an interrogation room. He sat straight-backed, elbows on the table in front of him, one leg jittering up and down as he stared intently at the wall. Jordan resumed his pace, pausing again two windows down. Roger Greenwood leaned forward across his table, face beet red, jabbing at the air as he yelled something at the woman who must be his lawyer.

Detective Jordan reached for the switch on the wall that would allow them to listen in, then pulled his hand back. "Nah. No one needs to hear that. But we're working on them both. Still waiting for King's lawyer to show up, so we're stalled for a bit with him. Even if we can't get a confession out of Greenwood, once the fingerprint results come in today, we'll have enough proof for premeditated murder. So far he's denying everything." He couldn't hide the hint of frustration in his tone.

"That's because he didn't do it," Savanna spoke.

Her sisters and Detective Jordan stared at her like she

was insane.

"Can he hear us at all? Can any of them?" Savanna peered into the little room.

"No. But hold on. Follow me."

In the last interrogation room on the right, Savanna leaned earnestly across the table toward Detective Jordan as she explained. "I don't think you'll find Roger Greenwood's fingerprints on that cellar door. They won't be a match for the unidentified partial prints on the knife. Or on my brake lines. He knows nothing about cars. And I don't believe he'd get his hands dirty. He didn't crawl around under my car, stabbing a hole in my brake line, because he was totally in the dark about those papers Yvonne had."

The detective shook his head. "That doesn't make any sense."

"Do you still have her phone?"

"It's in evidence." He hesitated a moment as he met her gaze. "I'll get it."

"Tell me." Sydney elbowed her when he'd left the room. "What are you thinking?"

She shook her head. "It's easier to explain with the phone."

When Nick Jordan returned, handing Savanna the cell, she opened the text message screen and scrolled down. She clicked on a thread, and then pulled out her own phone, going to her phone book. She turned both phones around and slid them across the table to the detective.

"The text messages from Greenwood to Yvonne asking her if she could bring John's files in," he acknowledged. "He asked her a couple of days in a row."

"Right. But they're not from Greenwood. Look at the number. It's obviously not a saved contact in Yvonne's phone. Compare the phone number to this number in my contact list." She pointed.

"Landon King. This is Landon King's number. In Yvonne's phone. Saying he's Greenwood."

She nodded. "And"—she moved a finger across the screen, scrolling the text message thread toward the end—"telling Yvonne to just leave the files in his mailbox in the parks and rec office. There's no way Mayor Greenwood would've told Yvonne to leave documents he suspected contained incriminating information in a mailbox out in the open where anyone could find it. This wasn't Greenwood. This was King, using the only method he could to get his hands on information he knew would expose both him and the mayor."

"Greenwood keeps saying he has no idea what we're talking about with Yvonne having those files. So maybe he's not lying," Jordan mused.

"There's more. Mia James is dating Landon King."

"What?" Both of her sisters reacted at once.

"All right," Jordan said slowly. "Officer Zapelli told me about your late-night antics when she came in this morning. You convinced her to look something up? She said she promised to let you explain first. But we've been through this. Mia James wasn't involved in Bellamy's death."

She nodded. "I know." She tapped her phone screen a few times, bringing up several photos of Mia with Landon

King. "But. Landon King is dating Mia, who, I might remind you, is John Bellamy's ex. We obviously have the money trail right, with Better Living paying off Greenwood to make the boardwalk development happen, and Greenwood putting money in King's pocket to help push the proposal through; they'd both continue benefitting, as long as the plan came to fruition. Everyone knows there was no love lost between John and Mia. If John went public with what Landon King and Roger Greenwood were doing, with proof, he'd have destroyed King's relationship with Mia on top of ruining both men."

She rushed on, glancing at her sisters and then back at Detective Jordan. "I believe John used that—the threat that he'd start by going to Mia with the information. Landon King killed John Bellamy. He had no choice. I'm guessing it was kind of a win-win for him, knowing how much Mia hated John for everything he'd done. And then he had to clean up his tracks. He slashed my tires, trying to scare me off looking into things. And he cut my brake lines yesterday so he could get the files he neglected to find last week, when he shoved Yvonne down her stairs. I think he'd hoped she'd just cluelessly bring them to the parks and rec office, but she kept forgetting. He ransacked her house but never thought to check her car." She paused, shaking her head. "I really thought he was so helpful at first. He was an open book. But only about the details he wanted me to have."

Savanna had the rapt attention of everyone in the little room. "The partial prints on the chef's knife are Landon King's, I'm positive. They're also on my car. Roger Greenwood wouldn't have a clue how to find a brake line. He can't even refill his own windshield washer fluid. I know, because Yvonne mentioned it once. And," she finished, sitting back, "I'm betting that gray SUV I kept seeing, first speeding by John's house with Britt that day, then when my tires were slashed, is the same gray SUV registered to Landon King. Officer Zapelli was able to look up the plate and confirm that's what he drives."

Detective Jordan sat completely still across from Savanna. His fingers were steepled under his chin as he stared through her, considering. A minute passed. Then two.

Savanna shifted in her chair, holding her cast above her head and wincing; her arm was throbbing. She should've brought the ibuprofen with her.

Skylar finally broke the silence. "Jordan? What do you think?"

He looked down at the two now-black phone screens on the table, and then up at Savanna. "Yes. All right." He pushed off the table with both hands, his chair sliding backward and hitting the wall. "All right," he said again, more to himself. "We can use this. I've got some work to do. Can I?" He pointed at her phone. "I don't need to keep it, but let me take it to evidence downstairs and bring it back to you later today, in case King's got more than one phone number. I'll walk you out." The detective's usual calm demeanor was now amped way up; Savanna could almost see him mentally ticking through each detail.

Skylar put a hand on his arm. "Jordan. I'll walk them out, it's fine. Will you please keep us updated? And let us know if there's anything we can do to help."

"I will. Thanks." He walked with them out of the room, looking at Savanna. "I'm going to check on the prints right now. But this makes each piece fit. I'll be in touch."

When the sisters emerged from the precinct, Harlan was leaning against his truck, talking with Aidan.

"Fresh out of heart surgery in another state, and here he is," Skylar said quietly, smiling at Savanna. "Doesn't surprise me at all."

Savanna's heart leaped. She'd wished him here, and it had worked. "He's pretty awesome," she agreed. She walked into Aidan's arms, resting her head on his chest and hugging him back. "I'm so glad you're here," she said into his suit lapel.

"I've got to get to work," Harlan spoke. "Sydney, hop in, and I'll run you home. Dr. Gallager says he can take Savanna."

"I'm not going home," Sydney protested. "I'm fine, Dad. I promised Willow I'd be in today. I'll just walk," she said, stubborn streak showing as she started off across the parking lot on crutches.

Harlan grumbled under his breath. "Sydney Marie, get in the truck. I'll drop you at the shop."

"Thanks, Dad," she said sweetly, hobbling past him around to the passenger side.

"I'm out," Skylar called, walking toward her law office. "Syd, I pushed all my meetings today. Text me if you need help, and I'll run across the street."

Aidan drew back enough to look at Savanna as everyone

left. "Are you really okay? You didn't hit your head or hurt anything but the arm? Let me see."

She presented her arm to him.

He cupped the bright pink cast, looking at her fingers and then her upper arm where the skin was visible. "No trouble moving your hand? Any pain when you rotate your arm?" He demonstrated with his own hand.

"You just can't not be a doctor, can you?" She looked up at him. She wiggled her fingers, which didn't hurt too much, and then tried to rotate her arm. She winced, pulling the arm back in to her body. "That hurts."

"Okay. It's probably a scaphoid fracture. Is that what they said? When's the last time you took something for pain?"

"I don't know, a while ago." She made a face and raised her arm up in the air like she was hailing a taxi. "It didn't hurt this bad this morning. It feels better elevated."

"Which is why you should be home, elevating it," Aidan said. "Come on, I'll take you. I'll write out a medicine schedule—the pain's getting away from you." He took a few steps to his car, holding the passenger door open for her.

"Aidan." She stopped before getting in. "Thank you for coming home."

He put a light hand at the side of her jaw and leaned in, kissing her temple. "I had to be first in line to sign your cast."

Chapter Twenty-Six

O PENING DAY OF Art in the Park was a perfect, sunny eighty degrees. Jessamina Carson was now fully restored, proudly watching over the festivities from her clean and gleaming pedestal. Savanna had obediently maintained a strictly supervisory presence last night, directing her able-bodied friends and family members in the event setup, right down to the small, warm white globe lights strung around the gazebo and art display tents. She'd even tasked Nolan with helping hang the flower baskets she'd gotten at the entrance to each tent, and he'd walked back and forth to Harlan's truck bed, carefully picking up overflowing planters of petunias and carrying them to Travis to hang.

With a solid forty-eight hours of rest and elevating her arm, it felt much better. As long as she followed Aidan's Tylenol and ibuprofen schedule, the cast was more a nui-sance than anything else. The opening festivities and announcements had gone seamlessly, the artists were still trickling in, as they had until tomorrow to arrive and display their work, and by the first evening, Savanna happily moved between the children in the small group she was helping paint a horse in a pasture scene. She'd left the activity open to all ages, hoping to interest as many kids as possible. It was only day one, with two new projects planned per day, but so far the kids around the long table under her tent were painting and having fun, chattering and giving each other opinions and compliments.

Sydney had proven a much better patient than Savanna had anticipated, still wearing her walking boot and taking care to keep the weight off her foot with the crutches. Savanna suspected she was being good due to Finn, her constant shadow. Every time she seemed to be getting a little too ambitious, Finn was suddenly there ahead of her, handling what she'd been aiming for or bringing her cups of lemonade. Right now, across the expanse of green lawn at the yoga ministation, Sydney sat in a chair with her foot propped up, giving instruction to four teenage girls and using Willow as a demonstrator.

Skylar and Britt came over from the art viewing tent next to Savanna. Britt walked around the table, admiring each child's work and pointing out a favorite feature or color combination in this one and that one, making the children smile proudly.

"Britt's fantastic," Skylar told Savanna. "They're going to let me use their employee discount for the Lansing Museum of Fine Art, which comes with a free membership to the Children's Museum!"

Savanna laughed. "Planning ahead, huh? How's she doing in there?" She looked at Skylar's barely noticeable baby bump.

"She or he is doing great. And I can finally keep breakfast down, thank God! Do you need any help here? The kids seem to love it."

She shook her head. "Nope, I'm wrapping this up soon, but thank you."

Britt made it around the table to Savanna and gave her a quick hug. "I'm heading home, but I'll see you here bright and early tomorrow, Ms. Officiator. Absolutely lovely opening day." Britt dipped their head and touched the brim of their white summer hat, smiling at her.

"Thanks, Britt, for everything," she emphasized. Her friend been indispensable last night and today, helping with setup and making sure all ran smoothly.

"My pleasure." Britt and Skylar were already into another topic as they walked away.

The horse scene session ended, and Savanna collected the paintings, carefully hanging them one by one on clothespins attached to string around the perimeter of her tent. She turned to find Nick Jordan approaching. She met him halfway, eyeing the sticky, cinnamon-sugar elephant ear on the paper plate he held in one hand. "Oh, that looks so good. I haven't gotten one yet."

"Get one soon, before they shut down for the night," he said, breaking off a portion and popping it in his mouth. He held it out to her. "Try a piece."

"Way too messy at the moment." She put a hand up, tipping her head toward the canvasses and paint supplies she still had to take care of. "But thank you."

"I wanted to let you know what happened, after everything came back from evidence. I tried to leave you alone yesterday—you and your sister need a minute to recover from all this," he said, motioning first at Syd to their right and then to Savanna's cast. "How's it feeling, by the way?"

"It's not too bad. Much better than it was. I've kind of turned it into an art project," she said, holding her left arm up and showing him. She had a few signatures, Aidan's the first—he'd scrawled *Dr. Boyfriend* in black Sharpie across the underside, smart aleck—with Nolan's name next across the top. Savanna had been filling the rest in with colored wild-flowers and butterflies anytime she had a free moment.

"Very cool," Jordan said, examining the work.

"So, you're going to tell me the partials on Joe Fratelli's chef's knife are Landon King's, as are the ones on the cellar door and my brake lines. And Mayor Greenwood was blissfully unaware of anything, other than his role in taking bribes from Better Living, right?"

Nick Jordan laughed, looking down and kicking the ground with the toe of his shoe. "I'm still not quite sure how you did that. You're almost a hundred percent right. The prints on the cellar door match no one. They must belong to one of the workers in and out of Bellamy's Michigan base-ment. But yes, the partial prints on the knife and your car are Landon King's. I believe he did come into the house by the cellar door, but he wore gloves when he killed John Bellamy. The placement of his prints on the knife are consistent with how he'd have picked it up to steal it during your banquet, not when he handled it as a weapon. He probably thought he'd wiped it clean after taking it, but he missed a spot. I'm sure he never thought to conceal any evidence on your brake lines. He didn't expect you to survive."

Savanna shivered. She still had trouble wrapping her mind around the idea of King trying to kill her.

"Roger Greenwood's arraignment hearing was this morning. He'll be tried on twenty-two counts of fraud and embezzlement. His lawyer has already posted bond for him," Nick Jordan said, rolling his eyes. "Landon King's arraignment is tomorrow. The prosecutor is pursuing first-degree murder, in addition to extortion and fraud charges. The court won't set bond for him. You were even right about his vehicle. We pulled Monday's parking lot footage from Anderson Memorial, and he was so bold, he pulled his SUV right up next to your car. It took him less than two minutes to tamper with your brake lines and get out of there."

"Oh, wow. And I just jumped in my car after seeing Yvonne, totally clueless."

Jordan chuckled. "You're anything but clueless. We got a full confession from Landon King, thanks to you. He's done, and he knows it."

"Good. Ugh," she said, a thought occurring to her. "Mia. She must be so upset."

"I'm sure," he agreed. "Better for her to know though. King wasn't a good guy."

"She's had some bad luck in that department," Savanna said. "Except for Chef Joe."

"Except for Chef Joe. We issued a formal apology to him, but he actually seems fine. He was glad to hear Remy was off the hot seat too. Fratelli wasn't happy we were looking at Mia's son. He thinks a lot of him. Anyway, thank you for your help."

"I enjoyed it. Most of it." She glanced at her cast.

"My wife and I will be at your beach scene class tomorrow," he said, beginning to walk away. He stopped and turned back. "Maybe you should consider moonlighting as my consultant," he told her, his tone half serious. "I'll let you know next time I need a sharp eye."

"I think you'd need a bodyguard for that job." Aidan's deep voice came from behind her, startling her.

She spun around, looking up at him. "Hey, you."

He wore jeans and a short-sleeve button-down today. He'd gotten his partner to cover the afternoon for him, and he and Mollie had been making rounds here at the festival.

"Where's Mollie?" She followed Aidan's gaze over to the yoga minis area. Mollie had joined the teenage girls, doing her best half-pigeon pose.

"Are you finishing up here?" he asked. "Finn's working the first aid tent right now, but he asked if he and Sydney could take Mollie out for ice cream. I think I'm off duty for the night."

"Nice! I'm almost done, just need to put this stuff away."

With Aidan helping, it only took a few minutes. She walked with him over to Sydney, whose little group was dispersing.

"You don't mind if we take Mollie?" Sydney asked Aidan, standing now with the crutches. "Finn wants a sundae from Lickety Split, and then they both want me to watch their favorite movie with them. *The Princess Bride*," she told Savanna.

"I can't believe you've never seen that! Sounds like a perfect evening. How's your ankle?"

"So-so. It'll feel better propped up on pillows while I watch a movie and eat popcorn with these two." Syd smiled up at Finn as he joined them. "Okay with you?"

"As you wish." Finn nodded. He turned and gave Mollie a wink.

The little girl giggled and spun in circles on the lawn. "As you wish as you wish as you wish!"

"We'll leave you to it," Aidan said, looking from his daughter to Sydney and Finn. "Good luck!"

Savanna let him lead her away on the path toward the beach. She could stay at the festival until after closing and micromanage every detail, or she could take the opportunity to sneak away for a walk on the beach at sunset. With Dr. Aidan Gallager, whose ability to make her heart race and leave her breathless seemed almost wrong for a cardiac surgeon to do. But she didn't mind.

The sky was a masterpiece of color, deep russet oranges and reds fading to yellows, pinks, and purples, and the lake was glass, the sheen reflecting the palette of the sunset. They'd walked hand in hand for several minutes when Savanna saw it.

Her house.

The house in her mind, the reason she'd turned down every single one she'd seen so far.

It was perfect.

Even from here, she knew it. The modestly sized house sat high on the dunes, overlooking Lake Michigan. The colors of the sunset shone in the large windows on the front of the house, a wide deck visible with cushioned benches around a small stone firepit. And a for-sale sign out front.

"Savanna?"

"That's the house. It's perfect. I think it might even be the one my real estate agent mentioned. It's exactly what I've been looking for." She squeezed Aidan's hand.

"I love it," he said.

"It probably needs work." She squinted at it. "I don't mind; it'll be fun. My dad will help." Her thoughts were running away with her. "Oh! My uncle Freddie and uncle Max are coming this summer. Uncle Freddie's an architect— I know he'll help me with plans. I could be in by the fall."

Aidan slid one arm around her waist. Savanna looked up to find him watching her.

"I can see myself there," she said. "Does that make sense? Do you ever just know you're supposed to be somewhere?"

Aidan touched the side of her neck, his fingers in her hair. "Every time I'm with you."

Her breath caught in her throat. She moved into his embrace. Less than a year earlier, due west across the lake, she'd run away from a life she'd thought she wanted. But she wasn't running away; she was running toward—her family, her town, and best of all, herself.

He kissed her, and she knew she was home.

The End

Acknowledgments

The Shepherd Sisters series wouldn't exist without my agent, Fran Black. Thank you, Fran, for pushing me, being honest with me, talking me through tangled plot points, and always believing in me. Thank you for never giving up on me.

Thank you to my husband and best friend, Joe, for being my constant. I couldn't ask for a better sounding board, champion, or overall source of support on this wild publishing journey and in life. Thank you for knowing things about me that I still sometimes forget about myself. Dude. I love you so much.

My kids have shaped my life, and I owe them worlds of gratitude. Katy, Joey, and Halle, you inspire me. I learn from you every day. I'm so proud of the adults you have become. I don't even have the words to express how constantly amazed I am by you (and you know I have a lot of words). I gain infinite joy watching you travel your respective paths. Thank you for being mine and for being you. I love you all immeasurably.

Thank you to Meghan Farrell and Kelly Hunter of Tule Publishing for falling in love with the Shepherd Sisters and allowing me to continue spending time with them in their little lakeside town. Thank you to the entire Tule Publishing team for an abundance of skilled support for this series. I'm thrilled to be on this wonderful journey thanks to Tule.

Every writer needs an in, a way to get through the door, if they hope to succeed. Stacey Donovan opened that door for me, and I'm eternally grateful. Thank you, Stacey, for giving me my shot.

Several friends and family had a role in bringing this series to life. Thank you, Ann Sullivan, for being such a dedicated concert wife and beta reader. I appreciate your assistance with all things wardrobe, style, and food, and your sharp eye and seasoned critique. Thank you, Rocsana Oana, for pushing me to finish an earlier book when I thought I'd given up; that completion propelled me forward into many more. Thank you, Jimmy Doyle, for your boundless vocabulary and support. Thanks a million, Suzette Nelson and Talia Wiley, for allowing me inadvertent use of some cool names. Thanks, Josh Howe, for very helpful law enforcement advice. Thank you, Thia Homer, for insider information on elementary art projects. Thank you, Jacob and Lilly, for being huge readers and the best cheerleaders ever!

One of the best surprises along this journey with the Shepherd Sisters books has been discovering the overwhelmingly awesome group of fellow authors who support and lift each other up. I'm so fortunate to be part of such a wonderful writing community. Thank you to all of you.

My mom, Joni Gardner, has been a writer ever since I can remember. From short stories and poems to an entire fabricated world about talking plants (Delores and gang), thank you, Mom. You cultivated the writer in me. And I believe my dad, David, an English teacher with a deep love of books, would be happy knowing all those books I read at the dinner table and well past bedtime finally led to me writing my own.

To my lifelong friend and fabulous sister, Julie Velentzas, thank you for giving me the foundation and tools to create these three loving sisters and their relationships. There's a little of us in each of them.

Lastly, thank you to everyone who's read, talked about, reviewed, shared, or in any way loved these books and characters the way I do. Thank you to countless readers who've reached out and asked when, for Pete's sake, there'll be more Shepherd Sisters books. Very soon! xo

Savanna's Mixed Berry Shortcake

Shortcake:

2 cups all-purpose bleached flour

½ teaspoon salt

1 tablespoon baking powder

6 tablespoons sugar, divided

½ cup butter, frozen

1 egg, beaten

2 egg whites

½ cup cold half-and-half

Berry topping:

1 (12 or 16 ounce) package unsweetened frozen raspberries, blackberries, blueberries or strawberries, thawed and crushed

16 ounces fresh mixed raspberries, blackberries, blueberries, or strawberries (hulled and sliced)

6 tablespoons sugar

15 or 16 ounce package or can of whipped topping

Directions

Preheat oven to 425 degrees

Mix flour, salt, baking powder and 3 Tbsp sugar in a medium bowl. Grate 2 Tbsp of the butter using coarse grater edge into dry ingredients; toss to coat. Repeat grating and tossing with remaining butter.

Combine 1 beaten egg and half-and-half. Pour into flour mixture. Toss with a fork to form large clumps. Lightly press clumps into a large ball; add a teaspoon more half-and-half to the bowl if dough won't come together.

Turn dough onto work surface; divide into 6 smaller balls. Place them 2 inches apart on a non stick or greased baking sheet and press each one to flatten slightly. Before baking, brush tops with 2 combined whisked egg whites for a golden sheen upon baking. Sprinkle with remaining 3 Tbsp sugar. Bake until golden brown, about 12 to 14 minutes. Let cool 10 minutes.

Mix thawed and fresh berries with 6 Tbsp sugar in a bowl; let stand until sugar dissolves.

Split each shortcake biscuit horizontally. Spoon a portion of berries over each cake bottom followed by a serving of whipped topping and cap with cake top. Spoon an additional portion of berries over the top, followed again by whipped topping. Enjoy!

If you enjoyed *Death by Deception*,
check out the other books in the

The Shepherd Sisters Mysteries series

Book 1: *Death by Deception*

Book 2: *Murder on Display*

Book 3: *Still Life and Death*

Available now at your favorite online retailer!

About the Author

Tracy Gardner is an Edgar Award nominated author of two cozy mystery series, one recent novel earning a spot on New York Public Library's Best 100 Books list. Tracy also writes book club fiction with heart and grit under pen name Jess Sinclair. A Detroit native with one foot in the sand of Florida's Gulf Coast, Tracy is a mother of three, the daughter of two teachers, and works as a nurse when not writing. She lives with her husband and a menagerie of spoiled rescue dogs and cats who inspire every fictional pet she writes.

Thank you for reading

Murder on Display

If you enjoyed this book, you can find more from all our great authors at TulePublishing.com, or from your favorite online retailer.

TULE
PUBLISHING